FIRST
LIGHT

ALSO BY LIZ KERIN

Night's Edge

NIGHTFIRE

TOR PUBLISHING GROUP

NEW YORK

LIZ KERIN

FIRST LIGHT

This is a work of fiction. All of the characters, organizations,
and events portrayed in this novel are either products of the author's
imagination or are used fictitiously.

FIRST LIGHT

Copyright © 2024 by Elizabeth Kerin

All rights reserved.

"Lethe" used with permission from Hannah Bonner.

"The Uses of Sorrow" by Mary Oliver reprinted by the
permission of the Charlotte Sheedy Literary Agency as agent for
the author. Copyright © 2006 by Mary Oliver with
permission of Bill Reichblum.

Title page art by Shutterstock.com

A Nightfire Book
Published by Tom Doherty Associates / Tor Publishing Group
120 Broadway
New York, NY 10271

www.tornightfire.com

Nightfire™ is a trademark of Macmillan Publishing Group, LLC.

The Library of Congress Cataloging-in-Publication Data
is available upon request.

ISBN 978-1-250-83570-3 (hardcover)
ISBN 978-1-250-83571-0 (ebook)

Our books may be purchased in bulk for promotional,
educational, or business use. Please contact your local bookseller
or the Macmillan Corporate and Premium Sales Department
at 1-800-221-7945, extension 5442, or by email at
MacmillanSpecialMarkets@macmillan.com.

First Edition: 2024

Printed in the United States of America

0 9 8 7 6 5 4 3 2 1

This dedication page has been blank for two years now.
So you know what?
This one was for me.
And now, it's also for you.

FIRST
LIGHT

In the predawn bluish milk
of forgetting, a bit more

green—and the dirt darker
where the leaves mulch over.

Every day a wilderness
my body can't contain.

Every day an other.
The clock ticks,

the sun salts air,
the light the light the light

—Hannah Bonner,
"Lethe"

NOW

MARCH 2024

My mouth is full of blood.

I clamp down on my tongue as we crest the hill. The Sara's remains are draped over the exit sign, dark and shapeless, like a black dress hanging out to dry.

I wonder how long it's been there. We drive closer, and all I want to do is look away, but I can't. I'm *supposed* to look. Long and hard.

Because I didn't the last time. When it happened to Mom.

It's probably been a couple of hours since the body was exposed to sunlight. It looks wet and dry at the same time: a stiff waterfall of charred entrails. There's no use trying to make out a face, so I don't search for one.

The exit sign reads BATEMAN STREET, but the hardened smears of sun-scalded viscera make it look more like BAT MAN. There's a stupid caped-crusader joke on my lips, but I'm swallowing too much blood to form words right now.

Beside me, Cora sucks a hoarse gulp of air. I feel the burn of her gaze in my periphery, but I keep my eyes on the road. On Batman Street.

"I need another pill," she rasps.

"You're fine. You took one at six."

"That was four hours ago."

I train one eye on her. She curls her purple-pedicured toes against the dash and buries her face into her knees. Rakes her nails through her thick chestnut hair, unraveling her messy bun to wisps.

"You know you can't be taking them less than six hours apart."

"Who died and made you my fucking doctor?"

She flashes her teeth. It's not a smile.

We're both trying to pretend we're not scared. But she's a bitch when she's terrified. Doesn't hide it well.

I think about reaching out to squeeze her shoulder or tuck the hair back into her bun. But trying to comfort her just pisses her off even more. It's best to let her simmer. That's probably the most important thing I've learned about her.

Batman Street shrinks in the rearview until finally, blessedly, it's out of sight.

"ADAPT's got people around here for sure," Cora says.

The name is a fist in my gut. "You think that was them?"

She nods and pops her long, swanlike neck. Flips down her mirror and pulls a tube of green apple ChapStick from her sequined backpack. I breathe the sticky sweetness as she applies the ChapStick in thick, generous strokes. A calming ritual. Next, she'll smoke a clove. And I'll pretend I don't want one. We've done this about a hundred times, now.

Right on cue, Cora negotiates with a cheap lighter and that warm, spicy fog rolls in. She switches on the radio. The last station we were listening to outside Pittsburgh has faded to unintelligible static.

"Mmm, 'merican as apple pie," she says as she drags the clove, scanning through the local stations. "You sure you don't wanna try?"

I shake my head. I get the appeal. The flavor combo. But cinnamon was Mom's go-to appetite suppressant. In gum form. Trident, specifically. I was never allowed to have a piece of her gum because she needed all of it. Actually, it was more like . . . I never allowed *myself* to have a piece.

It's still hard to untangle the rules from the things I did because I knew I should.

Cora finds a clear station—a country channel playing a twangy, retro Garth Brooks bop. She groans and presses her forehead to the window, leaving a halo of bronzer behind. "Think it's worth it to turn on my data and download a playlist?"

"Not unless you're trying to narc on us before we hit Ohio."

"Obviously, I am *joking*." She pulls from the clove. Quirks her head toward that black smudge in the rearview. Her energy softens. Like she can feel my fear circulating through the air vents. "I'd never let that happen. You know that, right?"

I hiss out a breath. Don't want to dwell on this. "How much further is the Red Market?"

Cora procures a huge, prehistoric road map from her backpack. Unfurls it like an unwieldy parachute. "We got a minute. It'll be exit one-twenty-two. That one back there was two-hundred-something."

She wrestles with the map, trying to accordion the thing back into place as Garth Brooks yodels about all his friends in low places.

"You or your mom ever go to one of these?"

"Uh, no. We didn't live near one."

"Right." She gives up on folding the map and just stuffs it into her bag. "Arizona, right?"

Shit, when did I tell her that? She keeps doing this. Making me say more than I should.

"Right."

I crack the window, letting the cold air pelt my face like a punishment.

Maybe it's fine. As long as I never said Tucson, specifically. I'm not *that* stupid.

The white lane lines pull my gaze as I drive, streaking past like lines of Morse code. *SOS. SOS.*

I concentrate on my poker face, but I'm afraid it's not good enough. Afraid she can see the seams as I weave together all the lies I've told.

"You think he's gonna be there?" I grapple for a new topic.

"Hopefully? I told him I was coming through." Cora expels a plume of spicy smoke. When it clears, there's a wistful smile on her lips.

My chest tightens. I hate the look on her face, when she talks about *him*. But listening to her talk about Devon is better than dodging her questions.

All the blood in my exhausted body curdles. I can still feel his flinty eyes watching me from the window. That ice-cold insolence thrumming in the air.

I have to keep reminding myself: This time, it's me watching *him*.

Cora kisses her clove. I'm aching to tell her the truth. She needs to know what kind of man he is. What he's done to me. Who he's killed.

Only the first time, Mia.

The hair on the back of my neck spikes.

The second time . . .

The second time . . .

No.

This was *his fucking fault* and he deserves what's coming.

I'm biting my tongue again, hard. Blood pools in the back of my throat. Cora glances at me as I sputter.

"You good?" She gently pats my back.

Unlike her, I actually *do* respond to comfort. To her touch.

I hate myself.

I hate myself for getting into this car with her. For starting this at all.

I hate myself for everything.

NOVEMBER 2023

TUCSON

There's no funeral because there's nothing to bury. Nothing I wanted, anyway. Most of what was left on the living room carpet that morning went to the Sara center in Phoenix, so it could be submitted to a study. Before the hazmat crew left the house, one of the technicians lifted the mask of his pillowy white suit, like a sentient Stay-Puft man, and gently asked if I'd like to "keep anything."

I said no.

I haven't been back since that night. June 6.

I was already packed, ready to move into Jade's minivan and accompany her on tour. Start a new life in New York. Get a little place with a terrace near a park, where we'd watch the puppies wrestle in the dog run and drink cold beer on hot nights, hidden in crumpled paper bags. At Christmastime we'd go to Radio City and see the Rockettes. We'd watch the icicles melt on our fire escape, sipping coffee—which she'd teach me to enjoy. The puppies in the park would grow up, and so would we.

What a fucking mess.

☾ ☾ ☾

There are laws about harboring a Sara. Most people get hit with a court date and a nasty fine, but there's jail time involved if they can prove you were helping them hunt. A lawyer from the Sara center calls to tell me they've reviewed my situation. Because I contacted them to surrender Mom, I'm in the clear. That, combined with how young I was when it first happened, helped them determine I was worthy of a clean slate. Legally, at least.

Sandy is good to me. The walls of her quaint adobe cottage are crammed with floor-to-ceiling bookshelves—a seamless extension of her store, the Book Bunker. Her wife, Alyssa, is an amazing cook, even though I barely eat anything the first month I'm at their house. She bakes corn bread in her cast-iron pan every morning, making a show of melting honey butter over the crispy golden top to lure me to the dining table. Eventually, I cave. It's still weird to go into their kitchen and open the fridge, though. Not because I'm living in a house that's not my own, but because there's just *so much food* in there. Only one person ate at my house, and it was me. I always knew exactly what was in our fridge, and I never had trouble deciding what I wanted. Choosing a flavor of sparkling water exhausts me. I pick up the cans and replace them a dozen times before making a decision. Keeping track of all the different milks gives me so much agita I've stopped drinking it altogether. There's almond milk, 2 percent, and oat milk. They use the almond for smoothies, 2 percent exclusively for cookie dunking, and the oat milk is for lattes. Actually, the *almond* might be for lattes. I don't know. It's just a lot.

I share the guest room with Sandy's elderly Boston terrier, Winnie, and she snores like a tractor, but I don't mind. I haven't had a pet since I was ten, when Cheddar the orange tabby cannonballed out our window in a blaze of terror after Mom's turn. Sometimes Winnie hops into bed with me, taking the shape of a doughnut between my shoulders. That's the best thing she does. Problem is, she's so old she can't jump down from the bed, so whenever she wants to get off, I have to wake up so I can carefully guide her back to the floor. But it's okay. It's never a deep sleep. It's an Ambien-induced twilight doze, which has been getting weaker and weaker by the day because I'm building such a resistance to the stuff and the doctor won't write me a stronger prescription. "You should ease off the caffeine," he says. "Try a guided meditation."

Every morning, Sandy cracks the blinds a quarter of an inch to coax my eyes open and whispers, "Time to head to the mines, buddy." I wonder if she knows I've been awake the whole time.

Sandy doesn't make me talk about anything. She has the bullet points. Getting those was hard enough.

Once the cops got settled to stake out the house the night it happened, they realized I had nowhere to go. I called the only person I could think of.

I waited for Sandy in the driveway, watching the sun fade. Keeping my back to our door, counting the donkey tail succulents in the neighbor's window boxes across the street. An old woman in a periwinkle bathrobe appeared, eyeballing the swarm of squad cars as I skirted her gaze. It's not like we knew each other. We never knew any of our neighbors. Never introduced ourselves.

They probably suspected us all along.

Sandy kept asking if I was *sure* I didn't want to keep anything. I didn't want what the moon men scraped off the living room carpet, vacuum-sealed in that heavy titanium vial. And she said no, not that. "I mean, what about something that was special to her? Some jewelry? Or a few pictures?"

No, I said. There's nothing here. I want to leave.

A couple weeks later, I put out an obituary because Mom's employees at the restaurant kept calling me to ask what happened, and I didn't have it in me to answer. Twenty-four words in the *Arizona Daily Star*: Isobel McKinnon passed away due to complications with Saratov's syndrome on June 6, 2023, in Tucson, Arizona. She is survived by her daughter, Mia.

There's no grave. No memory stone or anything. I don't know where I'd put it. What it would say. Having nothing to bury makes certain things easier. Then again, thinking about the *absence* of remains still means I'm thinking about them. And then I stop eating again.

I'm on my lunch at the bookstore, picking at a hunk of Alyssa's corn bread in the break room. I don't go to the Starbucks anymore. It's not like I'm trying to avoid Jade. She isn't there. But I go metal-mouthed with panic every time I walk past. Gag on the smell of espresso. I've started confining myself to a strict eight-foot radius around the Book Bunker.

Jade's in Seattle. I know this because of all the stories she's just posted. She hasn't reached out to me, and I've paid her the same courtesy. I don't know what we'd even say to each other, so it's honestly fine. Except, well, it's not. I'm on my phone way more than I should be. I've deleted all my social apps twice now, only to shamefully reinstall them in the dead of night when I'm wide awake with

Winnie snoring into my back. I don't like her posts and I *definitely* don't leave any comments. I don't know what I'm looking for. A crack in her smile as she poses for a selfie? Some sort of telltale, smudged asymmetry in her blue eyeliner? *A glimpse of Gabi?* The whole thing is pointless and I'm well aware. But something about it feels good and nothing else feels good right now. So.

I'm watching a video of her at the Pike Place Market, trying to master the icy fish toss with Tony, when my phone rings.

It's Sabrina. She's still saved as "Real Estate Woman" in my contacts because I couldn't retain any information back in June, when we met. In fact, I barely remember meeting her at all. I only remembered her real name about a week ago. My memory is full of holes, like the sun burned ultraviolet lesions into my brain that morning to punish me.

"Mia, honey, it's Sabrina." Her voice is staid but soft, with a put-upon breathiness she probably thinks sounds comforting.

"Yup."

"About the house."

"I know." Last time she called she might as well have been signaling an alien planet. A former version of me probably would've been embarrassed. But I didn't feel anything then, and I don't feel anything now. I guess that's growth or something. Who knows.

"We're planning to list it on Friday. But it needs to be cleaned out, before we can start showing it."

I sit up straight. There's a dry, scratchy feeling in my mouth. I paw around for my water bottle, but I left it up at the cash wrap.

"Oh um . . . I thought we were gonna like, get a big dumpster and just—"

"We are. But . . ." She sighs, right into the speaker. If she's trying to hide her annoyance, she's doing a miserable job. "This is going to be your last opportunity to save any items from the home. Before we dispose of everything."

"Right."

"If you want to make some time this week—"

"I got it. Thank you." I shovel a chunk of corn bread into my mouth, if only to fill the silence. "How long do you think it'll take, to sell?"

"That all depends if you're okay accepting a teardown offer."

I swallow. The corn bread clings thickly to my throat. "I guess that's fine."

It's November now, and we're starting to put the holiday stock on the shelves. Sandy likes to hang garland and tinsel from the end caps. Story Corner is going to be *A Christmas Carol* for the next six weeks. I'm already tired of doing the Tiny Tim voice.

My birthday was last week. Mom's is in six days.

Time feels like wind through my hair.

I tried to list the house immediately. Thought it was best to just rip off the Band-Aid. But, as always, Devon complicated things. Because I told the cops he would be back to check on Mom.

The stakeout the night of June 6 was a travesty. So was every one they staged after that. Night after night. All summer long.

The cops had no clue how to prepare for him. They kept the surveillance van parked directly across the street from our house, and they were in there all night chugging coffee. The thing reeked of stale, old Folgers the next morning. They said they were just trying to protect themselves, worried he'd be rolling a dozen Saras deep like he was at Cloak and Dagger. But I'm pretty short on sympathy. The whole thing was fucking amateur hour. He would have caught wind of the stench halfway down the block. If that didn't tip him off, the three cruisers stationed at the bottom of our hill would've done the trick. He came and left that first night, before they even knew he was there. Of course, the police don't subscribe to that theory. But they don't know him. Don't know *Saras*. Not like I do.

I told them about Montana. Where Mom said the group was headed. But I couldn't tell them much else. She never said which city. Just Montana. I scoured Facebook for bread crumbs, but the old Saratov Survivors group was deactivated before Cloak and Dagger. They closed ranks and cleaned house months ago.

There wasn't much on her phone, either. They asked me if she had another one, but if she did I'd never seen it. She probably went and cherry-picked texts and emails to delete, same way she pulled everything from Facebook. The night I came home for dinner and she didn't.

The only thing the investigation has turned up is a list of names. Twelve. Cobbled together from people's Cloak and Dagger photos and scraps of evidence on Mom's phone.

Turns out she had a lot of friends.

They looked for them in the desert, off-road in the wild, dusty sprawl. To the last place Devon dropped a pin for her. Nothing but an empty Airstream beside a cold, lonely fire pit.

After that, they told me it was okay to sell the house. But then came the fucking media blitz.

That was the second mistake the cops made.

They held a press conference and said everyone's name out loud. Some middling sergeant with a penchant for marketing branded them the "Tucson Twelve." I stood at the back of the room and listened, clenching my jaw. Outing Saras is pretty vulgar, but I decided not to fight them on it. I figured it might help get the job done.

There was just one problem: Every person who died at Cloak and Dagger was *shot*. There wasn't a single death you could pin on a Sara.

Seventeen people went missing, too. Seventeen new Saras—allegedly—abducted by ADAPT.

But that's just it—the thing that wrenches my goddamned soul from its socket. Without the Facebook group, without Mom, there's *no evidence*.

Not like those two and a half dozen gunshot wounds.

The police tried to walk back their stunt when they realized they couldn't actually *blame* Devon for Cloak and Dagger. But the genie's out of the bottle, now. All they did was make him famous.

Saras spent the summer lighting the internet on fire about how the whole thing was handled. How they so ruthlessly and publicly read those names.

I would have been livid, too. If I didn't have all the facts.

I've been wondering if Devon's face might pop up on my socials some random morning. If he'll expose himself because he can't resist the spotlight. I fantasize about the way they'll snag him: Some innocuous hint in the background of the video, like a bag from a local store or a street sign through the window. But he's a ghost. He's letting everyone else troll the comments and write the think pieces. Knows he doesn't have to say his own damn name if it's in everyone else's mouth.

Either that, or he's dead. But I don't think so. He's got a whole family to take a bullet for him now.

They didn't read Mom's name that day, considering she was already dead. But it didn't matter. I'd already published that obit. Already outed her myself.

I don't have a lot of friends here anymore.

Not that I had any to begin with.

Kayla's brother is sending me death threats. Her name was on the Tucson Twelve list. I keep wondering if I should report him to the police, but it's not like I'd trust them to do anything about it.

Luke, the chef from Mom's restaurant, is the only person who's been halfway decent. He asked if he could buy the Fair Shake. The offer didn't shatter any records, but I was thankful he didn't try to lowball me.

The house has been complicated, though. Sabrina said I should just wait till the new year to try and sell. But I need the money.

I need this to be over.

Tucson PD finally stopped calling me back in August, when they escalated the case to the feds. At first, I was relieved. But now . . . I don't know. I wish they'd give me an update. I have a right to be kept in the loop, if they find him.

On the other hand, maybe I don't. I'm just a girl with a dead mother.

And it's not like Devon is the one who killed her.

(((

On Tuesdays I leave work early so I can talk to Krista. I don't have much to say to her. But even when I don't talk, she takes notes. I actually think that's when she writes the most—when I'm quiet. When Sandy and Alyssa see Krista, they go together. I wish I had someone to go with, a person who'd lead the conversation so I could just nod if I agreed or, if I didn't, I'd know exactly what my beef was so I could argue my point without having to think too hard. "She never unloads the dishwasher." "Well, you never ask." "I shouldn't *have to ask*!"

I only go to Krista because Sandy and Alyssa are paying for my sessions and it would be ungrateful to ditch and I'd never want them to think I'm even remotely ungrateful. The whole thing feels dangerous, though. Disrespectful at best. These are secrets. *Our* secrets. Mom isn't here to defend herself. It isn't right. I sit there peeling tiny flakes of faux leather off Krista's cheap couch, rolling buttercream carnage between my fingers like dead flesh. She takes notes when I do that, too.

"How quickly do they expect the house to sell?"

"Not the house. It's more like . . . the land the house is sitting on."

"Same difference."

"Not really."

Krista squints at me through her chunky black lashes. They look so heavy. I wonder if it's hard for her to keep her eyes open. I've never worn that much makeup, even the night of Cloak and Dagger, when Jade attacked my cheeks and eyelids with pixie dust.

"Have you thought about what you'll do with the money?"

"I'm gonna go to New York." The words leave my lips like kids hopping a fence. "I was just . . . I was thinking about college. Like, that I should go."

Krista doesn't speak. Her unblinking eyes are like two black spiders on her face.

"I'd have to apply to some scholarships and things like that, but I'm pretty sure I can afford to move once they pay me for the house. Er . . . the land the house is sitting on." God, what am I saying?

After an agonizing hiatus, she resuscitates the conversation. "Do you know anyone in New York?"

"Um . . . I have this friend who might be headed there." My cheeks tingle.

"Mia, how's your sleep?"

"Okay, I guess."

"And how much are you eating these days?"

"More. Especially if Sandy or Alyssa reminds me."

"Nothing wrong with taking things slow, okay? There won't be anyone to remind you to eat in New York."

Sweat creeps down my chest and pools in my bra. Like I'm wearing ten pounds of extra clothes.

I don't know why I just said that. The thought of putting my whole life in a suitcase and boarding a plane for a strange city sends a hot spike of terror straight through me. Which, I realize, also feels a little like excitement. My body reacts in the exact same way. I struggle to tell the two feelings apart. Especially these days.

On the drive home, I get a text from Sandy, asking if I can swing by the supermarket and grab some eggs, tomatoes, and oat milk. I guess we made a lot of smoothies this week—or lattes? I hate it when she does this: when she asks me to run an errand after dark. It's been five months, but I'm still pulled home like a magnet every time those low, dusky fingers of light start pointing at me. But I don't want to disappoint her. She and Alyssa are letting me crash for free and paying for my therapy. The least I can do is pick up groceries. I need to talk to Sandy about this later, though. It's not cool.

Back in June, I used to sit in traffic and watch all the cars with a strange lump of nonsensical outrage in my throat. *Where the fuck are all these people going? Don't they know my mom just died?*

I don't feel that way anymore. Or if I do, it's become such a part of me that I don't even notice.

That old song "Spiderwebs" by No Doubt comes on the radio as I sit at a red light. I bob my head to the punchy horn riff and mouth the tongue twister lyrics. A cautious smile dances to my lips as the light turns green. The engine surges with the bass line. Fills my heart with something. Not sure what.

But it feels wrong.

This happens, sometimes. For a moment, I'm lighter. Till it starts to feel like a betrayal.

It's dark by the time I pull up at the supermarket.

I've been having this feeling lately. At night. Doesn't matter if I'm out or in Sandy's guest room, scrolling and tapping as sleep evades me. I feel like I have two shadows. No . . . it's more than a feeling. Sometimes I think I *see* her, stepping out from behind my own shadow for a timid peek at what lies beyond the darkness. She never shows herself for long. A split-second shudder, and my shadow twin is gone. I still feel her, though. That added weight.

Watching me. Is she watching me or is she watching *over* me?
There's a difference. Right now, I don't know.

I leave the car, and my breath catches as she dips a toe into a pool
of flickering light. Rides piggyback on top of my shadow as I turn
toward the store.

I wonder if she'll finally leave me alone once I manage to get
eight hours of unmedicated sleep. But part of me wants to see her.
I've come to expect her. Depend on her, even.

Saras die exactly twice. There is no evidence to suggest they live
a final, metaphysical life. Then again, there's no evidence to suggest *we* do, either. Doesn't stop people from believing it. There is
no word for "evidence" in the language of loss. A thing is whatever
you need it to be, as long as you need it.

That said, if she *is* watching me—or watching over me—she's
probably pissed as all get-out that I abandoned the house with all
our stuff in it.

Tucson has this whole "Face the Night Again" motto post–Cloak
and Dagger, though I'm not sure you can call it "facing the night" if
you're clenching your ass the entire time. Everyone heading toward
the grocery store has their eyes pinned to the ground, beelining for
the refuge of the scanner. Wondering if everything will start to feel
normal again if they keep pretending it is.

As I lock my car and turn to join them, a woman's voice croaks
across the darkness.

"Izzy?"

My breath catches as the syllables hit the back of my skull like
bullets. When was the last time I heard her name out loud?

A diminutive, middle-aged woman steps out from behind the
Jeep, wearing a shapeless sage-green dress and battered old Birkenstocks. Her long, salt-white hair hangs beside a purple crystal
around her neck, nestled in the center of a berry-sized hint of a
braless bosom.

I've seen her. Not in person. A photo. I don't remember her
name.

But she's one of them. One of Twelve.

I go boneless as she approaches. Her small, wispy build doesn't seem so small and wispy anymore.

"Just follow me and don't say a word. Okay, Izzy?"

I bite my mouth shut. My head spins like an out-of-control carousel, blaring manic calliope music. People at the restaurant used to call me "Fun Size Izzy" because we looked so much alike. But Mom dazzled in a way I never could, even as I caught up in age. Maybe it's the dim light. Or all the weight I've lost. Who knows. But this crunchy, delusional Sara is advancing on me, and I have about three seconds to decide what I'm going to do about it.

"O-okay," I whisper. Taking a step toward her. Toward the car.

I finger the key fob. One more step. She extends a hand . . . as I mash the unlock and panic buttons at the same time.

The alarm screeches, and so does she. Everyone in the parking lot stares. A guy walking toward his truck drops his bag and books it back to the store. Apples somersault across the pavement.

I flail for the Jeep as the woman pounces. She snags the edge of my jean jacket in her fist as I throw the door open. The entire sleeve tears at the seam. But I'm in. I punch the lock button as she starts kicking the side of the car. *Thump, thump, CRASH.* She's for sure just put a dent in it. I flip the ignition. The siren stops blaring, but she's still shrieking. Now that it's quiet, I can hear what she's saying.

"Fuck you, you fucking *rat bitch*—"

I yank the car into drive, and she scrambles up the hood on all fours like a deranged cat wearing Birkenstocks. Starts pounding the windshield with her fists. The glass spiderwebs and my stomach lurches. What happens when it breaks and she falls right on top of me?

I rev the engine. She's still hanging on, slamming her fists, and now her head, against the glass. Her lacerated forehead bleeds, but it barely leaves a smear, healing the instant the skin tears. She doesn't give a shit if she's still dangling from my hood when I scream out onto the freeway. But it's all I can think to do.

I cut my wheel hard to the left and roar toward the exit, driving over the abandoned bag of groceries. There's a pop under my tire, followed by a creamy white starburst of milk.

The woman slips, losing her footing against the curvature of the hood. One more forceful spin in the other direction ought to do it.

The old Jeep protests with an exhausted squeal as I doughnut clockwise. She twirls through the air, a tangle of arms and legs, before belly-flopping to the pavement. I wonder if I just cracked her spine. How long it'll take her body to recover, if I did. But she rolls upright, cradling her head. Blood drools from her furious, elongated teeth as she opens her mouth to yell after me. I ride the accelerator and tear out of the parking lot, squinting through the splintered, milk-spattered windshield.

Her words hiss in my ears as I pull onto the main road and hurtle toward the freeway.

Fucking rat bitch.

That's what she called me. No. What she called my mother.

I squeeze the steering wheel in my trembling fists. The cops have been spinning in circles, and meanwhile Devon's had people in Tucson all along. People who have been out looking for Mom.

Who are now looking for me.

The store is only about five minutes from Sandy's house. I'm about to merge into the exit lane when the pewter sedan behind me starts to purr and surges toward my bumper, as close as it can get without making contact. I weave toward my exit, keeping one eye on the road and the other on the sedan's headlights glaring savagely in my rearview. There's a man behind the wheel, white and pasty, with a thick, riotous beard. The woman from the parking lot rides shotgun.

They follow me off the exit, magnetized to my bumper. I fumble with my phone as I make a sharp left turn onto an industrial fire road. I need to stall. Can't lead them to Sandy's door. As expected, they spin to follow me, spitting up dusty rocks like shrapnel. I dial out, breathing past the shards of dread in my chest.

"What's up?" Sandy answers.

"Someone's following me. One of them's a Sara. Maybe both. I don't know. It's someone my mom used to—"

"Hang on, hang on. Where are you?"

"I'm in the car."

"No, I mean *where?*"

"Like, two minutes from the house. I'm trying to lose them. But—"

The fire road gives way to a dead end. Mountains of chalky white gravel and a Bobcat tractor stand at the edge of the star-spangled darkness. I'll have to loop back around. Or go off road into the desert. Shit.

"Lyss has a gun. Head for the house. We'll be ready."

"Sandy—" How does she know what it means to be ready? I'm pretty sure neither of them has ever faced a Sara before.

The car eats up road as I surge toward the gravel barricade. I toss my phone to the passenger seat, grip the wheel in both fists, and slice toward the desert beyond.

"Mia? Mia—!" Sandy's muted voice squawks from the phone.

The Saras are driving a crappy old Ford Taurus, low to the ground. Not ideal for off-roading. I, on the other hand, have a Jeep. They try to follow me, and hunks of limestone lodge in their undercarriage. Their engine whines as I head for the glimmer of the main road at the opposite end of the black sprawl.

After a bumpy, gut-twisting ride across the wash, dodging the glowing eyes of more than one nocturnal animal, I glance in the rearview. I'm alone again. The Saras' car hasn't moved. I breathe a sigh and snag the phone off the seat. Sandy's still on the line.

"I think I lost them. I'm in the desert."

"In the car."

"Yes. In the car, in the desert. They got stuck. Get the gun and I'll be there soon."

I hang up and make a hairpin turn onto Oracle Road, causing the entire left lane to slam their brakes to make space. But I can handle a couple of middle fingers.

Sandy and Alyssa stand framed in the light of the open door. Sandy gasps and points at my bloody, crystallized windshield as I roar up the driveway. I catch a glint of silver in Alyssa's clenched hand as I rush toward them.

"Get inside and turn off all the lights." I start pulling them through the door with me. "These people are fucking pissed. If they figure out which house I just—"

"What happened?" Alyssa whispers, adjusting her 9mm. The grip shines with sweat.

"I'll explain in a—"

Footsteps pound, hard and fat like hail. The two Saras burst toward us from the dark side of the street. Of course they opted to pursue my car on foot. I should have known they wouldn't give up so easily.

I blink, and they're in the driveway. The bearded man descends, arms outstretched in an anticipatory choke hold. The woman screams in my face.

"You're *fucked,* honey. It's over. He's gonna burn you alive when he fi—"

Alyssa fires the gun.

Two shots. One for each.

The man goes down, caught in the chest at close range. In an instant, his face bloats to twice its size. His eyes bulge from his head, capillaries exploding like they're pregnant with black ink. Breath scrapes across his lungs as he bucks on the ground, clutching his chest with swollen arms the color of combusted charcoal.

My gaze swings to the woman, on her knees but still very much alive. She cradles her arm as poisoned blood oozes down the front of her dress. She wails, catching sight of her partner, splayed across the stoop. Life ebbing from his black balloon of a body.

Rust is a bitch.

The woman rises. Alyssa's still got the gun trained on her. But her hand is starting to tremble.

"Alyssa . . ." Sandy whispers. She needs to finish the job.

Alyssa's gaze flicks from the rancid heap on the ground to the sobbing woman. Birkenstocks grasps the purple crystal between her berry breasts with her good hand.

"Paul . . . oh God. *Paul—*"

The woman's breath comes in frayed hiccups as her chattering teeth shrink dejectedly back into her gums. She doesn't look like a Sara anymore. Just a bloody, disoriented old hippie who just saw her man take a bullet.

Alyssa's lips part, but no sound comes at first. "I-I'm sorry—"

Sandy wrests the gun from Alyssa's grip.

I'm paralyzed on the stoop, knees locked tight, both hands clamped over my mouth.

Across the street, a door creaks open. Flip-flops patter on the pavement.

"Sandy!" a woman cries. "Are you—?"

The Sara gurgles, low in her throat, and the sound crescendoes to an anguished howl. Before Sandy can pull the trigger, she leaps the length of the driveway and sprints down the street, back the way she came. The toxic rust in her arm will start to spread soon, but it doesn't slow her down. She's just as fast as she was five minutes ago. Dammit, Alyssa. Should've shot her in the leg. Not sure I could have done any better, in the moment. But still.

There's a corsage of light as Sandy fires a useless round at the woman's back. She's already gone. Two more neighbors emerge from their houses. Commotion hums around us, like flies on dead flesh.

"Mia, go inside and call the police," Alyssa whispers, squeezing life back into my shoulders.

Finally, I release my hands from my mouth. Carefully step around the black remains.

There's a cop named Danny who came to the house on June 6, and he's back again tonight. He doesn't let anyone call him Officer Halstead, because that's his dad. He's just Danny. He has a round, rosacea-tinged face like ripe fruit and clear blue eyes. He can't be much older than me. He might actually be younger, I can't tell the difference. I still struggle with that, because of Mom.

Danny's the only cop who ever listened to my advice. When I told him to move that surveillance van, he agreed. He was also the only one who understood the risk of reading the names. But there wasn't much he could do. He's the rookie over there.

A black ambulance takes care of Paul. Through the window, I see Sandy turn on the garden hose. I'm perched at the far end of the breakfast bar as Danny enters the house. His radio crackles, announcing his presence before he rounds the corner into the kitchen. I remember how the evening of June 6, when the cops traipsed in like a herd of moose, Danny's footsteps were featherlight. He's got that same tread now, barely making a sound as he approaches the opposite side of the granite slab, leaning across to greet me.

"Heya." His smile is tight. "Sorry for the silence lately," he adds when I don't say anything back.

Danny used to call every couple of days to give me updates. Usually, the update would be that he didn't have one. But now that the FBI's in charge, there isn't even any news about the lack of news.

"I get it."

"So uh . . . Y'know we gotta take a—"

"Statement. It's fine."

He exhales and scratches his reddening cheek with a slightly too-long fingernail. Flips open a leather bound notepad.

"You ever meet Mr. and Mrs. Brightman?"

"Er . . . no. I didn't know that was . . . I mean, I knew *of* them—"

Veronica—Ronnie—and Paul Brightman were two of the names they found in Mom's phone. A couple of old yogis from Sedona who went missing back in April.

"Well, looks like we owe you one. Paul's toast. Eleven more to go." He quirks me a sympathetic frown, catching himself. "Er, sorry. I didn't mean—"

"If he were alive, we could've interviewed him."

"Look, you did what you had to—"

"And Ronnie got away."

"She'll slow down. She's hurt."

"Exactly. If she can't find anyone to help her with that bullet, she'll look just like Paul in a couple hours."

Danny absorbs my words.

"Did she say anything to you about uh . . ." He coughs, like he has to cushion it with something. "Devon?"

The cops are embarrassed for saying his name that first time. And they should be. Everyone's trying to walk it back. I hear his name less often now, on TV and on the internet. But it's too late. All anyone ever needed was the idea of him.

"She didn't. Specifically. Well, I guess . . . She said he was gonna burn me alive when he found—" I catch my breath. "I mean, my mom. Ronnie confused me with my mom."

Danny studies me, like he's mentally pressing Mom's face to mine on a sheet of tracing paper.

"I know. I don't get it, either."

"I was gonna say the opposite. Depends on the lighting, I guess."

"Yeah, depends on the lighting."

Danny taps the notepad with his pen. "They think she's alive."

"I don't know why. It's been all over the news that she's dead."

"You never buried her. If I'm Devon and I'm desperate to collect a head, I can do those mental gymnastics." He grinds his pen between his teeth as he works it out. "According to that obit, she died the same day someone ratted him out. A guy like that doesn't believe in coincidence. She could've faked her death and run off to Mexico, easy peasy."

"Okay, well if she's in *Mexico,* then why is she here?" I hold his gaze.

"To check on you, of course."

The pit in my stomach cracks wide open.

"We can put you up somewhere for a couple nights. That's not a problem. There's a hotel we can monitor." A tacit silence passes between us. "Is there anywhere else you can go, though? After that? Somewhere a little further?"

It's not like I wasn't considering it. I have a small nest egg from the restaurant sale, and once someone buys the house I'll have even more saved. But I was thinking I'd make the move in a year or two. Slowly inch my way out of Sandy's place over the next month.

Anguish thickens in my throat. It wasn't supposed to happen this way. I'm not ready.

"I'm sorry, Mia," Danny says after he's let the dust settle for a moment.

"I need to know Sandy and Alyssa will be okay."

"I'll keep an eye on their house at night. Me, personally."

"For how long?"

"Till we find Ronnie."

"Dead or alive?"

"Yes ma'am."

Guilt dances with the terror that's overstayed its welcome in my gut.

"I'll get my stuff so we can go to that hotel," I mumble, staring into my hands.

I wish I could go home instead.

NOW

The Red Market stays open 24/7 because it's underground.

Of course, any Sara looking to visit would have to enter during nighttime hours. But they can stay all day if they want. There's only one carefully monitored entrance to the abandoned parking garage, which is situated at the edge of a neglected, overgrown soybean field. The rough concrete façade looks unfinished and inconspicuous—another construction project lost to bankruptcy during the early days of Saratov's, tagged with faded old junkie graffiti and wreathed by grotesque, six-foot-tall spiked thistle. A guard wearing a Cincinnati Bengals cap paces outside as we approach, dumping the last few fries from a McDonald's carton into his mouth. I know the Red Market has uninfected employees on their roster, but still, I'm surprised to see him.

And he's surprised to see us.

He removes his scratched, douchey vintage Oakleys to get a closer look at our pickup as we pull around to the entrance.

"We have a parking spot in my name," Cora says. "Let me talk."

I meet the guy's probing stare through the windshield. "Fuck, we didn't plan this right, we can't enter during the day without causing a scene. This looks super shady."

Cora pops the storage compartment between us as he raps on my window. "We'll just show him the pills. He'll get it."

"What if he steals them?"

"He's not a Sara, he doesn't need them."

"He could sell them."

"You got a better idea?" We both know I don't.

The guard knocks again. This time, I roll down the window.

"This is private property, ladies—"

"We have a reservation. We're supposed to meet Nikita?" Cora reveals a ziplock bag. "We have stuff to sell."

Inside are five orange pill bottles with Sara center logos on each cap: a black cross inside a diamond. The label reads, "Recovery Center #48, Saratov Salvation of Manhattan."

"Shit, are those Daylights?" The guard sticks a greedy hand through the window. Cora withdraws. He whistles out a breath. "How'd you pull that off?"

"I work at Salvation of Manhattan," I reply coolly. Cora flips the bottle around so he can see the logo on the cap.

"You're a long way from home." He just stares for a moment. At me. Like he can't decide whether to let us in.

This keeps happening. I keep wondering who people think I am. Whether it's going to help me or fuck me in the end.

Cora leans forward to redirect his gaze. Smacks her gum and bats her lashes, blowing a weak bubble that deflates over her smiling lips. Sex appeal spiked with artificial sweetener.

I'd say I can't stand to look at her, when she's like this. But that would be a lie.

The guard cracks his stiff neck, eyeballing Cora, then the ziplock. "Niki buys those for seventy-five bucks a pop. If they are what you say they are."

Cora shoots him a disarming grin.

"If they're not, I've got one hell of a death wish workin' on this tan."

She waits for him to shudder as she runs her tongue over her teeth. A skin-crawling game of sexy chicken.

At last, he shakes her stare. "Uh, park on B1 only. Market's on B2 and B3. Elevator's a piece of shit and there's no one here to get it unstuck today so take the stairs."

He pulls a clicker from his belt clip, and the wrought-iron barrier yawns open. Cora smiles and squeezes my hand as I roll up the window.

"Nice." I meet her smug side-eye.

"We *do* get results, don't we?" She blows another bubble.

The garage below is pitch black, and I switch on my headlights. The gate clatters behind us with a resounding thud.

We creep forward. "Shit, I'm so nervous," Cora whispers across the darkness.

It's like someone's just stomped on my chest. I know what she's nervous about.

Granted, I'm nervous, too.

On one hand, if Devon is here, this entire nauseating charade can end. I'll be free. I'll slip away and call the cops and tell them exactly where to find him. On the other hand, seeing Devon requires . . . *seeing Devon*. Which comes with the risk of him seeing me first.

I drop Cora's hand.

She flips her mirror down, triggering the accompanying light, and starts touching up her makeup. She paints her lips a vivacious maraschino red and coats her lashes with mascara. I try to focus on the labyrinthian parking structure instead of what she's doing. My thoughts slide to Jade. Her peacock-blue eyeliner. The magenta kiss she left on my Starbucks cup. Cora subscribes to a lot of the same trends. But it's different. *She's* different. When Cora dresses up like this, she reminds me of a photo pasted to a fake ID, as if someone once told her this is how grown women are supposed to look. How they're supposed to look for *men*. I wish she weren't so desperate to impress. I wish she could see what I see, when her face is etched with freckles, acne scars, and old stories.

As I maneuver our pickup around a steep, shadowy curve, there's the muffled sound of distant music. Up ahead, a flashlight arcs in lazy circles. Someone's directing us forward and into a parking space. The lot is packed. Only a couple of spots remain.

As we exit the car, the music sharpens. There's some sort of country band playing beneath us. A harmonica warbles through the crevices. I tie my hair back and throw up the hood of my sweatshirt for a half-assed disguise. Red hair makes it tough to go through life inconspicuously. Especially these days. I should have dyed it, before we started this. But there wasn't time.

There's a spring in Cora's step as she leads us toward a dimly lit stairwell. I'm slower, securing the ziplock of Daylights inside my backpack. We've left one bottle behind, in the glove compartment.

My heart flutters as we approach the belly of the building. There's a scarlet arrow spray-painted on the wall, pointing us in the right direction. At least, I think that's spray paint.

I'd heard about Red Markets from the old Facebook group, but not a lot of people had been to one. At the time, there were only three in the whole country. The closest one to Arizona was some-where in Texas. I don't think Mom ever went. Then again, Mom did a lot of stuff I never knew about.

Six new locations have sprung up the past year alone, including this one, thirty miles outside Dayton. There are more free Saras than there were a year ago. A lot more.

A soft, muted wave of artificial light envelops us as we enter the market. Someone's rigged a grid on the ceiling and hung dozens of small floods, covered with different gels and diffusion paper, like we're in some kind of weird indie theater space. We might as well be. I feel like I've been dropped in the middle of a performance that's happening all around me, and I'm the only one who didn't memorize their lines.

The garage is congested with Saras, shoulder-to-shoulder, wend-ing their way past each other to visit different booths and tables. A quaint three-piece bluegrass band in the defunct elevator bank riffs on a Bob Dylan song—hence the harmonica. The whole scene makes me think of the farmer's market Mom and I used to visit in Salt Lake, when I was little. Except, instead of organic smoothie pop-ups, you've got pay-by-the-minute bleeders. That's where the longest line is. There are a dozen of them, sitting behind a ten-foot plexiglass barrier. Sipping juice and nibbling cookies with needles lodged in their forearms. One bleary-eyed guy finishes drawing half a pint, and the shopkeeper—bartender?—grabs the blood bag through a small opening in the plexiglass. He pours it into a plastic Solo cup, like it's cheap beer from a keg, then moves to sling the next one. I wonder how much the bleeders get paid. Whether they feel safe.

Bodies start colliding against me, and I realize I've planted my feet. The edge of my vision feathers and my legs wobble. I haven't eaten since we left New York. Adrenaline's kept me satiated, but it's not going to last. We should find Nikita and make this quick. I move along and pull Cora with me, following the current.

The market is an all-ages affair. I spot plenty of younger adults like us, but also elderly couples holding hands, trying not to get sep-arated, and even a few kids chasing each other through strangers' legs, attracting a few "where the hell are your parents" death glares.

There's no ventilation down here, just a smattering of industrial fans. The smell of the crowd tangles with those earthy notes in the blood, curling my stomach like gift-wrap ribbon. Then again, maybe it's not the smell. Maybe it's the sheer number of them . . . and the memory of the last time I was in a space with this many people.

Cora isn't bothered. She stands on her toes and scans the faces, adjusting her halter top so it hits her midriff just so. Her forehead glistens, and frizzy little ringlets blossom from her hairline, bidden by the heavy air.

My eyes comb the space for Nikita's table. She's supposed to be here selling hospital-grade burn remedies. Neither of us has met her, but Cora showed me her picture on the Red Market's Discord. She's a petite blond woman with sleeve tats and a septum piercing, and in her official shopkeeper's headshot she was wearing a bright caftan with tropical birds all over it. Clearly, she's not wearing the same outfit today. If she's on this level, she doesn't stand out. We're going to have to wade through the masses.

I sidle toward the guy juggling Solo cups at the bleeders' station, drawing stares from people who think I'm cutting the line.

"Hey, we've got an appointment with Nikita, do you know where she is?"

"Downstairs," he barks without looking at me.

As he clears the way, a shock of salt-white hair in the crowd pulls my gaze.

Ronnie.

She's standing at the end of the line, in a beat-up biker jacket. There's no mistaking those slender stems for legs. I can't see her face; she's turned in the opposite direction. Talking to someone who's just joined the line behind her. But it's her. It has to be. My nerves twist like a corkscrew as time stands still.

Tucson PD *claimed* they found her body in the desert. But it's hard to pull DNA from the shit that gets left behind after a Sara passes. For months, I wondered if they just called it a day so they didn't have to keep Danny posted at Sandy's house anymore.

I need to run. Before she sees me. Before she tells *him* she saw me—

"I'm gonna hang over there for a few minutes." Cora's voice pulls me back in. She points across the garage to a table with a screaming pink banner that reads "Frida's Flavors" in whimsical brush script.

I'm only half listening. I glance back over my shoulder, to the place I just saw Ronnie. The woman turns. Her face is . . . well, it's different. Wider. Softer. Her eyes are closer together. I think. It was dark when she attacked me. But—

"Mia?"

"Er . . . yeah. You're gonna—"

"I'm gonna wait over by Frida's. I told him that's where I'd be."

Panic lunges up my throat. ". . . Wait, he's *here*? Did he reply to you?"

"Uh, I don't know, seeing as that would require me to turn on my data to check my DMs and I'm not *a fucking moron*—"

I release a breath. "Right."

"I'll meet you back on this level when you're done with Nikita, okay?"

If I'm going to bolt, this is my chance. I keep one eye on Cora. The other on the white-haired woman.

"Wish me luck." A nervous smile plays on her lips, like she's about to ask a celebrity on the street for a photo.

"You look great." I wonder if she's clocked the flat distance in my voice.

Cora trots off, and the woman's eyes sweep over me. Once. Twice.

But there's no stumble of recognition. No stiffness in her gaze. Because it isn't her. I *know* it isn't.

I unfurl my clenched fists. I'm just exhausted. Hungry. Scaring myself for no goddamn reason. I have to stop freaking out like this. Can't quit before we get to the outpost. That's the end of the rainbow. Unless, of course, I see him here today. Either way, if I run, I'll never know how this ends. If *I* could've ended it.

I wind my way back toward the stairwell, securing my hood around my face.

B3, the market's lower level, is a darker, quieter space, illuminated by the glare of work lights on lopsided stands. There's no bluegrass band down here. The air is muddy with cigarette smoke and the stench of mildewed concrete. None of the booths have signs or banners. You either know who you're looking for, or you're not doing business.

There's an RV parked along the far wall with its side hatch propped open. A group of bleeders gather around a plastic folding table, having just wrapped their shift. Some wear bandages on their arms, but most just leave the hole gaping, unfazed. I remember that feeling. They silently count their cash as they split a large pizza heaped with toppings.

I turn, and a gust of smoke fills my lungs. A woman passes as I cough, heading toward the stairwell, wearing a black caftan with a cascading pattern of plump marigolds.

"Oh hey, um . . . Nikita?"

She spins to face me, cigarette pincered at the side of her mouth.

"I'm here with Cora, er . . . QT_Core?" I remember to use her alias from her socials. Nikita's eyes rest on me as tendrils of smoke twist through her open lips.

She looks like somebody's "cool mom" with her shaggy, textured bob and septum hoop, fine lines and crow's-feet only just starting to reveal themselves. If she's a Sara, she was turned in the nick of time. If she's the kind of person who cares about that sort of thing. I can't help but remember the way Mom used to claw for that silver lining.

"We uh . . . we have Daylights—"

"Follow me." I detect the hint of an accent in her voice. Eastern Europe, maybe. She leads me behind the RV.

There's a mini fridge plugged into the RV's grumbling generator, flanked by two tattered camping chairs. She settles into one and gestures I sit across from her. I sink down, carefully, afraid I might tear a hole in the seat.

"What center?" The "w" comes out from under her front teeth, not quite a "v" sound, more like a soft "f."

"Forty-Eight."

"Manhattan. Fancy girl."

"I guess." I fish the ziplock out of my backpack. "This is a new formula, by the way. They rolled these out a couple months ago."

She ashes her cigarette into an empty, red-ringed Solo cup by her feet and takes the bag from me. She's silent as she opens a bottle and dumps a hill of sea-green capsules into her palm.

"It's an extended-release blend," I go on. "The Saras at Forty-Eight could stay outside for up to seven hours on one dose. Six hours was the recommended limit, though."

Nikita knits her brow, then pops a pill into her mouth.

"We'll see." She smiles as she holds the pill in her cheek and sucks on it. "Part of my commission."

"Fine."

She pulls a small metal trash bin from behind her camping chair, followed by a book of matches from the deep V of her caftan. "I give you seventy-five for each pill, minus my commission," she says as she takes all four bottles from the ziplock, then pours their contents back into the bag like hard candy. "Ten percent."

"And the one you just took."

Nikita shrugs, dropping the empty bottles into the metal bin, one by one. "It's a good price."

She lights a match and adds it to the pile, melting the incriminating empties to a gelatinous paste.

"I pay you in cash. Okay?"

"Actually, what I really need are Saranasia shots. Two of them." Her face hardens. It's a bold request. "Whatever the difference is, cash is fine."

Nikita stands, catlike, arching into a stretch. Lets a moment pass before breaking my stare.

"I will see what we have."

She moves off, sealing the bag of loose pills. I notice her fingers are tattooed with delicate, tiny violets and black stars. She's missing three-quarters of her right pinky. I wonder if she lost it before she got infected. Either that, or she had some kind of rust accident. Which, I remind myself, isn't always an accident.

As Nikita ambles over to the RV, a figure comes down the dark staircase, into the scattershot glow of the work lights: a withered white guy with silver and gold hair, wearing glasses and a puffy green ski jacket. Probably one of the bleeders, taking his break; he's not a Sara, if he's wearing glasses.

There's a security guard posted toward the far corner of the

garage. Yellow vest. Badge. All very official. Carries a sidearm.
Instead of joining the other uninfected people on their break, the
bespectacled bleeder heads his way. Hands him a Solo cup with a
friendly pat on the back.

That's nice. Seeing people with friendships like that. I watch their
casual body language. The bleeder doesn't seem tense, and the guard's
in a good mood, now that someone's come through with something to
eat. I wonder how long they've known each other.

A moment later, the guy in glasses frowns. Murmurs something
to his friend from the corner of his mouth.

He's staring right at me.

No.

. . . Yes.

It's not my imagination this time.

The security guard follows his gaze to me. Wrinkles his nose.
Like he's trying to suss something out.

I don't recognize either of them. Never saw their photos in Tucson.
Still, I fix the RV with a pleading stare. Like I'm begging it to spit
Nikita back out.

The guy in glasses whips out a cell phone. Starts typing. I stand
and turn around, showing him my back, in case he's about to take
my damn picture or something. I don't know. I should leave. Now.
I don't need the shots. Don't need the money.

. . . Except I do. I *really* do.

I pace in tiny spirals, wringing my hands. Nikita alights from
the RV clutching two brown paper bags. She offers the lighter bag
first, but doesn't release it right away. "I'm supposed to make sure
you know what these are," she whispers. "What they're for."

"Of course I know," my voice cracks as I tug the bag. "Sorry, I
really gotta—"

"Yo, Niki—" The security guard shouts at her from across the
room. Waving to get her attention.

I don't know what's about to happen, but I don't like it. I'm electric
with horrible certainty.

Nikita sighs and thrusts the second bag toward me. "Anyway.
One twenty left over."

I should haggle. She's shortchanging me. By a lot. Instead, I spin
to face the stairs. Don't say thank you. I walk as steady as I can,

keeping my back to the security guard. Break into a run the second I turn the corner.

I hurtle up the dark staircase and trip on the top step, blasting my kneecap against the unforgiving concrete. I rocket through the pain and pick myself back up, stabbing my way between the bodies on B2. Retracing my steps to Cora and Frida's Flavors.

I could leave without her. That'd be the smart thing to do. I can still head to the outpost. I know where I'm going, and I have the car keys. I don't need her anymore.

But I stay the course. I'm not ready for us to separate. Not yet.

Not till we have to.

Cora materializes, holding a Solo cup. She chats with the booth's Tinker Bell–sized owner—the eponymous Frida, no doubt—who presents a small, translucent pink square between a pair of tweezers. Cora sticks out her tongue.

"Oh . . . *wow,*" Cora closes her mouth over the strip, dramatically rolling her eyes. "That's amazing, I'll take a dozen. Do you have any in peach?"

I seize her arm and she coughs, swallowing the strip too quickly. "Shit, Mia!"

"We have to go."

"What's wrong?"

"Just come with me. Now."

I'm still deciding what to tell her. Which lie to slot in.

Frida hands Cora an envelope. "I don't have peach today, sorry. That'll be twenty-two fifty."

Cora's stare hops from me, to Frida, then back to me.

"Cora. We have to *go.*"

"Tell me why."

My heart gallops as I scan the stairwell. I grab for her, yanking the strap of her halter top. She slaps me away, trying not to spill what's in her cup.

"Mia, what the fuck! We can't go. He's not here yet."

"He's not coming! That's not even him you've been talking to, and you know it."

Cora spears me with her wounded gaze. I know, in an instant, that I've said the wrong thing. I'd do anything to shovel it back into my mouth.

"Fine. Leave," she says, "I don't need you."

My breath catches and unravels.

At that moment, the bleeder in glasses crosses the room, trailed by Nikita. Headed right toward us.

I elbow my way past Cora, forcing the crowd to part for me. Pound back down to the level where we parked the truck, feeling for the keys in my backpack. The headlights gleam as I unlock it, guiding me like a tether as a wall of tears builds in my panicked eyes.

I dive into the truck, but I don't turn it on. Not right away. I'm transfixed by the middle distance, reading the darkness like tea leaves.

What, exactly, just happened?

What did I see?

What did I *think* I saw?

For all I know, Nikita's the one who's in trouble. Not me.

This is shameful. Melting down like this. Thinking everyone's put a target on my back—first "Ronnie," and now this rando.

Even if they have, I can't afford to flinch.

A cynical laugh rises to my lips. Devon wouldn't act like this. Wouldn't fucking *dare*.

Then, three hard knocks pelt my window. My hand flies to my mouth, stifling a yelp.

Cora stands outside, haloed by the light of the stairwell. Folds her arms across her chest. When I don't move, she knocks again, blowing a rogue wisp of hair from her face.

I paw around to unlock the door and she collapses to the front seat, still gripping her half-full Solo cup. She spikes it into the nearest cupholder.

"Thought you wanted to wait."

She angles her body away from mine, facing the window.

"Just drive, okay?"

I turn the key in the ignition. My slippery hands shake as I clutch the wheel, flooded with relief. Because she came back? Because we're leaving? Both, I guess.

I think about saying sorry. Saying *anything*. But I don't know where to start.

That's fine, though. Because she doesn't say anything either.

NOVEMBER 2023

Everything in the yard is dead. I'm surprised. It was mostly cacti. We haven't had any rain since June, but that shouldn't matter.

I have another ninety minutes of daylight, give or take. It's safe to be here now, but once the sun goes down the police want me back in my hotel room. Guess I finally got the hours I wanted.

I sit in the car for a minute. Then two. Studying the cracks in the stucco. The husks of our succulent garden.

The curtains in the big picture window were never put back up. Sunlight cascades into the living room. I've never seen it look that way before. Sabrina's hung a trailing plant there.

This was a nice house. It still is, it's still here. But I understand why Sabrina thinks the only offers might be teardowns. People are weird about that stuff. Houses where Saras lived—and died. It is what it is, I guess. It'll still be more money than I've ever had at once.

It'll still help me start over.

I didn't park in the driveway. Doesn't feel right. The house doesn't belong to anyone new yet, but it's not mine, either. Not really. I've been banished, and today I'm returning with my tail between my legs. I shift my weight on the front steps, fingering my key like I'm flashing a weapon I don't want to use—but I will if I have to.

The dead bolt gives way, and I half expect the door to open on its own with a nefarious creak. As I step inside, I watch my shadow from the corner of my eye, waiting for it to split in two. To confirm I'm not alone. It doesn't. It follows, dutiful, drifting across the living room mural.

I stop to take it in: Those spiny, geometric suggestions of mountain peaks, so satisfying in their symmetry. The seamless gradient of violet, tangerine, and blush behind them, like dawn on a distant planet. Creamsicle-orange mist crowns the tallest mountain peak. I remember carefully sponging that part as Mom steadied the ladder.

Maybe whoever buys the house will like the murals and decide not to knock it down. That would be nice.

I inch toward the wall till my nose touches, appreciating all the pockmarks and pores in the plaster. There are places where the brushstrokes are still evident, probably whenever Mom took a break and I picked up where she left off. Her brushstrokes were flawless. Invisible. Like she breathed all that color into the wall.

I shuffle back, zooming out to absorb the entirety of the piece. My middle school art teacher used to have a print of Monet's *Japanese Bridge* in her classroom, and I used to do the same thing every Thursday afternoon before the bell rang, appreciating the chaotic pink parabolas, thick like icing on a cake, as they morphed into lilies on the water. Chaos at a distance starts to feel like intention. Destiny, even.

Mom wasn't an impressionist. Come to think of it, I don't really know what her style was. She did it all. Maybe that was what held her back, when she tried to pursue a career. She couldn't pick a lane. But she had talent. I imagine what people might say about this particular mural, fifty, a hundred years from now. What message was Isobel McKinnon trying to send here? What was she *saying*, with these mountains?

Who knows. I never asked her. Never thought to.

My gaze tilts to the bottom of the painting, where ombré plum deepens to indigo and kisses the white base molding. The old carpet is gone. I hadn't noticed before. Maybe the moon men from the Sara center took it with them that day. I can't remember. But I'm relieved. I was sure there'd be some kind of noxious fog hanging in the air, hypnotizing me, dragging me back to that moment. But the sun sterilized the whole house in my absence. We left our things behind, but things are just things. She was gone in an instant, and I went with her.

All I did for thirteen years was wonder how this story would end: if she would die, *how* she would die. Whether I'd be there when it happened. Now I know. Everything. How strange it is, to finally know. I wonder what I'll wonder about now.

I wander over to the kitchen, surveying the cabinets but not opening any. Sabrina's gotten rid of the sharps container next to the recycling bin.

I don't know why I'm here. There's nothing I want to take with me. I only came because it was my last chance. Before Sabrina lists the house. Before I leave for New York City. Alyssa, who has family in the area, did some aggressive digging on my behalf this past week. Her uncle's friend's colleague hooked me up with a sublet near Columbia University through next May.

I'm beyond thankful, although I'm starting to wonder if a city like New York might be too big for me to swallow. Sandy and Alyssa have bolstered my confidence, helping me apply for jobs and study the subway map. But I keep imagining what Mom would have to say about it.

I sit at the table. Don't even realize I've done it till I'm in my chair.

I'm like a nonplayable character in a video game, programmed to move through the world in exactly one way with no deviations. Mia goes to the cupboard. She gets the blood kit. She sits at the table. She sits in this chair. Not the other chair. Never the other chair.

I rise and move to the opposite end of the table. I don't know why, but I want to sit in that other chair. I *need* to.

Her seat is exactly like mine. Dark walnut with a blue-and-white-striped cushion. This one is thicker, though—less worn down. She only sat there once a day, after all.

The room feels wrong from this angle.

What did she see, when she looked at the girl sitting across from her, with the needle in her arm? She used to feel sorry. She said so, every night. But after a while, she stopped. I told her it was my job. Said I was happy to do it, over and over. Finally, she started to believe me. And she kept believing, even after it wasn't true anymore.

I stand. For some reason, I feel drawn to my old room.

I thought I took everything I'd need for my new life the morning of June 6. Before Jade arrived. I could use some more warm clothes, though. Yesterday I looked up the weather in New York and my jaw came unhinged.

I turn down the hallway, but freeze midstep. Like the whole world just glitched.

There's a light on in Mom's room.

Did I miss it when I walked in? Maybe I couldn't see it from the door. Or . . .

Or.

I shiver as I approach the doorway, one painstaking step at a time. The room is silent aside from the nearly imperceptible electric

murmur of Mom's bedside lamp. Maybe we had a power surge. Or
Sabrina left it on last time she was here.

Or . . .

Stop it.

I skitter toward the lamp like I'm moving across thin ice. She usually kept things tidy. But not that last week. Half her drawers hang
out, with open tubes of makeup strewn across the dresser. The bed is
unmade. A tuft of stiff, soiled gauze sits on her nightstand. My memory flares, like brushing a hot stove. I feel her labored breath hitting
my neck as I drive my fingers into her bloody gunshot wound, desperate to free myself. I hear her scream—that gut-shredding, god-
awful scream that goes on forever.

My ears ring as I stretch toward the lamp to turn it off.

A second item on the table pulls my gaze.

It's a sketchbook, open to an unfinished drawing, charcoal stub
still tucked in the spine for safekeeping.

It feels inappropriate to look. Obscene, even. For years, my
world was sharply divided into two categories: things Mom allowed
me to see, and the rest of it. That's where all the trouble started. I
blurred that line when I confronted her about Devon. Nothing was
the same, after that.

These drawings won't change anything. If I flip through the
book, it won't take back what I did.

But it won't hurt me, either. Not anymore. I already know everything. What she did. Who she became.

I reach for the sketchbook, carefully. Like it might crumble to
ash in my hands.

The drawing is rough, difficult to make sense of. There's a
figure on a boxy couch, in repose. The jagged angles representing
knees and elbows give the subject an almost robotic sensibility, like
they're not entirely human. That, or she hadn't finished softening
the curves. Or giving it a face. There's a blank void beneath its
humanoid head. The figure's lazy arm drapes over the side of the
couch, clutching something in its crudely rendered hand. A flower.

I pull back from the drawing like I did the mural, trying to add
it all up. The tiny flower is the only discernible object on the page.
Probably the last thing she ever drew.

My throat closes like a vise.

She loved yellow tulips and the month of April. Disneyland and Julie Andrews. *These are a few of my fav-or-ite things.* Her heart was tender and naïvely raw—open to attack. She might have called it fearless.

I turn the sketchbook over and open it to the first page. I'm startled to see my own handwriting. *Merry Christmas! Hope you enjoy using this whenever inspiration strikes!* This was my gift to her in 2016. How could I forget? I had the leather cover monogrammed with her initials.

I am once again forced to reckon with all the dead air in my memory: places where the movie cuts to static and nobody knows how to fix the frayed cables. I've forgotten Christmas. Long-ago birthday parties. Smiles and sing-alongs and late-summer sunshine—back when we could enjoy that together. I have forgotten anything that resembles joy. That morning in June, my mind built a makeshift bridge for me to cross and survive this moment. It would collapse under my weight if I stopped to look back at anything beautiful. My only clear memories of us are from this past year: somersaulting down that dark, inevitable hill, hand in hand. Letting go and watching her fall to the bottom.

There's a framed photo on the dresser: the two of us at the zoo, posing in front of the panda exhibit. I'm ten years old, holding a massive bag of caramel corn. Mom's a knockout in her distressed cutoffs. Another exiled memory. We traveled all the way to San Diego to see the pandas because they were my favorite, and one of them had just had a cub. This would have been May, right after school let out.

On July Fourth, we met Devon.

The people in this photo had no clue what was coming. There was no nightmare twisted enough to conceive it. Things weren't perfect. We didn't have a lot of money. Gram had just passed. Mom was lonely and still mad at my dad. But what does perfect even mean, when you're a family? Good is good enough. For the first time in years, I dare to wonder what our life might have been like if we'd skipped the fireworks that year.

My knees go soft. My body and my brain so firmly reject this line of thinking that they're refusing to keep me upright as a form of protest. I hold a sharp gulp of air as I let the bed catch me. Wondering if I'll feel the shape of her in the mattress. If there are threads of copper hair between the pillows.

I make myself small and knead my eyelids with the heels of my hands. The pressure creates swirls of color across the blind dark. Like fireworks.

We were hunted. *Mom* was hunted. I remember what Devon told me the night he cornered me outside the Book Bunker: "I wasn't *hunting* her. I bit her." I asked him what the difference was, and he rolled his eyes and said I didn't get it. But there's no other word for it. He had a strategy. Knew how quickly she'd trust him, that she was the kind of woman who'd try anything once. What he didn't count on was that she'd ultimately choose me—the first time, any-way.

What we had wasn't built to last. Another thing he probably knew.

I turn onto my side, and a hard object grinds against my hip.

I reach between the sheets. My hand brushes cold, rectangular plastic.

It's a phone.

I stare at my reflection in the black screen. It's dead. Been dead as long as she has.

Of course. She *did* have two phones.

The police asked me about it. If I hadn't been so eager to abandon our house, if I'd just cleaned out her room, I would have—

I squeeze my eyes shut. Pressing it between my clammy palms.

I need to charge it.

Need to decide what I'm going to do with it.

Give it to the cops. Obviously.

Yes. But I'm going to charge it first. Just to see.

See what?

I blink, letting light bleed back into my surroundings. Drop the phone into my pocket. I stand, considering the sketchbook . . . and tuck it under my arm.

Finally, I turn off the lamp.

As I head for the bedroom door, I pick up the panda photo, and dust scatters like dandelion seeds. I should take it. But I can't stand to look at it. My gap-toothed smile. Her sun-kissed arm around my freckled shoulders. Clouds of red hair tangling in the wind.

I don't want to remember.

I still need that bridge. Haven't made it all the way across yet.

Haven't even begun to consider what's on the other side.

((((((

It's a scratched-up old Motorola with a flip screen.

I race to the mall to buy the right charger before the sun goes down, half expecting the officer outside my hotel to write me a speeding ticket when I get there.

I should be packing. Preparing for tomorrow's journey.

I'm watching the phone charge instead.

The battery hits 10 percent and the screen flickers. Blood rushes my ears as I sink to the floor beside the outlet and turn it on.

There's no email or 5G on this fossil. The network connects, and the text icon in the corner starts pulsing with frantic red notifications. 1, 2, 3, 4, 5, 6—

All the air leaves my lungs. Twenty-four new messages.

My finger trembles over the text icon. I know I'm not supposed to pull back that curtain.

But this is my inheritance. And nobody's here to stop me.

June 6
7:58AM
 ok I have everyone
 HELLO
 ?????
 Pick up
3:44PM
 Are you ok?
7:29PM
 gonna come thru in 30 are you THERE?
 Im really worried please pick up
8:33PM
 WHAT TH FCUK IZZY
 HOLY FUCKING SHIT
 WHY R TEH COPS AT UR HOUSE WHAT THE
 FUCK IS THIS
 omg
 PICK UP

New day, new phone number.

June 7
8:15AM

> **Babe**
> you better pray to god you never see me again
> i still cant figure out why you did this but i promise
> by the time im done with you youre gna fcking
> BEG ME for a bullet
> and don't you even TRY to imagine what Im gonna
> do to your daughter
> YoU ARE SO FUCKING FUcKED YOU BITCH

Two weeks later, another new number.

June 21
3:36AM

> Hey. It would mean a lot to me if we could talk. I
> know this number is still connected, i know youre
> reading this.
> i love you, ok?
> i am not too proud to tell you that
> Ive had a long time to think. i know why you felt
> like you had to do it
> This was my fault, if im bein honest w myself.
> you had every right to be upset. I'm so sorry for
> everything Iz
> please call me

4:49AM

> Fine, youve made your fucking bed
> sleep well

Finally, from another new number, more than four months later:

November 1
6:52PM

> **Hi**
> Ronnie just called me

Ngl im a little offended you were hanging out w/o
me lol
anyway how are you?
alive, clearly 😊

I'm drowning in cold sweat as I close the phone and let it drop to the dingy carpet.

He keeps changing his number. There's no way that last one is still in service, even though he just used it. But for an unhinged, out-of-body moment, I want to dial it.

I don't know what the hell I'd say, if someone answered. I think I'm just dying to see him do something stupid.

It was definitely stupid of him to keep texting her after all this time. I might have given the phone to the cops months ago. He's desperate for her to surrender. He did something stupid because he hoped she'd react by doing something even *more* stupid.

Not because he still loves her. Or ever did.

Then again, maybe that *is* love. To a person like that. The breathless intimacy of plotting someone's death.

I can't sleep. The phone glows from the floor. A hundred percent charged now.

I'm going to swing by the police station tomorrow. Give it to Danny before I leave. That's the right thing to do.

Isn't it?

What the hell am *I* supposed to do with it?

I scroll back in time to the beginning. April 17. She texts him first.

Umm YOUR SHIRT

???

I told you, PLEASE dont leave stuff here

jesus relax ill get it tmrw

No you don't get it. I promised her you would never be at the house.

Stop

Izzy
its insane the way you let her run things its YOUR
HOUSE

I clench a pillow to my chest, like it will keep me from being sick all over the cheap scratchy bedspread. How many times was he at our house? Was I *there*?

You're ashamed of me
      Absolutely not
that really hurts
      Devon
you have so much SHAME about all of this and tbh
youre kinda making me feel like a piece of shit
      I'm so sorry i never meant to make you feel that
      way
      i'll fix this i will talk to her
      babe?
Idk Iz im starting to feel like i need some space
from this situation
      No no please don't say that
      come over later ok?

I don't want to keep scrolling. But it's like tapping through Jade's stories. Masochistic autopilot.

There's some stuff I quickly swipe past. Salacious words that leap from the screen and stab color into my cheeks.

I understand enough to see the pattern, though.

They will fight, and it will be about me. He refers to me as a "shrill little dictator." Demands Mom stand up for herself.

This makes me sick u need to own this. you guys
live by this horrible code of self pity and it's so
fucking sad it makes me want to light ur house on
fire. you deserve better.
She doesnt know you
      well maybe i dont want her to

After that, he'll ghost. Let her stew a few days, till she apologizes. He'll humor her, followed by a too-private section I scroll past, holding my breath. And then things even out. Till they fight again. About the shrill little dictator. Playing bloody knuckles with each other's hearts, week after week.

Things crescendo as Cloak and Dagger approaches. A different kind of argument.

> What does that bitch from montana kno about me?
> Wtf were you gonna do when i CAME UP THERE
> w you??

tell her the truth of course

> what does that even mean
> the truth?
> jesus christ after everythng i ducking did for u

lets have this convo in person i dont wanna do it
this way ok?
gimme 10 min, watching sun

Dark, ironic laughter seethes in the back of my throat. Guess we were both someone's third wheel this past summer. I'd feel sad for her if he'd been someone worth feeling sad about.

After that, things get quiet between them. Just a few tense, truncated messages the night of Cloak and Dagger:

we're here
meet us downstairs
be safe

And then June 6 happens.

I read the whole chain again. This time, I don't skip anything. Somewhere between the lines, I know he's given something away. I feel it at the center of my fucking bones.

I also know this phone is going to ring again someday.

It doesn't make any sense. But I want to be there, when it does.

NOW

The Red Market is about twenty miles behind us when Cora finally speaks again.

"How much did Nikita give you for the pills?"

I race to pull an answer out of thin air.

"Like, eight hundred dollars?"

"Seriously? The guy said seventy-five a pop."

If she only knew.

I can't reveal how much money we really have because I can't risk any questions about that second brown paper bag. Those shots are a dead giveaway I'm up to no good. They're going to check us for weapons when we get to ADAPT's outpost. These things are much easier to conceal than a gun.

The Saranasia formula was developed in a lab run exclusively by Saras somewhere in Poland. They're suicide injections, packed with highly concentrated toxins and, surprisingly, human stem cells. But people get queasy about that stuff, even if it's being used to save a life. Forget using stem cells to benefit Saras. To put them out of their misery. The lab had to operate in secret, without proper approvals and all that, so once people got wind of it, the whole project disappeared overnight. The injections *do* work, though. It's unclear how many shots were salvaged. How many knockoffs are on the street. But I guess Nikita has her sources. I did some digging using Cora's Discord account one morning after she'd fallen asleep and sussed out who'd be selling them.

I steal a glance at her. Wondering if she's going to say anything else. Whether I'm supposed to blink first. I probably should, considering what I said to her earlier.

"Cora, I'm sorry."

She lights up a clove in the silence that follows. "It just sucks because you're the only person I could really talk to about this."

"We can still talk."

"Not if you're judging me."

"I'm not." And I mean it. This was never about judging her. There's so much more than she knows.

"I'm not an idiot," she mutters, clove tweezered between her lips. "I know I'm probably talking to some mouth-breathing chatter with his dick in his hand. It's just . . . Look, you don't get it. How this stuff works."

It stings, but I try not to show it. "I mean, you could tell me. We've got time. Five hundred miles of it, give or take."

I cast her what I hope looks like an appeasing smile. She lets out a breath.

"The stuff I do on the internet isn't real. That's what makes it fun. For me, and also the people who look at it."

"Right. That makes sense," I reply, cheeks burning.

For a while, I pretended not to know about her torrid alter ego. We don't talk about it. But of course, I see the stuff she's posting. I know how she makes her money.

"The people who message me and subscribe to my stuff . . . they don't care that it's not really *me*. I mean it's *me*, but it's this whole other—"

"I get it."

"The realness isn't the point. That's what I'm saying. It's the *idea* of what I am. What I might do to them. It makes them happy. It's enough."

"Is it, though? I mean, isn't having someone physically *there* the goal? Ultimately?" The steering wheel slides like a snake through my clammy fists, and I tighten my grip. I feel like a child, eavesdropping on an adults-only conversation from behind a locked door.

"That's what I'm saying. A lot of these people . . . their lives are too tiny for that. They *can't* have someone physically. Maybe they tried and they're bad with women. Maybe they're trapped in a marriage they don't want to be in. Shit, maybe they're Saras, too."

I nod, slowly. I think I see it now. But my ears are still on fire. I wish I weren't so goddamn squeamish. Wish I were an *adult*.

"When I first heard from him . . . Devon or—y'know. Whoever. Obviously I knew right away, that it wasn't him. But that's just it. I wished it were real, so fucking bad. Just wanted to live in a world where it was true. And I'm really good at that. Creating a world for myself. It's not like, *hurting* anyone. And it's definitely not hurting me." Cora fixes me with a bruised stare. "It only hurts when someone reminds me it isn't real. And I feel stupid."

"Then what I said sucks. And I apologize."

"You were right, though. To call me out." I watch her clenched jaw soften from the corner of my eye. "I'd rather focus on what's real, from now on."

A light rain kisses the windshield. Not quite enough for me to turn on my wipers. I just watch for a moment. Letting the moisture bead together in the wind.

"Pull over."

The sudden intensity of her voice sends a spasm through my soul.

"Wh . . . what?"

"Pull over. I need you to look me in the face, when I say this."

What the fuck just happened? What did I say? Terror ping-pongs to every corner of my body as I tap the blinker with a trembling hand. God dammit, I never should've gotten into this car with her. I know better. She's a Sara—she's one of *them*. She's—

"Mia."

"Okay, okay . . . I'm doing it—" Gravel groans under our tires as I veer to the right shoulder. My heart pounds my ribs, and she stares at me as though she can hear it like a jackhammer.

"We need to talk about what happened."

". . . What happened?"

"*You* know. I want you to say it. Acknowledge it. With words." She holds my stare.

"You mean like . . . When we—" When we . . . what? Slept together? *Fucked?*

My entire vocabulary retreats to the pit of my twisting stomach.

"I got the feeling you were having second thoughts, and like . . . that's your right. But—"

"No, I'm not having second . . . I just . . . I didn't know how to like—" Couldn't even begin to "like."

"Why are you so weird about sex, Mia?"

I draw my lip under my teeth and start chewing. She sighs and breaks my gaze.

"Sorry. I don't mean to put you on the spot. I just want you to feel safe. When it comes to this stuff."

I slide the car into park and remove my foot from the brake. A truck whizzes past—the only other vehicle I've seen for the past thirty minutes. It's quiet. Desolate. Just two girls at the edge of a cloudy cornfield, awkwardly dodging each other's gaze.

"Did something like . . . happen to you? When you were younger?"

"No. Not to me." God, what I'd give to have the words for this. "I'm just like . . ."

A person who wasn't allowed to grow up.

"A person who doesn't have a lot of *experience* in that department."

"Neither do I," she murmurs with a wry smile. "You're not alone."

I arch a brow in her direction.

"You think I let my subscribers come visit me? C'mon, Mia."

"What about the other Saras?" There's no dearth of attractive tenants at Salvation of Manhattan—even if they're under lock and key.

She snorts. "You know how those assholes feel about me. And it's fucking mutual."

I think about shifting back into drive. But the rain is starting to intensify. And I'm thrumming with certainty that she's not done with me. I always seem to sense those things.

She sparks up a second clove in her mouth and threads it between my fingers. Not giving me a choice this time. Her hand lingers there, tantalizing. Teeming with intent.

"You wanna know how many people I've slept with?" she asks with an insinuating side-eye. At last, she moves her hand. Lifting her clove to her lips.

I take a drag in the spellbinding silence. I want to cough, but I'm afraid it will ruin something. Not sure how, or what.

"Is this like, a trick question?"

"No. I want you to ask me."

I bite back a scandalized smile.

"Okay. How many people have you slept with, Cora?"

"Three. My high school boyfriend, Carlos. My friend, Natasha. And . . . *well*."

She smiles. The tone of her voice tickles me between the lungs.

It's not that I don't want to know these things, about her. But it feels unsafe. Like I'll reveal too much about myself in exchange. I think back on those first few nail-biting conversations with Jade at the bookstore. The way I'd keep the ball in her court at all costs. The feeling ricochets across time, hitting me square in the chest.

"What happened with them? Carlos and Natasha?"

They've got to be in their thirties by now, if they managed to avoid Saratov's this long. She thaws, tense posture relaxing. Allowing me to change the subject.

"Me and Carlos dated all through high school. We were both scholarship kids at this like . . . *super* nice private school downtown and kinda bonded on day one. We broke up midway through college. Like ya do. As for Natasha . . ." Cora laughs darkly. "It's 'cuz of Tash I'm sitting here with you."

She cracks the window. Now she's the one who's not looking at me.

"Was Natasha the one who lifted you?"

"See, that's the thing, about how it happened. I don't actually remember. *Who.*"

She swallows. Ashes her clove in the cup. The crisp smell of cold rain fills the air between us. She's told me a lot, in the short time we've known each other, but this topic is sacred.

It is for most Saras.

"There was this big group of us who went to the Hamptons for Natasha's twenty-first birthday. Her aunt had this crazy beach house and she let us throw a party there. Everyone was really fucked up. A lot of friends of friends got invited . . . and, well. You get it."

I realize I've stopped smoking my clove. The tip withers to a precarious gray column. I stub it in the cup.

"Where is she now? Natasha?" I choose my words carefully, unsure if she wants to continue.

"Uh, dead. Unfortunately."

"I'm so sorry."

A gentle hiatus passes.

"She tried to run right after, and the sun was out. Didn't know any better."

"Are they all dead? Everyone from that party?"

"No. There were a couple people in the pool house who didn't get lifted. Slept through the whole damn thing." Suddenly, she brightens. Only a few degrees, but I'm keyed in. "I'm still friends with some of them. On Instagram, anyway. They're doing okay."

The rain finally yields. A chasm of light opens across the sky.

"We should probably—" I jerk my head toward the road. Shift us back into drive.

"Yeah, for sure."

I ride the accelerator, preparing to merge back onto the freeway.

"It's so weird, seeing them get older," she goes on. It takes me a second to realize she's still talking about her old friends. "But I love all the pictures of their kids."

She starts picking at her manicure. I don't think I've ever seen her do that. "My friend Alex had twins last year, a boy and a girl. She named them Roger and River. It's funny because I know they're not *identical* twins but whenever I see them in pictures they're just these two little jellybeans and I don't know which is which and I'm just . . . I mean, I'm obsessed." She rambles like a fountain.

I glimpse her in my periphery. She's pried a sizable chunk of metallic pink off her thumb.

"D'you ever think about having kids?" Something shimmers in Cora's voice. It's timid, all of a sudden. Vulnerable.

"Oh. Uh, I don't know if I . . . I never thought I'd be any good at it so I don't really—" Her eyes elicit the question. "Do you?"

"I mean, that's kinda what happens, right? When you get to be thirty?"

It takes me a second to realize she's talking about herself. She'll be thirty-five in April. Technically.

Becoming a Sara at twenty-one must be so strange. You're stuck in a moment where the world says you're ready to be an adult, and you want all the things adulthood promised.

But those things aren't promised to Saras.

She slumps in her seat. Starts spinning the radio dial.

"When the twins were born, I sent Alex some presents, and they got mailed back to me. For months I had a whole closet of Winnie the Pooh shit before I finally trashed everything. I don't know why I hung on to it. Not like I was gonna give it to my kids or anything."

I want to reach out to her. Even though I know she's going to flinch, even though I know she's deathly allergic to every soft thing. But she draws back before I can.

"Anyway, what was up with you at the market? Why'd you bail like that?"

My spine goes taut. Reminding me to start lying again.

Reminding me what this is.

"I should've told you. I've had some experiences that really make me hate crowds."

I can live with that. Because that one's not a lie.

(((

Cora's sleeping now. The low-fuel light is flashing. It's been on for the past thirty minutes or so, but it wasn't flashing before. I imagine the truck sprouting manic green Kermit arms, flailing them to get my attention.

I pull off at the next gas station: a shiny new Shell at the edge of a dilapidated, tornado-torn farming town. A fractured silo in the distance tilts to the side like the leaning tower of Pisa, split across the middle, gushing a metric ton of corn. Jagged hunks of white fence are strewn like bones across a barren brown field that was probably once filled with cows, or horses. From the looks of it, the gas station is the only thing anyone's had the heart to rebuild so far. I wonder what happens to horses, in a tornado. Even the sturdiest creatures are no match for nature's massive, unforgiving middle finger.

I give Cora a poke as I pull up to the pump, but she doesn't budge. She's a heavy sleeper when the Daylights start to wear off. But I'll need to wake her soon and make sure she takes another one. We're not safe yet. The sun won't be down for another couple of hours.

The breeze punctures my thin hoodie. Spring is taking its sweet time out here. I zip it up and head toward the mini-mart, surveying the entryway for a scanner. There isn't one. But that's not a surprise. A lot of these small Midwestern towns don't have scanners on their doors. Instead, everything just closes before dark. I doubt enough people live here to stage much of a protest.

I'm the only person in the store aside from the beleaguered, pumpkin-shaped old woman at the register, cat's-eye reading glasses slung around her neck. She reeks of barbecue sauce. Jesus, I'm salivating again. I grit my teeth as I fork over half the cash Nikita gave me.

"Sixty dollars on number two, please. Also, do you have a sewing kit?"

She raises an arthritic finger that's somehow bloated and bony at the same time and points toward the aisle behind me. "Housewares, by the soap."

As the truck gasses up, I quietly snag my backpack from the back seat, along with that second crumpled paper bag. I'm careful not to disturb Cora. I let my door come to rest without shutting it all the way.

Outside, I unpack the sewing kit, using the pickup bed as a table. Mom was always good at sewing, but whenever she tried to teach me how to patch my jeans or replace a button, I couldn't get past threading the damn needle and we both gave up. It takes me a good five minutes to feed the cheap, flimsy black thread through that microscopic cleft. My eyes are itchy, stinging in the afternoon sun. I've just realized how exhausted I am. It's all starting to hit me at once. I'm envious of Cora, the way she can just crash. She's a city girl who never got comfortable behind the wheel, so I volunteered to do all the driving. Of course, I never considered when the hell *I* would sleep.

I open my backpack and take the seam ripper to one of the small, interior pockets. The sewing kit comes with a comically small pair of scissors, but they'll do. I stab an opening in the fabric behind the pocket and secure the two tightly capped Saranasia shots to the other side, tucked into the lining. I pad them with a wad of toilet paper so they don't break, then stitch around the haphazard bundle in circles till it's tight. Then, I sew the pocket back up. It's perfect. You'd never know. Mom would be proud.

The gas pump clicked off a few minutes ago. Cora hasn't stirred. I drag my heavy feet back to the car, making a bit more noise this time to encourage her to rally and take her pill. She groans and drags her fingers down her exhausted face.

I uncap the bottle and shake two teal capsules into my palm. I place one into Cora's cupholder for her when she's ready.

I place the other one on my tongue.

NOVEMBER 2023

My flight is at three o'clock. I figure I'll sleep on the plane. Because I sure as hell didn't sleep last night.

Sandy comes to the hotel to pick up the Jeep first thing in the morning. She's got a friend who wants to buy it for scrap. I resisted at first, but it has to happen. Another cornerstone of our life better off as rubble.

"I'll be back in an hour to give you a ride to the airport." Sandy whirls the keychain around her finger. I watch Mom's Minnie Mouse pendant spin and I feel nauseous, as if I'm strapped to it.

"Could we make time to swing by the police station first?"

"No prob." She gives me a captain's salute before ambling toward the Jeep.

"Hang on, Sandy?" She faces me. "Can I keep that keychain?"

Danny's taking lunch at his desk when I get to the police station: a bummer of a meatball sub on a thin, soggy roll.

Mom's phone burns a hole in my Book Bunker tote.

"Sorry," he says, wrapping the chaotic sandwich as best he can, shoving it to the side. "I keep drawing the short straw, being on call through lunch. Like they think I don't know what gentle hazing looks like."

"At least it's gentle?" I take a seat beside him.

"Ready for takeoff?"

"I guess. I dunno."

"Glad you came by."

It's like I can hear someone stage-whispering: *And now, you give him the phone.*

"I'm really sorry things went . . . y'know. The way they went," he says. "Wish I had some good New York recommendations, but I'm not nearly cool enough."

I try to laugh. Slide the bag from my shoulder. But I don't open it.

"Anything I can do? Before you jet?"

"I guess I just came here to . . ."

To give you the phone.

"I wanted to ask if you've like, gotten any updates. Even if it's stupid. I know you kinda don't get them anymore. But—"

He rises, wipes his hands with a ball of rough brown napkins, and moves to close the door. Like he doesn't want anyone to hear us. I sit up straight in my chair, studying the indecisive wobble of his head.

"Look, there is this one . . . weird thing. Not *stupid*, necessarily. But—"

I prod him with my stare.

"I just don't have enough background to interpret it in a meaningful way for you." He's suddenly all business. Which makes me think he's sitting on something bigger than he wants to let on.

"Danny, you have to tell me."

He reclines in his chair, glances at the ceiling, then back at me.

"Earlier this week, we got a request from Phoenix PD to go interview a local florist down here. Apparently, the Phoenix Sara center had some sort of . . . *threat*?"

"From a flower shop?"

"I mean, I guess it wasn't really a . . . One of the patients there got an arrangement for her birthday and the card was, well, basically, the card included a set of instructions for how to escape. Give ya a hundred bucks if you can tell me who signed it."

"Uh—" My heart pounds.

He pulls a stack of Post-its from his drawer and uses a scratchy, half-dead Sharpie to draw a lopsided Jesus fish supported by two stumpy legs.

It takes me a second to put two and two together as Danny offers an expectant, cynical chuckle to the silence. It's the Darwin fish. I've seen it before, on bumper stickers and coffee mugs—a rallying cry for like-minded intellectuals. Understanding rushes through me.

Devon founded ADAPT based on a half-baked work of Darwinist

fan fiction he wrote last year. It makes sense that his group would start co-opting the same symbolism.

"Oh, wow."

"Right?" Danny holds my gaze.

"Who wrote it up, who arranged the flower order?"

"The owner of the shop said this would've been done by his assistant, who was out that morning. He gave us her information. The feds took over from there."

"How was it paid for?" I keep his feet to the fire.

"Prepaid gift card. Online."

"So . . . What does that mean, what do we do?"

"I told you, right now there's not enough information to assume—"

There is no way in *hell* I'm letting him off the hook. Not this time. "Can't you guys like, do some shady NSA stuff and trace the IP address of the—"

"The feds will likely get into that. They'll contact you right away, if they need you for anything." He sighs. "I'm sorry, Mia. I wish I had more for you. I always do."

I sag in my cold metal folding chair, and it creaks in response. God dammit. Why did I let myself hope? I should know better. This will never be anything more than an endless pile of leads that turn to dust till *I* turn to fucking dust.

I hug my bag to my stomach. Feeling the phone against my ribs.

They won't know how to decode what's on it. What they said to each other, what it all means. I'm the only one who can do that.

I'm the only one who knew her.

I hang the bag back over my shoulder and stand.

"You'll call me if they find him, right?"

"Of course. You won't hear it on the news, you'll hear it from me."

I know I should thank him, before I go. But I don't have it in me.

"Listen, my door's always open," Danny chirps as I shuffle toward the door. "Er . . . phone. You know."

I nod with a thousand-yard stare.

"Good luck, Mia."

I don't need luck. I need this to end.

☾ ☾ ☾

My last plane ride would have been that long-forgotten trip to California to see the pandas back in 2010. My nerves are like an upside-down soft drink. Am I anxious about the flight itself? It's been over thirteen years and I've never been on such a long one before. But no—I think I'm actually looking forward to it. I hope we fly over the Grand Canyon or the Rockies while it's still light out. I made sure to get a window seat.

It's everything that comes after the flight.

Sandy subjects me to a rapid-fire New York geography quiz as we drive to the airport.

"Is Fifth Avenue on the east or west side?"

"Trick question, it divides the city in half."

"Which train runs local to your apartment and which ones are express?"

"The 3 train is local. 1 and 2 are express." Wait, no. "Actually, it's—"

"Get on the wrong train, it's gonna blow past your stop."

"I know, I know. Um . . . the 1 train. Is local. Right?"

"Look it up, 'cuz now you got me second-guessing myself."

I wish Sandy were coming with me, even for a little while. Just to help me get settled. But I've already asked so much of her. Probably too much.

I hug her goodbye and promise I'll text every morning. She swears the same thing, up and down. They mean everything, those daily check-ins. Proof of life after another tense night.

Neither of us wants to start crying, so we keep things brief. But that's okay. It's the fact that we would have cried. That I have someone here worth crying over.

I scan in to the airport, then scan in a second time once I reach the front of the security line. The whole thing is overkill for a daytime flight. Then again, they're still making people take off their shoes and randomly inspecting tiny shampoo bottles, so it feels on-brand for the TSA. There's a third scanner I've yet to encounter, at the gate. They prick you right before you board. I remind myself to use my other hand and give my sore right index finger a rest.

I arrive at my gate and spot the plane parked on the tarmac outside. I'm not even on it yet, and I already know I am entirely too far from home. I should not be here. I can't just *leave*. Why should I get to do that? After what I did? What makes me think I deserve a clean getaway? Self-loathing hangs on my shoulders like a filthy coat.

I unravel into a seat against my will. Study the faces of my fellow passengers. There's a harried mom and dad corralling two rowdy kids around an iPad, riddled with grubby fingerprints. One of the kids spills Goldfish all over the floor. At the end of the row sit two ladies in designer blazers and buffed black boots, deep in conversation, sipping lattes. Everyone seems to be adhering to the buddy system but me.

There's a TV mounted on the wall a few rows ahead of me. I stare like the screen might anchor me and keep me from bolting toward the exit. National network news plays on a loop, muted with the captions activated. I hold my breath, waiting to see the words "Tucson Twelve" flash across the screen. Instead, the ticker announces CONTROVERSIAL NEW MEDICATION, over and over, in screaming capital letters. There's footage of some sort of lab. People hustling in and out of frame wearing white coats. I squint to read the poorly timed autogenerated captions.

> *Dr. Moore estimates the medication will be available nationwide by*
> *December 1*
> *Those infected with Saratov's will have to self-report to a recovery*
> *center in order to receive a prescription*
> *There is no way to access a prescription outside of a recovery center*

The broadcast cuts to a new image: the front entryway of a Sara center somewhere in New England, framed by umber fall foliage under blue skies. Two black wrought-iron crosses have been grafted to the vintage brick pillars flanking the driveway, and the camera lingers there to make sure we get a good look. Then, the focus shifts to the background: the building's courtyard, where six figures hunch around a picnic table, engrossed in a board game.

The groundbreaking formula allows the infected to be exposed to
sunlight for up to four hours at a time

The camera zooms in. A man laughs and rolls a pair of dice. The woman beside him pulls from her cigarette with a smug grin, counting her Monopoly money.

Holy shit. This is the first footage I've ever seen from inside a Sara center. Although technically, I suppose this is *outside* the center.

How long have they been developing this medication? How come we never heard anything? I'm flooded with regret that surges to my eyes. If we'd known about this trial, maybe that would have encouraged Mom to self-report. And then maybe . . .

Maybe . . .

I rip my gaze from the TV. I can't watch anymore, I feel sick. I start digging around in my backpack for my book. Or my phone. Hell, *Mom's* fucking phone.

I wonder how I'll feel the day they find a cure. If they find one. The internet will erupt with joy and the news ticker will flash REVOLUTIONARY BREAKTHROUGH! and NIGHTMARE ENDS! on repeat all day.

It'll change the whole world. But it won't change mine.

"Now boarding group A," a flight attendant warbles from a static-laced intercom.

My ribs contract like a straitjacket. Tight, tighter, tightest.

I'm group C. I still have time.

Time for what?

To turn back?

There is no back.

Please stay home with me tonight. I'm so sad.

I force-feed myself a sip of air.

We could bake cookies. Or finish painting the bathroom?

Exhale.

You want to watch a movie? You pick.

"Now boarding group B."

The Wizard of Oz flickers across my mind's eye. A desaturated Dorothy lies unconscious in bed as her house spins like a top, tossed by the twister, then lands with a thud. Dorothy startles, clutching Toto with an astonished "*Oh!*"

She stands. It's quiet. Too quiet. She tiptoes toward the door. Wraps a cautious hand around the doorknob. Shielding her eyes from the sun.

"Now boarding group C."

And then, without a warning . . . Technicolor.

☾ ☾ ☾

The best thing about New York is knowing you'll never be alone again. Depending on who you ask, it is also the worst thing.

I have no idea what I expected. Didn't have time to *expect* anything. My studio apartment is a pied-à-terre owned by a Columbia law professor out on a semipermanent sabbatical. I have just now learned what "pied-à-terre" means: an overpriced closet in an enviable city that you get to call home whenever you swing through. For me, though, it's *home* home. I have enough money socked away to make rent till March 1, in four months. After that, though, I'm going to need a job. And, once the professor gets back, a new—cheaper—place. But I think I can make it work. I've already applied to a bunch of job openings.

I'm safely tucked away on the ninth floor, and the building is a towering brick fortress gilded with gleaming raised-relief borders around each door, like a statuesque woman dripping with gold jewelry. Never in my life did I think I'd live in a building like this. Even if my apartment is just one big room where the hum of the fridge sings me to sleep.

My first full day in town is Mom's birthday. As soon as I wake up, I turn on her phone. Waiting to see if Devon might text her. Figure he might want to tell her to have a great day and watch her fucking back. I take an initial, timid stroll around the neighborhood and explore the nearby park, keeping Mom's phone in my pocket the whole time. But it doesn't make a sound.

I shouldn't be surprised he forgot her birthday.

Having a spring in my step starts to feel like less of a betrayal as the days go by. Probably because I'm in a new place. My favorite thing about my neighborhood is the stroll past Columbia to the train station. The cathedral-like spires. The smell of roasted nuts and street coffee. The chattering students, roving in packs. Everyone's always *out,* day and night. Like the terror of Saratov's passed over the city like a cloud.

I understand right away why people here walk so fast—at least, this time of year. It's too damn cold to meander from A to B. But I like the way the freezing air fills the pleats in my lungs and hardens my blood. I've learned to take longer strides so I don't get mowed over. I imagine I'm reaching for something with each step. It's what everyone else seems to be doing. Reaching. It's contagious. I've never felt connected to people like this before, never knew I *wanted* to feel it. The space between bodies crackles, as if everyone's wired together like a circuit. People don't come here to settle. People come here to chase something. I love that. I just wish I knew what my something was.

Well, I do. But I'm not going to find it here.

I'm taking some classes while I look for a job. Not at Columbia. There's a community college downtown that's letting me audit a couple of courses till I can officially enroll next semester. One of my instructors practically did a spit take when I told her I was interested in taking finals "for fun." I ride the 1 train—*not* the 3—from 116th Street every day. I'm not quite comfortable with the subway yet. Not because I keep confusing the local with the express. The subway is shielded from sunlight 24/7 and packed to the gills with oblivious, headphone-clad sheep. Ice shoots through my veins the first time I glimpse those dark tunnels twisting past the platform.

The city has, of course, taken this into consideration. You have to prick your finger and scan in after you pay to board the train. They have these slick, rapid-sanitizing machines I've never seen anywhere else, connected to automated eight-foot double doors made of steel where there used to be turnstiles. I spot some of the decommissioned entry points at the shoddier stations. There are black 911 call boxes on the platform, as well as in every train car, in case of any Sara-related emergencies. In fact, as far as I can tell, you can find those same black boxes on every street corner up above. The first time I board the train, I study the movements of every person on the platform. Marinate in their shared body language. Somehow, everyone seems relaxed. I mean, as relaxed as New Yorkers can be for their morning commute. They sip their coffee and nod to the beat in their headphones. Turn the pages of their paperbacks. If anyone's broken a sweat, I can't tell. The only suspicious bystander is me. I imagine people probably behaved differently when the disease first started spreading here. But that was thirteen years ago.

The heart of New York keeps pumping blood.

My first week of class, I'm crossing Canal Street toward the BMCC campus when I receive a text. On *my* phone.

> **Hey Mia i was thinkin of you today. how are u doin? X**

Jade.

I swell with hot air.

What does this mean? Why was she *thinking of me*? Today?

I'm already lost and running late. Can't stop to engage with this. But my feet are fused to the pavement like melting candy. A kid on a skateboard screams past, clipping my shoulder.

I'm not going to answer. What do I say, how do I start? Well, *she* started it. It's up to me, whether we continue.

What did I think, that we'd just vanish from each other's lives forever? After everything that happened? Maybe that's exactly what I thought. What I hoped.

She's half the sin. A destructive force I know I'm responsible for. I'd take it all back, if I could. Every glance, every whispered secret, every kiss.

In a way, I guess I can. If I leave her on read.

I swing by the store on my way home from class to pick up some dinner staples for my mouse-sized kitchen. I'm on a tight budget till the house sells. But that doesn't stop me from snagging a few *additional* provisions: a bottle of Jack Daniel's, some cheap tequila, and a six-pack of weird stone fruit sour beer that's on sale. I'm still learning what I like to drink. How much. I figure I'll conduct a little experiment tonight. I'll do some light reading for my Intro to Journalism class, pound a few funky beers, and stop trying to compose a reply to Jade's text. A nice, quiet night in.

And it works. To an extent. Except, after three funky beers and a sleeping pill, I pick up the *other* phone. As if my altered state might help me spot something I missed before. I turn it on and read the whole damn saga.

It's all the same. Maybe even uglier. Everything feels ugly tonight.

I fall asleep with the lights on. Both phones on my chest.

(((

The nights eat the days and spit them back out again. I'm trying to focus on my classes. I like having deadlines. But it's started getting weird, when the sun goes down. Everyone seems to be out on the street. As if I'm the only person in the whole city who knows to be afraid. I nervously watch my neighbors from my window like I have the ability to swan-dive and save a life if the moment calls for it.

After a few weeks, December arrives. And the feeling darkens. I'm not nervous. I'm jealous.

I want to join them. Want to feel like it's safe to feel *safe*.

This isn't the life I imagined, when I wondered what it might be like to move out of our house. It's like I'm right back where I started. Except now I'm alone.

One night, after I finish a paper and four Jack and Cokes, I put on my boots and slip out the front door. Wearing my intoxication like armor.

I know it's a bad idea. Caffeine won't protect me from a rusted bullet intended for Mom, or the jaws of some prowler hoping to turn a new friend, Cloak and Dagger style. But all I want to do is capsize. Fall headfirst into the arms of a death wish.

From the corner of my eye, I think I see my shadow split in two.

It's a Friday. Bars are open and the students are out. If anyone tries to grab me or threatens me in any way . . . someone's going to notice. I traipse down Broadway all the way to Eighty-Sixth, cross over to

Riverside, and hoof it back up again. I've never felt so powerful and so stupid at the same time. I wish this delusion could last forever.

Wish he weren't still keeping me from living half my life.

Holiday break sneaks up on me.

I get an A– on that paper. Probably would've nabbed the A if I hadn't written half of it drunk. My instructor asks if I've thought about applying to one of the more prestigious four-year colleges in the area next semester.

"NYU's got a great journalism program," she coos.

But I don't have the money for a place like NYU, even when the house sells. I guess I could research scholarships, if I felt like getting serious. But I don't know how permanent any of this is. Like I'm expecting I'll be called home any day now. Or someplace else.

I haven't given any thought to my holiday plans. I've applied to several jobs but I haven't gotten any interviews. Which is what happens when all your experience is in retail but you don't want to work fucking retail anymore.

I should have tried to make some friends at school.

I'm riding the train home after my last lecture, absently scrolling through my phone. I leave Mom's phone at my apartment now. Don't need to look at it anymore. I know every word of that text chain, like a horrible song in my head.

I thought Jade might send me a follow-up message, but she hasn't. Not like I was going to respond. There's something delicious about the restraint. If I wanted her to talk to me, I could *get her* to talk to me. All I have to do is text her back. Maybe that's what feels so good. Knowing I have something she wants.

I'm still watching her stories, though. I'm not made of stone. And she's posted a boatload today.

She's got a new set of tour dates, handwritten in artful calligraphy on her bedroom mirror. In a GIF, she kisses the mirror, leaving a stain, then waves. Kiss, wave. Kiss, wave. Over and over.

She's dubbed this the "Dagger Stabs Back" tour. For obvious reasons. Her follower count has exploded since that fateful night. That said, she's still driving a van cross-country. Hasn't leveled up to private jets or anything. I've also noticed a gradual rebrand take shape over the past few months. Instead of those white fishnet gloves with the fingers cut off, I see her playing piano wearing these spiky leather wrist bands. She's swapped her blue eyeliner for thick, matte black and pierced her lip. Could be fake, though, I can't tell.

I tap to the next story, which shows a clearer picture of all her tour dates. Atlanta. Baltimore. D.C. All East Coast dates through the end of January.

December 26, the day after Christmas, reads New York, NY.

The dagger stabs back, right through my gut.

She's playing a club on the Lower East Side. I don't know it. But why would I? Good thing I'm so afraid to go out at night so I don't do something dumb, like buy a ticket to this show.

I shove my phone into my bag. Like my self-destruct code is subliminally buried somewhere in her stories. Anyway, my stop is coming up. I redirect my gaze to the subway ads.

Three different therapists have bought ad space here. All soothing, toothy headshots on sunny park benches. It's become quite the profession du jour these past thirteen years. You'd think that would help make sessions more affordable, but apparently inner peace is still a luxury item. I still feel bad Alyssa and Sandy paid for mine.

116th is next. As the train slows with a silvery groan, my gaze flicks to another ad, above the black emergency call box.

Dignity. Safety. Transparency.

Beneath the slogan is a photo of a spindly young man and a girl-next-door blonde playing cards together. My mouth turns to sandpaper when I see the tourniquet around the boy's arm. The needle lodged in his elbow crease. Blood gathers in an inconspicuously placed reservoir, under the table.

Now hiring volunteers and paid bloodletters at all recovery centers across New York state. Visit our website today for more information.

I read the caption a second time. My head swims, and I nearly miss my stop. I wedge through the closing doors half a second before they clamp down on my backpack and hop the stairs to the street, two at a time.

The centers are recruiting. Opening their doors to the public for the first time. I think of that news footage I saw at the airport. How *shocking* it was.

Transparency.

Of course.

They're making a point. Actively working to change the public tone on these places. They want to show free Saras these aren't the clandestine torture chambers the internet has led them to believe and get them to surrender—fast. But why now, after all this time? Why do they feel like they have to do this?

As if I don't know.

The number of free Saras must be exploding. Exactly as he planned.

My laptop roasts my knees as I hunch on the couch with a dozen different tabs open.

There is no way to trace rate of infection because free Saras don't self-report. But what you *can* count are deaths. It's pretty obvious, when a Sara feeds and kills someone. If they do a shitty job dumping the body—and so many do, when they're flustered and blood-drunk—the coroner can easily puzzle it out. That information gets added to a national database, broken down by state and county.

If the number of free Saras is increasing—and ADAPT is to blame for that—it should be pretty obvious where they've been hunting. All I have to do is follow the blood to his door.

I don't know why I didn't think of this.

I mean, the FBI probably thought of it. But if they knew where he was, they would have caught him already. There's something they can't see.

The first state I check is Montana. Over the past three months, they've had 794 Sara-related fatalities. It's not nothing, for such a sparse population. But it doesn't feel like a smoking gun, either. I check all the bordering states. Idaho, 543. North Dakota, 620. South Dakota, 758. Then, I check Wyoming. 2,457.

Iowa: 6,872.

Colorado: 12,439.

Nebraska's even worse. 13,032.

Something needles me about Colorado.

I start making a spreadsheet. I look up all fifty states, including Hawai'i.

Iowa, Colorado, Nebraska, and Kansas are the big winners.

But why is Colorado the one gnawing at me?

I go to the kitchen to pour myself a drink before I turn on Mom's phone. Don't like to do this sober anymore.

I chase cheap tequila with a swig of week-old Gatorade and start scrolling. There was something he said at the end of May. Right after they brought Kayla into the fold, around the time Mom lied to him: the lie about turning me into a Sara, which ended up not being much of a *lie,* when all was said and—

> wait who's gonna pick me up
>
> **Gareth will be tehre at 730**
>
> **he drove down from Boulder last night**

Right there. Boulder, as in Boulder, Colorado. I think.

It's not much. And I have no clue who Gareth is. They never mention him again.

But . . . maybe?

I take another shot and dissolve to the couch. This isn't evidence. It's barely even a hunch. I laugh and chuck the phone across the coffee table.

So there's something shady going on in Colorado. So what? What do I think I'm going to do? Corner him with a rusty samurai sword like I'm in a fucking Tarantino movie?

He's not the same foulmouthed, chain-smoking lunatic who held my head underwater thirteen years ago. He's worse. He's got an army now. And I'm all alone getting drunk with a spreadsheet.

☽ ☽ ☽

I order delivery from the Chinese place down the street on Christmas Eve.

I slurp shrimp lo mein as I watch *A Charlie Brown Christmas* on TV, oddly soothed by the kids doing their weird little loop dances to Schroeder's piano. This wasn't a movie Mom and I watched during the holidays. We preferred the stop-motion Rudolph films and *A Muppet Christmas Carol.* Mom didn't like Linus's religious monologue at the end. "Ye shall find the babe wrapped in swaddling clothes, lying in a manger . . ." et cetera. Mom loved the magic of

Christmas, but she kept Jesus at arm's length. The older I got, the more I understood. I wonder if Christmastime made her sad. If she ever wished she could go back to church.

I drink half a bottle of wine and pass out on the couch. A couple of hours later, I swim out of sleep when my phone rings. Sandy's FaceTiming me. I consider my own image onscreen before swiping to answer. How gnarly do I look? Will she have any commentary about it?

Probably not. It's Christmas, after all.

It's nice when people call you on Christmas.

"M-Merry Christmas-Christmas Mia-ia!" Alyssa and Sandy attempt to shout in unison as I pick up.

I can't help but laugh. "Merry Christmas. Sounds uh . . . festive over there."

"We miss you!" Sandy chirrups, a tipsy lilt in her voice. Wish mine sounded the same.

"I know, I do, too."

"Sorry, are we calling too late? You sound tired."

"No, I just . . . I think I'm getting a cold."

"What have you been up to over break? Are you doing anything special tomorrow?" Alyssa asks.

"I'm just gonna like . . . catch up on rest. Like I said, I'm getting sick."

"Did you go see the tree at Rockefeller Center?" That's Sandy.

"I think you can ice-skate there!" Alyssa butts in front of the camera.

"I actually haven't. I kinda forgot. School has been really hectic."

"I thought you were auditing?"

"I decided to take finals."

"Which she *crushed*, by the way," Sandy says, sotto to Alyssa. "Gonna transfer to NYU next year for sure."

"Stop." And I mean it.

"Fine. Columbia. Those *are* your stomping grounds."

I nuzzle a quilted throw pillow under my chin as my eyelids droop. Want to go back to sleep or finish that bottle of wine. Maybe both. "Anyway, what's new with you two?"

"We have some news, actually," Sandy says. "We decided we're gonna be moving in January. I'm selling the store."

I sit up. "Wait, Sandy, is this like . . . a thing I say congratulations about or—?"

"Why not? I'll take a congratulations. I've wanted to head to California for a couple years now to be closer to my dad. Felt like the right time." There's a twinge in her voice.

"Things are just a little weird in Tucson," Alyssa says. Sandy cuts her a look.

They're moving because of me. Because of what happened with Ronnie.

"I'm really sorry. I wish you didn't have to sell the store. I wish—"

"Mia, don't say sorry. It's not your fault," Sandy leaps to my rescue. "Arizona's changed since you left."

"Changed how?"

"Just . . . the laws are a little sketchy right now while everyone decides what to do—"

"About *what*?"

"Someone escaped from a Sara center," Alyssa lets slip. My stomach snarls.

"We don't have all the information, that's not—"

"There was an attack in Scottsdale. *During the day.* They have these pills now—"

"I didn't hear anything about that," I choke out. Fucking Danny. Why didn't he call me?

Is this yet another thing he didn't "have enough background to interpret"?

"News hasn't been covering it. Probably trying to keep everyone from panicking. But when was the last time that worked?" Sandy mutters.

I feel like the room is shrinking.

"Anyway, California has a way better handle on things. Come visit. We'll go to the beach, it'll be great." There's a forced smile on her face.

"Sounds awesome," I reply, robotic.

"You take care, okay? Enjoy the rest of your break. Go out and do some cool stuff in the city. I'd *kill* to be twenty-four and living in New York, good God."

"You say that like I've been invited to the Met Gala."

"Just go to the ice rink, Mia."

We try our best to laugh. Feels good, for a moment. Till it feels wrong.

I guzzle the rest of that bottle after we hang up. Nibble on fried rice, even though I'm not hungry anymore.

The police *knew* people were trying to escape. Those Daylight pills are *everything*. That's why ADAPT sent those flowers last month. They had intel the centers were about to roll them out.

The cops had intel too, but they did nothing.

I may not have anything but the digital carnage of an endless hate fuck and a stupid hunch about Colorado. Still, I'm glad I never gave them Mom's phone.

I turn it on. But black out before I remember why I did.

Christmas Day. Night. Day?

I'm on my third festive tequila sunrise and the Muppets are on. Not a bad start.

Around midnight, I start thinking about church again. I wobble upright. There's a cathedral nearby—this looming Gothic tower sandwiched between brownstones, overlooking the river. It's probably open late for Christmas. I'll make some coffee and walk over.

But when I start scooping the grounds, I spill the entire bag, and as I hunt for the vacuum I recall I have actually never *been to church* in my life and they will probably be singing songs and saying prayers I can't keep up with and everyone will know I'm just a sad drunk Christmas interloper.

Sleet starts to fall outside. For a second, I think it's snow. I crack the kitchen window and extend a hand, but it's just a cold, wet letdown. I weave back to the couch and refresh my glass. I've switched back to wine. Cabernet and Cuervo don't make for the most pleasing brew in the pit of my stomach, but at this point I'm just filling the tank.

Fa-la-la-la-la, la-la-la-la.

I should've decorated. Everything's so sterile. I could have at least hung a wreath on the door. Mom was a devoted day-after-

Thanksgiving decorator. She made little lanterns out of paper bags and placed them all over the garden. Strung the cacti with hundreds of glimmering fairy globes.

I'll be home for Christmas, if only in my dreams.

We had a fake Christmas tree for a few years, but once I was old enough to drive, she put me in charge of procuring the tallest, fullest evergreen I could find. I'd hit every nursery in the county, texting her pictures of our prospects. Finding a perfect Christmas tree in the desert is a blood sport. But I always delivered.

I've started to cry, but I'm not sure when. My face is like a fat fuzzy peach, numb and bloated, and I can barely feel the tears trailing my cheeks.

Fuck it. I'm walking to the church. I don't need coffee. Don't need anything.

I fumble with the laces on my boots. Drying my tears with my sleeve.

A phone is ringing.

But I'm holding my phone.

Oh.

Oh . . .

Mom's phone writhes across the coffee table as it buzzes.

The caller ID reads 000-000-0000.

Oh shit.

An alien hand that is not mine reaches out. When it vibrates in my palm, I feel it everywhere.

I do not say hello. Don't say anything.

Someone exhales.

It takes me a second to realize it's not buzzing anymore. That's my hand shaking.

"Izzy?"

I liquefy. Collapse to the couch.

"I know it's you." Devon's voice slithers over me. "I can hear your heart beating."

What do I do, what the *fucking shit* do I do?

I chew my lips into a line, holding my breath like it will slow my racing pulse. But it's probably just making it worse.

"Don't be nervous. It's okay," he says, honeyed like a trap. "I'm just glad you answered."

Is there a mute button on this thing? Maybe I can keep him on and call the cops *right now* and get them to tap the line and—

"I know someone's probably tapped this piece of shit and that's fine."

A scream boils in my chest.

"I just wanted to see how you were doing. Y'know. Considering the Christmas of it all."

A door opens on his end. Like he's stepping outside. Or maybe inside. I try to listen to the background for something that sounds significant. Anything to pull focus from his voice.

"I have this guy I've been working with—actually, you met him. Bjorn. You might not remember. Anyway, Bjorn used to work in IT and he says it's *real* easy to figure out which cell tower you're pinging if you have the number."

Is he lying? I don't know. I don't—

"But I don't think that's gonna be necessary. I feel like we can work this out between us."

I try to fight it, but my breath comes out with an audible tremor. His quiet laugh is a blade through my ear.

"Babe, where the hell are you?"

"Where the hell are *you*?" I'm in free fall. Why, why, *why* did I just—?

"God, you sound so sad." There's a pang in his voice. "Smile, babe. It's Christmas."

He sighs when I don't speak again.

"Are you in a Sara center?"

Nothing.

"Iz."

Never again.

"Hope someone buys your house soon. Although, whoever's been lookin' after it kinda let the garden slide. Thought you should know."

I shiver. Of course he went to Tucson, after Ronnie called him. Jesus, when was he there? For all I know, he was sniffing around the same night I made my final visit.

"Anyway, how's Mia?"

He says my name like a dirty word. Sucks air through his teeth in the silence.

"Well, I'm sure you're busy. But here's where we're at, in case you're keeping score." All the tenderness leaves his voice. "If you come home right now, I can make this real easy on you. But that door's closing in about . . . well—" He waits for me. "Shit, it just closed. Guess I'm gonna have to come to you."

The whole room blinks, like I'm being throttled in and out of consciousness.

"Merry Christmas. I miss you."

I snap the phone shut. The scream I've been stomping on comes rushing up my throat. Tearing the paper-thin veil that keeps my past in the past.

I get older but it doesn't feel like it. And he stays the same. The same but worse.

I hurl the phone against the wall and it cracks in half.

I stare at the broken pieces, then lurch across the room and twist into my boots. My heel descends, splintering the cheap old screen. I kick the shards aside like a dead roach.

Scream again.

Scream till I'm on the floor. Till I don't have the strength to get back up.

NOW

This address doesn't seem right. It's a movie theater.

After a nerve-shredding final stretch with less than a quarter tank and only ten dollars cash remaining, we've reached the outpost. But the parking lot is deserted. The multiplex's red logo is riddled with holes and exposed wires. Peeling posters for a ten-year-old movie flap in the breeze like rags on a clothesline.

"Did they er . . . did Devon say this was a movie theater?" His name is acidic in my mouth no matter how many times I say it.

"No, all he gave me was the address," Cora replies.

My foot rests on the brake. Neither of us budges. I think she's as nervous as me.

All I can think about is turning my phone on. Making that call.

Granted, we're not in Colorado. We're on the outskirts of Omaha, Nebraska. But this was within that bloody radius. No reason this couldn't be it. Except for the fact that nobody's here.

I remove my foot from the brake. "Let's just see if someone comes out."

We park across from the revolving front door, a fractured glass cylinder, chained shut with a heavy padlock. All the windows are boarded up. Our high beams cut the darkness. There's no other light.

I don't need it, though. My eyesight has made a quantum leap. Dim light, like a dying flashlight or the moon, is more than enough to guide me. Muted colors are more pronounced. And then there are the auras. I didn't know what I was looking at, the first time I spotted a heat signature in the darkness. I was woozy and liquorish with new blood, still seeing and hearing things that weren't there. But this was real: a glittering lemon-lime specter rising from the heating vent. Cora had to pin me to the ground to keep me from kicking a hole in the wall.

I'm used to it now, though.

That's also how I know we're alone here. If there were anyone lurking nearby, we'd be able to tell. It's hard to hide from Saras at night. But I already knew that, because of Mom.

Cora uncaps her apple ChapStick. She's shivering. I turn up the heat.

From this point forward, I can't afford any missteps. I have to listen more than I speak. Have to start separating from her. When it's time to run, she can't hold me back.

I could do a little recon right now. Without her. That might be smart. After all, the key is to spot him before he spots me. I'm still sitting in this car because I'm afraid of what's out there. I have to keep reminding myself: *I am* what's out there.

From the bottom of the well in my mind comes a tiny voice. It's been yelling at me since we started this. I already have a sizable piece of serious evidence, if this is the outpost. I don't need to involve Devon at all. The FBI could raid this place and find someone to squeeze information from. It doesn't matter if he's here tonight. But I didn't come all this way to catch one of his lackeys. It needs to be *him*. And he needs to know it was me who did it.

"Why don't you stay here and I'll take a lap around the building." I unbuckle my seat belt. Cora clutches my arm.

"Be careful, Mia." The gravity in her voice catches me off guard.

"What, are you scared now? Of your own boyfriend?"

A wry smile plays on my lips, but she doesn't react. Just keeps holding my arm.

"I'll be back." I reach for my backpack in case I need to make a run for it. She furrows her brow and I understand, too late, that it's weird if I bring all my stuff to "take a lap around the building." Dammit, she's still staring at me.

"I've got pepper spray in here somewhere." I pat the bag and smile at her, hoping I'm cute enough to misdirect. Never mind that most Saras find the stuff mildly irritating at best. Never mind that as a Sara, I don't even need pepper spray to defend myself.

I hop out of the car before my whole-ass leg is in my mouth.

There's no way inside from the front. The only door is padlocked. If anyone's here, they've been using a side entrance. I keep my back pressed to the frigid concrete wall of the building and inch along. My breath catches and burns through me as I turn the corner. There's a vehicle in the rear lot: a white cube truck with Colorado plates.

I should take a picture. I'll keep my phone on airplane mode till it's time to make the call, but this feels important. Slowly, quietly, I place my backpack on the ground and unzip the front pocket. The sound screams across the emptiness. I pause, scanning my surroundings. Left, right, front, and back. No luminous heat signatures. No footsteps.

I fish out my phone and open the camera, but it's too dark to get a clear picture of the plates from here. My naked eye is much more powerful. I'm going to have to get closer. But the instant I creep away from the building, exposing myself, a body torpedoes on top of mine.

I hit the pavement face-first and howl as my cheekbone shatters with a hideous *crunch*. It takes me a second to realize I'm crying out in shock—not pain. My body is so eager to heal that my brain hasn't even received the distress call.

The person on top of me wrestles my arms behind my back and kneels to keep them pressed against my spine. Where the hell were they hiding? I swear I looked everywhere.

Except up. I didn't check the fucking roof.

"You carrying any weapons?" a female voice snarls. She pries my cell phone from my hand.

"Uh . . . no. That's my phone—"

"Can't have that either."

A pair of hiking boots slam the ground, inches from my face, as a second person hops down from the roof.

"I-I'm here with Cora? We were sent here. She's in the truck." My jaw is tight and tender as my face knits back together. I spit a mouthful of blood as I try to buck the woman off my back. My tongue caresses my teeth and I catch the points of my elongated canines. They do that on their own, whenever my heart rate climbs. I can't believe they didn't chip when I hit the ground. Must be stronger than I thought.

"Hold still," the second figure sighs, like he's already exhausted with my theatrics. I don't recognize his voice. It's thick like mud and deeper than Devon's. The woman on my back tosses him my cell phone.

"Excuse me. I need that." I really, *really* need that. . . .

"Have you used this device in the past twenty-four hours?" The man taps his dusty boot, impatient. Doesn't crouch down to show me his face.

"It's been in airplane mode. We haven't used data since we left New York. Can I please have it back?"

He doesn't answer. Because the answer is no.

"Search her bag," the woman barks.

"I told you, I don't have any weapons." Unless you count those Saranasia shots. I hope to God I did a good enough job concealing them.

"Mia?!" Cora squeals across the parking lot.

Bloody drool slides down my chin. "Core, I'm back here!"

She sprints toward me, arriving in a flash with a ragged yelp when she sees me on the ground. She's got her own security guard at her side—a skinny young man with a shaved head and a pencil-thin, droopy mouth.

"It's okay, she's with me," Cora tells him.

The woman on my back finally withdraws and I wobble to my feet, wiping blood from my mouth with my dirty sleeve.

"I'm Shea," she says. "You ladies want to come inside, you gotta go through me."

Cora and I both nod. I swallow a hard kernel of unease.

Shea's frowning eyes scrape over me then rivet to my face. She opens her mouth, and I swear she's about to say my mother's name.

"We gotta search you," she says instead. "Turn around, guys."

She indicates we start stripping down. Shit, it's cold enough to see our goddamn breath.

Cora looks to me with a helpless shrug. We chatter and shake as we peel off our layers, down to our underwear. Shea turns our pockets inside out. I hold out my arms and let her pat me down as my bare feet protest against the freezing concrete. She does the same thing to Cora. At least she's quick. Knows what she's looking for. Nods to let us know we've passed.

As we dress, the two men dig through our backpacks.

"You're the ones we were expecting from Forty-Eight, yeah?" the skinny guy asks.

We nod, still shivering.

"How many Daylights you got left?"

"So uh, the thing is . . . I'm really sorry, but we used them all." Cora sheepishly chews her cheek. That's not true, though. We had at least a dozen pills on us. "We sold most of them at the Red Market like we were supposed to, but the rest . . . Sorry. We couldn't get a lot, the day we left." I meet Cora's eye, but she looks right through me.

Shea jerks her head toward the guys searching our bags.

"All phones, weapons, and medications are now communal property. You make that hard, we can make things hard right back."

"I swear, we don't have anything. Just our phones. And you can take those, it's fine, we don't care," Cora blubbers.

The guys toss our bags back to us. I breathe out a sigh. Those crude stitches securing the Saranasia shots to the lining of my bag are still intact. I could cry. Losing my phone is a nightmare, but at least I still have my last scrap of leverage.

"I'm Moose." The hulk with the huge hands quirks his chin in my direction. Of course he is. "You two can't be wandering around outside without an escort. This is strictly an indoor operation. Can't risk people seeing any activity."

"Bernie, search the vehicle," Shea squawks at their third, squirrelly cohort. He darts around the corner. I glance over at Cora again. Are the Daylights in the car? But her poker face holds firm.

"Gonna need your names so we can process you," Shea goes on.

"Cora Quinto."

"Izzy McKinnon."

It just comes out.

Shea's lips part. I feel the corner of Cora's eye like a paper cut.

I don't understand what I've done at first, like my panicked mind is on autopilot—rerouting me before I know where I'm headed. But everything makes sense a second later.

Devon isn't going to risk revealing himself for Cora. He doesn't care about her, doesn't even know her.

But he cares about Mom.

He asked her to come home. He'll show himself right away, if she's ready to surrender.

This approach is a lot riskier, especially considering I just lost my phone. But it could still work. What I need is a guarantee he'll come to me. Then, before he arrives, I'll bolt. Take the truck and make the call from the nearest gas station.

Everything's unraveling but I can grab just enough to braid things back together.

I think.

"You called her by a different name a minute ago," Moose says after a tense hiatus. His stare arcs between Cora's face and mine. God dammit, he's right. She yelled "Mia" when she got out of the car.

"I'm sorry." I squeeze Cora's shoulder, and she stiffens. "I should've told you the truth. I didn't want anyone to know my name till we got here."

Cora pulls her canines under her lip. Her eyes are two rings of fire. Is she angry? She's definitely confused. But she doesn't ask any questions. She just nods, staying the course.

"I'm here to see Devon."

"He ain't here to see you." That's Moose.

"Tell him where I am. He'll come."

Mom makes herself at home under my skin. I feel her rush through me, straightening my posture, chiseling my gaze.

"I'll handle this," Shea says to Moose. Her voice is softer now. But her stare stabs at me like shards of glass.

"Will you call him?"

Shea makes a raspy sound in the back of her throat that's almost a laugh. Shakes her head. "Shit girl, if that's what you want."

I'm half expecting her to slap a pair of handcuffs on me or lead me inside at gunpoint. But she's casual as she guides us toward the side entrance. Riffles through her jingling keyring.

I guess she knows better than to mess with me. Knows he wants me alive.

Her. Wants *Izzy* alive.

As we approach the building, Shea fishes a pack of cigarettes from her pocket. She lights three of them. Gives one to Cora, one to me, and keeps the last for herself. Cora's gawking at me again. I meet her eye with a deliberate blink. *All will be revealed.*

"You got some *brass* on you, walking up like this," Shea whispers as she unlocks the door. "I gotta respect that."

I smile at her as I take a drag. That nectar-sweet reaper grin Mom was famous for.

"I was ready to come home."

These cigarettes are nice. An aftertaste like warm butterscotch.

I forgot how hungry I was. Now it's all I can think about.

There's no electricity in the movie theater, but ADAPT has a whole army of generators, just like the Red Market. There have to be at least a hundred people in the lobby alone, working on laptops in little makeshift plywood cubicles: a hidden hive of Saras, clacking away on their keyboards, lit by camping lanterns and construction work lights. Probably shutting down accounts and relaunching them every five minutes. Chatting up a dozen sad, lonely Saras at once, just like Cora. *I feel like I can trust you. Do you want to know who I am?*

It's freezing cold, so everyone's wearing puffy winter parkas. Except us. Shea hands me the knit cap from her own head.

"Here. We'll get you some more gear once you're assigned to a bunk."

She doesn't give anything to Cora.

"Thanks." I pull it on. It's still warm, with a musty smell like dead flowers. She probably hasn't washed her hair in a while.

I can't smell the other scent Saras have anymore.

"You ever meet a gal named Kayla, out in Tucson? Think she used to roll with you."

"Uh, yeah. Kayla used to work at my . . . I mean, she's—" My head spins. If Shea knows Kayla, she knows more than I anticipated. "She and I go way back."

"Bitch nearly got me killed a few months ago. Someone needs to take her out for target practice."

My antenna shoots up. "Where is she now?"

Shea laughs. "Shit, who knows? Russia? Wherever he tells her to go."

I wonder why she said that. My mind churns, but it's not safe to ask too many questions. I need to keep playing my part. Keep looking for my chance to make a break for it.

Who has the car keys? Cora?

I glance her way and she falls in step with me, clearing her throat. Impatient to get back on the same page. She's barely smoked the cigarette Shea gave her.

As she walks, I notice she keeps adjusting the band of her bra, over her shirt. Pulling it like she's sweaty and trying to air it out.

Shea leads us to the defunct ticketing window, where four bedraggled bleeders sit behind the glass with needles in their arms. Two others have already finished for the day, and are sharing a box of dry Cap'n Crunch in the corner. They're all in their teens, wearing stained, mismatched winter hand-me-downs. A couple of them look strung out: too thin, with watery red eyes.

"Figure you two haven't eaten yet," Shea says as she knocks on the window. One of the kids with the cereal box rises to grab a cup from a stack of old movie theater accoutrements with Coca-Cola logos on them.

I'm grinding my lower lip between my teeth the way Mom used to. It's not an act.

"Thanks," Cora exhales, loosening for the first time. "We split a drink from the Red Market but that was all the way back in Ohio."

"Are these people clean?" I whisper to Shea as the kid fills our cups from one of his friends' blood bags. "They look kinda . . . I dunno."

"We drug-test them every day. Pay 'em better than the Sara centers do. They're just a little dry lately. Doing a lot of business. The towns around here are uh . . . well, they're kinda picked over," she explains. "I mean look, if you wanna sing for your supper, go for it. But designating a permanent food source is part of our new strategy. We need to keep some of these townies alive." I watch as the boy seals the cup with a lid and sticks a straw through it. Now all I need is a large buttered popcorn.

"That's nice that you pay them a living wage."

The window slides open and the kid hands a cup to me, then Cora. She's still fumbling with her bra.

I take the cup but hesitate before I drink. I'm still not comfortable with this whole exchange. Sitting on the wrong side of the dinner table.

"For now," Shea says from the side of her mouth. "Eventually, we won't have to."

I chew my straw. I want to ask her to elaborate. But Mom wouldn't have to ask, and I can put two and two together. For these people, the world is divided between those who want to become Saras, and those who do not. According to ADAPT, that balance will invert one day. Saras will outnumber the uninfected, and if you're not a Sara, you're food. Given the choice between certain death and farming out your blood, you'll choose the latter. And you won't ask for money.

I can't resist any longer. My lips quiver. I sip from my straw.

It's awful and mesmerizing, the way my body restores itself the instant the blood hits my lips. Healing energy surges to my wounds, and my pulse races as if I'm in line for a roller coaster. My injured cheek tingles, flashing hot and cold. I take another, deeper drink. I know I never gave Mom quite as much sustenance as she needed. It was the bare minimum. Four ounces. She was always hungry. Barely getting by. Every time I drink, I'm reminded of that.

Trancelike, I suck down the entire cup. Wash it down with one last puff from Shea's fancy cigarette. Crush it at the bottom.

Cora sounds like she's shouting into a pillow when she turns to me and says, "Izzy, you coming?"

I don't respond right away. Not just because of the blood high.

I blink and reorient myself as Cora follows Shea toward one of the theaters. The empty frame where the featured movie poster should be holds a cardboard sign that reads BUNK A.

"My buddy Alan will get you checked in here." Shea drops us off at the door to the theater. I remove her hat from my head and try to give it back, but she waves me off.

"I'll get it later."

I plant my feet. "When will he be here?"

"I gotta touch base."

"But he'll come."

Shea looks me up and down as she holds the door open. "I can't decide if you're absolute batshit or the bravest dumb bitch I've ever met. Either way. Good luck."

Her exacting gaze lingers as we pass. My stomach lurches. Like I've said the wrong thing, but I don't know what.

"Stop. You have to talk to me."

Cora yanks my arm and pulls me against the trash cans as we enter the vestibule of the dim theater.

"Not here. Wait."

"Just tell me if it's true."

"No, Cora. You know who I am."

"But then how do you . . . *Oh my God*—"

"Core—"

"She was your mom."

I told Cora my mom was a Sara. Even told her how she died. But nothing else.

I guess even that much was a mistake. Too late now.

"You guys were from Arizona. Holy shit—" She paces in a circle as the pieces interlock. "Why didn't you *tell me*—"

"Stop talking. We can't do this here."

She nods. Starts fussing with her bra again.

"What the hell is wrong with your—?"

"God dammit, they're melting," Cora whispers as she snakes a hand underneath her sweater. "Give me your empty cup."

Of course. The Daylights are in her bra. I pull her behind the trash cans. For the moment, we're alone. But probably not for long.

"Why didn't you keep them in the bottle?" I hiss, blocking her from view as she whisks a dozen sticky pills from her underwire and into her palm.

"So they wouldn't rattle around, obviously. Haven't you ever like, snuck drugs into a concert?"

"Have *you*?"

She rolls her eyes. "Just help me."

The pills are intact, though their color has started to fade, leaving sea-green freckles all over Cora's chest. She's damn lucky Shea didn't make us strip completely naked. I can't help but laugh as I hand her the cup.

"What's so funny?"

"Nothing. Just . . . I'm glad you did this. You never know."

"Never know *what*?"

There's that flicker of fear in her eyes again. The way she gets mean when she's scared. I'm not going to say it, and I don't have to. She and I both know we're not safe yet.

A pair of Saras with overstuffed camping backpacks make their way inside the theater. We wait till they've passed to say anything else.

"By the way, where are the car keys?"

"Should still be in my bag, I don't think they took them," she replies, but doesn't offer them to me. And why would she?

I'm going to have to steal them. When I leave her. Soon. It has to be soon.

It's time for me to cauterize my open heart.

"So . . ." she says under her breath. If looks could kill. "You know him."

I'm not ready to have this conversation. I haven't had a chance to prepare, to decide what to include or redact. We were never supposed to get to this point.

Holes burn the edges of my vision, like lace, and my legs suddenly feel as though they're filling with water. It's like the overture to a panic attack, but different somehow. I need to lie down. Need to catch my breath.

"Let's just go inside and sit." I pull her along with me.

"And then you'll tell me."

I nod.

"Everything?"

". . . Yeah."

It's a pretty brilliant strategy, to set up a campground for Saras inside a movie theater. Artificial darkness, soundproofed, and plenty of space, once all the seats are removed. This place is a multiplex, with twelve different theaters, each housing clusters of tents, cots, and sleeping bags. In Bunk A, they're even playing a movie—which seems like a huge expenditure for the generators, but I guess these people deserve some entertainment. It's *Mean Girls*, of all things. Cora murmurs half the lines under her breath as we unroll two thin sleeping bags in a dark corner. Instantly snaps into a lighter mood.

I didn't realize this was one of her comfort movies. It would have come out when she was in high school though, so it makes sense. It's funny. I thought I knew all her anchoring rituals. That's something I learned about at the Sara center. Everyone has them. There was Ingrid, who had a miscarriage when she got infected and passed the time knitting hundreds of baby blankets. Franklin, a former athlete who cultivated a savant-like knowledge of obscure MLB stats. Cora would wear her threadbare Duke hoodie to bed every night without exception. Kept herself calm watching old episodes of *Survivor* and *The Bachelorette*. God help you if you tried to put on a season that aired after 2010.

Anchoring connects you to the person you used to be. The person who, paradoxically, you will *always be*. All this time, I thought that kind of behavior was specific to Mom, like the Disney movies we watched till we knew them by heart and the murals all over the house. I always figured she got into that because she was stir-crazy. But the rituals go deep.

I was an anchor, too. Until I grew up.

It's strange. I don't know what mine are.

God, maybe it's *this*. Hating him. Hunting him.

Cora curls into her sleeping bag, using her backpack as a pillow. I keep one eye trained on it. Wondering where the keys are.

Maybe she'll fall asleep. But I know she's not tired. Not yet.

Her expectant glare spurs me across the darkness.

The movie's still playing, loud enough to muffle our words. The tent next to us is empty.

"Why didn't you say anything before?"

That bizarre, lacy effect returns to my vision. For some reason, my lips feel hard. Cold and slippery, like ice.

"Look I uh . . . I knew how you felt about him. I didn't want to make things weird for you." Is that good enough? I have no idea. My brain is getting swampy. Is this still a panic attack? I'm so tired all of a sudden. . . .

"But we had to jump through so many goddamn hoops to get here, when all this time you *knew* him—"

"I never had an in. That's what you need to understand. He and my mom . . . they have this *history*, you know?" She does, if she's got a working knowledge of the Tucson Twelve drama. "We didn't get along, because of that."

"So then why did you come with me? Why do you want to see him so bad?"

"Because I'm—" I'm *what*? Shit.

The screen looks like a wall of multicolored Swiss cheese.

"I uh, I have information for him. None of that stuff from our past matters now. I'm trying to help." The words ooze out of me. I can barely keep my eyes open. "It's important that we help him."

"Right."

My head comes to rest between my knees. I am *not* well. Maybe those kids were strung out on something after all.

But Cora seems fine.

"Is your mom really dead?"

"Yes. That part is true," I think I say. I can't lift my head anymore.

"Mia, what's the matter?"

"I'm uh . . . I'm really—" I'm slurring, like my tongue is too large for my mouth. "I think I just . . . I haven't slept—"

"Okay?"

"I'm gonna just—"

Sleep slaps me across the face before I can say anything else.

I'm levitating. Someone's carrying me. The world rocks like a cradle. I must be dreaming.

"Shit, let go of me!" Cora's voice cleaves the darkness, and my eyes slingshot open.

I *am* being carried. I part my lips to scream, but someone's put tape over my mouth. There's rope coiled around my arms and legs, mummying me inside my sleeping bag. My heart spasms and my canines shoot from my gums, but they're fucking useless. I crane my neck, desperate for a glimpse of Cora. Somewhere behind me in the blurry, Swiss-cheese blackness.

There's the sound of a struggle as someone tackles Cora to tape her mouth shut. She's putting up more of a fight. Wasn't sleeping as deeply as me.

Because Cora barely smoked that cigarette.

We're still in the movie theater. Nobody stands to defend us or even asks what's happening as our captors parade us past.

We float through an emergency exit that empties into the rear parking lot. The sky is briny with clouds. Snow flurries prick the exposed skin on my cheeks.

The cube truck with Colorado plates idles outside, hatch hanging open like an expectant tomb. I'm pathetic, twisting around in my prisoner's cocoon. I'm stronger than I've ever been in my life, but strength is relative, when it comes to Saras. I finally glimpse the person carrying me. It's Moose.

How did I miscalculate so tragically? Horror squalls in my chest as I think of Batman Street and those sun-scalded entrails. How stupid I was, assuming I could weasel my way around these people. Like I knew something they didn't. There's no one to blame but me.

Moose tosses me into the truck first, and Cora lands on top of me. The hatch slams shut. Cora's sleeping bag strangles her faint heat signature. My eyes are powerless against this kind of darkness.

There's nothing to light our way now.

DECEMBER 2023

At some point in the night, I scatter a fortress of coffee grounds in front of the door. I don't remember doing it. Only realize I did when I slip on my way to the bathroom to throw up.

I rest my head against the bath mat, breathing rubber and mildew and the smell of my own sweat. As the fog clears, I remember the other thing I did. I destroyed the phone. The only lead I had is gone.

But I had to. Didn't I? He said he could track it. "Said" being the operative word.

I wish I'd been sober. Wish I could remember his exact words, not just the way they felt.

I shamble toward my bed as a thought spreads across my mind like a stain.

I know Devon the way a child knows the scary parts of her favorite movie. The scenes you watch between your fingers. I know my memories of him. Which is not the same thing as knowing him.

I do not know the person who called me.

My body calcifies, brittle as glass. Like he poisoned me through the phone and I'm already dead.

I wake sometime in the late afternoon. Try to eat some leftovers but I can't keep anything down. An hour later, I manage to swallow some chicken broth. I'm determined to regain my strength. Clean that coffee up off the floor and step outside.

If he's coming after me, I can't stop him. I don't know where he is, what he's planning, or how he's planning to do it. I have nothing, not even the phone. And the FBI has even less. The whole of my existence boils down to two choices: Hide till he finds me. Or seize whatever time I've got left.

I have nothing to lose. If I die in this apartment without seeing Jade one last time, it'll be the coward's death I deserve. I'm going to that show.

Even if Devon was telling the truth about pinging cell towers, he won't be looking for me at a random club on East First Street. For all I know, I might actually be *safer* there.

I gouge my scalp with my nails, staring at the event page on my phone. Jade's black-ringed eyes stare back. It's twenty-five dollars to get in, with a two-drink minimum, but my liver can't fathom another night of abuse. Maybe they'll let me order Coke, or a cranberry juice.

It's not like I'd be showing up unprompted. After all, she texted *me*. The reminder of it is a constant pulse. A cut in my mouth I can't stop running my tongue over.

Hey Mia i was thinkin of you today. how are u doin? X

So brutal in its casual approach. "Hey how ya doin' since your mom spontaneously combusted and I told you I had a girlfriend?"

Maybe I should finally reply. It might be prudent to let her know I'm coming tonight. Prudent. Wow. She can't even keep "you" and "u" consistent and I'm over here trying to be *prudent*.

I peel off my stale PJs, wondering what I ought to wear. What message I'm hoping to send. Is this *Look what you fucking did to me* or *Your loss, bitch*? I'd love to find something that screams the latter. But that's not me. Never was. When I went to Cloak and Dagger, I stole one of Mom's outfits, that sheer black shirt with the bare midriff. I wonder what happened to it. It's not with the rest of my stuff. By the end of the night, it was caked with so much blood and dust and sweat I probably balled it up, chucked it across the room, and hoped I'd never see it again.

I'm going to be late. I slap some concealer under my eyes and settle on a fuzzy blue sweater over a new balconette bra I bought a few weeks back. It's made of smooth black satin and I've never owned anything like it in my life. I thought it would be fun, that I might feel sexy or something, but I'm not convinced. I'm too aware of it, like I'm a top-heavy Barbie doll fighting to keep my spine straight. I don't know why I'm wearing it. No, that's not true. But

I'm trying not to think too hard about what I want out of this. What happens when she sees me. If we talk. What talking could lead to.

I haven't taken the train after dark before, and I'm not about to start now. I pace the lobby, waiting for my Uber. Wishing I could have steeled myself with something stronger than chicken broth.

☾ ☾ ☾

The club is fairly intimate, resplendent with Edison-bulb fixtures and exposed industrial pipes for that oh-so-trendy Steampunk Lite feel. A couple of round copper tables flank the stage. Standing room is over by the bar. I expected it to be bigger. It's dark, but it's also small enough that she'll probably spot me from the stage. I'm not sure if that's how I want this to happen. I want to reveal myself, like a secret, at just the right moment. I decide to immerse with the crowd and hang toward the back. Find a nice cozy corner to lurk in.

I tell the bartender I'm not drinking tonight, so she's cool with giving me a Coke to fulfill my drink minimum. She's a petite, raven-haired firecracker, and for a moment my thoughts drift to Kayla. I wonder where she is. If she's still alive.

I slink toward a dark, cavernous booth, sipping my soda with pride. I will get through this without being drunk. As I take a seat, a familiar face materializes onstage. It's Tony, checking his cables. He's lost weight and shaved his mustache, but that Tigger tattoo is eternal. The pitch and roll of my gut sends me racing back to the bar. I present my glass.

"Actually, could you please add some rum?"

There's a lanky, dour-faced girl with glasses and baby bangs who will *not* stop staring at me. I'm being as inconspicuous as possible, here in my little fortress of solitude. But her beady eyes are tracking me like radar. I have no idea who she is. She looks older than me, maybe in her mid-thirties, wearing this yellow jumpsuit that's like a whimsical mechanic's uniform. I avert my gaze and snag my phone, scrolling through the same Instagram posts I already looked at three minutes ago.

At that moment, the lights dim. The woman springs to her feet and cheers, like she's been cued. The rest of the audience follows her lead. I do the same, though I strategically scoot behind a taller guy in front of me.

It's weird, when there's someone you've been thinking of non-stop and you finally glimpse them in the flesh. Your brain short-circuits for a second, rebuilding fragmented neurons to help you understand that this is, in fact, your person. You've gotten too used to imagining them: this ethereal Frankenstein's monster your memory cobbles together.

Jade floats onstage, and she's tinier than I remember. She's flattened her nest of curls and sliced them into a jagged, devil-may-care shag—part of that Dagger Stabs Back rebrand. She confidently struts toward her piano in emerald-green platform boots and black pleather culottes. The girl in the yellow jumpsuit sticks two fingers in her mouth, and her shrill, enthusiastic mom-whistle dominates the applause. I want to cheer louder, but I'm suddenly afraid Jade might recognize my voice. Her scream is seared into my memory. Just like mine must be, in hers.

Or maybe I just hope it is.

"New York, how we feelin' tonight?" Jade purrs into the mic. Tony and Steve file in behind her, getting situated at their respective instruments. "I've been waiting a long time to come play for you. Thanks for making me feel at home here. If we've just met, we're Landshark."

I wonder if she's ever going to change that name. It almost feels silly now, a strange contrast with her thorny new vibe. I mean, it was always silly. She said that was the point. But she seems like she's evolved past that brand of detached, ironic humor. Then again, how would I know? It's not like I've talked to her.

She opens with a song I haven't heard before. I know she's been releasing new stuff, but I've taken great pains to avoid listening to it. Steve pounds the toms: low and ominous. Jade growls into the mic, cupping it with her hands like a chalice, muffling her voice just enough to dull the edges of her sparse, jagged lyrics.

> *"I see, I see, I see a light, light, light*
> *We take flight, flight, flight*
> *Come and get me, I'm ready for a fight, fight, fight—"*

I don't remember her songwriting being quite so basic before.
The words are almost vapid.

> "*I see a light, light, light*
> *The moment before we take flight, flight, flight*
> *I'm ready for a fight, fight, fight, fight—*"

Something else about the song jabs at me, like a pebble in my
shoe. It's not just the simplicity of the lyrics. I don't know. I'm probably imagining it.

None of these songs are going to be about me, or what happened.

Jesus, if they were, I don't know what I'd do. Find the closest
emergency exit and bolt? Trigger the fire alarm and all the sprin-
klers? I wouldn't be flattered. I know that much.

I waterfall the dregs of my drink into my mouth. I want to get
up and grab another. But if I do, I risk her seeing me. And I don't
want that to happen yet. I've decided on my moment: Right before
her last song ends, I'm going to stand up and walk toward the front
tables. I'll hover and lock eyes with her, making sure she knows it's
me, then promptly swoop through the door. But I'll just be in the
bathroom or something. I won't actually *leave*. Just want to make
her think I would. I imagine her flubbing the words to her final cho-
rus when she sees me. The awkward squeal of her mic. The rum
gives my brain a warm, encouraging squeeze. I can't remember the
last time I was so excited for something.

She plays an older song next, one I remember. Ghost hunting
in Tokyo and Paris. I suck the astringent flavor from my melting
ice, tamping down my excitement long enough to ask myself what
I think this dramatic move will accomplish. What am I trying to
say to her? Am I still angry? About Gabi, about the lie by omis-
sion? Or am I angry for the way she followed me into the house?
I picture her crying in the kitchen, that bead of blue eyeliner
rolling down her face. I can still hear her begging me to come
with her, promising we'd figure it out. That howl from Mom's
bedroom.

But the fault line goes deeper than that. Farther back in time.
The night I rode my flat-tired bike to the Starbucks in a nervous fit
and she kissed my cup. No. Rewind again. The first time I saw her

behind the coffee bar and she gave me a free strawberry drink and pretended it was an accident, that she'd made too much. I decided she did that on purpose, that it wasn't an accident. I never asked her about it.

She forced herself into my life. Made me feel this way, made me burn everything down. That's why I didn't want to respond to her text. I can't rehash the past, or suss out what *really happened* between us. There's no point, because there's no answer—no magic number that solves the equation. It wasn't Gabi, or the lie about Gabi. It wasn't the moment she entered my house. It was everything. The fact that she exists at all.

Yellow Jumpsuit is staring at me again.

After about forty-five minutes of propulsive, moody earworms, Tony hands Jade an acoustic guitar and she climbs up onto a stool. The room falls into quiet reverence as she performs a quick tuning check.

"This is my last song of the night, and it's a new one." Her voice is a little hoarse—maybe because of all the singing she's done. But it feels like something else. "Thanks for supporting me after the year I've had. I appreciate you all so much."

I was hoping she'd close with a loud banger so I could slip toward the door without disrupting the audience. I don't want her to notice me till the *exact moment* she's supposed to. There's a method to this, but now I'm all out of sorts. My plan feels wrong now.

Her final song is raw and stripped down, and the lyrics are . . . well, they're *her* again. She's not trying to simplify her story for the sake of a hook. She gets so close to the mic it looks like she might swallow it. The whole room, and all the people in it, fall away. It sounds as if she's whispering in my ear.

> "I wanna save you, the way you saved me
> Don't got a plan, but I got you a cup of tea
> Goin' to New York, gonna sleep on the rooftop
> But the building burned down before we woke up
> It burns and it burns and it burns
> And it's all I can see
> The world turns and it turns and it turns
> But it turns without me."

I go wooden and tremble at the same time. The song is beautiful. It's everything it should be. I absolutely fucking hate it.

This isn't her song to sing.

She was there. But it happened to *me,* not her. She's not allowed to use this as her muse.

> *"It burns and it burns and it burns*
> *And it's all I can see*
> *The world turns and it turns and it turns*
> *But it turns without me."*

She should've asked me if this was okay. Maybe she was trying to, the day she texted me. Which, if true, actually makes this even worse. She wasn't interested in how I was doing. She wanted permission to reference the worst day of my life in a song.

Maybe.

I could be wrong. This might not be about me at all. But I don't want to hear any more.

> *"The smoke in my eyes*
> *Becomes my disguise*
> *She burns and she burns*
> *And takes me all the way down*
> *Till I'm nothing but ashes wearing a crown."*

I feel myself stand. But I'm not executing the plan. I'm just leaving.

I squeeze past the loud hanger-on in the yellow jumpsuit. "'Scuse you," she hisses. Good riddance.

The exit sign beyond the stage glows like a lighthouse. I'm almost through the storm. But as I reach for the door, the back of my neck prickles. Certainty coils around my body. I didn't stop to look at her, but I already know—she's looking at *me.*

I turn, and she's still singing. Hasn't forgotten a single word. She's a professional. I should've known she'd keep her cool. But her pleading gaze makes a wordless bargain. *Stay and I'll fix this. Stay and all your pain will be a bad dream.*

This feels like a victory. What I wanted. Not what I told myself

I wanted—the secret want, concealed beneath my convictions. I don't know who I'm kidding. I'm not *really* trying to leave. We both know that.

I spin toward the bar. And that's where I wait for her. She doesn't take long. Knows not to test my patience, or her luck.

"What're you drinking?"

I can't face her. There's too much emotion packed into this moment, an entire universe on the head of a pin. I keep my eyes glued to Tony and Steve as they break down their gear.

"Uh, rum and Coke."

"I'll allow it." She flags down the bartender. I regard her from my periphery. "Can I get a Skinny Pirate, please?"

"What's that?" I swallow a generous mouthful from my glass.

"Captain Morgan and diet."

". . . I'll allow it?"

She laughs and sits down. Spins her stool to look at me straight on. I stare into my drink. A robust floral aroma wafts toward me. I wonder if she put on perfume before she came to meet me or if she was already wearing it.

"I didn't know you were in New York," she pours into the silence.

"I mean, I didn't tell you."

I meet her gaze. She exhales with an audible hiss.

"I'll go, if you don't want to do this." A gentle concession. No judgmental barbed edges.

"Do what? What are we doing?"

She winds a strand of her flat-ironed shag around her finger. "Saying hi, I guess. I dunno."

"Hi."

Her drink arrives. She takes a long, desperate sip from the straw.

"I moved here like, six weeks ago." The rum helps nudge the conversation along. "Would've come sooner but I had to list my house and stuff—"

"That's awesome! I mean, that you're here. Not that your house . . . you know."

We both pull from our straws in the same breath.

"Where's your place at? Where you working?"

"I'm looking for a job. Taking classes at BMCC in the meantime."

"Mia, that's great! You're going to college!"

I squirm. There's a grace note of pity in her enthusiasm.

"It's different than like, *college* college."

"Don't knock it if they offer a degree."

I'm aching to slice through the preamble and ask her about the song. But I don't know what to say, where to start.

"That was a great set."

"I'm glad you came out. It means so much to me. Why didn't you tell me you were in town? We could've . . . I mean, obviously we're gonna hang out. But I just . . . shit, it would've been great to . . . y'know—"

She keeps rambling, hoping I'll interrupt. Purses her mouth shut when I don't. I watch her as she watches me take a drink.

"I texted you last month. Did you change your number?"

"Nope." The word is delicious in my mouth. I don't know why I'm being like this. But she isn't walking away. Like she knows she deserves it. I'll dish it as long as she can take it.

"Hey, J—" A voice pipes up behind us. Jade whirls around on her stool.

It's yellow jumpsuit lady. Her gaze nips mine before she turns back to Jade.

"Steve's loading out and needs to know if you're storing your keyboard in the van tonight."

"Yeah, he can take it. Thanks."

"My place is safer."

I turn my back to them, but I'm still listening. The bartender mouths "Another round?" at me and I nod.

"If you want to take it, go ahead. I appreciate that." Jade's voice pitches up with forced professionalism. I've never heard her sound that way.

"Okay. I'll call us an Uber."

"I'm gonna hang downtown tonight."

"Oh."

The woman's stare hits my back like an electric prod.

"J, can we talk for a sec?"

"Not right now. Text me when you get home."

Jade spins her stool back into my gravity as Yellow Jumpsuit violently slings a phone charger across the bar. Jade intercepts it without looking at her.

"You'll fucking need this, then."

Jade stuffs the charger into her purse as the woman stomps back toward the stage. Doesn't say anything else.

"If you have to help them pack up, it's fine—" My refill arrives. Nick of time.

"I finished my load-out already. She knows that." I already suspect what Jade's about to tell me. "That's Gabi, by the way."

I'm not sure how to respond. I swirl my straw around my drink and gore the lime, filling the glass with pulpy green gristle.

"We're not together. Just so you know."

"Jade, I don't fucking care." She flinches, startled. I do, too. Not sure if I deserve a pat on the back or a slap across the face.

If I'm trying to make this happen between us, I'm doing a miserable job.

"She's managing us. For now. Her aunt lives in the Bronx and she's crashing there for the holidays, but I've been staying with the guys. She's here 'cuz she's *working*—"

"I *said* I don't care."

She studies me. No—more like vivisects me. "God, you're weird now."

"What's that supposed to mean?"

"I mean you're just . . . not the same. The way you talk. The way you . . . I dunno." She fixes me with a sad smile.

"Sorry?"

"Listen, I get it. Why *would you* be? The same."

"Maybe I should go," I sigh. "I live up in Morningside Heights. I have a long ride home." I don't think I mean it. I might just be saying it to elicit a response, the same way I pretended to walk out during her last number.

She seizes my wrist. "No. There's only one other person in the world who knows what I've been through, and that's you. I'm not letting you leave."

Wait. What *she's* been through? Like this whole thing was *her* tragedy? The anger is volcanic in my chest. But I push it down.

It's been so long since someone looked at me this way.

"If you're still mad about Gabi, I understand." Her grip on my wrist tightens.

"It's not that."

"I told her about everything that happened in Arizona. I needed to let it out, and I knew you weren't the right person to . . . y'know. I had to give you some space. So I spilled my guts to her, which meant I had to tell her about *you,* and after I let that slip—"

"Jade, I don't want to talk about Gabi. A lot has happened since then."

Finally, she releases my hand.

"Did you really like my set?" She bats her lashes before they start to droop. I wonder how long she's been drinking.

"It was awesome."

"Where's Morningside Heights?"

"Uptown, by Columbia."

"Why the hell do you live all the way up there?"

"My boss's wife knew a guy who knew a guy."

She polishes off her Skinny Pirate, and I race to catch up, even though my glass is still full.

"I want to leave," she announces. "Do you want to leave?"

"Um . . . I mean—"

"Let's take a walk. I don't like to sit still, after a show."

Her credit card is already out.

"Fuck, it's fucking cold! I love it though, don't you?"

She links arms with me. We're heading south. I wonder if she knows where she's going. If there's even a destination.

"You're so lucky to live here," she goes on. "God, I wish I could stay."

"You're not going to? I thought that was the plan—"

"It was, but I think LA might be better for me. I need a real manager. I have some leads out there. Gabi isn't *really* my manager. I mean she's doing the job and she's fine, 'cuz we needed someone and she knew the basics 'cuz she used to work in PR, but—"

A black ambulance whizzes past. No sirens, no flashing lights. But still, it's enough to stiffen my stride. Jade stumbles. I forgot we had our arms linked.

"Whoa now." Jade snorts as she loses her footing. Spins me in an awkward circle as she rights herself. She realizes I'm not laughing. "What's up?"

"Just sorta . . . I dunno, I wonder if we should go inside?"

"You cold?"

". . . I guess." I'd rather not elaborate.

I can put myself in as much danger as I damn well please. But I'm not about to take her down with me.

We're in a stuffy basement that serves exclusively mezcal, lit by a parade of paper lanterns dangling from the ceiling. It's meant to feel like a secret grotto, I imagine—a beachside cave you might stumble into after midnight somewhere in Mexico. But it's not Mexico, it's New York in the middle of winter, and the ventilation is so bad I swear I can smell everything everyone had for breakfast, lunch, and dinner. At least it's warm, though. Warm and behind a scanner.

Jade and I are on our second round of Palomas, crammed into a booth near the kitchen. Spices hang in the air like ghosts—cumin and chipotle. Adobo and red onion. Kind of like the Fair Shake. I drunkenly dance with my sense memory as Jade spews gossip for which I have no context.

". . . And then, when I finally charged my phone, I had sixty-two texts from her. Sixty-fucking-two. Which is when I realized, she *needs me* to be a disaster. If I'm always a tire fire, she'll always be there to hose me down and she'll always feel useful. And even though I'm not the same person I was when I met her, I feel like I *have to be* or I'm gonna smash her heart into a million pieces." Jade groans between gulps. "Tony says that's textbook codependency and I agree. It's so hard though."

I hate that we're talking about Gabi again. "I dunno, it sounds like you guys are just afraid to break up."

I reach for my glass. Jade intercepts my hand.

"I told you. We *did* break up."

"Right. Just like before." I signal to our waiter as he passes. One more round.

"This time it's true. She lost her shit when she found out about you."

"Well, she's still here. So she must not be *that* pissed."

Jade grabs a fistful of her hair with a dramatic moan.

I'm feeling bold. I'm about to make this interesting. I lean across the table, closing the distance between us with a whisper. "Have you ever *actually* cheated on her?"

"I mean, would you call what we did cheating?"

I mirror the way she rests her chin on her hands. "Some people wouldn't. Maybe someone like Gabi, who's looking for a reason to stay."

"God, that's so true, though." Jade's face slides down her palm, smudging the kohl on her left eye. Her hair has started to thicken back into a tumbleweed in the damp, musty air.

"I guess the thing you have to ask yourself is . . . what would really, I mean, *really* break her heart?"

She holds my gaze, but my eyes slide off. Who the hell am I? I don't just . . . *say things* like that. But it feels so good, holding power this way. A sac of darkness opens inside me. I want more than whatever this night is building toward. I want to blow up her life like she blew up mine. There's nothing that could even the score. I know that. Still, I'm craving chaos. Want to make a mess and leave her to clean it up by herself.

A moment passes, and our third round arrives. She chews her straw.

"By the way . . . I just wanted to say thank you. For being so amazing and cool about my song." She rolls her paper napkin holder into a tiny purple caterpillar. So, she admits it. And she's anxious. Guess she's human after all.

"Oh I mean . . . it's great that you have a way to express yourself when you're going through something." My cheeks burn. Why am I conceding like this? This is my chance to put her in her place.

But if I put her in her place, if I acknowledge what she did was wrong, then I acknowledge that *she is wrong,* for me, and none of this happens. I go home alone. The only way I get what I want to-night is if I forget how she hurt me.

"I really appreciate that, Mia. I was afraid of how you'd react. This is just how I deal with all the noise in my brain, y'know?"

I just drink. Keeping my mouth soft so it's almost a smile.

She coughs and digs a compact mirror from her purse, followed by her lipstick. As if she's desperate to direct her gaze to something other than my face. She fumbles with her lip ring, like it's bothering her, and removes it. It's not pierced. I knew it was fake. I watch as she smooths blackberry stain across her mouth: almost the same shade she wore when we first met, but darker. I imagine biting down and drawing blood. The taste of it.

The Mexican grotto bar cuts us off three rounds later. We pay up—I think?—and leave. Jade hobbles against me, using my weight as a crutch. Are we still on the east side? Walking uptown or downtown? God dammit, I think I need to pee again.

"Should . . . get us an Uber . . ." I let a brick wall catch me as I pat myself down for my phone. She keeps walking. I kick a clod of filthy slush in her direction and she pirouettes back toward me.

I find my phone, but the screen is blurry. Why can't I see my damn screen?

"Wait . . . I think . . . my phone is broken? Or—"

She kisses me and my body seizes. I fight for balance as emotion jackknifes up my throat. Am I crying? Why am I crying? Maybe it's relief. That this finally happened. But it's something else, something more. She's filling my emptiness, but whatever she offers just spills down my face.

I don't want to blow up her life. I want to *be* her life. Any power I thought I had was a fantasy. And I'm too drunk to care, much less fight it.

"You okay?" she murmurs into my mouth. I don't answer. Just pull her back in.

☾ ☾ ☾

Getting on the train is Jade's idea, not mine. But it's right down the block and Uber is taking too long. Rather, *I* am taking too long, because my screen is still blurry. Well, no. It's not the screen. My soggy, drunken eyesight is to blame. The train will be fine, though. Other people are scanning in. There's no difference between riding at night and riding during the day. Not really. As long as you're not alone. Besides, Jade assures me it's only four or five stops to the place she's staying. Hell of a lot better than the long, sleepy haul up and across the island to my apartment.

A few people board the train with us, maybe half a dozen. More than I expected at this hour. But what do I know? I'm the girl who doesn't go anywhere at night.

Our fellow passengers all seem tipsy, either laughing in a huddle or slumped in an upright fetal position, so we don't feel particularly obnoxious by comparison. I pull a breath as we collapse onto a corner bench, a tangle of limbs, and immediately start kissing again. My fear melts like ice in an empty glass. I roll my hips from side to side, luxuriating in that silky feeling between my legs as she sucks my tongue.

"This is. East Broadway," our automated guide announces. I crack a reluctant eye open.

"How many more stops?"

"Um . . . I dunno. We get off at Smith Street so just keep an eye out. Ear out. Ear up." She reaches out to touch my lips. Wipes a blackberry smudge from my mouth with her thumb. "Oh shit."

"It's okay—" I worm my arms inside her coat, searching for the bottom of her shirt and the promise of warm flesh.

"No, I mean *him*." Jade points over my shoulder.

My breath catches and terror grips my chest as I follow her gaze. For a second I think she's talking about . . .

Oh.

A doughy white guy in a moth-eaten parka sits at the opposite end of the bench, wrist squirming down the front of his pants. I leap to my feet with complete disregard for the inertia of the train and my current blood-alcohol ratio. Jade catches me before I fall and smack my face on the seat.

"C'mon." She guides me toward a pole and helps me grab on, sneering at our degenerate audience of one.

"Eat shit, you fucking goblin." She yanks open the door at the end of our car and leads me through.

My vision's still sloshing around like watercolor. The wheels shriek and spit up sparks as the track curves. Jade's already bouncing to the adjoining car. She holds the door open for me. I gape at the narrow steel bridge beneath my feet, bound by two loosey-goosey ball-and-sockets.

"Mia, you gotta jump. Ready?" Nope. "One, two . . . three!"

I make the leap with a childish squeal. Heads turn as Jade catches me and I explode with laughter.

We search for a seat, but there's a stream of frothy yellow vomit on the floor, trickling toward the car's center of gravity. A girl on the corner bench retches, gearing up for another round. Her two disgusted friends, wearing matching Santa hats with blinking LED lights, reluctantly pat her back and breathe through their mouths.

"Keep going," Jade whispers. We hopscotch around the vomit.

The next car already has a pair of booze-blitzed face suckers—a young woman and a guy twice her age in a tweed jacket. A doe-eyed college freshman and her professor, I decide, cheating on his long-suffering wife. An image flashes across my mind: Mom, barely twenty years old. My father, a faceless smear of an older man with a wedding ring and a Ph.D. A stolen kiss during office hours that gave me life twenty-four years ago.

I hurry past, and Jade trails after me. One more car ought to do it. They're getting emptier the farther we go.

We cross one last chaotic threshold and reach the end of the train. Jade hip checks the door and draws me through.

A wine-dark, syrupy tide surges across the floor, ankle-deep. For a moment, I don't know what the hell I'm looking at. But then I realize: The car is filled with blood.

I've never seen so much at once. My fuzzy brain blinks. This has to be a dream. But dreams don't have a stench. The air is redolent with a thick, cloying coppery smell. Jade gags. The blood ebbs and flows with the train's jerky rhythm, splashing our boots. My knees go slack, and Jade hooks her elbows under my arms to prop me up.

Neither of us screams. We're past that, immunized; our bodies know this fear. But that doesn't mean we don't feel it. Jade's heart drums against my back and reverberates along the length of my spine.

Danger, danger, danger.

The car is empty, aside from the blood. A dozen people must have been drained here. How many Saras fed? How the hell did they remove the bodies unnoticed? Then again . . . if they'd fed, they would have *fed*. They wouldn't have wasted a drop. The blood wouldn't be on the floor. The patina clinging to my vision falls away like a shed skin as my mind shakes itself awake. A dozen people drained—but not consumed. This is a *statement;* a grisly new brand of street art.

A seat at the end of the car pulls my gaze.

Someone's sitting there: a disheveled old man with holes in his clothes, covered with a ragged blanket. I point at him. Jade follows my gaze, slack-jawed.

He's not moving. It takes me a second to realize he's been duct-taped to the seat to hold him upright. There's something stuck to his limp, lifeless fist: a paper coffee cup. One of those blue ones with the kitschy Grecian font: *We Are Happy to Serve You.*

Beside him, scrawled across the fiberglass bench, is a message. The artist has signed their work in his blood.

Adapt or die.

My stomach roils like a snake pit.

I know what this is. But it's not meant for me. Has nothing to do with me at all, in fact. It would be a waste of time for Devon to orchestrate something like this just to intimidate me. And there's no way he could know I'm on this train. This is for everyone else: all the stupid sheep seduced by safety in numbers. In a way, I guess it *is* meant for me.

I should have figured ADAPT had a contingent here. How could they not? They're everywhere the internet is. I have no doubt this has happened before. That it's *been* happening. And nobody knows. Or nobody wants to. I'm not sure which is worse.

"What do we do? Do you think they're on the train?" Jade hiccups.

I scan the car. The closest black box is on the opposite end of the bloody floodplain. I snag Jade's hand and pull her back the way we came.

The horny couple in the adjoining car seethes at our second interruption. I lunge past and slam my fist against the black box above them, triggering the distress button in the center. It glows red and pulses in time with a shrill, wake-the-dead alarm.

"Holy shit," the girl gasps, seizing the lapel of the man's jacket. "Are there Saras on the train?"

"Uh . . . no. Just a lot of blood," I mutter, a laughable attempt to reassure them.

Jade paces the car, wringing her clammy hands. We've both left a trail of crimson footprints all over the floor.

The man jumps to his feet and pulls the young woman along with him. "They have to stop and let us off. Right?"

"I've never pressed the button before, I don't know," she whimpers, competing with the wail of the alarm. "Shit, my mom thinks I'm at Maggie's house."

The train howls and punches to a halt. Jade collides with the wall and rights herself against a nearby pole.

"They'll evacuate us now," I say to everyone, but mostly to myself. A soothing improv. "They're gonna pull into the nearest station and they'll have cops waiting there and everything will be—"

The lights flicker.

"Attention passenge . . . please remain . . . the train is being held . . . the next station—" The intercom crackles in fits and starts. An actual human this time. "The MTA police will be—"

The weak lights flicker again, then go completely dark. The train powers down with a heavy sigh. I squint in the sudden, crushing blackness.

"Oh my God, Mia—" I hear Jade stumble. I think she's coming toward me, but it's impossible to know for sure. I extend a hand. I can't even see it.

I shouldn't have pressed that button. This is my fault. We could have calmly exited the train at the next stop and reported the incident when we got above ground. Now we're stuck.

The guy in tweed starts sobbing. It's contagious; my throat twists. I've never felt so helpless. Jade and the others may as well be shouting from a parallel dimension. I wonder if this is what death is like. Impenetrable darkness, surrounded by the voices of the living, unable to reach them.

"Attention pass—" the intercom sputters again. "The MTA po . . . please re—"

A light appears. Jade's got her phone. She turns in a circle, shining it like a lantern, and falls into my arms. We were right next to each other, almost touching, back to back.

"Please re . . . the tr . . . being held momentarily—"

The young woman bolts toward the double doors and assaults the plexiglass with her fists. "Let us out, let us out, let us *out*!"

Jade buries her tiny frame inside my unzipped coat and wraps it around both of us. I think about kissing the top of her head, but I'm paralyzed. Last time we were in danger, I knew how to save us. I saw a way out. This time, there isn't one.

"We could jump out between cars," Jade whispers through tears.

"No. We don't know what's in the tunnel."

The man must have overheard us. He knifes toward the door at the opposite end of the car, away from the crime scene.

"*Peter!*" the girl shrieks. He doesn't even look at her.

"Dude, I wouldn't—" I yell at his back. But he's already jumped out into the tunnel. We watch the light of his cell phone bob across the void until suddenly, it goes out.

"Oh my God . . . *shit*. Peter—" The girl joins our trembling huddle, as if the two of us were a shield.

I'm not sure how long we stand there, fused together as a pack— three women who thought the only trouble they'd encounter to-night was the trouble they'd made for themselves.

It's shameful, the way I bought into the scam of my own safety. I learned a long time ago: My fear is there to protect me. I deserve to be punished, for ignoring it.

Jade gasps and squeezes my hand as a coin of light hits the tun-nel wall. Someone's coming, but I can't make out a face in the glare of the plexiglass.

Our companion fumbles with her phone, dialing out. Not sure how much signal she's going to get down here, but it's more than we've managed.

"C'mon . . . c'mon . . . Please—"

She clutches the phone like a string of prayer beads as a crowbar breaches the double doors.

I shut my eyes as tears burn down my cheeks.

In that moment, I think of Mom.

I imagine her face in the window. Her teeth against my skin. Somehow, it calms my racing heart. Better someone I love than a stranger. Better to keep my eyes closed and pretend it's her. That's what I'll do. I'll block everything out and . . .

"Everyone all right in here?" a husky voice calls out.

I crack an eye open. Jade releases a breath that comes out as a yelp. Two NYPD officers force the doors apart, panning across the car with their high-beam flashlights.

"Got a distress call from this box," one of them barks as he boards. "Sorry 'bout the lights. Conductor panicked and triggered an emergency shutdown when he saw the signal."

All we can do is stare: awash in the afterbirth of terror.

"One of you ladies press the button?" The second cop shines his light in our faces.

"Uh . . . me. I did." I step forward, stuffing my trembling hands into my pockets. "We found something."

The cops quickly escort us out into the tunnel. One of them stays behind to take photos. I hear him radio out for assistance.

"Have you ever seen anything like that before?" I whisper to the husky cop as he guides us along. His badge says PRINGLE. Like the potato chips.

He doesn't answer. I wonder if he heard me.

"It said 'Adapt or Die,' you saw that, right?"

"Yuh-huh." He pulls his sidearm. Doesn't say anything else.

There are six cops in all, forming a perimeter around all of us as we make our way above ground. We weren't far from the next station. Just a hundred yards or so. Maybe Peter made it out. But I don't see him anywhere.

Two NYPD vans idle on the corner with their lights on. We're in Brooklyn somewhere. Bergen Street. The buildings here are smaller and older. Almost quaint. The pavement shimmers with freshly fallen sleet.

"We'll give you folks a lift wherever you're headed." Pringle opens the sliding door to one of the vans. But before he allows us entry, he snags a clipboard from the back seat. "Just gonna need y'all to sign this before we head out."

Jade receives the clipboard first. She barely reads what's on the form before she grabs the pen, attached with a frayed piece of old dental floss.

"Hang on, what's it say?" I whisper, glancing over her shoulder.

"I don't care, I just want to go home." Jade's teeth chatter as she signs her name. She flips the paper over to reveal a fresh form underneath. "Here."

"Sir, can you give us a little info here, before we sign?" I chirp, waving the clipboard.

"Mia—"

"We've got a press moratorium, when it comes to this kinda stuff."

"What 'kinda stuff'?"

"Like the *kinda stuff* you found on that train. If the press contacts you, you tell 'em you're not at liberty to discuss an ongoing case."

"So if we sign this, that's what we're agreeing to."

"Yes ma'am."

"Why, though?"

Jade jabs me with her elbow. I shake her off as Pringle rolls his eyes and mutters "Damn" under his breath. "Because it's an *ongoing case* and we'd prefer you not discuss it."

I think back on what Sandy said, about the incident in Scottsdale. How the news wasn't covering it. This is a national gag order. It's not enough, that the press has stopped saying his name. The goal is to delegitimize him by refusing to cover anything with his stamp on it. They're hoping they can kill his platform. But ADAPT doesn't need the mainstream media. Never did. In fact, that's the whole reason people trust it.

"What's wrong with you? Just sign the thing so we can go home," Jade hisses.

The guy standing next to me wrests the clipboard from my hands as I bend toward Pringle. "Listen, I can help you," I whisper. Maybe the cops in New York will be more productive than the ones in Tucson. "I just moved here from Arizona. I know about ADAPT." Fuck it. I'll bite the bullet and say his name. "I know Devon Shaw."

Pringle makes a face like I just stomped on his foot. "Ma'am, I can promise you, we have this under control. We don't need your help."

"But—"

"Please, either comply with the nondisclosure or feel free to walk home by yourself."

I'm the last person to sign. It's fine. Whatever. Not like I wanted to talk to *The New York Times* or anything. But still, I'm fuming. Jade grips my hand as the van shepherds us across Brooklyn, to her place. My eyes bore into the back of Pringle's stubbly bald head as he drives. He has no idea what I've seen. What I'm capable of.

But what *am* I capable of?

I know this much: I didn't leave home so I could hide in my apartment, drink myself stupid, and sign nondisclosures. Heat rises in my blood. Nobody—nobody except *me*—has any right to tell me how the hell to live my life. It's mine now. That's the gift of being alone in this world. I can't afford to keep wasting it.

☾ ☾ ☾

Jade's rental is a fourth-floor walkup above an Italian restaurant. The lobby smells like garlic bread and cats. I want to gag, but that might be all those Palomas answering back. We trudge up the stairs, each one groaning with a prehistoric creak. She doesn't try to kiss me. Doesn't touch the small of my back or take my hand. She's silent aside from a muted "This is us" when we reach the door to her apartment.

Tony and Steve are still out. Their shit's strewn all over the kitchen and living room. The sleeper sofa is piled high with dirty laundry. Jade got the only proper bedroom. The décor is frumpy and dated. Way too much burgundy—including the walls. There's a curio cabinet filled with porcelain plates, painted with frogs and kittens and baby deer. A lopsided framed poster for *Gypsy* starring Bette Midler hangs above the dining table. Mom and I had that one on DVD.

Jade beelines for the fridge and rips open a cardboard case of beer. She tosses me a can, and I almost drop it.

"I'm freaking out, I need a Klonopin." She shakily cracks her beer. "Do you want one?"

"I guess. I mean . . . I've never tried—"

She digs through Steve and Tony's laundry pile with one hand, her beer in the other. I haven't opened mine. She uncovers a black leather toiletries kit, from which she procures a bottle of pills.

"Hold out your hand."

She shakes out a round, buttercup-yellow pill. Folds up my hand and gives it a kiss.

"Everything's gonna be okay."

I nod and open my beer, waiting for her to swallow her pill. When she does, I take mine. We stand on opposite ends of the living room, almost looking at each other but not quite. Avoidance at an acute angle.

"C'mon, it's cold." She opens the door to her room. But her tight smile doesn't float to her eyes. "There's a heater in here. We can watch something stupid."

Do I still want this? Does she?

I think the answer is yes. For both of us. It feels weird now, though. *I* feel weird. How quickly does this pill take effect?

"Mia?"

She's halfway through the door, and I haven't moved.

"Is this okay?" She tilts her head, and her curls bounce with it.

"For sure," I croak after a moment. "It's freezing out here."

We're only about ten minutes into whatever it is we're doing when the Klonopin starts to kick in. I'm almost relieved. I'm out of my depth. I know what I want. What my body wants. But I have no idea how to ask for it, especially at the pace she's moving. I wish we could go slower. Wish she'd let me take the lead. Should I ask her? No. That feels strange. Like it'll ruin something. When she touches me it's almost the right thing, but it's *off* somehow—like a dream where everyone's speaking a foreign language and you can *almost* understand them if they'd just slow the fuck *down*. She tries with her mouth. It's better. I like it. I can feel her smirk against me as I rise to meet each luscious stroke. But my thoughts are just too damn loud. I fake a dramatic sigh to drown them out, but it gets stuck in my throat. I can't stop wondering how the hell I'm supposed to do this back to her. She'll have to stop and give me fucking *instructions*. God, she knows so much, and I'm like a child. I can't . . . I'm not . . .

She falls asleep. I think. Or maybe I do. I don't know. The whole thing is sponge-painted onto my brain: the impression of intimacy.

After a few hours—minutes?—she wakes up and pulls the blankets around us. She's crying.

"It's okay." My lips shape the words, but I have no idea if I said them aloud. I paw around for her in the darkness. No wait, it's not dark. My eyes were just closed. We left a lamp on. Everything feels furry. The sheets, the blanket. Oh, that's her hair.

She kisses me, breathing life back into my corpse of a body, and slips two fingers inside of me. I slide a hand up her leg, and it feels like it goes on forever. Fuck, she's still crying. This seems wrong. I withdraw my hand, and after a moment she does, too.

We fall asleep again.

Around 6 A.M., I jolt awake. I might have been having a dream, but I don't remember what it was about. I can't get back to sleep. Jade snores, light as a feather. I gently tip her over onto her side. I once read you're supposed to do that, if someone falls asleep and they're really drunk.

My thoughts sway to Tony and Steve. Whether they're asleep in the living room, how awkward it will be when I leave in a few hours and they see me. I know Tony knows I was at the show. I hope he doesn't try to talk to me.

The show. The song. Everything I tried to forget, everything I *did* forget, thanks to those Palomas and that nightmare subway ride. I find my underwear crumpled at the foot of the bed and pull them on.

She wasn't even sorry. Doesn't know she should've been. And what's worse, it was a good song. There's a reason it's stuck in my head.

I close my eyes again, but I can't get comfortable. Don't want to be here anymore. I have more important things to do than lie here and ask myself why I did this. Whether I got what I wanted. I could sit around and wait for her to apologize about the song—but first I would need to tell her I was hurt by it. I could wait for her to force Gabi out of her life, wait for her to call me up and say, "I'm ready. Let's do this." But then I'd have to accept that we began with a lie—and we'd probably end with one, too.

I never knew how easy it was, to want someone so wrong for you.

When it happened to characters in movies, I'd turn up my nose and say, "God, what an idiot." When it happened to Mom . . . Well, the first time, I forgave her. She didn't know any better. Didn't know what he was. The second time . . .

Back then, all I felt was betrayal. I *hated her* for going back to that well. But I was angry because I was scared. I knew how intense her feelings were. Not because they were perfect for each other. Because they *weren't*.

She wanted someone who would destroy her. Because I refused to let her destroy herself.

Jade and Devon don't have a damn thing in common. But maybe I wanted to know what that was like.

I stare at a water stain on the ceiling. Wondering if I'll ever reach a point where I can no longer trace all my feelings back to my mother.

Jade hasn't moved since I turned her onto her side. I don't want to wait here till she wakes up. Don't want to talk about the night we just had, the same way I don't want to talk about Cloak and Dagger or Mom or anything that happened in Arizona.

I creep out of bed, hunting for the rest of my clothes. I'm careful to peel back the comforter just enough so I can grab my sweater while still keeping her covered.

I'm taking too long locating my left sock, and she stirs. Her eyes flutter open. I plaster a smile onto my face.

"You leaving?" she rasps. She could use a drink of water.

"I was gonna get us some coffee."

"You're so sweet." Her eyes shut again.

I grab my shoes even though I still haven't found my missing sock.

On my way out, I swoop into the bathroom and fill her toothbrush cup with water. Place it on her bedside table.

I march outside, bracing myself for that bright spank of cold morning air. I like it. I'm awake now. I don't want to sleepwalk through the fear like Jade does. Swallowing strange pills till I feel safe again. Till I don't feel anything at all.

My phone's dead, so I can't order an Uber. It takes half an hour to flag down a yellow cab, but it's worth the wait. I won't be riding the subway anymore. Even if I'm drunk and it's below freezing. I know how those Saras boarded the train. They came from the tunnels and bypassed the scanners—just like I feared the morning of my first commute. The police have probably been sweeping the tunnels this whole time, uprooting innocent unhoused people just trying to stay warm. Thinking they're doing their due diligence. Meanwhile, ADAPT stays hidden, using the unhoused as decoys—and prey. It's cruel and strategic and makes perfect sense.

I get home and plug my phone in. Jade's texted me a few times, wondering where I'm at with the coffee. She gave up about an hour ago. I'm relieved, if not a little empty inside. Her last message says:

k, I get it. I'm sorry if I did something.

My email pings. I have a reminder to make my first tuition payment on the thirty-first and, lo and behold, a job interview. Some hostess gig I don't even remember applying for. I close my email and Google a phone number instead. When I dial out, I'm surprised my palms aren't sweating. My breath is steady.

I was wrong, when I thought I only had two options: hide till he finds me or enjoy the time I have left. There's a third.

Someone answers the phone.

"Saratov Salvation of Manhattan, how may I direct your call?"

"Hi. I'm interested in your volunteer program."

NOW

I squint through the darkness, desperate for anything that will help me get my bearings. My arms are strapped to my sides inside my sleeping bag, but I'm able to wriggle to a seated position and inch along till my back is against the cold steel wall of the cube truck.

I sigh into the hot, sticky tape covering my mouth and try to stretch my knees. My foot hits something soft and oblong: a bag of some sort. Hope crops up like a weed. Maybe they threw our backpacks in here with us. At least then we'll have Daylights. Daylights and those shots.

I caterpillar across the ground, toward Cora's muted heat signature. I hear her shuffle from the opposite direction. We meet in the middle. I can hardly see a suggestion of her, but her warmth is unmistakable. We feel for one another and curl together like melted spoons. She sniffles against her gag.

"Mm-mm." I force a soothing sound between my constrained lips and shake my head. *Let's not cry yet. This isn't over.*

If they were going to kill us, it would have happened already. That's what I wish I could say to her. We've been driving for a long time, though the aftereffects of that poisoned cigarette and the dark make it hard to tell exactly how many hours it's been. I think we've stopped for gas twice? Three times? Whoever's behind the wheel is either uninfected or loaded with Daylights; the sun is definitely up by now. Which means they could throw us out of the truck and execute us just about anywhere. But we're driving with a purpose. A destination.

I'm hungry. Like, ravenous, gnaw-your-lips-to-shreds hungry, even though I drank a full cup at the outpost less than twenty-four hours ago. Might be another symptom of whatever the hell I smoked last night. I'm aching to sleep again, but the lancing pain in my stomach keeps stabbing me awake. It's like watching myself in a mirror, smacking the shit out of my own face.

I'm grateful I don't need to pee more than once a day. At least there's that.

(((

I'm fully alert once we hit the dirt road. I moan as my hip slams the floor, over and over. Never mind how quickly the bruise will heal.

The rugged turbulence drags on. Where the hell are we? Who goes off-roading in a cube truck?

At last, the brakes squeal.

Then, stillness. Nothing but the blood in my ears and the wind hissing through the truck's undercarriage. Cora makes a weak sound through her closed lips, pitched up like a question. As if I have an answer.

A metallic shriek cuts the silence. Someone's unlocked the doors.

I squeeze my eyes shut, bracing myself for that first murderous blade of light. Cora thrashes with a muffled scream.

But it's nighttime again.

Stars burn holes through the blackness as the doors swing open.

A gangly man with gold and silver hair clambers into the cargo, shining a flashlight into our faces. My vision whites out after a day in the dark, and it takes me a moment to make sense of his features. I didn't see him earlier, at the outpost. But I've seen him somewhere else. I recognize the glasses he's wearing.

I saw him at the Red Market.

He hunches his slight shoulders with a nervous upturned lip. Cora and I could definitely take him if we weren't strapped inside our sleeping bags.

"You." He trains the flashlight on me. Yanks my hood and drags me across the floor of the truck.

My breath catches. He's separating us. This can't happen. Not like this.

He heave-hos me out the door like a bag of trash, then tosses something on top of me. A backpack. Guess I was right: they allowed us a carry-on for our troubles. Cora is crying again. I flip myself over like a fish, desperate for one last glimpse of her before the man slams the door.

The air is sharp and cruel, and there's the rush of a river nearby. We're tucked into a nest of hills, covered with a dark blanket of evergreens. On the shoulder of the dirt road is a black, mud-spattered Chevy Suburban, idling with its lights off.

The man with glasses tears the tape from my mouth, taking a layer of skin along with it. I'm careful not to react. Snot drips from my nose, stinging my bloody lip, but I don't move.

I'm not going to talk first. I need to know the rules of engagement. I wait for the man to speak. He doesn't.

But someone else does.

"You're too late, babe."

I gulp cold air but it's like a spear through my lungs.

"I told you the door was closed."

I crane my neck. Can't get a sense of where Devon's voice is coming from. I'd do anything to be able to stand.

I was supposed to slip away like a wraith and watch his doom from some distant hilltop. How, how, *how* could I have been so naïve?

A footstep. Behind me. The crunch of pine under boots.

I struggle to a kneeling position and whip around in a circle till our eyes lock. He laughs through pursed lips. But only for a second.

He's just seen my face. Knows exactly who I am.

Who I'm not.

He just stares. Mirroring my stillness. Or maybe I'm mirroring his.

Emotion flares across his flinty eyes. Bewilderment. Fury. Something like dejection. His lower lid twitches.

His hair is longer, roving past his neck. A dead-grass beard prickles across his face. But he's the same. He is *always* the same.

He lowers himself to one knee, studying me like an explosive he's been tasked with disarming. I didn't see it before, but there's a butterfly knife in his hand. Whether it's new or rusted, I can't tell.

Without breaking eye contact, he says to the man with glasses, "Gareth, you can go."

His lackey nods and trots back to the cube truck. He's leaving. With Cora. I shatter my silence with a terrified yelp.

"Wait! There's someone else in the—"

Devon holds the knife to my cheek. My voice dies in my throat.

Gareth starts the ignition and peels away, back down the bumpy dirt road. The moon behind the mountains casts an eerie penumbra, like a mouth yawning open to swallow the whole world.

"Did she send you in her place?" Devon finally speaks again. "That sounds like something she'd do."

"N-no." My voice is a wisp. "Devon, she's—"

He slices my cheek. I hold my breath, waiting for the horrible scorch of rust to swarm my system. But nothing happens.

He wipes the blood from my face with his thumb. Stares at it. Tastes it.

My empty stomach twists.

"Had to make sure. Considering how you lied the last time."

He cleans the blade on my sleeping bag.

"Who did this to you?"

I don't respond. Don't know how I'm *supposed to* respond, to a question like that.

"I can tell it wasn't her."

I watch as he paces, twirling his knife open and shut. Like he's considering whether to cut me loose.

"Can you please just . . . tell them not to hurt Cora, okay?" I hate the way I sound, begging like this. "She didn't do anything wrong. She's a good person. She's—"

"Who?"

Of course.

He glowers down on me. "Where's your mom, Mia?"

"She's dead."

I'm waiting for him to react. He holds my stare and I wonder if he's finally going to accept the truth . . . till he laughs darkly and rolls his eyes. "Did you come all the way here to tell me that?"

"No. I came here because—" I never decided what I was going to tell him. We were never supposed to have this conversation.

". . . Or did the FBI send you?"

"You seriously think they would send someone like *me* after *you*?"

"I dunno, Fun Size. You always were a little fucking narc."

The knot inside of me tightens. I hate hearing my old nickname is his terse, raspy voice. But I can't show it.

I fix him with a hard stare, careful not to blink. The wind pulls tears across my face. I might be on my knees tied up in a sleeping bag, but if I can reassure him and tell him what he wants to hear . . .

"I came here because I was scared. When *this* happened to

me . . . When I . . . you know. I didn't want to live in a Sara center, or hide the way my mom did. I wanted to be free. Like you."

There's nothing in his eyes but the icy reflection of stars.

"I knew you could help me."

I let the tears roll down my cheeks. I know what I have to say next.

"Because of how you helped my mom."

He stuffs his hands in the pockets of his parka. Shows me his back. His sigh surrounds him in a cloud of white vapor, haloed with its golden heat signature. If I weren't so terrified, I might think it was beautiful.

When he turns back around, he's unfurled the knife. He hooks it underneath my restraints, serrated side up, and starts cutting me loose. But only halfway. Like something stopped him.

He peels the hood from my head, letting my hair spill out. Studying me like a bomb again.

"If she's dead, then how did it happen?"

I make sweaty fists inside the sleeping bag. He doesn't deserve my truth—my dark, private shame. Same way he doesn't deserve to know how I became a Sara.

I want to make him think this was *his* fault. Because it is.

"She um . . . well, she was hurt. When she got home that night."

"What night?"

"Cloak and Dagger. Someone shot her."

"I remember."

"And I know you took the bullet out. But it was already spreading really fast—"

"It was her leg. She should've healed."

"I'm sorry."

"I was coming back to help her."

"I know."

There's a flash of raw anguish in his gaze. Like he's picturing it. Like he almost believes me. But it's gone in an instant.

He takes a step backward, holding the knife between us.

"The night you're talking about . . . that was in June. I have a source who saw her in Tucson in November."

"Ronnie. No. That was me she saw."

"Okay, well, a month later your mom and I spoke on the phone."

"That was me, too."

He looks at me with an upturned lip, like he just tasted something rancid. "Why did you answer her phone? That's fucking weird, you know that?" Before I can respond, it dawns on him: "You didn't give it to the police."

"I couldn't. I needed to talk to you."

"Well, you did a shit job, once you had me."

"I guess . . . I just got nervous." I stare at the ground.

"Not too nervous to haul ass all the way to the outpost, though. Lie to my guys."

"You wouldn't have agreed to meet, if you knew it was me."

"You don't know that."

He lifts my chin and redirects my gaze to his. Lightly touches the cut he made on my cheek. Where it was, anyway. It's already healed. I don't know what he's searching for, in my face. But after a moment, he decides he's found it. Finishes slicing me loose.

I kick off the hot, clingy sleeping bag. I'm free, but there's no point in running. Not till I know what he's going to do. How any of this works. Has he decided to trust me? What did I do, or not do, to make him decide that? Would *I* trust me?

I step forward. He takes me in and starts twirling the knife open and shut again.

"They searched you at the outpost, yeah? No phones?"

I'm slow to respond. I realize I've been grinding my teeth. My head swims and my feet feel like they're sinking into the earth.

I need to eat.

"Mia."

He snaps his fingers in my face. Something scratches the paper-thin wall of my gut with a long, pointed nail.

"Y-yeah. They took our phones. Searched all our stuff."

I pick up the sleeping bag. My movements are slow like sap. I shake it out to show him it's empty, shivering in my thin, sweat-drenched hoodie. Lift my arms and turn my pockets inside out as an extra show of compliance. My head lolls to the side, like it weighs a hundred pounds.

"You're hungry."

I don't want to answer. I hate how he knows.

"Okay. C'mon." He lifts the backpack off the ground. I almost forgot it was there. "This yours?"

My mouth goes dry, now that I can see it clearly. It's *not* mine. That one belongs to Cora.

That means she's got the Saranasia shots. And I've got her Daylights. But I can't react. Devon's going to search that bag if I can't claim it. And I'm going to need those Daylights when I make a break for it.

"Yeah . . . thanks." I take it from him.

There's still a chance I can get out of this in one piece. I don't know where we are, but I can identify his vehicle. All I have to do is start running.

My knees buckle as I shuffle forward, and he catches me before I crumple to the ground. I fight the reflexive urge to swat him away. Clench my teeth as he bears my weight and leads me toward the Chevy. I wasn't wearing any shoes, when they took me. Freezing mud seeps through my socks. Maybe Cora has something I can wear in her backpack.

"When'd you last eat?" he asks, guiding me into the passenger seat. Drapes the sleeping bag on top of me for warmth. Which might pass for kindness if this didn't still feel like an interrogation.

"Um . . . yesterday. But I was . . . Someone gave me something at the outpost that made me—" I think I'm still talking, but I'm just chewing the underside of my lip.

"Keep the blood in your mouth, please. This is a new car."

He slams my door and gets in on his side. Lights up a cigarette as he yanks the gear shift. I cut him a glance, sucking my teeth. New car, but of course he's entitled to fill it with smoke.

He misinterprets my stare. Offers me a cigarette as he steers one-handed.

"N-no thank you." Not about to fall for that again.

"It'll help."

I cradle my head in my hands, pinching the pressure point between my eyes. I don't like this. I've never spent this much time alone with him. Not since those terrifying forty-eight hours after I found Mom dead on the couch. Taping down the curtains. Perusing the Facebook group. The past parades across the middle distance. There's Devon at the kitchen counter rolling cigarettes. The smell of Mom's bedroom. The blood pooling in her eyes. His hand on my scruff, dragging me away. *"She's gonna* fucking *kill you."*

And yet, for the first time all year, I feel like my feet are touching the ground again. His presence is like an artifact—something lost to time, unburied. Here to translate the dead language ringing in my ears.

"There's a spot we can go, about half an hour from here." It takes me a second to realize he's talking to me again. "If you can't handle your shit, you're walking."

"I'm *fine*." I catch a wad of bloody drool in my palm.

"God, can't you at least chew some gum or something?"

He grips the wheel with both hands as we navigate a craggy pothole. My head smacks the window. I realize I forgot to put on my seat belt.

"Look, I'm just not used to . . . I came from one of the centers."

"Gareth mentioned."

"The schedule there was . . . predictable."

He drags from his cigarette in response.

"I'm dying to know, by the way."

". . . What?"

"How it happened. Who lifted you. If it had been your mom, I would've tasted it."

Silence stretches thin between us.

"I have to admit, I'm a little jealous."

He laughs, like he's waiting for me to join in. I swallow more blood.

"Fine. I get it."

He cracks a window to toss his butt. The air between us hardens.

"I guess I'll have one."

He presents the pack of cigarettes to me without a word.

"Thanks."

Neither of us says anything else till we get to the Walmart.

The store's incandescent blue sign is the only light for miles. The lonely main road hems the frosty foothills, vacant aside from a few dark, half-finished housing developments left to ruin. Once upon a time, people tried to build a life here. The last fourteen years have not been kind.

There are a dozen cars in the Walmart lot, ostensibly the only store servicing the area these days. Devon parks on the street, away from the lights.

I'm not sure what we're supposed to do. Is the Walmart like the movie theater? Another outpost, where bleeders with skateboards wait to service us?

"I'll wait here," he says. "Take a couple laps around the lot first. Pretend you lost your keys or something."

"Wait, where are the . . . ? At the outpost, they had people who—"

"Does this look like the outpost?"

"I just . . . I need you to clarify."

He tilts his head, nostrils flared like he's about to breathe fire at me. "Teach a man to fish."

I lean back in my seat, wringing my hands. "I just thought you—I mean *we*—were trying to like, bring more people into the fold? As opposed to . . . y'know."

"Sometimes it's about head-hunting. Other times it's . . . well, it's just hunting." A smile plays on his lips. "I need you to find someone who smells right and make the first move. Incapacitate, but don't kill. You got me? We need to take them back with us. Alive."

"So you *are* recruiting bleeders."

He runs his tongue over his teeth with a tired laugh. "Wouldn't exactly call it recruiting."

More like abduction, I almost say.

"If you're gonna hang with me, I need to know you can pull your weight."

My nerves sputter. I promised myself I would never break flesh. I had a plan. Cora and I knew where to find the Red Market so we could eat. I wasn't supposed to be on the road for this long.

Wasn't supposed to end up with Devon.

"Let's fucking march, Fun Size. I don't have all night."

"Please stop calling me that," I say into my hands as I try to formulate a plan.

He can't make me do it. The second I leave this car, he loses all his power. This is my chance to run.

I unzip Cora's backpack, digging for a pair of shoes. Hell, even some fresh socks. There's nothing but a flimsy pair of rubber shower sandals. But they'll work.

I pick up the bag to take it with me, but Devon shakes his head.

"Leave it. You got mugged and you need someone's help." He rolls his eyes when I don't reply. "You're welcome."

Fine. Doesn't matter. I don't need the Daylights or anything else in that bag. I just need my wits, a kind stranger with a phone, and the strength to keep my jaws to myself.

"Can I have another cigarette?"

"If I say yes, will you go?"

Nicotine rattles inside me like pebbles in an empty jar. I pace around the lot. The clock in Devon's car said 9:20. I need to make my move; the store probably won't be open much longer. I'm surprised it isn't closed yet—it's well after dark. But this is a corporate superchain, the lifeblood of this whole crumbling county. They've got scanners. I'll have to intercept someone as they exit.

We're definitely somewhere in Colorado, judging by the license plates of the surrounding pickup trucks and horse trailers. A ray of pride shines through my dread. I fucking knew that's where he'd be. We're miles out in the sticks, though. This doesn't look like Boulder, or anything close to it.

A harried young woman around my age with bottle-blond curls rolls her cart outside. A toddler bundled in a snow suit rides on the shelf, trying to unwrap a chocolate bar with his mittens on. The emptiness in my stomach metastasizes, like a black hole.

I crush my cigarette under Cora's sandal and hobble toward them, breathing deep to ignore the howl of my body. She's a mom. She'll show me sympathy. Let me use her phone.

Just need the phone. Nothing else. Just the phone. . . .

"Excuse me . . . I'm sorry to bug you—" I stumble on a patch of half-melted ice.

The woman startles and instinctively pulls her child out of the cart, hugging him to her breast. Starts walking at a faster clip. The kid drops the candy bar he's been wrestling with and wails.

"Sorry, sorry, I just want to know if I can please use your phone." I stagger after her. "I got jumped by some guy on my way over here, he took my bag. I think he might've been a Sara." A subtle misdirect feels like the right move. "I need to call the cops. And my mom."

The woman pauses and studies me as she rocks her son. I definitely look the part: dazed and disheveled with crusted blood all over my face.

"Um, I guess . . . Yeah. Gimme two seconds—"

My teeth chatter. Her eyes comb over me, coming to rest on my thin sandals and soaking-wet socks.

"God, you must be freezing."

She starts leading me to her car. Her son stares at me over her shoulder. Suddenly stops crying. My shivering intensifies.

God dammit, she smells amazing. They both do. Fragrant like sweet orange blossoms. There's a bitter hint of caffeine under the surface, but it's weak—hours old. Not enough to deter a Sara. She should've chugged a Coke before she left the store. My heart races, anticipating the ruinous thrill of a full belly.

"I just need a phone. You really don't have to—"

She pulls her keys from her pocket, balancing the kid on her hip.

"Just a sec. I think I left it in the car."

Jesus. Okay. Just breathe. . . .

She approaches her vehicle—an old, rusted white Jeep. Kind of like the one we had.

"Where'd you say this happened to you?"

"Just like . . . up on the main road. I was walking to the store." I shift my weight to hide the way I'm fidgeting.

"From where?"

"My house."

"Coming east or west?" At last, she unlocks the car.

"Uh, west."

"Cops aren't gonna come, y'know. I mean, you're welcome to try 'em. But—"

My canines shift in my gums like retractable spikes. My arms stretch toward her of their own volition. I force myself to take a step in the opposite direction.

"Please, please, please, fucking hurry!"

She freezes and faces me, eyes glistening with confusion. Then terror. She knows.

I can't help it. I lunge for her. For the kid.

She draws back with a scream that slices straight through me and shoves her cart between us.

"I'm sorry, I'm sorry . . ." Saliva wells in my mouth, making it hard to shape the words. "Get out of here. I'm not alone."

I double over as I tear myself away. Start running.

I lose a sandal as I scale a grimy gray snowbank, hurtling toward the shadowy hillside beyond. I don't know where I'm going or what I'll do next. But I'm not taking a life tonight. And I'm sure as shit not getting back in that car with Devon.

I can still smell them: a tantalizing sweetness on the breeze, luring me back like a cartoon pie on a windowsill.

I've stopped running.

Why the hell did I stop running?

I'm being pulled in the opposite direction. I turn and skulk forward, like sleepwalking.

"*No*—" I scream into the wind. Bite my own wrist to jolt myself awake.

It's like clawing my way out of a nightmare, gouging layer upon layer of darkness with my bare hands. Finally, my legs obey. I topple over the guardrail into the brackish, muddy wilderness surrounding the main road.

I think of Mom, making her escape from the hospital in Utah. Barreling across the freeway with me on her back. She was exhausted. She was hungry. But she kept going till she knew we were safe. My body's no different. I can do this.

I bank to the left, toward the safety of a dense pine thicket . . . as a sickening *pop* blazes through the trees.

I take cover, face-first in the dirt.

But I should've kept running.

The toxic bullet shreds my pants and comes to rest under my skin. A fiery ache scythes across my calf.

I'm seismic with pain, writhing on all fours, breathing mouthfuls of mud.

I wait for another bullet. The one that's going to take my life.

I wait. I sob. And I wait.

But it doesn't come.

I moan into the dirt. A second later, my own name ricochets between the trees.

"Mia . . . ?"

My wound flares as if bidden by his voice, belching hot, black blood. It simmers all around me like I'm sinking in a tar pit of my own filth.

A branch snaps in my ear as he approaches.

". . . Fucking *shit*—"

I feel the spectral suggestion of his fingers against my neck, checking me for a pulse as he rolls me onto my back.

"You're okay, I gotcha. Open your eyes, Mia."

I need him to kill me. Right now. God, please let it be now.

I don't want to know what happens to me if he doesn't.

DECEMBER 2023

I stand outside the Sara center for a good five minutes before I enter, gazing up at the mammoth concrete façade where a grid of windows ought to be. There's something unnerving about the building. Not just because of what's inside. The lack of windows is oppressive, unnatural, like the architect fell asleep on their watch. I wonder what it must be like to live in such an iconic city and never get to see it. That is, unless you've taken a Daylight pill. But even then, I'd have to imagine you're not getting past the courtyard. This place is still a prison.

I'm supposed to head to that job interview at three this afternoon, but I never confirmed it. Don't think I'm going to. Standing on this spot feels resonant. Like I've been called here.

Recovery Center #48, Saratov Salvation of Manhattan, is built entirely on a pier that juts out into the Hudson. I have to cross Eleventh Avenue to get to it, reaching the western edge of the island. The winter wind cracks across the water like a whip, burning my eyes and drawing moisture across my red face. Apparently the city voted that the only suitable place for a Sara center would be somewhere on the river, where they could easily cordon the area if there was some kind of emergency. The driveway is actually a drawbridge. It's a hulk of a building, a ten-story concrete eyesore that probably wrecked a lot of people's views across the Hudson. The only exterior embellishment is a gigantic black cross inside a diamond painted on the southern wall, likely pitched as a "tasteful, minimalist mural" when the artist presented their plans to the city. Mom would've had notes. Minimalism can start to look clinical, even cruel, in the wrong hands.

I expected the building to be surrounded by an electric fence and barbed wire, like Riker's Island or something, but it's wide open. The only discernible security is a checkpoint by the front door, where a guy in a bulletproof glass booth asks visitors to show their ID.

Around the back is a remote-controlled gate to access the loading dock. A fleet of potted Christmas trees stands at the entryway, strung with tinsel and little red bows. It's surprisingly low-key. Maybe even pleasant. I guess that's the point. If I didn't know better, I'd guess this was an ordinary hospital—albeit a hospital with no windows in the middle of the Hudson River.

There's a monstrous amount of paperwork to do before I pass the lobby. This is the only area with windows: floor-to-ceiling rectangular glass broiling with sunlight. All the Saras must be on the upper floors. The windows provide an extra, subtle layer of security.

Saggy-eyed Beatrice, a sleep-deprived supervisor who's had enough of me before I even introduce myself, presents me with an iPad. She insists I "read it, please don't just sign it and hand it back to me," and says she'll know if I didn't. I get through the documents pretty fast, but I don't want to ruffle her feathers. I sit for a few extra minutes, skimming the contract a second time. Trying to ignore my jangling nerves.

All volunteers agree to vacate the premises from 5–7pm each day.

Of course. Saras aren't hungry till nighttime and they're safe once they've eaten—relatively speaking. There must be a night shift for volunteers as well.

Any volunteer who wishes to participate in bloodletting must submit an application and pass training protocol. These are the only non-staff individuals allowed on campus from 5–7pm. No exceptions.

Bloodletting is the paid portion of the program. I could use some extra cash, considering I still don't have a job. But I don't think I could bring myself to do that again. I shudder as I reread the paragraph. Like I can feel the needle's cold incursion.

Please limit your interaction with patients. Keep conversations brief and <u>avoid physical contact</u>. Report any suspicious behavior to your supervisor.

Cuts must be properly bandaged and covered by an article of clothing. <u>NO OPEN WOUNDS</u>. If you have had a recent surgical procedure, please stay home until your stitches have been removed. If you are a person who menstruates, we encourage you to request time off each month. You will not lose your place in our program.

I get that. Mom was always a good 10 percent meaner whenever I had my period. Which didn't help my mood, either.

By signing this form, I release Saratov Salvation and its affiliates from liability. I acknowledge that I am engaging in these activities at my own risk.

Sounds a lot like that Cloak and Dagger release form. The grain of anxiety in my stomach thickens to a pit. I wonder how many people hand Beatrice the iPad without signing and bolt for the door.

I hesitate. But only for a second. Don't want to lose this beautiful blaze of invigorating purpose. My fingertip skates across the screen, carving twin arches to mark my initials—M.M.

(((

They pair me with a volunteer named Mandy, a diminutive thirty-something with boxy glasses, mouse-brown hair, and a tremulous voice. Reminds me of the skittish desert rabbits who'd take cover in the brush whenever I rode my bike on the trails back home. Maybe she's here to conquer a phobia. Exposure therapy.

Mandy leads me to an elevator bank at the far end of the lobby, folding and unfolding her hands behind her back.

"So . . . where ya from?" she squeaks as the elevator pings. We step inside.

Mandy scans her badge to access the second floor. Beatrice gave me a badge, too—a skeleton key to an uncharted world. But I'm not ready to use it. Not yet.

"Arizona."

"Wow, what brings you all the way out here?"

"Just like, family stuff."

We ride up in silence.

As the doors open, Mandy holds my gaze before allowing me to step into the hallway.

"We're on mail and visitor duty today. Nothing crazy. But just . . . y'know. You read all the rules. They're there for a reason."

I reassure her with a confident nod. Her mouth takes the shape of a tightrope as we leave the elevator and turn the corner.

"Oh." My breath catches.

I don't know what I was expecting—anesthetized Saras in drab hospital gowns, shuffling up and down the hall like *One Flew Over the Cuckoo's Nest*? Sad gray linoleum floors, stained pink like Mom's old cup?

This place is like a hotel. Aside from the nurses' station beside the elevator bank, you'd never know this was a medical facility. Tastefully mismatched vintage Persian carpets line the hall. They've just been vacuumed, judging from the lines in the fibers. The nurses' station is resplendent with tropical plants, several in bloom. It takes me a moment to realize they're fake. They have to be, there's no sunlight. It's easy to forget there aren't any windows up here; the artificial recessed light is warm and natural, seamlessly mimicking the morning glow outside. Farther down the corridor are a dozen doors stained a dark mahogany color, marked with pewter signage in clean, modern Helvetica. I can read one from here: FRANKLIN STEWART. These are their rooms.

"Take off your shoes and leave them here."

Mandy leads me toward a cubby made of that same dark, sturdy wood. Everything here matches. "We have to keep quiet during the day. Some of the patients get up around noon and they'll want to socialize and do activities. But a lot of them just sleep till dinnertime."

"Aren't they hungry though? When they wake up?" I think of Mom's blue lips every evening. The way she used to pace around the kitchen. Dishes slipping through her shaky hands.

"Our portions here are pretty big. Keeps them satisfied for twenty-four hours. The early risers don't get up because they're hungry. Some of them have jobs they do remotely. The rest are just bored and want to hang out."

Mandy removes her frumpy, scuffed clogs. Doesn't see the way my mouth is hanging open. I'm slow to untie my shoes.

The Saras here have big dinners. They make their own money. They have friends next door and hang out with them every day. I picture Joey and Chandler's apartment across the hall from Rachel and Monica on *Friends*. Shit, for all I know I'm on the set of a sitcom.

"You coming?" Mandy watches as I fumble with my laces.

"Yeah, sorry. I'm just kinda . . ."

"Shocked?"

"It's like you've done this before."

"C'mon." She quirks her head toward a parallel hall.

"I just mean . . . this is *super* nice." I shove my Chucks into the cubby. Scurry along to keep up with her.

"Not all the centers are like this. New York has a lot of generous donors." Mandy keeps her voice low as she ambles along. "There was this guy who was one of the higher-ups at Goldman Sachs, and his daughter landed here a few years ago. He paid for a bunch of the upgrades."

"Must be nice."

"The rooms here on Two are the best. Soaking tubs, memory-foam mattresses, all that kinda stuff."

"Jeez."

"You get to live down here if you get all tens on your weekly Behavioral. If they dock any points, they can move you upstairs. Every floor gets a little sketchier. We're not allowed past Four."

"How many floors are there?"

"Nine."

I let out a breath that leaves a frown on my lips. Of course, not all Saras get to live like Rachel and Monica. I wonder what floor Mom would have been on.

I follow Mandy into the adjoining atrium, decorated in the same classy, modern style. Another crop of convincing plastic plants. There's a colorful "Happy New Year!" banner stretched from one end of the hall to the next.

"Down here we got the gym, a little screening room for movie night, and the library. Ballroom's over that way. We've been setting up for a New Year's Eve party. Although they might have to cancel it if they can't get enough volunteers. It's hard enough to get people to come at night, let alone on a holiday."

"You ever work nights here?"

She snorts, "Ha. No, thank you."

"Why not? Aren't they safe after dinner?"

"They're just . . . *different*. At night. Like, that's when they want to get to *know* you."

I clear a scratchy twinge in my throat. Mandy opens the door to the ballroom, where tentacles of silver streamer dangle from a wrought-iron chandelier. Speakers flank either side of the space, surrounded by a dozen half-decorated high-top tables. I wonder what they put on them. It's not like they need a place to leave champagne flutes or little plates of hors d'oeuvres while they dance. It probably just looks nice. Less empty. Less desperate.

"Anyway." Mandy shuts the ballroom door. "I'm outta here by five every day. Four thirty, if I can help it."

"You ever think about giving blood for extra money?"

"Nooooo. This is a community-service thing for me. I'm logging my hours till my probation is up."

I almost laugh. Mousy Mandy, a criminal? What did she do, steal twenty cats from an animal shelter?

"Anyhoo, mail's due any minute so we should get to our post." She shimmies her unkempt brows, underlining the pun.

"Is it anyone's birthday today?" I think to ask as we head back toward the nurses' station, remembering those flowers ADAPT sent to the Sara center in Phoenix. Mail duty, as dull as it sounds, could be a decent place to start sniffing around.

Mandy looks at me like I just said something in Japanese. "Uh . . . I don't think so? Hope you didn't bake cupcakes or anything."

"I mean, around here I think *I am* the cupcake." I chuckle to myself. But Mandy's face is ghost white.

I follow her in silence, dragging my socks against the grain of the carpet.

I've changed a lot this past year. But I guess I've still got work to do, when it comes to first impressions.

The first Saras start to wake around twelve fifteen, just as Mandy said. Alonzo, the head nurse on Two with the tanned, sinewy arms of a bodybuilder busting from his scrubs, trots down the hall to greet his patients. A middle-aged guy in gym shorts and a New

York Jets hoodie emerges from his room, and they exchange a high five. *You catch the game on Sunday? Fuckin' brutal.*

I know I'm gawking, but I can't help it.

Mandy nudges me. We've got an avalanche of packages to dig through.

Here's the thing about being locked up in a Sara center. You might have money, but you can't spend it on experiences. You can't go out to fancy dinners or take vacations. The centers are a public health initiative, which means you don't pay rent. So you spend your money on everything else. And I do mean *everything.*

Opening the boxes presents a privacy issue, but we log the return address of every shipment the residents receive. Mandy points out an unremarkable PO box I've logged a couple of times and whispers, "That one's a sex shop."

Clothes, makeup, and jewelry are a big hit. Electronics, too. There are a lot of boxes from Apple and Amazon.

"I swear people here get a new phone every damn week." Mandy rolls her eyes. "Kinda makes you wonder if it might be nice to get infected, move in, and save all that money."

The back of my neck itches. *Might be nice to get infected.*

"I mean, from the looks of it they're not exactly *saving* money." I gesture to our cardboard tower. "I didn't know they had phones in here."

"How do you think people hold down a job?"

Another layer of ignorance comes loose. This isn't prison, where the inmates all wait in line at the pay phone to call their mom or their lawyer.

"They used to check 'em and block social media and all that stuff. But that got changed these past couple months."

I nod. Transparency's the name of the game, just like the volunteer program. No more locked doors. No more secrets.

"You'll see though, how easy it is to screw up and lose device privileges," Mandy explains with a grunt, lifting a bulky box up onto our desk. "Like, if they get moved above the fourth floor, they have to surrender their phones and they can't get them back till they pass Behavioral again." She peers at the return address label. "This is another one from Apple. Computer, probably."

"What happens if they get moved up to Nine?"

"Dunno."

"Who lives up there?" Figure it has to be the people who didn't self-surrender—Saras with serious criminal records.

Mandy cuts me a sidelong glance. "What're you, a reporter or something?"

"Nope. Just interested." I chew a tender spot on my lip.

She fixes me with a shadowy stare. I suddenly get the feeling she could do a lot worse than steal twenty cats.

Mandy and I ride up to Four with a cart full of packages to deliver. She's antsy again, doing her one-woman patty-cake, clasping and unclasping her hands.

Four is slightly shabbier, with dated, unfinished décor. No blooming plants up here. I notice a security camera as we pass the nurses' station. Watchful eyes wedged into the crown molding.

"Are there cameras in their rooms?" After all, this is Four. The "sketchy" floor.

"When I first started here, yeah. People started getting salty about them on the internet though, so now they're gone."

Mandy clutches the cart with white knuckles as she leads us along.

We don't knock because we don't want to wake anyone, but the first woman we deliver to is already waiting, listening for the gentle patter of our socks on the other side of the door.

"Mandy! Hey!"

She looks like she's in her forties, with infectious, quirky mom energy, wearing puffy, oversized SpongeBob SquarePants slippers and a shamelessly generic pink tee that says, COFFEE, KISSES, DOGS, AND NAPS. The word "COFFEE" has been crossed out—either by her or the shirt's designer.

"Hi, Ingrid," Mandy mumbles, skirting eye contact. "Delivery for you."

"This is amazing, thank you. This color was backordered for months, I was so bummed it didn't come in time for Christmas but better late than never, right?"

She seizes the box from Mandy and tears it open in front of us.

It's filled with bundles of thick goldenrod yarn, flecked with pink. Reminds me of a grapefruit.

"That's pretty," I say.

"Isn't it? I can make you a hat or a scarf or something, if I have any left over. I'm knitting a blanket for my nephew," Ingrid warbles, breathless. "What's your name? I don't think we've met."

"Mia."

Mandy nudges me. We need to move along. This is already too much socializing.

"Oh my God. *Mia.* I was considering that name for my daughter, actually! My mom's best friend growing up was named Mia and she died when I was little and I always thought it would be nice to . . . anyway. We ended up settling on Ariana. But—"

Mandy starts rolling the cart down the hall.

"Nice to meet you!" I skitter away to catch up. "Your uh . . . your shirt is funny."

Guilt rises in me, having to leave Ingrid like that. I think of the early days of Mom's infection, barricaded inside the Tucson house. Not going to work or school. Just painting and watching our movies. Every day, I'd wait for that blue and white mail truck to putter down the block. There was always a box to open. New housewares from Ikea, or art supplies. Birthday presents Mom didn't think I knew about. The mail was everything when we didn't have anything else.

Afternoon approaches, and Mandy takes us back down to Two: the safe zone. We're allowed a lunch break, but we have to eat in the private staff café off the courtyard. Mandy goes to grab a bite downstairs, but I tell her I'm not hungry.

"You only feel that way because of the Saras," she says. "You need to remember to take breaks to eat and drink."

She's right. I've completely forgotten what that's like. With Mom, the dinnertime ritual helped keep my appetite grounded, but most of the time I would only get hungry at work, when she wasn't around. She was just one person, though. This is a whole building filled with Saras. Saras and their pheromones.

Still, I decline Mandy's invitation. I need a moment alone to soak it all in. Start formulating something like a game plan. She leaves me on my own at the mail station.

"Don't forget to have some water, at least."

I can't believe I thought the residents here would be wandering around in hospital gowns and grippy socks. A few more people are awake now, and they're dressed to impress. A young man with a jawline that could cut glass parades past, wearing a tailored chambray suit and alligator loafers, like he's about to jet to the French Riviera for lunch. His eyes are an impossible, luminous pale blue: an enchanting contrast to his deep copper skin. I wonder if they're contacts. He links up with a svelte senior woman in a silk headscarf who's just emerged from her apartment. A spotless blush Chanel handbag hangs from the crook of her elbow. Probably brand-new. We might have delivered it to her room this morning. She checks her claret-red lipstick in the hallway mirror before her blue-eyed prince whisks her toward the nurses' station, conspiratorially whispering into her ear. She erupts with laughter.

The two of them exude a powerful gravitational pull that keeps my eyes tethered to their every move. I have tunnel vision, like the entire hallway is a desaturated still frame and they're the only thing in color.

Pheromones again.

It's not like I imagined when I was younger, like when I first met Jade and thought she was a daywalking Sara who'd hijacked my brain. Sara pheromones only increase your attraction to someone you've already got your eye on. It's not a seduction in the literal sense—it's this catch-all, hypnotic magnetism. An unshakable urge to stare with your mouth agape, like how I used to gaze at Mom while she curled her hair, telling her she was the prettiest woman on the planet. I felt it upstairs with Ingrid, so easily absorbed in her effervescent chatter. I've felt it with Devon, too. Like rubbernecking as you pass a car wreck.

Coco Chanel and the Alligator Prince approach Alonzo at his station, and he hands each of them a tiny pill cup.

They don't swallow the Daylights. They suck them like mints. A

Sara's digestive tract is built for only one thing, but as Mom discovered with Ambien and cigarettes, the bloodstream can still absorb certain chemicals if you keep your stomach out of it.

"Give it about five minutes before you head to the courtyard," Alonzo instructs the pair. "This is a new formula, so you should get an extra two hours. But if you start to sweat or feel light-headed, come right back in and let us know, okay?"

Coco and the prince stroll toward a second, smaller elevator bank I didn't see before, different from the one Mandy and I were using.

As they wait, the man pulls out his phone and they pose for a selfie together. He snaps another. And another. I'm gaping again.

"Hey, do you uh . . . want me to take that for you?"

"No thank you, honey," the prince answers, flashing his pearly whites. He poses one more time, holding his phone just so. Seems to know his angles.

"God dammit, Topher, delete that. I've got chicken neck," the woman grumbles.

Well, he knows *his* angles.

Alonzo waves, pulling my attention away. I'm sure he's used to this: fishing rookies out of the pheromone vortex.

"Good first day, Froshie?"

"Yeah. Mandy's been super helpful."

"Here's the list of everyone who's outside, if you get visitors for them." He hands me a clipboard. "Just send them to the courtyard. Most of 'em know where to go. That elevator over there takes you straight down."

"It's freezing today."

"Doesn't stop anyone." I follow his gaze to the elevator as it opens. "A lot of 'em have a standing date to play chess or pickup basketball or whatever. It's been good, letting them get out during the day. We're trying to plan more activities. Once the weather gets warmer, one of our residents is gonna teach sunrise yoga in the rose garden."

"That sounds nice."

"Topher and Lisa just like to gossip and read, though. They've got a little book club. It's *very* exclusive," he says drily. A smile slides to my lips.

That sounds like something I'd do, if I lived here. Form a very exclusive book club.

I get my first visitor while Mandy's still on lunch. I fumble with Alonzo's clipboard and the basket of lanyard badges, trying to remember the protocol for check-in. But this woman is a regular. Hardly even needs me. She smiles, and I can see the faint sheen of an Invisalign over her awkwardly spaced teeth. She looks like she's in her late fifties—maybe sixties?—but the braces throw me off. She's pale, soft, and round, like an underbaked dinner roll in a pea coat.

"Hi, you must be new here! It's so great to meet you, I'm Cheryl. Franklin's mom."

"Hi, Cheryl. I'm Mia. I uh . . . Sorry, I don't think I've met your son yet—"

"Franklin Stewart. He's in 203?" She grins proudly, like he's a burgeoning celebrity I ought to have heard of.

"Okay, um . . . Let me see if he's gone outside—"

"No, Frankie always waits for me. I'll just grab my badge."

She reaches past me and paws into the basket of lanyards. Hangs the neon-yellow VISITOR tag around her neck.

"Thanks, Mia!"

She's gone before I can get any other information. I think I'm supposed to check her ID. I scribble "Cheryl—Franklin's mom?" on the visitation log. I look for Alonzo, hoping for some guidance, but he's stepped away from his post.

A moment later, the door to room 203 opens, and Cheryl leads Franklin into the hallway. He's young, probably around my age, with sandy curls, an athletic build, and the awkward posture of a boy who has yet to find his footing among men. Cheryl starts fussing over a stain on his white shirt. Digs a Tide stick out of her purse. He's tense as a live wire as he bites his lips together to keep his teeth hidden. His annoyance is palpable. But there are rules here. And he needs to keep things airtight if he wants to hang on to his cushy apartment.

He busies himself with his phone as Cheryl finishes cleaning his shirt, furiously tapping the screen like he's trying to demolish a horde of ants. "This isn't a good time, Mom," he mutters. "I told you to wait. They're about to announce a new coach for the Braves and I have to change all my—"

"I promised Aunt Kathy we'd FaceTime her for her birthday—"

"Trust me, Aunt Kathy doesn't give a shit—"

"Frankie—"

He shakes her off, dropping his phone. As he curses and bends to grab it off the floor, his eyes shoot to the end of the hall. To me.

He pockets his phone. Smiles.

He's coming over here. Cheryl scuttles behind him.

I'm bowled over by the need to say something to him. Yes, I am definitely supposed to say something—*anything*.

"Hey! Uh, Alonzo should be back in a second if you haven't taken your medication yet."

"You're new, aren't you?"

Cheryl butts in before I can answer. "This is Mia. It's her first day."

"Cool. I'm Franklin. But I'm sure my mom already told you that." His gaze sways to Cheryl, admonishing.

Cheryl definitely seems like the meddling type, but her presence gives me some relief. Franklin's energy is heavier than Topher's and Lisa's. Like he's the kind of person who might need their mom to remind them of the rules now and then.

My tangled nerves loosen as Alonzo rounds the corner with a fresh tray of pill cups.

"My man, how'd ya make out with that parlay last night?" Alonzo intercepts Franklin, handing him a cup.

"Dude, the parlay hit! Walked away with ten Gs." Franklin shakes the pill into his mouth.

Cheryl pats him on the back. "I don't know how he does it."

Franklin's gaze reels my attention back in like a tractor beam. Like he knows the question I'm about to ask.

"I used to play minor league baseball like, a million years ago," he says with a self-deprecating laugh. "Nowadays I make about twenty times the salary just sitting on my ass here betting on other people's games."

"Wow, that's . . . a great way to use those skills? I guess?"

He smiles and runs a hand through his butterscotch curls.

I would really, *really* like to stop staring now.

I wonder if he knows he's doing this.

Cheryl clears her throat. If he doesn't know, *she* certainly does.

"Uh, what kinda stuff can you bet on, when you do that?" The words stumble from my lips. Trying to keep the conversation afloat against my will.

"Oh, it's hilarious, you can bet on *anything*. Like, last year a buddy of mine won five thousand dollars guessing what color Gatorade the team was gonna dump on the coach when they won the Super Bowl." He chuckles, eliciting the same response from me.

"Mia, Beatrice was asking if you could give her a hand in the ballroom with some of the New Year's stuff." Alonzo quirks his head in the opposite direction.

Finally, permission to disengage. It's like coming up for air.

"Later, Mia," Franklin says to my back as Alonzo leads me away.

"Sorry 'bout that," Alonzo sighs. "You'll be old news around here in a day or two."

At four thirty, Mandy and I gather our things. I glimpse our visitors clipboard and notice Cheryl hasn't signed out.

"Are we supposed to like, go get all the guests and tell them to leave?"

"They'll make an announcement at five o'clock. But Cheryl stays through dinnertime, for Franklin. They'll bring her to the kitchen in a few."

I remember the nurse with the saccharine accent who answered the phone when I called the Phoenix Sara center to admit Mom. "Will you be comin' to the center to bloodlet for the patient?" There's a foul, corrosive taste in my mouth and I can't seem to swallow. Probably because I forgot to drink water all day.

☾ ☾ ☾

I walk all the way back to my apartment, same way I walked this morning, along the river. I'm trying to be careful with my transportation budget. I don't want to take the train, but I can't blow my savings on cabs and Ubers, either. Besides, the cold helps me think.

ADAPT is going to try to get Daylights however they can. Someone in that building knows something. All I need to do is find out who that someone is.

On my way past Columbia, I swing through the school bookstore and buy myself a belated Christmas present: a slender red Moleskine notebook.

I collapse to the couch with my phone the second I arrive home. Open my socials to search for the Sara center geotag. I'm curious how many residents I'll be able to look up. There's no official label for the building, but someone's created a tongue-in-cheek alternate: Blood-Bath-on-Hudson. There are hundreds of hits.

Mandy said the Sara centers used to block social media, so this is a new phenomenon. At the top of the search results sits a photo of Topher. A gleam of sunlight creates the perfect lens flare off his shades as he lounges on a bench in the courtyard, gazing out at the river. *Everyone deserves their moment in the sun. #RayBans #sponsored*

Jesus. He's being paid for this—or getting free sunglasses, at the very least.

I navigate to his profile, a muted "What?" on my lips. The guy's got over 200K followers.

The centers must love people like him. *Come self-report and spend your afternoons with this handsome gentleman! We'll even throw in some free Ray-Bans.*

I scroll through Topher's grid, marveling at his beautifully curated, color-coded fashion photography. His prepossessing smile, over and over. Like a goddamn supermodel. Not *like* one—he *is* one. Sara center residents can do pretty much anything if they have a phone. They can win gobs of money gambling. Show off their photography, release music. Hell, they could even shoot a whole movie if they were feeling ambitious.

An image materializes: the account I could have helped create for Mom's art. My heart twists. She could have sold her paintings online. Who knows what she could have become.

I stand and gulp water from the sink, washing the thought away. Still parched from the daylong pheromone high.

I create a throwaway account and start following all the residents I can find. Open my Moleskine to its first, fresh page and start making a list of suspicious followers and comments. Devon's first attempt at organizing happened on Facebook. There's no doubt he's still using social media to corral people. This is a new game, with new tactics. But I'm patient enough to watch the snake hole and wait for something to lunge out.

And something does.

Not the thing I'm looking for. A different sort of something.

The photo rolls into view halfway down the top posts on Blood-Bath-on-Hudson. I swallow a bubble of air with my water.

Her username is QT_Core. Her ginger-gold eyes are downcast, shaded by an umbrella of thick black lashes. She's lounging in a lacy scarlet bra-and-panties set on an unmade twin bed without a headboard. The sparse, dingy setting seems intentional—as though it's meant to look like some kind of holding cell. Two loose, red bra straps ring her shoulders, expertly draped for lackadaisical effect. She's spilling from her cups. The corner of her plump, glossy lip is clenched between her teeth, and there's the hint of an exposed, razor-sharp canine. I zoom in on the photo. Transfixed by the ripe bead of blood on her mouth.

My body lights up like a tinderbox. I reflexively flip the phone over.

I know the internet is full of cheap thrills and thirst traps, but I'm still not comfortable with how I factor into all of that. I don't look at stuff like this. My hand quivers as I suffocate the phone against the couch cushion. She's Bloody Mary in the black mirror, waiting for me to whisper her name ten times.

I wonder what floor she lives on.

After a moment, I turn the phone right side up, holding my breath. Navigate to her profile. Her photo grid calls to me in flashes of amber flesh and red lace. Five years' worth. I avert my gaze. Determined to maintain clinical distance.

She doesn't list a name. There's just a black heart emoji beside a red one, and a link below. I tap it.

Oh. No thank you.

Her silken lips smile from a black "Subscribers Only" page. That same suggestive hint of a pointed tooth.

I pound the little white X at the corner of the screen, desperate to close the page.

Guess not everyone can subsist on free Ray-Bans.

She doesn't have as many followers as Topher, but it's still a respectable 20K. The appeal is obvious: she's naked, she's deadly, but most of all . . . she's *safe.* She'll never hurt you. Rapunzel with a taste for human blood and Wi-Fi. Still, I want to scream at every person who's clicked that Subscribe button . . . and maybe her, too. Don't they know this is a fucking *disease?*

God, ADAPT must love people like her.

QT_Core, I jot her name down in my Moleskine, followed by: *Camgirl?? Whoring out bloodlust since 2018?*

Guilt rises in me as I stare at that last sentence. It's harsh. But it's not like she'll ever see this, it's just research. I don't even know her real name.

I start taking note of her top commenters. Jot down a few usernames. One of them, s_a_r_a_lebrity_001, has left the exact same comment on every one of her recent photos:

» omg gorgeous ilysm xxxxx

The account has 150K followers but doesn't follow anybody back. Clearly a bot or something, with no original content. Just a patchwork of poached infographics.

ACTION ITEM—*SARA CENTERS STILL RUNNING CCTV IN RESIDENCE HALLS: Dallas, TX; San Diego, CA; Chicago, IL; Portland, OR. FLOOD THOSE INBOXES. CALL TILL SOMEONE PICKS UP. DEMAND PRIVACY.*

I've never seen stuff like this on my own feed. The algorithm decides which corner of the internet you inhabit. And this definitely isn't mine.

The adjacent post shows a grainy picture of a tiny girl curled in a ball on the floor with tears in her eyes and a bloody rime all over her face. The superimposed text reads:

It's been 300 days since Samantha Corbin was surrendered to Salvation of Miami by her abusers. She's locked up. THEY'RE STILL FREE. #JusticeforSammi

I hate myself for wondering if it might be fake. Of course, there are awful stories like this. How could there not be?

I sift through the comments. They use terms I've never heard before, even on the old Facebook group. Instead of "infected" or "turned," they say "lifted."

> there's a special place in hell for people who lift kids for this kinda shit

A lot of them also refer to something called Inversion. With a capital I.

> Inversion will NOT BE KIND to these sick mfers
> keep em alive post-Invo so they can feel the pain they deserve

Context helps me connect the dots; they're talking about population inversion. The day Saras outnumber the uninfected. Sorry. "Unlifted."

You're cool if you're a bleeder, though. That's *bleeder,* not blood-letter. It's funny: Mom and I never had a word for what I was. That, or she never said it in front of me.

There's another word they keep using. One that makes my whole body blush. When a Sara engages in a sexual relationship with an unlifted partner who provides blood, it's called "banking." As in:

> 911 ive been banking this guy for the past 6 months and i think he told his family I'm a Sara wtf do I do???

Or:

> Remember guys ALL BANKING IS CONSENSUAL. If it's not, it's SA. NO EXCEPTIONS.

There's something in it for the unlifted party, too: that sweet, narcotic afterburn when a Sara leaves its mark. Textbook symbiosis, if you're chasing a good high. Plus you both get laid.

I gulp from my glass of water to wash the taste of bile from my mouth. All consent aside, they chose a pretty crude term to describe this. I doubt the unlifted party came up with it.

Mom shielded me from so much of this. I'm thankful. I think.

As I shake it off and keep scrolling, one stark, simple post in particular pulls my gaze. A plain black square emblazoned with white text.

> "Darwin says 'the crust of the earth is a vast museum.' The natural processes of extinction and renewal define life on this planet, and our own births and deaths are a microcosm of this rhythm. But it's difficult to see the forest for the trees when it's your own species on the verge of extinction—or, if you do, you refuse to accept defeat. Such refusal helps us survive. But we can't forget—To survive is to adapt. Even if it feels like surrender."

A memory rubber-bands from the back of my mind: Mom at the dinner table, gushing like a schoolgirl about his fucking *epilogue*. "You can't write an epilogue to someone else's book," I say like an ignorant snob.

I swipe to the second half of the post. Black text on a white background this time.

> "If I keep thinking of myself as something to be feared, something to be hidden away and silenced, I will not survive this. And, statistically speaking, I'm going to survive a very long time. Longer than those who silenced me."—Devon Shaw, On the Origin of a New Species

This is the unknowable person I fear. Not the man who made my mother cry. Not the creep who watched my first kiss across a dark parking lot. The most terrifying and mesmerizing version of Devon continues to be the *idea* of Devon—and everything that idea represents.

If he dies, does the idea die with him?

❨ ❨ ❨

The next day, I opt for a night shift. It's New Year's Eve.

I walk downtown to avoid surge pricing on rideshare. I'm not as keen on strolling around at night anymore, so I leave at four thirty, while it's still light out. The Sara center won't let me upstairs till seven. But I can kill time in the lobby. Keep tabs on my little research project.

As I bide my time in the lobby, I pull out my phone to check if any of those shady accounts have updated. But I can't seem to find s_a_r_a_lebrity_001. The page has vanished overnight. I cross-reference with my notebook and realize a few others from my list are missing, too.

QT_Core posted something late last night: a shadowy, almost artistic black-and-white self-portrait in a full-length mirror. She's got her bare back to the camera in a pair of skintight Lycra shorts, hair trailing between her shoulder blades like a black vine. She's got to be on one of the lower floors, if she has a phone and posted this yesterday.

I pull up her comment thread. I'm looking for something . . .

» omg gorgeous ilysm xxxxx

Same vapid wording. Different account. This comment is from a user named li_fted_gifffft.

They're killing accounts and launching new ones simultaneously. How often, I don't know. As I add the new username to my list, Beatrice emerges at the front desk and waves me toward the elevators with a foggy frown.

"Happy New Year. Glad someone showed up tonight."

The party is nice enough. Lighting is festive. Music upbeat. But the mood is a little bit . . . *hygienic*. Like a middle school dance—or at least, my *impression* of a middle school dance, considering I never went to mine. The residents flock to the sidelines, fused together in tight, impenetrable cliques. Nobody's on the dance floor. My job tonight is to keep things clean and tidy as the party rages on, but there's nothing to eat or drink, so there's not much to do in that department.

I scan the faces, clocking the ones I recognize from all my stalking. It's still early; Topher and Lisa won't deign to arrive for at least another hour, if they come at all. I spot Ingrid in a far corner, sporting a massive, chunky scarf she must have knit herself. And then there's Franklin, with his mom. She dons a pair of cheap plastic "2024" glasses and bobs her head to the music, encouraging him to dance. He scowls and pulls out his phone.

Alonzo sails past, wearing a gold sequined tuxedo vest over his scrubs.

"Didn't realize there was a dress code." I take a sheepish glance down at my Chucks and the frayed cuffs of my old jeans as he slows to face me.

"Eh, figured I should help boost morale this year." He thumbs the corners of his vest so the sequins hit the light. "Not sure it's working, though."

A plume of creamy, neon-stippled smoke from the corner of the ballroom catches my eye. Ingrid's pulling from a vape. She passes it to the person next to her, wearing a similar chunky scarf that must have been a gift from her. I recognize them from Instagram. I think their name is Kai. They draw raunchy comic strips and read a lot of self-help books.

"Damn, I'm not supposed to let 'em do that," Alonzo sighs. But he doesn't march off in their direction. "You won't tell, right, Froshie?"

"Is that . . . Are they smoking weed?" This really is like a middle school dance.

"Probably. A lot of them do it in their rooms, or in the courtyard when they think nobody's watching. Technically any kind of intoxication is a no-no. But, y'know. It's a party." He turns in a circle with a dismayed shrug. "I mean, it's supposed to be."

He lumbers away, half-heartedly snagging a pair of "2024" glasses from a nearby high-top table. I watch Ingrid and Kai, transfixed. I wonder if Mom ever smoked weed after she got infected. I know she missed drinking wine, and she definitely enjoyed her cigarettes.

She probably did with Devon.

Another secret. I'm still drowning in them.

I feel exposed, just standing here in the middle of the room. I sidle toward Ingrid and Kai. If they're cutting loose, they might start to feel chatty. My palms twinkle with sweat as bass assaults my ears. I hate that my plan of attack relies so heavily on my ability to socialize.

Ingrid meets my eye as I approach and conceals her vape, disappearing into her voluminous scarf like a turtle. She exhales, and smoke escapes through the stitches.

I shoot her my most disarming smile. "It's okay. I won't tell anyone."

"Oh God, thanks." Ingrid snorts into her scarf. Hesitates before revealing the rest of her face. "I swear we don't do this a lot. Only on special occasions."

"Ingrid—" Kai cuts her a warning glare.

"No, she's cool. This is Mia. We met yesterday, I'm knitting her a hat." Ingrid stealthily passes the pen to Kai as she spins them to face me. "Mia, this is Kai."

I pretend not to know them as I smile and wave. No handshakes. No touching. I won't tattle about the vape, but that rule is ironclad.

Kai wears an ironic purple tutu and sneakers that light up blue in time with their steps. The thick Technicolor scarf from Ingrid completes the offbeat look. They remind me of an eccentric elementary school teacher you'd find in a storybook. Miss Frizzle from *The Magic School Bus* with a buzz cut.

"Surprised to see you here for a night shift." Ingrid studies me. "Figured Mandy would've talked you out of that."

"You're shadowing Mandy?" Kai lets loose a derisive laugh with a puff of smoke.

"Leave Mandy alone, she's fine." Ingrid snags the vape back, then quirks a look in my direction. "Sorry, you want? I don't mean to be rude, but I know you're on the clock—"

"No, you're not being . . . I'm good. Thanks." I'd kill for a shot of tequila, though.

"The hell you mean she's *fine*?" Kai sneers, still stuck on Mandy. "You know why she's here."

"She's done her penance."

"I thought she was nice," I meekly offer at the same time.

"She's a nasty, judgey little shrew and her dumb face looks like a moldy-ass piece of white bread." Kai turns to me, mouth half open, as though they're considering whether to continue in mixed company. "Also, she's a murderer."

"Kai—"

"We can't call a spade a spade?"

"Wait . . . *What?*" I bend toward the two of them, as close as I can get without touching.

"Mandy's boyfriend was a Sara. When he cheated, she shot him and called it self-defense," Kai hisses. "All she got was community service."

"O-oh." I don't know what to do with my face.

"That's a very simplistic way of putting it," Ingrid interjects. "She didn't shoot him *because* he was cheating. He got infected by the other woman and *that's* when Mandy shot him."

I can't help but notice Ingrid's word choice. She said "infected." Not "lifted."

"Anyway, please don't tell Mandy we were gossiping about her," Ingrid whispers. "She's in charge of our mail."

"Hey, Mia."

I whirl in the opposite direction. Franklin's right behind me.

"Happy New Year, it's great you came."

There it is again—that aggressive, aggravating magnetism. So different from the infectious energy radiating from Kai and Ingrid.

"Uh . . . yeah! Happy to help. It's a nice party."

I figure he must have come over to try and bum some weed. But he just stands there, chasing my gaze all over the room. I notice he's not holding his phone.

"Where's Cheryl?" Kai intervenes on my behalf, casually scornful.

"Went home. I told her I had some work to do." He smiles. Right at me. "Would you maybe like . . . wanna dance? Or something? I dunno, is that stupid?"

Ingrid sputters and Kai stomps on her foot. Franklin is like a statue as he waits for my answer.

"I'm kinda not supposed to like . . . fraternize. Or whatever the rules say. I'm sorry—"

"Ooookay, well what would you call what you're doing with these two delinquents?"

My eyes meet Ingrid's. She sighs dramatically, then hands me her vape.

"She's writing us up, if you must know."

As I turn to pocket Ingrid's contraband, a face in the crowd wrenches my gaze.

Bloody Mary just stepped out of the mirror.

She enters the room with an uncertain gait, on spiky silver stilettos. She's on her own. Everyone else here seems to have a tribe or a partner, but she's flying solo. Her chestnut hair falls in waves across her back like a bolt of chiffon, and she keeps tucking and untucking it behind her ears as she approaches the dance floor. Her dress is long and high-necked, surprisingly modest, save for a slit up the side to make way for her leg. It's a lustrous pearlescent white, like the inside of a seashell. She wears a fragile string of a smile, trying to make eye contact with anyone who'll have her.

Franklin coughs. Shattering my stare. "Well, have a good night, I guess."

"I'm sorry—" I mutter to his back. Even though I'm not.

Ingrid eyes my pocket as he moves off. "I'll have that back, if ya don't mind."

I hand over the vape without looking at her. QT_Core hovers at the corner of the dance floor, still panning across the room for a friendly face. Her dress absorbs all the light it touches like a crystal in an open window, spilling tiny spectrums across the floor.

"You're welcome for the rescue."

"Yeah. Thank you. Sorry, um . . . what's that girl's name?"

I point a subtle, lightning-quick finger in her direction. Careful not to draw attention to myself. Ingrid lets loose a thoughtful "mmm" as she takes a drag. Like there's a story here. But of course there is. Everyone here has a story.

I just want hers.

"I just . . . I think I might know her from somewhere? But I'm not sure—"

"That's Cora." Kai picks up the slack. "She bounces around floors pretty often, so we don't know her that well. We first met her maybe like, two years ago?"

"Yeah, that sounds about right," Ingrid says.

"At first we thought she was a brand-new resident but it turns out she was being moved *down* to Four after having been upstairs for the past few years."

"What floor?"

"Shit, who knows. Like, she'll tell you it was Nine, but she's probably just fucking with you. That's kinda her thing."

"And she keeps getting moved," Ingrid adds. "She'll show up on Four, then disappear again a few weeks later. Next month—*poof,* the bitch is back on good behavior."

"How come?" A quiet thrill moves through me.

"You fail your Behavioral, you move upstairs."

"No, I mean, why does she keep failing?"

"Not sure. That's what I'm saying," Kai goes on. "Nobody knows her. She's never downstairs long enough to make friends. Though I can't say I'm interested, all things considered. She ate her whole family like it was fucking Thanksgiving. Nobody wants that kind of vibe around here. It's contagious."

"Thought you said nobody knows her," I say.

"Sure, but everybody knows *that.*"

Cora dips a toe onto the dance floor. She performs a slow, cautious twirl, lifting the corner of her opalescent skirt. Her shoulders sag. Nobody's coming to dance with her.

She's gone in the next flash of light: through the doors, back the way she came. My breath catches. I almost forgot she was a Sara till she moved like that. Maybe I could have danced with her. Could have done it without touching.

My taut body goes cold, like death just passed straight through me.

It's a good thing she gets moved so often. It's not safe for me to see her again.

I unfollow her on my way home the next morning.

☽ ☽ ☽

I sleep through the day and leave my apartment at four thirty for another night shift. It's a holiday but I'm welcome to put in my hours 24/7, 365.

January 1. Two months' worth of savings left. Maybe less, considering how much I've been spending on alcohol. I never realized how expensive it was, even though Mom owned a bar. It's hard to grasp till you're the one drinking it. So far I've managed three days of sobriety, thanks to the memory of that blackout catastrophe with Jade. But that's only going to make a small dent. I need something resembling income. Fast.

I shadow Alonzo's rounds after dinner. On my water break, I shoot Sabrina an email about the house. *Any teardown offers?* I try to reschedule that stupid hostess job interview, but I'm not optimistic. I feel like an idiot. Small and childish again, like I did that night I spent with Jade. Mom always handled this stuff. I had a job, but I never had to worry about keeping a roof over my head. We took care of each other, and we were good at it.

Everything I've done since her death feels so shameful. Reckless at best. I'm pathetic without her.

I wipe down equipment in the gym, silent and robotic. Kai swings by to say hello. I want to ask them about Cora. But I don't. Because I know I shouldn't.

I need to get my priorities straight.

And yet, I return the following night. And the night after that.

I don't see Cora again, and there haven't been any leads. Just gossip. But that's fine.

I think I'm just lonely.

I learn Lisa used to be on Broadway and even has a Tony Award. She keeps it on her shelf and loves to show it to anyone who asks. I wonder if Mom knew who she was. She was the theater aficionado in the family.

I discover Topher receives conjugal visits from three different long-term boyfriends who don't know about each other—and that second-floor residents are allowed to receive said visits from uninfected partners. I'm more than a little shocked, the first time I sign someone in. I can't help but remember what I read about "banking." How easily something like that could go wrong. But I guess the people on Two are on their best behavior. Alonzo says they've never had an unsavory incident. I think of the way Franklin fought to conceal his teeth in front of Cheryl, even though she was driving him up a wall. People downstairs know how to keep themselves in check. Residents also don't hook up as often as I imagined. Transferring to another Sara center can be complicated, so people figure they ought to protect their friendships if they're here for the long haul. It *does* happen, though. Ingrid had a fling with a guy on the third floor last year, but then the staff was going to make them sign a hill of paperwork acknowledging the relationship and she decided to back off.

I've learned a lot of things. But it's all useless. There's not a whiff of ADAPT's signature poison anywhere. Just a bunch of bots on social media and a beautiful girl who never comes out of her room.

I decide Friday is going to be my last night shift. I just applied to another dozen restaurant jobs, and if any of them hire me my evenings will be spoken for. I'll do as much research as I can online and volunteer during the day when I have free time. I resolve to re-enroll in my classes, meet some real friends, and find a new therapist. Whatever normal people do to get over something.

I head upstairs at seven, and we've had a late UPS delivery during dinner. Beatrice asks me to log and distribute the packages. Nothing out of the ordinary. Apple Store, Nordstrom, and that sex shop again.

I'm up on Four with the delivery cart. There's no one else in the hall except a couple of nurses keeping watch. It's quiet upstairs after dinner. Most of the residents are on Two in the common rooms or enjoying an evening cigarette in the courtyard. I knock on a door but there's no answer. I leave the box.

As I wait for the elevator with my empty cart, a primal shriek splinters the silence. I crumple against the wall with a sharp intake of breath as two nurses sprint past.

"Stay back."

My heart plummets to the ground. There's another scream. Louder this time. A woman appears in the hallway, struggling against the nurses just a few yards behind me.

Cora.

Run, run, run, my mind cries. Instead, I plant my feet. In thrall to the sound of that wail.

"Fuck you, you shit-eating cunt rags—Fuck. *You.*"

Her voice throbs between my ears as a third nurse joins the

fray to restrain her. They push her face against the linoleum as the elevator opens with an urgent *ping*. Alonzo bursts forth, brandishing a needle.

"No, no, no, please don't," Cora moans. "I promise I won't do it again, I promise, I—"

Alonzo slides toward her on his knees. Plunges the syringe into her arm.

"*No!*" she and I both howl. Like she forced my mouth open across the distance and stole the word from me. My legs are buttery soft as my body shimmers with empathy.

Alonzo's eyes dart to mine. Like he didn't realize I was standing there. Cora's scream dissolves to a pitiful whimper as the three nurses drag her upright. She slumps against them, toes grazing the floor. They carry her to a waiting gurney and strap her down.

As they push the gurney toward the elevator, Alonzo looks at me, then my empty mail cart. "Froshie, can you help us with something?"

"Uh . . . sure. Of course—" I shake out my legs, fighting to get the blood pumping again.

I knew I'd have some sort of chemical reaction when I saw her again. What I didn't anticipate was how disorienting it would be. The elemental toll of it.

"We need to search this room for contraband. Do me a favor and grab any electronics you can find. Bring 'em down to Two and wait for me at the nurses' station."

"I thought they were allowed to have phones and stuff?" I wonder if this has to do with the content Cora's been posting. Feels like a pretty shitty double standard, considering they allow unlimited banking for people like Topher.

"She's on a watch list. We still gotta check those devices."

Maybe that's what set her off.

"Okay, I'll see what I can find."

Alonzo nods his thanks and trots off toward a locked stairwell. He scans in with his badge, leaving me alone in the hall. I pull a ragged breath, preparing to enter her domain.

The room is surprisingly spartan. I guess she hasn't been here long. I remember that cold, empty "holding cell" vibe from her photo. The walls are white and bare except for a framed photograph on her shelf: four girls on graduation day throwing their caps into the air, embellished with sequins and silk flowers. Cora stands in the middle with a thousand-watt grin. The only other décor is a vase of dead yellow lilies on her nightstand. A ring light sits on her dresser, and she's left her curling iron on. I reach over to unplug it. Rosewater hangs heavy in the air. She doesn't have to hide her smell here, but old habits die hard. Either that, or she just likes it. I do, too.

There's an iPhone on her pillow and a laptop on the floor. I grab both and place them in my cart. The phone lights up at my touch, asking for a passcode. Like it knows how much I wish I could look at it.

And that's when I spot it: the tassel of a bookmark peeking out from under her bed, wedged between the pages of a thick hardcover book. I can't help it. I want to know what she's reading. I'm starved for insight. Maybe it's something I've read before, something we could chat about sometime.

On the Origin of Species, by Charles Darwin.

My hands go numb around the book.

I sink to my knees and open to the page she's marked. Force myself to get a grip. Let's not jump to conclusions. Maybe she's taking classes, getting her degree or something. Maybe—

A single passage draws my gaze, highlighted with pink marker:

"One general law, leading to the advancement of all organic beings, namely, multiply, vary, let the strongest live and the weakest die."

She's underlined the word "multiply" three times.

I slip the book underneath my sweater, switch off the lights, and wheel the cart of contraband into the harsh glare of the hall.

NOW

The moon bears down on me like a searchlight. I'm sprawled across a tarp in Devon's open trunk, caked with blood. The resonant ache of the rusted bullet screeches across my leg, and I swear I can feel the poison creeping toward my heart. Did I black out? I must have. I don't know how I got to his car.

"I'm sorry. I should've warned you," he says as my eyes flutter open. He perches on the edge of the trunk. Leaving an inch of space between us. "These fucking townies have started packing after dark. But I can't say I blame the lady. I mean, you went after her kid."

Is that who shot me? The woman from the parking lot?

"I'm gonna take it out, okay?"

He reaches out, and I recoil. A parabola of pain arcs from my toe to my hip and back down again. I don't want to scream, but it just comes out. He clamps a hand over my mouth.

"Don't touch me," I whisper through his fingers.

"C'mon, you know what happens if we don't—"

"I can do it myself."

He raises a brow. Lifts his hands, conceding. I can't help but notice the edge of a derisive smile.

I heave myself to a seated position as another scream simmers in my throat. But I keep it inside as I twist around to inspect the wound. It's on the back of my lower thigh, just above my knee crease. I can touch it, but I don't have a good visual.

I have no antiseptic, no tools. My hands are filthy, but my only choice is to extract it with my fingers. Do it by feel.

Jesus, he's just *watching* me.

I don't want him to help. But does he have to stare like that?

I caress the tender wound with my thumb and pull a deep breath—which somehow invites even more pain. Has the rust already reached my lungs? How long before it's too late? I make a shaky scissors shape with my index and middle fingers and move the fabric of my jeans aside. Slowly part the folds of my shredded flesh. I retch as my fingertip brushes rusted copper.

He inches all the way inside the trunk. Directs my trembling hand away from the wound.

"Stop. You're pushing it in."

I can't decide if he sounds angry. His voice is steady, like still water.

He reveals his knife. The tarp crunches as he crawls over my listless body so he's facing the back of my leg. I don't like this. Not being able to see him.

I realize I smell blood. Not mine, though. And not ripe, either. The tarp is plastered with it. Bone dry and long dead.

"This is gonna suck but it's gonna be quick. Deep breath."

"Wait—"

"Don't scream."

The bullet sizzles and clings to my poisoned sinew as he pries it out, using the knife as a fulcrum. Of course, I fucking scream immediately.

His hand flies to my mouth again as he tosses the bullet into the woods with the other.

Sweat weeps down my face, mixing with fresh tears. He locks me in place, squeezing my jaw as I hyperventilate into his palm like a paper bag.

"Shh, you're okay. We got it."

His voice needles the back of my skull. He's still behind me and I want him to move. But if he lets me go I'm pretty sure I'll start convulsing so hard I'll fall right out of the car.

After a moment, I regain control of my lungs. He peels his hand from my parched lips. "We're gonna go see a doctor, okay? She can bandage you up."

He snakes toward the hatch, putting space between us so he doesn't nudge me in the wrong direction. Swoops into the front seat and grabs my sleeping bag.

"It's probably better if you stay where you are," he says as he lays it over me. "I'll drive slow."

"Um . . . okay."

My eyelids shudder as echoes of pain bounce up and down my leg.

"You did good, Fun Size."

His gaze is soft but loaded with expectancy. Like he's waiting for me to answer.

". . . Thanks."

He shuts the trunk. Careful not to slam it.

The ignition turns. As I breathe the stench of stale blood, my mind swerves to Cora. The ache in my thigh rises to my chest. I hope to God nobody's put a bullet in her leg, or someplace worse.

☾ ☾ ☾

He keeps his word and drives slow. The desolate mountain back roads are paved, but they're dark and monotonous. Swaths of identical moonlit trees streak by, minute after minute. Mile after mile. It's impossible to tell how far we've come. And we're the only car on the road.

We pass through a town. If you could call it that. Is it still a town, if nobody lives there? Faded signs swing on rusted hinges above broken storefront windows. There's an empty Goodwill. The skeleton of a diner. A derelict silo emblazoned with flaky yellow script that reads DAWSON'S DAIRY FARM.

As we approach the outskirts, a mildewed, hand-painted sign sways in the wind.

Thanks for Visiting Clark
Est. September 16th, 1889
Elev. 7271
Pop: ?

I'm waiting for Devon to speak, or put on some music. Anything. But he's mute. A chain-smoking phantom behind the wheel.

I was so sure he was the one who shot me.

At that point, I was across the street from the Walmart, in the woods. I have no idea what kind of gun that woman had, if she could have reached me even if she was the straightest shot in all of Colorado.

But he was even farther away. The car was parked down the block.

Unless he wasn't *in the car.*

But if he shot me, why the hell would he save me?

Why save me *at all*?

Letting me die in the woods would have been the most elegant solution, if he thought I was some kind of mole. But no.

An icy finger of truth strokes my spine.

If I'm still alive, it is because he *needs me* alive. Regardless of who pulled the trigger.

I shiver, sweat, and vomit bile all over the sleeping bag.

We make a sharp turn, and the cruel, luminous throb of my leg answers back.

He finally speaks. "Hang on to something. Dirt road up ahead."

I slowly worm to a seated position and grab the back seat for balance. The pit of my belly croaks, sending a distress signal up between my ears. The resulting migraine takes my breath away. I still need to eat. Can't fight this infection on an empty stomach. He said we were going to see a doctor. Is this a *doctor* doctor, or another lunatic with a pocketknife?

It's another fifteen minutes on the dirt road before we start to slow down. Devon cuts the headlights as we approach a padlocked gate at the bottom of a steep hill. He hops out to unlock it, and I glimpse a sign behind the glimmering heat signature of the car's exhaust.

Lost Moon Mountain Ski Lodge

He slides back into the car, pulls up a few yards, then jumps back out to lock the gate behind us.

Before we climb the hill, he twists around to look at me. I study his gaze, but there's nothing in it.

"You know I saw you run, back there."

His accusatory tone shanks my heart.

"I didn't . . . I-I ran because I saw her gun," I lie.

A shadow smile crosses his face. I have no idea how to interpret it.

"Anything else you wanna tell me?"

My gut lurches. I have no idea what he's fishing for.

"No." That feels like the safest answer. For now.

A moment passes before he shifts the car back into drive.

"Is Cora here?" I whisper to his back.

"That your friend?"

I nod. He meets my eye in the rearview mirror, but doesn't

answer. His attention tilts back to the road. "Hold on again, it's bumpy up here."

The rusted ghost of a ski lift looms as the Chevy grinds up the hill. I watch the ancient chairs swing perilously in the wind, hanging by a thread. The faint glow of civilization dances in the distance. Firelight and heat signatures.

A stately yet rustic log A-frame sits at the center of the forsaken resort, surrounded by a cluster of smaller cabins and weatherworn trailers. A barricade of evergreens guards the perimeter, and someone's taken care to shovel the cobblestone walkways.

The buildings are all dark, dead monoliths with boarded-up windows. There's only one light on, outside the main lodge on the first floor. It's an old, flickering neon sign that says CLINIC beneath a screaming red cross. A generator hums nearby, like this is the only part of the camp being serviced with electricity.

That's good, I think. The clinic is open for business. Maybe that's where my so-called doctor is, right now.

A bonfire roars at the center of the ragtag neighborhood, where a dozen people hold court in camping chairs. As we drive past, I scan the faces for Cora. Gareth. Kayla, too. But I don't recognize anyone.

Muted music fills the air. Someone's strumming a guitar. I can't help but think of Steve's compound out in the desert, where I came to watch Jade play that afternoon. Smoke signals from another life.

We hang a left, circle around behind the trailers, and park beside another vehicle: Gareth's cube truck. I could howl with relief. That has to mean Cora's here somewhere.

Two figures emerge from the darkness to meet Devon as he hops out of the car. He shuts the door, muffling his voice as he trots toward them. I wonder what he's telling them. About me.

Seconds later, the trunk opens. Devon stands flanked by a tall, unsmiling young woman with hair like glossy black crow feathers. Her home-hacked pixie cut accentuates the jagged diamond shape of her petite face. She wears a camo-print jacket and a cautious grimace. Gareth stands beside her.

"Mia, this is—"

"Where's Cora?" My eyes jerk to Gareth. "I need to see her."

Devon ignores me, and his acolytes follow suit. "This is Dr. Lacie. You've already met Gareth. I'll leave you to it."

He spins on his heel with a short-fused sigh. Gone is that steady, still-water tone he used on me in the car. Like he snipped the cord between us as soon as he killed the ignition.

"C'mere and slide on out, we gotcha—" Gareth offers his hand as Devon stalks off. But I don't take it.

"Don't try to walk. We can carry you," Dr. Lacie adds.

My disbelieving stare toggles between them. I guess I understand the change in Gareth's energy. Before he knew it was me, Devon told him he was transporting the person who betrayed them—the vile spiderwoman herself. But any generosity here is a poisoned apple.

Dr. Lacie makes a careful arc with her long, lithe frame and ducks into the trunk. I draw back, instantly regretting it as agony radiates across my leg. I shriek, and her mask of gentle professionalism falls away.

"Mia, we need to bandage that wound," she snaps like a whip.

Gareth intervenes, in a softer tone. "Listen, we got drugs. Injectables. No pill sucking around here."

He gingerly places a hand on my shoulder. Trying not to startle me. I think of that nurse with the Sunkist hair at the hospital in Utah. The one who tried to take me away from Mom. Bedside manner's always going to feel like a threat to me.

"You need to eat and get some rest."

He leans forward, preparing to help me to my feet. And that's when I smell him. I mean *really* smell him. That sweet orange-blossom elixir wafts toward me, but somehow salty this time. Earthy and aromatic. I grind my teeth.

His gaze rises to mine, and I know we've understood one another.

I figure we're headed toward the clinic, but instead we cross the main lodge toward a back door, at the opposite end of the building.

I hop on one foot as the two of them bear my weight and help me stumble inside. I can tell we're in the old ski shop; the space is lined with shelves of moldy, mismatched boots, and the room is musty with shoe polish and ski wax. Someone's nailed boards over all the windows. There's a wood-burning stove in the corner of the room, beside a cot. Dr. Lacie eases me into it as Gareth rushes to light the stove. To my relief, there's a generous stack of wood against the wall.

I collapse to the cot, out of breath. A fifty-yard hobble across the camp—even with two people helping—is too much for me. And my migraine is back with a vengeance. I wonder what would happen if I just pounced on Gareth, right here and now. But I have the sense to recognize his importance. What the consequences might be if I opened him up without permission.

Gareth pulls a stool from behind the defunct rental counter and offers it to Dr. Lacie. In exchange, she unzips her cross-body first aid pack and hands him the holy trinity: a needle, a tourniquet, and a rubber reservoir.

Both of them silently get to work as my consciousness contracts to a pinhole, then expands back out. The stove glows with warmth, illuminating the space. Gareth hops up on the counter and removes his jacket, then his fleece pullover. He shivers in his thin T-shirt as he tightens the tourniquet around his arm with his teeth.

His spindly arms are studded with scars, but not tiny, telltale pricks with a constant needle. Not like the ones I had. These are fat, raindrop-sized scabs like rubies, marching two-by-two up and down his flesh.

Someone feeds from him directly. Someone he trusts, if they haven't torn him to shreds by now. The poor guy's probably tapped out. And yet, he's giving of himself to save me. Well—he's saving me because Devon told him to. But I'll take it.

Gareth eases the needle into his elbow crease, and in the anemic half-light I spot a tattoo on his inner biceps: "167" in simple black font. I focus on the numbers to keep myself from salivating after those scabs. After a moment, he turns his back. I think that's interesting. Shows self-respect. I used to hate it when Mom watched me draw.

Meanwhile, Dr. Lacie preps her own needle. She presents me with two injections from her first aid kit. The first one burns when it hits my skin, and I reflexively kick her with my good leg. But she's stoic. Unfazed.

"It'll probably be a couple weeks till you can put weight on it, but you'll heal," she says, flatly, like she's reading from some sort of manual. I can feel the reluctance radiating from her. Her touch is iron cold as she hacks away at my bloody jeans with a pair of scissors to access the infection.

Gareth rises, offering me the blood bag. I yelp, involuntary, not sure if the sound came from my body. I hardly feel the rubber reservoir he places between my shaking hands.

It's gone too fast.

"Is there more? Someone else?" I whisper, sucking sweet copper from my teeth.

"Sorry. All the others are tapped out."

God dammit, I'd do anything to rip into those scabs.

At that moment, Dr. Lacie injects me with the second needle and a soft, downy weightlessness rushes over me. Relief at last. Any lingering hunger abates with my pain.

"Good?" She stares down at me, still wearing that stormy, impatient gaze. But I hardly care what she thinks of me, or why. I'm safe and warm as the womb. I could cry. I think I am.

After a moment, she starts flushing my numb leg with antiseptic. Her frigid touch is like baby's breath.

"I gotta go clean out the Chevy," Gareth whispers to Dr. Lacie, handing her the empty blood reservoir.

"Wait . . . my uh . . . my . . ." My mouth droops, like it's melting down my face. "My bag. Is in the front . . . s-seat."

That's all I have the strength for. I think I hear Gareth say, "Okay," but I have no idea.

Night two.

Or, I guess it's night. I can't tell what time it is, thanks to the boarded-up windows. My sleep was grave deep. At some point, I think someone came back to put more wood on the fire. I saw a dark figure cross the room through my half-moon gaze. On their way out, they dropped something at the foot of my cot and took a knee next to me on the floor. Dr. Lacie, probably. Maybe Gareth.

I don't want to think about the other person it might have been.

It takes me a moment to realize someone's here with me, right now. Sitting beside me on the bed. That's what woke me.

"Oh my God, Mia—" A woman's voice.

Her arms stretch toward me as I blink my surroundings into focus.

Cora? It doesn't sound like her. . . .

"I can't believe you're here. I'm so happy to see you."

Kayla.

She fumbles me into a hug. She's thinner, judging by the jut of her cheekbones, and all the pink is gone from her long, dark hair. She wears mismatched winter outerwear, and when she unzips her coat, I spot a holster around her waist. The silver wink of a pistol.

"Is your leg okay? Gareth said you slept all day so that's good."

I hope Gareth's on his way back, right now. I'm starving. Now that I'm awake, I feel that empty churn again with twice the force.

"Y-yeah—" I muster, still gawking at Kayla.

"God, I'm so glad you're all right, you have no idea—"

Of course, she's here. But seeing her still feels incorrect, like when you have a dream you're back in school failing an algebra quiz and you start to panic, till you remember you're an adult now and you wake yourself up.

Kayla helps me sit, propping a pillow behind my back.

I glance down at the foot of the bed and realize my backpack—no, *Cora's* backpack—is waiting for me. I need to sort through it as soon as I'm alone in here. See if anyone confiscated that cup of Daylights.

"I want to hear everything," Kayla says, squeezing into the space next to me.

I have no doubt Devon's put her up to this. She's an effective little postcard from home—I'll give him that. When she speaks, I can almost hear the rhythmic *shhk-shhk* of her cocktail shaker, calling me back to a simpler time.

"Have you seen my friend Cora?" My voice stumbles back to life. "I know she's here." *I can feel she's here,* I almost say. But it seems wrong. Too revealing. "She and I came together. She's about my age with long brown hair, I think she was wearing a green—"

"Sorry. I haven't seen her yet." A benevolent half smile hangs on Kayla's face like a crooked painting.

"When did this happen?" she asks after a moment. Reaching for my hand.

"Uh, last night. Someone shot me at the Walmart."

"I don't mean your leg. I mean—"

"Oh. It was like . . . a little over a month ago?" I stare into the middle distance. "I was working at a Sara center and there was an accident."

"Jesus. Does your mom know?"

My canines squirm inside my gums. "My *mom*?"

She nods, a sweet vacancy in her eyes.

"Kayla, my mom's dead. Didn't Devon tell you?"

"Look . . . I get why you'd want to protect her—"

The puzzle snaps into place.

That's why Devon didn't leave me for dead. Why Kayla's here right now.

"Read my lips. She *died*. Okay?" My frayed voice lodges in my throat. "She was gonna kill my . . . my friend. So I opened the curtains and . . . Look, it was horrible and I don't want to talk about it. Please don't ask me again."

"Wait, really? But Devon said—"

Fuck. I told him something else, didn't I? I'm not thinking straight. Too distracted by my hunger and that fleecy medicinal fog.

"I told him she died from rust poisoning, when she got shot. So he'd feel like it was his fault." That much is true. I pull my good knee to my chest and smother myself against it. "But it was mine."

Kayla places a hand on my back.

"I believe you."

"I don't care if you do."

"No, I mean . . . What you just said about your friend, how she was gonna—" She lets out a breath. "Your mom was . . . she just wasn't who I thought."

All I can do is nod.

"Y'know how it happened, when it happened to me?"

"Devon, I guess? She like, told him where you lived or something?"

"Try again, honey."

My breath catches. "No. That doesn't . . . I mean, you were—" Mom adored Kayla. For years, she was the closest thing she had to a real friend.

"I guess I understand it now. Like, that's what you're *supposed* to do, if you feel close to someone. But . . . at the time? That shit was *deeply* fucked."

I want to kick through that boarded-up window and run till the sun eats me alive.

"She wouldn't have done that to you. I mean, unless someone *told her to*—"

"Who? Devon?" She laughs. "I would've died if it hadn't been for him. She freaked out after she lifted me and left me down in the wine cellar for two whole days. I was trapped in the storage locker, where nobody could hear me. That's the thing that hurts the most. She abandoned me. On the third night, Devon came with Gareth."

I don't say anything. I'm picturing it. It gets so cold down there. She must have been scared out of her damn mind.

"Izzy . . . er, your mom apologized and we tried to patch things up. But it was just like . . ." She shakes her head. "I thought we were friends, you know?"

The stove groans and crackles, filling the emptiness between us.

There's a cramp in my bad leg, but when I try to adjust, I shift the bandage by accident. Pain blossoms across my thigh and I clench a scream between my teeth.

"Oh shit, you okay—?" Kayla helps me lie back down.

"Uh, yeah. I'm just—"

"I'm sorry, Mia. I shouldn't have brought it up."

"It's not that. . . . C-can you go see if Dr. Lacie's around? I need more medicine. And . . . I know you guys are short on bleeders but I could really, *really* use Gareth one more time—"

"Oh my God, of course. Hang tight."

She rushes for the door, summoning her full speed. Shuts it behind her.

Now's my chance: I reach for the backpack at the foot of my bed. Struggling upright with a snarl.

"Ow, ow, ow, *fuck me, ow*—"

It takes me a whole minute to eel toward it. At last, I'm able to grasp the strap between my fingers.

I rip it open and dig through Cora's clothes. To my relief, the treasure is still intact, buried inside the sleeve of her crumpled leather jacket: one crushed paper cup from the movie theater with a dozen Daylights inside. I pull it out and give the stupid thing a kiss. Once I'm strong enough, I can start walking back down that dirt road the way we came. Leave during the day so nobody can chase me. There's hope for me yet, dammit.

The door creaks open, and I shove the cup and dirty clothes

back into the bag. Hurl it underneath the cot. My leg yowls, protesting all the jerky movement, as someone rounds the corner.

Devon is back.

I freeze, like he's just caught me doing . . . what? The Daylights are hidden. All the same, my heart thrashes.

His face is an impassive mask. Far from happy to see me, but he doesn't look upset, either.

"What's up?" There's that shadow smile again.

"Um. Hi," I babble. "Kayla was here. She said she was gonna try to find Gareth and—"

"I just saw her." He plants his feet. Doesn't move toward me.

I swallow. The distance between us is cold and barren.

"You changed your story." He hisses out air when I don't respond. "Night your mom got shot, I took that bullet from her leg within about two minutes. You thought you gave me a plausible explanation. But now you see for yourself: A person in your position—in *her* position—can't die."

At last, he takes a step in my direction.

"That car ride was exhausting. Waiting for you to own up to it."

"Listen, I didn't want to tell you what *really* happened to her because—"

"Because you wanted to make me think *I* killed her? Because talking about it makes you too damn sad?" He smirks. "Little bit of both?"

"*Yes*. Because that's the truth. It doesn't matter *how* it happened, okay?"

"It does, though. Actually it matters a *great fucking deal,* and here's why. Instead of admitting I caught you in a lie, you doubled down. Told another lie. You know who else used to do that?"

He paces in a neat, measured rectangle, waiting for me to answer. But we both know I don't have to.

"I can't let you be a part of this family, I can't *protect you,* if you keep protecting her."

"I'm not. She's *dead*."

I study his dark, bloodshot eyes as they sear mine. I wonder when he last slept, or fed. In that moment, I glimpse his true age. The years of haggard, paranoid ruthlessness.

"I had a long time to think about this, while you were sleeping.

And here's where I'm at." He starts walking the rectangle a second time. "You two were attached at the hip. But now you're separated. Someone lifted you, and it wasn't her. Which tells me something horrible must've happened between the two of you."

"Yeah. She *died*."

"Could you at least dignify this conversation with some fucking creativity?"

I curl my lip, exposing my teeth. As if that could possibly intimidate him.

"I have an idea. But maybe you can help me fill in the blanks. The night of that festival was when the whole thing started. She was pissed I didn't stay with her, after she got shot. She was pissed about a lot of things, by then. At that point, I figure, she decides it's time to rat me out and fakes her death. Meanwhile, *you* . . ." At last, he pulls a breath. "Somehow end up in New York."

"Because I moved there," I retort, colorless.

"Alone." He smiles. "You finally had enough of her and decided to fuck off. Which—hey. Who could blame you, right?"

My breath catches. That "right" hangs between us like the final chord of a song left unresolved. Till he starts pacing again.

"Thing is . . . I know her, which means I know you. There's no way in hell you're not in touch. You're still hiding her. It's what you've always done." At last, he's still. "She had you trained like a dog."

A memory staggers out of the past: Danny stands at Sandy's kitchen counter while the EMTs scrape Paul's curdled remains from the front stoop.

If I'm Devon and I'm desperate to collect a head, I can do those mental gymnastics.

He's so hungry for comeuppance he'd rather weave his own sketchy story than accept what really happened.

I open my mouth to fire back . . . till a thought smothers my words. If he accepts the whole truth, then *I'm* the rat, and I inherit her punishment. My insides torque under his gaze.

Whatever I say next, I need to say it *very* fucking carefully.

"Look, a lot of what you said is true." I finally speak. "About like, what happened after Cloak and Dagger. She was upset. But after she made that call—"

"Mia, you need to tell me where she is. Now." He kneels beside my cot. "You came here because you were in trouble and you knew she couldn't help you. Your own mother. What's that tell you?"

He tries to reach for my hand. I squirm out of range.

"You don't owe her anything. Not after how she treated you."

He's using that placid, still-water voice again. Manufactured reassurance.

"Call the Phoenix Sara center," I say, matching his tone. "They saw what happened to her. They'll tell you."

He stares at me—like he's considering it—then springs to his feet. A jarring tactical switch that punches me off my axis. "Know what, we're done here."

"Wait. No. You have to believe me—"

He laughs. "I don't *have* to do anything."

The air between us festers. I follow his gaze as he peers at my soiled bandage with predatory, catlike detachment. My wound throbs in time with my racing heart.

"Is the doctor coming?" I dare to ask. "Or . . . or Gareth?"

But there's no reply.

He backs away. Slowly, then all at once.

"Shit. Devon, you can't just—"

He lunges for the door. I fight to gather my body upright, but it capsizes to a flaccid heap. "I'm telling you the *fucking truth*, Devon—"

The door slams.

"You can't just *LEAVE ME HERE*—"

But of course he can. And why wouldn't he?

I roll out of bed, landing with a nauseating thud against my bad leg. I steel my ribs and hoist myself onto my opposite hip, dragging my body across the floor using only my arms. I knock into a wall of old skis and daggerlike metal poles. A cruel, comical hailstorm of equipment rains over me as a key groans in the dead bolt.

"No, no, no, *no*—"

My throat burns as I wail, pounding on the door. I hope the whole camp hears. Not like anyone's coming to help me, though. Not if he tells them to cut me off.

I'm dead. Worse than dead. He's just buried me alive.

JANUARY 2024

Lisa commits suicide two weeks after New Year's. A Wednesday night.

I wasn't there. I had a job interview. As if I could have done anything.

Topher is inconsolable. The second-floor mail station explodes with flower arrangements. They announce a memorial service in the chapel over the weekend.

When Mandy tells me what happened, I'm not sure I've heard her correctly. It's damn near impossible for a Sara to take their own life. You're likely to make a full recovery unless you're dealing with sunlight or rust in the bloodstream. But this was something else.

"Alonzo says she ordered these injections online. Some friend-of-a-friend referred her," Mandy whispers as we try to find space for all the condolence florals. "It's got this cocktail of stem cells that disable regeneration so the lethal stuff can take effect. Quick and painless."

"God. Wow."

"There are worse ways to go."

Can't argue with that.

The energy the day after Lisa's death is chaotic, with no discernible schedule. Nobody notices when I slip up to Four to see if Cora's been moved back down to her room. She hasn't posted anything since the night of our encounter, which means she's still upstairs somewhere without a phone. Still, I keep checking, with her book tucked into my tote bag. Ready to return it to her. My plan is to say I found it with her confiscated stuff and tell her how wrong it is for the nurses to go through her belongings like that. I imagine she'll thank me. Introduce herself. Flag me as a person she can trust.

But the door to her dark room hangs open. I don't know where they've taken her. Whether I'll see her again.

In the meantime, I run some light reconnaissance. I need to be ready to connect with my target. I pull up her patient profile on the computer at the center, but volunteers don't have access to any sensitive information. All I can get is a last name, a date of birth, and a YOI—year of infection. Corazón Quinto, born April 11, 1989. Became a Sara in 2010. It's dizzying, how she is technically ten years my senior and yet, I am three years "older."

That night, I Google her—now that I have her full name. There's not much, considering she's been using an alias on social media this whole time. But an archived article from a student-run publication at the Dalton School pulls my attention. I recognize the photo from the shelf in her room: four smiling girls at their high school graduation, tossing their decorated caps in the air as the sun sets over the river behind them. It's a sweet little puff piece about her graduating class, from May of 2007. Cora has a quote in it:

> "I'm really excited to head to Duke this fall—my plan is to work like crazy to get a pre-law fellowship. But I'm going to make sure to keep in touch with everyone no matter what. My friends and I all promised our kids are going to play together someday."

My eyes devour Cora's flushed face in the strawberry-blond sunlight. Her hopeful grin, all teeth and squinty eyes. She never smiles like that in the pictures she posts. There's a prominent dark brown freckle at the corner of her left eye, like a little black jewel. I've never noticed it before. She probably covers it with makeup, or edits it out.

I jot down her quote in my red Moleskine; I've got whole section dedicated to "QT_Core." Though at this point, it's starting to take over the entire journal.

All the residents, even those above Four, are allowed to attend Lisa's memorial on Sunday night. I have a second interview for that server job, but I call in sick and ask to reschedule. I can't afford to miss Cora, if she shows up.

I take a seat toward the back of the sleek, white-walled chapel, waiting for everyone to arrive so I can help Beatrice usher people to their seats. The second-floor residents are the first to arrive, as the first to finish dinner. Feeding always happens in ascending floor order. She won't be with the Fours. Maybe Five? Six? Still, she doesn't show.

Nobody comes down from Nine. I only count seven arriving groups—four of which come with a dedicated regiment of watchful nurses, armed with sedatives.

Shit, maybe she's not coming after all. I feel like an idiot. Should have gone to that interview. March first is in six weeks and I've only got two grand left in my savings account.

I pull Beatrice aside as we head down the aisle, handing out programs.

"How long does it take to pass training for the bloodletting program?"

I never thought I'd ask about this. My blood is my own now, and I wanted to keep it that way. But bloodletters make $250 per pint. That's four times as much as I used to draw for Mom, so I can't do it every night. But that could help bridge the gap in my savings. Till the house sells. Till I figure out what I'm supposed to do with the rest of my life.

"It's a two-day crash course," Beatrice replies, folding a fresh stack of programs. "We could get you the materials this coming week, if you're interested. Do you drink or use any drugs?"

"Um . . . no. Not like, heavily—"

Maybe signing up for this program will help me stay sober.

"No alcohol at all, the week you give blood. Same goes for caffeine."

"Of course."

"See me next week if you want in."

"I do. I already know."

She sniffs, like she's disturbed by my eagerness.

The service is about to begin when, at last, Cora appears in the doorway. I beeline toward her, ready to direct her to an open seat, but the nurse accompanying her—guarding her?—has it covered. She's sluggish and misty-eyed again, like they shot her with another sedative before letting her come down here. I should feel safe. But I just feel sad.

I try to catch her eye, but her woozy gaze wanders. She wears a black turtleneck and slacks, and her hair spills down her back in a limp, messy braid. I spot that little black jewel of a freckle. She's not wearing makeup. And yet, the hollows beneath her tired, red-ringed eyes give her face a different sort of depth. There's a dark, unsteady beauty in her detachment. A prelude to danger.

Lisa dabbled in Buddhism and astrology, but she wasn't what you'd call religious, or even "spiritual." The service is mostly just people standing up to share a few words. There aren't any family members, or friends from her golden years in the theater. It's all residents and staff. A woman plays piano and sings "Send in the Clowns." She forgets the words to the second verse, but I don't think anyone notices. I only know because of Mom.

A surge of emotion takes me by surprise, and I breathe deep to hold it back. I hardly knew Lisa. But this is the only funeral I've been to aside from Gram's, when I was eight years old. I didn't have it in me to organize one for Mom. Didn't think anyone would come. But I never did anything for me, so *I* could say goodbye. Unless you count walking through our house one last time. Taking that phone and sketchbook from her room.

At that moment, Cora's vacant gaze sweeps across the crowd and lands on me. My lungs harden as I try to draw air. The corners of my mouth bend into a smile. But she doesn't smile back.

It's a long, quiet night at the center. A few residents gather in the courtyard for a smoke, deep in a sea of private whispers. Topher goes to his room and shuts the door.

I perch at the volunteer desk beside the nurses' station, eavesdropping on a conversation between Beatrice and two night shift nurses.

". . . If it's a safety issue, then we have to—"

"Obviously it's more complicated than that," Beatrice scoffs. "If it doesn't concern *our* safety—"

The second nurse interjects, "I just think . . . we have a responsibility to—"

Beatrice lowers her voice, making it harder for me to hear. I make a show of rearranging the florals lining the hallway so I can hover a little closer. Start picking out the dead stems.

"The board's gonna meet tomorrow," Beatrice says. "But I wouldn't count on anything changing. We don't open mail. If we started doing that, and people talked—"

"Isn't it worse if our residents are *killing themselves*?" the first nurse snaps.

I twirl a wilted yellow lily between my fingers as my mind circles the conversation. Inspecting the mail could accelerate the FBI's investigation—a welcome side effect of saving Saras from themselves. But ADAPT would get wise to it fast, if they've got eyes here. And I'm sure they do.

As I stare at the flower in my hand, an image blinks from the corner of my memory—a vase of dead yellow lilies on Cora's nightstand.

Nobody needs to inspect the mail if gifts from ADAPT are hiding in plain sight.

There are cards taped to most of these condolence arrangements. Many unopened. The staff figured—and so did I—that they were all from Topher's followers because they all came in after he posted about Lisa's passing. We didn't distribute them to any other residents.

I scan the hall to make sure nobody's watching and tear open the miniature envelope attached to the yellow lilies. *Dear Topher—May her memory be a blessing.*

Fine. Not that one. But there are at least fifty more of them all over the second floor.

As I inspect the arrangements outside the chapel, a quiet voice snares my attention.

"Hey there."

"Oh um . . . hi, Franklin." There's a thorny feeling at the back of my neck as he forces my gaze to his. I redirect my eyes to the flowers, fighting the urge to ask any questions that might lead to a longer interaction.

I'm getting better at swimming upstream through the pheromones. Just takes practice. It's still freakishly disorienting, though.

"Thanks for being with us tonight," he goes on. "It's cool that you're here so often. Like, you really seem to care. We don't get that a lot."

"I mean . . . I'm happy to—"

"I guess, if you don't mind my asking . . . I was wondering *why*?"

"Why what?"

"I just mean, during Lisa's service, I kept looking over at you and thinking . . . God, she's so cute and so cool, like, she could be anywhere tonight, but she's *here*."

"I'm just trying to give back," I stammer. Desperate to return to my task.

"Are you doing community service like Mandy?" God, he's being nosy. Am I not sending strong enough cues?

"No. Nothing like that."

He closes the distance between us and expels a breath, running an anxious hand through his curls. His sudden nervousness disarms me.

"Sorry. I didn't mean to—"

"My mom was a Sara," I blurt. How the hell did he pull that from my mouth? "I guess I just . . . yeah. That's what I mean, when I say I want to give back."

"She *was*? You mean she's . . ."

"She passed away last year."

"That's awful. Shit, okay. I won't ask again. I'm really sorry—" He backs away, releasing me at last from his psychic grip.

"Um, it's okay—"

"I'm sure tonight was hard for you. I'll give you some time alone."

"Yeah. Thank you."

"If there's ever anything you need . . . you know where to find me." He smiles. My face is a sheet of ice.

When he realizes I'm not going to say anything else, he turns back toward his room. I unclench my shoulders and rub the back of my neck, like I can still feel it prickling.

Back in Tucson, before I met Jade, I kept to myself. I never gave men the opportunity to pay me unwanted attention. I stonewalled any guy who looked like he might approach me. I don't know what to say to Franklin. "Thank you"? That feels wrong. But so does telling him off. It's not like he said anything vulgar. In fact, aside from asking me to dance at New Year's and mentioning I was "cute and cool" just now, one could argue he's just being friendly. Next time he tries to chat me up, I'll let him down easy by insinuating I'm not interested in guys and that will be the end of it.

There's a cube-shaped vase of understated lavender mums on the table. I can't seem to find a card at first. It's lost somewhere among the stems. I tweezer it out between my fingers—and my throat slams shut.

It says "Cora Quinto" on the envelope. My hands tremble as I peel it open. *Core—Be strong. We'll be together soon.—D*

I forget to breathe.

A hundred competing thoughts volley across my mind as I whisk the vase off the table. Shove the card into the pocket of my jeans.

We'll be together soon. Is this person coming here? Or does she have plans to go to them? How soon is soon?

Should I report this? Would anyone else think it's significant?

. . . What does "D" stand for? I know what I *want* it to stand for . . .

But something feels off, when I imagine it. The person I know— the person I *think* I know—wouldn't send a gift like this. I need more information.

I remember what Danny said about the arrangement ADAPT sent to Phoenix, which included instructions for how to escape. But there's only one card. Nothing special about it. Unless it's been written in some kind of code. But I don't think so.

I place the flowers on the volunteer desk. When Cora comes back to her room, I'll deliver them upstairs with her book. But I keep the card in my pocket.

I race home at the first hint of sunlight, hungry to call the flower shop listed on the back of the card. I hit record on the conversation as I listen to the other line ring.

"Good morning, Bloomstead."

"Hi, I work at Saratov Salvation of Manhattan and we had a delivery yesterday for a resident named Cora Quinto? They were these really beautiful purple mums. Problem is, the card fell off, and she has no idea who they're from. Can you help me?"

"Sure, let's see . . . I can pull up the file for the greeting here," a chirpy young woman responds. "It said, 'Core, be strong. We'll be together soon. D.'"

"Right but . . . do you have a *name*? She doesn't know who that is."

"Well, she ought to, if they're supposed to be together soon," the woman chuckles. I don't indulge her.

"Maybe there's a name on the credit card. Would you mind checking?"

The woman sighs into the phone, followed by the irritated clack of a keyboard.

"So, there's no name on the credit card. This is actually one of those—"

"Prepaid gift cards." I bite down on the pen I'm holding.

"Yeah! How'd you—"

"Thanks for your help."

I toss and turn all morning, intermittently checking my socials to see if Cora's posted anything. She was well behaved at the service last night. They might move her soon. But nothing pops up.

The person who *has* posted a lot is Jade. She's got a new set of tour dates.

I realize I haven't thought about her all week.

I wait for that all-consuming rush of reluctant emotion as I stare at her photo. But it doesn't come. I push the screen against my nose, so close her smiling face becomes partitioned into a thousand, tiny pixelated boxes. Still. Nothing. Only the dull ache of phantom pain; the quiet knowledge of a feeling that's flown.

☾ ☾ ☾

I head back to the center earlier than usual to train for the bloodletting program.

They upgrade my badge; regular volunteers can't access the kitchen. Every day at five, about a hundred people queue up at a private entrance around the corner from the lobby, where the kitchen is. Residents and bloodletters are forbidden to interact during dinner, and you can't leave the kitchen till everyone's fed. Every couple of minutes, the nurses divide the fresh blood into individual cups and send it up to Two in a heated dumbwaiter. The dining room is directly above us.

When the nurse fits me with my needle for the first time, a wave of sweet calm washes over me. I wasn't expecting this. The other rookie bloodletters tap their jittery feet, distractedly scrolling their phones or thumbing through magazines. I go slack in my chair as dopamine twinkles in my veins. I hate how good it feels. I try to think about that two-fifty.

By the time Cora starts posting again, the flowers are dead. Someone throws them away.

Thankfully, I've kept the card. I buy two dozen purple mums and spend way too much money having the florist arrange them just so.

I take the flowers and *Origin of Species* upstairs with the post-dinner mailroom packages. Adrenaline rockets through me as I grip my cart with slippery hands.

Her door is closed. I knock, but there's no answer. If a resident is asleep when their package comes, I just leave it at their doorstep. But that's not why I'm here. I knock again, louder.

At last, there's movement on the other side. I press the vase against my sternum, as though it will muffle my pounding heart.

She opens the door wearing gray sweatpants and a rumpled blue button-down, face halfway made up with her hair in rollers. Before I can speak or offer her the flowers, she scowls with a flash of teeth.

"You were in my fucking room."

I draw back from her. Slowly. Nearly dropping the vase. "I'm sorry, I don't know what you're—"

"I *smelled* you. You came in and you went through my shit."

I can't hide the way I'm shuddering. "I didn't . . . Alonzo asked me to . . . Look, I'm sorry—"

"Are those for me?" Her fiery gaze flicks to the flowers. I release a breath and thrust them toward her.

"Yes! Yeah. Here ya go—"

She spins back toward her room without so much as a grunt of thanks.

"Wait! Er . . . sorry—"

She cranes her neck, slashing me with the corner of her eye.

"Someone took this out of your room that day and I found it and I thought . . . maybe you'd want it back?"

I offer her the book: an explosive olive branch.

She scans the hall for watchful eyes before she snags it from me.

"It's definitely like, an invasion of privacy for them to take stuff from your room," I start blathering. "If I were you, I'd be—"

A brazen, wolf-white smile spreads across her face. As if she's trying to scare me or something. I realize she's staring at my hands.

"What're you so nervous about?" she asks.

I didn't notice before, and I don't know how long I've been doing it. But I've been biting my nails again. Half my cuticles are inflamed. Red with faint whispers of blood.

My eyes float to hers. Or maybe she's pulled them there.

Her gaze prods me, like she's telling me to come a little closer. And I do.

She quirks her head. A quiet snicker on her lips. "You should really be more careful."

She spins and shuts the door. Like a slap across the face.

My feet fuse to the ground as I shed her spell and the unstable air settles. For the first time, doubt creeps in. This feels incorrect. Unsafe. *She* feels unsafe. But I knew that. I'm not stupid. That's just how she makes me feel.

I rush to the staff restroom and wash my hands with soap and scalding hot water. Swaddle my shredded fingers with Band-Aids.

I don't know what to do, now that I've given her the book and the flowers. I'm all out of inroads. And yet, I keep showing up. The ball's in her court, after all. If I stop coming, I might give up the same day she decides I'm more than just a squirrelly volunteer with a nail-biting problem.

February shambles in, sullen and gray. Every day is the same. Sandy and I text each other good morning. I check my email for a job offer that doesn't come. And then I head to the Sara center. I'm trying to give blood as often as I can now, praying I can stretch my savings another couple of months and make rent. One night, when I head upstairs after the dinner draw, Beatrice pulls me aside to inform me that, per the board, we have begun opening residents' mail.

"You're only gonna open a package if you can't confirm the return address." She walks me through the new procedure, brusque as usual, halfway through the door to the stairwell. "The box those Saranasia shots came in didn't have a return address, so nobody logged it. We can't have that happen again."

Because they care about the residents' well-being? Or the center's reputation? I stare at her back as she marches down the stairs in her kitten heels, all business. Pretty sure I know the answer.

My nighttime duties, aside from sorting late package deliveries, consist of evening visitor registration and keeping the common rooms orderly. When Beatrice and Alonzo don't have a specific assignment for me, I'm in the library, reorganizing the center's collection by genre. The room is usually empty. Most people here just order what they want online or read on their devices, if they read at all. But there are a few residents who enjoy the library's quiet ambience. Lisa was one of them. I want to keep it nice.

I'm alone, sitting on the floor alphabetizing the memoirs, when the door whispers open. Before I can raise my head to see who it is, Cora's standing beside me. My body crackles with gooseflesh as I meet her eye.

"Hi." She's expressionless. Monotone. I almost wonder if she's been sedated again, but she just moved so fast.

"Um . . . hey. How're you—"

"Ingrid said you'd be in here."

"Yeah I'm just shelving all the . . . I used to work in a bookstore—"

"I'm Cora. But you knew that." Her shadow looms over me. I want to stand, but her gravity keeps me beneath her. "What's your name?"

"Mia?" Like all of a sudden I'm not sure.

"Okay, Mia. I need your help with something. You seem cool. Are you cool?"

"I-I think I'm . . . yeah. What do you—?"

"My birthday's coming up on Friday."

No, it's not. Friday is February ninth. Her birthday isn't until April.

"Oh, that's great. Happy—"

"My boyfriend sent me a special present. It's *private*. Do you get what I mean when I say private?"

"Sure." I shape the words, but my mind sprints away. Boyfriend. The person who sent her those flowers?

"They're opening our fucking mail now because of Lisa." At last, there's some musicality in her voice. But her phrasing is still sharp. Truncated. "I'll be so embarrassed if anyone sees what he sent me. These assholes are bad enough. I'm sure you've heard the shit people say about me."

"People don't gossip as much as you think."

"That's nice of you. You're wrong. But still. You're probably the nicest person who's ever worked here."

"Thanks?"

"If you get any mail for me, between now and my birthday, I need you to take it straight upstairs and not open it." Then she adds, "Please."

"I'm not here all the time, y'know—"

"True. But it's better than nothing." She bends to my level. Her gossamer whisper is like spider's silk, holding me captive. "And if I find out you told anyone . . . I promise I'm *really* gonna give you something to be nervous about."

She whisks out the door, quick as she came. Ending the conversation fast and on her terms. Mom and Devon both used to do that.

I slump against the wall and catch my breath. She wouldn't threaten me if this weren't a big deal. Wouldn't risk *involving* me at all. Whatever's in that package, she's desperate enough to ask a stranger to break the rules for her. Granted, she saw me break the rules first, when I handed that book to her. Both of us knew what it meant. The cipher buried in that title. I stagger to my feet, buzzing with smug exhilaration. I can't believe it. I got her. She's *mine*.

I can't keep spinning off into her vertigo, though. Not if we're going to do this. I need to get stronger, maybe come up with some sort of mnemonic device whenever she's around.

I seed my plan as I finish alphabetizing the memoirs. It's physically impossible for me to be here all the time, not if I want to sleep, but I can be here when the mail arrives. That means taking all the daytime shifts starting at 9 A.M., plus early evenings. It's a lot, but it's only till Friday. Only till that package comes—and I find out what's in it.

That night, my sleep swarms with flashes of amber flesh through a veil of red lace. A shining black jewel pulses in the sky like a cruel, dead sun. Pulsing. Pulsing. I swim through a sea of sweat and come back to my shivering body. Lie awake till morning comes.

Thursday is a bloodletting day for me. It is also the day Cora's present arrives with the afternoon mail.

Manic elation cuts the fog of my sleeplessness. It's been a grueling week, but it's all been worth it. I tuck the padded manila envelope between two larger packages on my mail cart. Mandy is over at the nurses' station talking to Alonzo. I don't think she saw me add this one to the pile. Didn't notice I left it unlogged.

The envelope, predictably, has no return address.

I'll wait till it's time to do the delivery and slip it into my shirt once I'm alone in the elevator.

I lean back and reward myself with a grin. Sneaking around gave me no pleasure back when I was living with Mom. But maybe that's because I knew, even then, that I was good at it—just like she was. A wicked birthright I didn't want to acknowledge.

A visitor steps off the lobby elevator and I wheel my chair across the bullpen to sign him in. We exchange the usual pleasantries.

When I spin back to face the mail cart, it's gone.

Mandy, too.

I spot her a dozen paces down the hall, pushing it toward the elevator.

I stifle a gasp and scramble in her direction, nearly tripping on one of those priceless Persian runners.

She shoots me a puzzled glance as the elevator arrives and we both step inside.

"I thought you were doing visitors."

"It's pretty dead. Figured I'd give you a hand."

Silence rankles as we ride up to Four. I eyeball the padded envelope with sniper-like intensity. God dammit, there's no way I'm going to be able to grab it. The best I can do is get it to Cora and try to look at it later.

The elevator bounces to a halt, and Mandy hip-checks the cart into the fourth-floor atrium. I scoop an armful of packages—including Cora's envelope—from the top of the pile.

"I got these."

Mandy clears her throat. "Oh uh, thanks."

It's weird, what I'm doing. We both know she's perfectly capable of delivering everything on her own. I hold my breath and scurry toward Cora's door before Mandy can say anything else.

At least today is a blood day. I'll make sure to feed in the first group so I'm done by the time the Fours go to dinner, allowing me a few precious minutes to enter Cora's room. I'll use the restroom, then sneak upstairs via the private stairwell. Of course, I'll have to disguise my smell. Maybe I'll run out on my break and swing by the nearest Sephora. Grab some sort of perfume. It might not work, but improvising is my only option now.

I knock on Cora's door, keeping Mandy in my periphery as she deposits a box outside Ingrid's apartment at the opposite end of the hall. As I wait for Cora to answer, my mind chews the mantra I came up with to stay out of her gravity: that quote from her high school newspaper. Something to remind me she's just an ordinary girl who lost everything.

I'm really excited to head to Duke this fall—my plan is to work like crazy to get a pre-law fellowship . . .

I knock a second time when there's no response. Hoping she'll realize it's me. She flings the door open, prancing on her tiptoes. Wearing a smile like the one in her graduation photo, all ebullient teeth and crinkled eyes.

I'm really excited to head to Duke this fall—my plan is to—

"Oh my God, it came—"

"Shhh . . ." I tuck the envelope into her waiting arms.

"Thank you so much. Holy shit. You have no idea what this means to me."

—work like crazy to get a—

I wait for that abrupt pivot, heralding the end of our conversation. The slam of her door. But she's still standing there looking at me.

—pre-law fellowship.

"This is weird, but can I hug you? I know you're not supposed to. But—"

Her gaze pleads, so vulnerable and earnest. Like the girl in the white dress on New Year's. God, when was the last time someone gave her a hug?

My friends and I all promised . . .

"I really can't . . ." And yet, my feet shuffle forward. Into the rose-tinted haze.

My friends and I . . .

She stretches toward me and my breath seizes. What the hell am I doing? I can't let this happen. I can't—

No matter what . . .

Mandy's clogs squeak across the linoleum, parting the clouds. I withdraw as her gaze comes to rest on the two of us.

"Sorry," Cora mumbles.

"No, it's okay—"

"Thanks again."

Slam. Door in my face. My heart deflates as I trail Mandy back to the elevator.

The hour approaches. Dinnertime. I make sure to line up early so I'm in the group feeding the residents on Two. I absently study a centipede of traffic as it inches up Eleventh Avenue, trying to concentrate on my new plan. But Cheryl's wound up right behind me in the queue, and she's *chatty* tonight.

"I just don't know what to do anymore. He was *never* like this," she sputters, to anyone who will listen. I'm just the closest set of ears. "He's lost in his phone, doesn't even acknowledge me when I come to visit—"

"I mean, he's technically working, right?" I'd rather have a hundred needles lodged in my skin like a porcupine than stand here in the cold talking about Franklin. A nurse opens the door and ushers us into the kitchen. Cheryl keeps rambling, a nails-on-a-chalkboard counterpoint to our footsteps.

"But he's been doing that for years. Something's changed."

"I'm sorry. That sounds hard." I have experience with this type of distant, textbook empathy because of Mom. Usually that was all she needed to hear if she was spiraling. She just wanted validation. But it doesn't seem to placate Cheryl.

She plops down in the chair beside me, offering her forearm to the phlebotomist.

"What's he like, when I'm not here?"

"Um . . . He's nice. Says hello to everyone. Seems happy."

"He's not like that at all, when I'm around. Do you know what he said to me last night?"

The phlebotomist cinches my tourniquet and sticks me. I flinch, which Cheryl takes as a cue to continue.

"He told me to stop coming at dinner because my blood tastes like an old woman's sandy, dried-up . . ." She glances over her shoulder, scandalized, and whispers, "*P-word.*"

I try not to laugh. "That's . . . rude of him."

Tears rise in her eyes. Dammit, we're here for another three minutes.

I didn't realize you could taste the difference between people, unless someone had caffeine, drugs, or alcohol in their system. I always figured blood was just blood. But everyone's working with different chemicals and cell counts. Some bodies might be more compatible than others. I never thought of it that way.

"I wouldn't take it personally," I say after a moment. "He's probably just bored of the same thing."

Cheryl groans, ushering in the sniffles. Not sure why I thought that was the right thing to say. It probably wouldn't have worked on Mom, either.

"He loves you, you're his mom. That'll never change."

"You'd think that." She dries her dinner roll cheeks with her free hand. "People dump their kids at places like this all the time. I promised it would never be like that, between us. But if he keeps pushing me away—"

"I'm sorry. That sounds hard."

She narrows her eyes. Oh. I already said that, didn't I?

At last, the timer pings, and the first wave of bloodletters stand. I split as fast as I can, leaving Cheryl to unload on someone else.

We're all supposed to hang out in here till every floor has fed. We sip juice and eat cookies, watching videos on our phones or reading magazines. Bathroom breaks are permitted, though. We have a secure, adjoining restroom right outside the door.

I use my badge to scan into the bathroom, and nobody bats an eyelash. But when I'm done, I don't go back to the kitchen. I tiptoe into the hallway, toward the locked staircase that leads to the second floor.

I'm not sure how long it will take them to notice my absence. And I'll probably get fired if I'm caught in Cora's room. Can you fire a volunteer? Same difference, I guess. Badge revoked. Persona non grata.

I hesitate on the bottom stair before I ascend.

This is what I came for, isn't it?

I creep out onto Two and cross the empty hall to a second, separate stairwell that leads to the upper residences. I don't want to make any noise, so I let the door come to rest, gently, against the latch as I patter upstairs. Driven by my racing pulse.

There's no staff up on Four during dinner. It's all hands on deck while the Saras feed. I have somewhere between ten and twelve minutes till everyone starts heading back up.

As I make my way out of the stairwell, there's a faint tapping sound at my back. I turn, scanning the dimly lit staircase below. But I'm alone.

I can't stall. Every second counts. I have no idea where Cora might have put her gift, or if I'll know what it is, now that she's opened it. I dig into my pocket and fish out the rollerball of rose oil I bought during my break. I apply two dabs to both my wrists and check my cuticles for traces of blood. I've taken great pains to avoid biting my nails this week.

As I sail toward Cora's room, I'm suddenly aware I didn't hear the stairwell door close behind me. I'd let it fall instead of resting it against the latch, thinking it would click shut on its own. I pause in Cora's open doorway. Peer over my shoulder.

Franklin is right behind me. Two inches from my face.

"Hey!"

What the hell is he doing on Four? It's not like residents from the lower floors don't come up here, but everyone's at dinner. There's nobody to visit.

Except me.

"Mia?" He leans in, and I recoil. Stepping backward into Cora's room.

"Um . . . hi. Aren't you supposed to be—?"

"Aren't *you* supposed to be? Down in the kitchen?" He fixes me with a surreptitious smile. "Why do you smell like that?"

"Like what?"

"Never mind. It's nice." I try to inch past him, back the way I came, but he blocks me. "Listen, it's been hard to find a second to talk to you alone so I thought this could be a good time to . . . uh—"

There he is again, nervously running his hand through his curls to disarm me. But it's not going to work this time. He needs to fucking leave. Now.

"Franklin, I'm sorry. I'm kind of up here on some official business and—"

"Just hear me out, Mia. I'm not stupid, and you're not either. There's . . . well, there's a vibe here. Isn't there?" He stirs the air between us with his hand. Smiles when I don't reply, as if I'm agreeing with him. "I want to figure out if we can like . . . make an arrangement. I gotta double-check all the rules, but—"

"Sorry, I-I don't know what you're—"

I realize, too late, that I've wedged myself into the corner of Cora's room, between the foot of her bed and the dresser. "We should go. We're not supposed to be in here."

"No, we're not." He reaches out for me, a furtive glint in his eye. His grip on my shoulders is tentative, but powerful all the same. Combustible electricity thrums from his hands.

Fuck.

"They let you designate your blood for someone, if you sign some papers." His voice shrinks to a whisper as he chews his lip. "But it has to come from you. I can't ask for it. You see what I'm getting at?"

"So that's . . . the arrangement."

He nods. "I promise, it doesn't have to be weird. Like, I figured we could start there and then . . . see how we feel about things?"

He slides his hands down my arms to braid his fingers with mine. White-hot dread tears through my veins as I try—and fail—to shake him off.

"I'm on Two, so it's cool if I have visitors who—"

"Listen, Franklin. I think you have the wrong idea. About this . . . *vibe*. Between us. I like girls. I'm sorry."

I hold my breath as my eyes rake over him for a reaction.

He loosens his grip, and my entire body sighs with relief.

"Oh . . . shit—"

"It's okay—"

"No, I feel stupid."

"Don't. You couldn't have known."

Finally, he releases me. "I mean we could still . . . *you* could still give me your—"

"I don't think that's a good idea, Franklin." I try to keep my tone as even as possible. Like an authoritative kindergarten teacher. "C'mon, we should go back downstairs."

After a moment, he nods. Politely moves aside to let me pass without looking at me.

I wince as I shuffle toward the door, clenching my fists. Cora will be back in five minutes, maybe less. I don't have time to look for the package. So much burned-out, wasted buildup, all because of—

In one heart-wrenching, supersonic movement, he's on me. All around me, *in* me. He snags my shirt, reels me in, and plunges his teeth into the back of my neck, where my spine meets my skull. His canines scrape bone, and yes, I feel it . . . but it doesn't *hurt*. Not the way it should. In fact, I'm not even fully aware of what's happened till I feel the river of blood pouring down my shirt.

A scream stands ready to burst from my open mouth. But the horrible speed of the attack outpaces my simple, defenseless reality. Suddenly, I'm on the ground. Time flattens, then curls tight like a snake.

Franklin turns me over and bites again, piercing the hollow at the bottom of my throat.

I can't just let this . . . No.

Stop. Get up. Scream.

Where is my scream? Where, where, *where*?

Where am I?

I have the alien sensation my entire body is a huge, ancient drum: nothing but dead skin stretched across an endless echo chamber. No sense of self but the distant flail of my heart.

He pulls from one of my wrists, then the other. Little more than a kiss. A quick, sweet death for a sweet, dumb girl.

The room kaleidoscopes around me in flashes of ocher and magenta and peacock blue. Fourth of July fireworks. Lipstick on a coffee cup. The eyes of a girl whose name I can't remember anymore.

There's a great black wave building and building, crashing through the doorway, filling the room like the cargo of a sinking ship. No . . . not water. A shadow. Two?

Just one. There's only ever been one.

My body aches to submit to her. To let her drag me to the dark side of the moon.

The shadow becomes a tree. Becomes a branch, becomes a hand made of brittle black glass. A filament-thin, insistent finger hooks me like a fish.

Please, please, please, don't tell my mommy.

She'll be so mad. Please don't—

At last, a scream.

But not mine.

In an instant, the weight of him is gone.

Someone howls. The room shakes and shattered plaster rains down on me.

"What the fuck are you doing in my *fucking room*?"

A girl. There's a girl here.

I lurch an eye half open. Feel like I should know who I'm looking at, but I don't recognize either of the figures looming over me.

The girl pulls the red-mouthed boy to the floor in a blood-slick choke hold. His frantic shoes scuff black gashes all over the linoleum.

She bashes his skull. Once, twice, three times. "Get. The fuck. *Off her*—"

The glass shadow returns. Kisses my eyelids shut. Cold and

smooth, like a tongue of ice. She scrawls a message across my skin: *Someone's been waiting for you.* Yes. I'm ready. I'm

No.

No, no, no.

This is wrong.

I am warm and I should not be warm I was supposed to be cold. I was—

A wrist bears down on my wilted lips. My pulse rallies, called up by the warm drink. There's no taste, just heat. My mouth is on fire. Burning, burning, all the way down.

My eyes slide open. Someone's hovering over me, but I can't make sense of a face. There's a faint murmur of roses in the air. I can hear the way they smell.

My vision grays out, hazy and fragmented, as the lights blink on. The boiling cup of life leaves my lips. Whoever's beside me melts away as footsteps assault the room, pouring in from all sides and the ceiling, too.

Arms lift me off the ground. I feel threads come loose inside me: a thousand taut strings rupturing, one by one.

Gray flashes to unsteady, trembling white. Implosion imminent. Death of a universe.

Or the start of one.

Someone I loved once gave me
a box full of darkness.
It took me years to understand
that this, too, was a gift.

—Mary Oliver,
"The Uses of Sorrow *(In my sleep I dreamed this poem)*"

FEBRUARY 2024

"I'm looking for my daughter. Please, ma'am, can you help me find my daughter?"

The room is full of people but no one answers.

I try to stand but they've tied down my legs. No, no, no . . . I can't go, not without my daughter. They can't take me. I promised her I'd come back. She's downstairs drinking chocolate milk.

"Mia! Where did you take Mia—"

Wait. We told them a different name, at the front desk. What was it . . .

Who are we?

What's *my* name?

Something's in my eye. Thick and heavy. God, it stings. Can't see a thing.

"You have to let me say goodbye, where is she?"

Downstairs drinking chocolate milk.

I'm upstairs and they're going to kill me.

Downstairs . . . drinking chocolate milk . . .

Drinking chocolate milk.

The thick stuff spills down my face. My tongue reaches for a taste.

No. Bad, bad, bad. Hot, bitter mire in my mouth.

Bad blood.

"Mia?"

☾ ☾ ☾

They take the straps off my legs too soon and I kick two holes in the wall. I only vaguely remember doing it. And I'm not sure why. I think I wanted to run. Not *away,* though. I know I'm safe. Being fed. They must be used to all the wall-kicking nonsense; my foot collides with a steel plate underneath the plaster.

I still don't know who did this. Even though I'm starting to re-member how it happened.

I wish it had been Mom.

I can't speak yet, but I can cry. That's what I cry about the most.

Someone's been sitting next to me. There's too much blood in my eyes so I can't see who it is. But there's an angelic rosewater haze in the air.

Cora starts asking me questions. I still can't talk. I want to, but I'm not capable—like my brain's still building bridges to all the different parts of my body. Sometimes my whole skull has goose bumps—especially after I eat.

"Is there someone we should call? You said something about your daughter?"

I shake my head with a weak grunt. A little embarrassed. Guess I *was* speaking, at some point. When I was halfway out the door of my old life.

I slurp from the plastic cup I'm holding till it's empty, disgusted with myself. Crumple it in my fist. Cora gently pries it from my tight fingers.

"When you're ready, I'll make sure they give you your phone so you can get in touch with everybody. Okay?"

I nod. Grateful I can't speak so I don't have to tell her the truth. Nobody's waiting to hear from me.

Well . . . that's not entirely true. I've missed my morning check-in with Sandy now three days in a row. I imagine the terror and dismay in her voice, when I finally tell her. How could I even begin to explain, when she asks how it happened? Maybe it's better to disappear. After all, that's how it goes. When you move into a Sara center.

I haven't asked, because I already know. I'm going to live here now.

This is the seventh floor. Cora has temporarily moved into my room, stationed on an air mattress next to my bed. It's day four and I'm still not talking. I know that's bad. Mom had all her facul-ties back after about forty-eight hours, and she didn't have a whole squad of doctors fussing over her. Just Devon and *Beauty and the Beast*. Cora says she'll keep talking to me till I start talking back. She sits on my bed, brushing the tangles out of my wet hair. I just had my first shower. It was a long one.

I can't remember the last time someone brushed my hair. Mom, probably. With a purple bottle of that Aussie detangling spray that smelled like berries. Sitting on the living room carpet watching cartoons, at the old house in Salt Lake City . . .

"Seven's actually a pretty decent floor because it's mostly people like you. People in recovery who got hurt," Cora says as she pulls the brush across my scalp. "Sometimes if you're in really bad shape, they'll let you have two dinners. We should ask them, tomorrow."

I nod with a sleepy half-smile.

"I lived up here for a few weeks last year, after I had a little rust incident. It was dumb, I did it to myself. Anyway." She deflects, turning me to face her. "Which side do you part your hair on? Or do you like it in the middle?"

I point to the left hand side and she gets to work. I can't help but think back on the day Jade came to visit me at work and I let her braid my hair. How it was the most breathtaking, dangerous thing. How danger has changed me, forever.

"By the way, you should know," Cora whispers. "Franklin's up on Eight, and he's gonna fucking stay there. You should ask for his room, once you're feeling better. There's a wait list for Two, but they owe you."

She picks up the remote and turns on the TV. "You wanna watch something?"

"Why isn't he on Nine?" The words erupt from my lips. I am reborn.

Cora squeals and wraps me into her arms: our first legal embrace.

"There she is! Hell yeah—" She rubs my shoulders, careful to avoid the lesions on my arms. I'm elated I've done something to make her smile. But she hasn't answered my question.

"Franklin should be up on Nine, right? For what he did?" I carefully shape my speech, loosening my viselike jaw. "Isn't that like . . . maximum security?" I don't know if this is actually true. It's just what I always assumed.

"Er . . . nah, they wouldn't have put him on Nine." Cora withdraws from the hug with pursed lips. "That's not really how it works."

"So then who lives up there?"

She takes a moment before answering.

"Kids. The kids live on Nine."

"There are *kids* here?" I close the distance between us. "How come I never saw them?"

Cora laughs darkly. "You ever see a toddler throw an absolute shit fit at the grocery store 'cuz her mom won't buy her a cookie?"

I nod.

"Imagine that kid is strong enough to snap your neck."

I let her words sink in. She stands and starts tidying her side of the room. She's strewn dirty clothes everywhere. A well-meaning but messy guest.

"Why didn't anyone tell me?"

"Volunteers don't interact with the kids, so I guess everyone figures it's better to keep it quiet? Plus, I mean . . . It's *really* depressing."

My weak, half-mended mind whirrs.

"You can meet them, though. If you ever feel like it. I go up there to babysit whenever the nurses need a break. I used to nanny, back when I was in college. I knew like, CPR and all that stuff. Not like Sara kids need CPR, though. All they ask is that I know my Pokémon." She offers a half-hearted laugh.

So *that's* why she's up on Nine so often. God, there's so much I want to ask her. She's finally turning her pages for me, but she's doing it too fast. I barely have time to skim the words.

At that moment, her smile flatlines.

"Now that you're talking again, I need to ask you a question." She lowers her voice and sits down beside me. "Actually, it's three questions."

"Okay?"

"First off . . . Are you upset? About what I did?"

I meet her eye as the truth shines down on me. Emotion sticks in my throat.

It wasn't Franklin. It was *her*.

Thank God, thank *God*.

"I tried to ask you if it was okay," she spills, like she's dreading my answer. "But you didn't say anything. You were already dead. And I just, I couldn't—"

"I'm not upset," I finally whisper. "You saved my life."

"Good. Okay."

Silence swells between us. I cough and shake my gaze away, like I'm afraid I'll burst into tears if we keep talking about this.

"What's the second question?"

"Well, it's not a question, really. I need you to keep this between us. I told Alonzo Franklin did it."

"But you saved me."

"They don't care. You get punished for lifting same way you do for drinking."

I nod with a queasy frown. "I promise, I won't tell anyone."

"Okay. Number three. And this one *is* a question."

"Shoot."

"What were you and Franklin doing in my room?"

The temperature between us plummets.

"Well . . . Y'know, the truth is—"

My brain isn't ready for this. I fight to recall how it all happened. What led to that moment. Her birthday—*not* her birthday. The package. The boyfriend.

My mission's off the rails forever. I know that much. But I have to keep my secret if I want to keep her.

"Franklin uh . . . he knew we were becoming friends. He lied and told me you were in trouble. Told me to come upstairs."

"But you were in the kitchen."

"I left to go to the bathroom."

Her stony gaze relaxes. Slowly.

"You broke the rules to check on me."

I nod. She sighs and pats my bare leg. Her metallic manicure glitters in the lamplight as she kneads my skin—tentative, like gentle cat claws. Warmth blooms across my chest.

"Shit," she says.

"Yeah."

A lawyer calls me the next day. Someone who works with the residents pro bono. It's not like *being a Sara* is a crime, he explains.

It's everything Saras do in order to survive. Causing bodily harm to source blood. Trying to bypass a scanner and enter a business. I haven't done any of those things—yet. But I *am* on the registry. The center already knows I'm a Sara. Living free only works if nobody knows who you are.

I already knew this, because of Mom. But I never fully recognized the ingenuity of her survival till this moment. We didn't think about how impossible it was—we just did it. But maybe that's how it seemed to me. I wasn't the one who had to hide who they really were.

The lawyer says I don't have any grounds to sue because I signed that waiver when I first started volunteering. I'll never sign another one of those things again as long as I live.

The center's going to make things nice for me, though. So nice. Yes, of *course* I can have a room on Two. Oh, and I'll have access to all the latest medical trials. I'll have friends. A community. Isn't that so much better than survival on the outside?

Later that day, there's an email from Sabrina after a month and change of silence. We finally have a teardown offer on the house. Eighty-five thousand, cash, from some corporate flipper.

She apologizes for the disappointing news. "I wish things had turned out better."

If she only knew.

After I sign the paperwork she sends me, I order a present for Cora: a buttery brown leather jacket from Neiman Marcus. I imagine her wearing it outside on a sunny spring afternoon, overlooking the Hudson. I hope she likes it. Figure it's the least I can do. Besides, it's not like I have to make rent anymore.

I send the landlord a text, asking if someone can please mail me my laptop and Mom's sketchbook from the apartment. I don't need anything else. But he doesn't respond. As if he knows what I am now.

《   《   《

It's my last day on Seven. I move down to Two tomorrow night. Cora's still camped out on the air mattress, hunching over her computer. Helping me shop for artwork and paint for the walls. This should be fun. That's what she says, exactly: "This should be fun."

But I'm staring into space, absently rubbing lotion on my fading lesions.

"We should order a few samples, just to see. Without sunlight, these colors might look really different in person."

"Mhmm," I reply.

"Or—and this is something kinda crazy but I've always wanted to try—we could like, paint a mural or something?"

My heart slides to my feet. All of a sudden I can't breathe.

"Mia?"

I roll onto my side, turning my back to her as the dam breaks. For the first time, I notice my tears aren't salty anymore. My eyes don't sting. I don't taste anything when they hit my lips.

Which just makes me cry harder.

She's beside me in a flash, folding me into a hug from behind. Her knees meet the back of my legs and she bends them in place, locking us together.

She doesn't ask if she did something wrong, or if there's anything she can do to make it okay. She knows better.

We stay that way till my alien tears dry without a trace. I glance down at her arm, interlaced with mine. There's a thin, grayish-green line running parallel to her elbow crease, raised like scar tissue, stretching from one side to the other. Straight, then jagged. Like someone started drawing and suddenly couldn't keep their hand steady.

She notices I've noticed.

"Don't let me catch you back on Seven again, after this."

The rust incident. What's unsaid could fill an ocean.

Eventually, we doze off. Nobody's ever held me in my sleep before. At least, not since I was a child, in Mom's bed with her noise machine blaring sounds of summer rain.

I dream about a tea party. The Mad Hatter and the Queen of Hearts. A fragrant rose garden. *We're painting the roses red. We're painting the roses red.*

We move downstairs. I say we because, even though Cora still has her own room, we're fused at the hip. I don't need her help anymore, not like I did those first few days. But I feel bound to her by this strange, glimmering web of fibrous oxytocin. I've never had this kind of connection with another person before. It didn't feel like this with Mom. And it's not how it was with Jade, either. It's familial, yet somehow foreign. Kinetic eroticism tempered by platonic dependability. Whenever she goes to her own room, I physically shudder and my joints ache, like I'm coming down with some sort of malaise. When she returns, renewed health floods my body. I was drawn to her, before all this. But everything's magnified now.

I know, now, what an impossible request I made, the night I begged Mom to make Devon leave and never see him again.

This is different, though. Toxic as it was, there was a *reciprocal* element, when she bonded to him. I don't have that with Cora.

We share a bed, sleeping the day away, back to back.

She's seen me get undressed. I wonder if she notices the color rise in my cheeks. The way I crave her eyes on me.

But nothing *happens* between us.

She showers in her own room. Goes upstairs to take pictures in private. I glimpse them on my socials in her absence. It feels a little skin-crawly, now that I know her. But I can't stop.

And then of course, there's the "boyfriend." Whoever he is.

I don't know where I stand anymore. Don't know how I'm supposed to feel about ADAPT, about *him,* about any of it. All the fight's gone out of me.

But he still haunts our conversations.

We're in the resident salon one evening, where Cora gets her nails done every other Friday with Alanna, a perky stylist who lives on Three. She insists I come with her, considering the horrible state my nails were in the first time we spoke.

The cuts and inflammation have healed, though. All over my body. Even the places Franklin bit me. My hair and nails will grow at a normal pace if I cut them, but only to the length they were the night I became a Sara. Alanna suggests acrylics because of this, but I decline. It's never been my style. I just ask her to paint them blue.

I realize, as she works, that the only person who ever painted my

nails was Mom. We used to have those at-home spa nights back in
Tucson. My mind skips away. It does that a lot these days.

Cora's voice draws me back in. "This is bullshit."

I glance her way. She's scrolling through her phone with her free
hand as Alanna files.

"I haven't heard from David in almost two weeks." She stares at
the screen like she can conjure a text with her unblinking eyes. "I
don't know what I did wrong."

"D" stands for David. Apparently. They met online about six
months ago. He was a follower of hers, an uninfected law student
from Michigan with big dreams of fighting for Saras' rights in front
of the Supreme Court. A real noble, stand-up guy. One—virtual—
thing led to another and now, she's in love.

She's shown me exactly one photo of him—a twentysomething
guy in a polo shirt with dark ringlets and a winsome smile, sipping
a beer at a pub somewhere in Europe. But when I try to look him
up, I can't find any of his social handles—even though she says
that's how they met. Before all this happened, I'd been taking notes
on Cora's followers. I know which users interact with her content
most frequently. He's not one of them.

He's also never come to visit. In fact, I've never even seen him
call her. They only talk via text. The whole thing is a little shady.
But whenever she brings him up, I try to put the more sinister ex-
planations out of my mind. Try to forget about *Origin of Species* and
the mysterious birthday gift.

It's not shady. It's sad.

She deserves better.

The following afternoon, I take my first Daylight pill. I pace around
my room, wringing my hands, waiting to feel . . . what? High? *Off*
somehow? I'm too scared to go outside. I don't trust it. But Cora
wants me to go with her today. There's supposed to be a parade
along Eleventh Avenue and we think we'll be able to see it from the
courtyard.

She comes down to my room wearing her new leather jacket.
Performs a twirl in the doorway to show it off.

"This is *so* nice. You seriously didn't have to." She strokes the lapel. "It feels extremely expensive."

"I mean, you spent your birthday wiping bloody vomit off my face so—" I shrug. "Happy belated?"

We're both still committing to that lie about her birthday. I think that's interesting.

She laughs and tosses an arm around my shoulders. Leads me out into the hallway. "You ready?"

"Oh, I-I don't know if the pill's kicked in yet—"

"You took it half an hour ago, you're fine."

She pulls me toward the elevator to the courtyard. I don't say anything as we ride down.

We approach the exit, and a knife of sunlight shines between the double doors. I freeze, letting Cora walk ahead of me.

"What's up?"

"I just . . . I really can't—" I slump against the wall and slide to the ground. Like I'm bracing myself to pass out.

"Whoa, whoa, hang on—" Cora tries to tug me to my feet, but I pull back in the other direction.

"You go ahead."

"What's wrong? I told you, the pill is—"

"I can't go out there. In the sun." I rasp into my hands, "That's how my mom died."

In an instant, she's on the floor next to me.

"Hang on. How'd your mom . . . *oh*."

I have to say it. If I don't, I'll never survive this. Never walk outside again. Never find any peace in my body the way it is now.

"I killed her."

Someone passes through the door and the sliver of light expands to a chasm. I make myself tiny against the wall, but Cora reaches out a hand. Her fingers dance along the sunbeam, unharmed, catching dust motes and pollen.

I watch, and she meets my fascinated gaze.

"I killed my mom, too."

I just stare. Don't know how to react. It's so stark, so naked, the way she says it.

"I didn't know—"

"Bullshit. Everyone talks about it."

After a moment, I concede. "I mean, they said you killed your whole family."

"Nope. Just her." The door eases shut and the sunlight evaporates. "I just tell people I bit my sister and my dad too 'cuz it's easier than saying they dumped me here."

The space between us glistens with urgency. She's waiting for me to elaborate. But I'm waiting for her.

"My parents decided it was better if everyone thought I was dead," she finally says. "And one day my mom and I had this huge fight 'cuz I stole my sister's phone and texted some of my old friends." Her mouth forms a line. "She was starving me as punishment. When it happened I kinda . . . I blacked out. I don't remember doing it."

"I'm sorry—"

"Hang on. This isn't about me. Sorry if it sounds like that. I was trying to make a point. I never meant to hurt her. It happened because she hurt *me*. Which, if I had to guess, is how it was with your mom, too."

I nod. Slowly. Hoping to make it stick.

"When you're ready, you can tell me more. Or not. Your call, okay?"

She pushes the hair out of my face. I rest my cheek against her creamy leather sleeve.

After a moment, she places her lips against my temple. Electricity explodes through me, igniting every synapse. I don't move. Couldn't if I wanted to.

Then, she stands, holding fast to my arm. This time she doesn't let me pull back. I have no choice but to rise with her.

"I love you. Let's go outside."

I know that's not how she meant it. I know, I know, I know. But in this moment, watching the sun skim the Hudson with my head in the crook of her neck, reality feels obscene.

Please just let me have this. Only if for a night.

Topher swings by to ask if I'm doing okay. Offers us both a cigarette. Cora sticks to her cloves, but I take him up on it. I've never had one before. Hitting Jade's flavored vape was different. There's nothing to disguise the taste. This is death, straight-no-chaser. I can't decide if I like it.

The parade peters out along Eleventh Avenue. I wonder if the kids up on Nine were able to see it. Maybe they have some sort of private roof deck. Probably not, though.

"What are the kids like?" I spill into the silence.

Cora shoots me a look of surprise. Like she didn't expect me to ask about this. But it's been pirouetting in the back of my mind since the day she mentioned it.

"I mean, they're *kids*. That's the first thing. People don't understand that. It's not like they're adults in children's bodies. Which is . . . y'know. How a lot of the trouble starts. How a lot of them end up here."

I shiver. It's not the wind. I think of that awful post I saw— #JusticeforSammi.

"If your brain gets stuck before it's done growing, then that's how you vibe. But that's why they're fun. They like to play and do dumb kid stuff. But then, of course, the littlest thing sets them off. I'm a good babysitter because they can't hurt me."

"I'm sure it's more than that."

She scoots closer to me so our hips are touching. "I wanted to get into Child Welfare, actually. Go to court on behalf of foster kids and things like that. I was studying pre-law, when I was in college."

I soften my face, hoping it belies all the things I already know.

"You could probably like . . . practice online? Right?"

"Not if you never graduated."

Cora lights herself a second clove as I ash Topher's cigarette.

I take her hand. This is our language, now. We leave quiet space for the pain, knowing the other person will fill it with something else. Something better.

But a moment later, she lets me go. Distracted by a muted *ping* from inside her jacket.

My cheeks burn and my eyes shoot to the ground as she fishes her phone out.

"Oh my God, it's him." She leaps to her feet. "You mind if I run upstairs for a little bit?"

Do I *mind*. What a question. Do I mind if she strips naked and gets on camera for him? Do I mind if she does whatever she does when she's all alone in her room and he's telling her everything she wants to hear and she starts calling him fucking "baby" or "daddy" or—

"Yeah um . . . That's fine. See you after dinner?"

"For sure." She flings her butt into the water and trots away, already typing a reply.

It's colder now. But I don't want to go in yet. Don't want it to look like I'm following her. I wonder if this is better or worse than Jade. At least I know about him. She's not actively deceiving me.

This time I've cut out the middleman. I'm deceiving myself.

When I return to my room, I've got an email. My landlord—no, the corporation my landlord represents—has blessed me with a form letter.

> Dear Ms. McKinnon—
>
> We regret to inform you that, due to your inability to pay rent within the 7-day grace period, your belongings have been cleared from the apartment on W. 116th Street.
>
> We send our regards and wish you well.

I sag to the bed. It's not like I had much. Just some clothes and my laptop. All of that's replaceable, and I can afford it now. But Mom's sketchbook was there. Tears quiver in my eyes.

My earthly possessions keep slipping through my fingers, every time someone forces me to start over. All I've got now is the backpack I was using the day I got attacked. My wallet. A stale, half-empty water bottle. My phone. And that little red Moleskine.

All that remains of me.

I hate the color we picked for my wall. I fell in love with this soft, sage-green swatch, but without any sunlight it takes on this sickly, yellow pallor that reverberates across the entire space. Cora warned me that might happen. It makes me want to throw up.

I glance across the room and notice the center's done my laundry for the first time. Well, Cora's. I've been wearing her clothes. They've left everything fluffed and folded on top of the dresser in a neat stack.

How *nice* all of this is. How very fucking *nice.*

I rise to inspect the pile. They tried their best with the clothes I was wearing that night, but they're permanently bloodstained. I really loved those jeans. Yet another thing I'll have to replace.

As I move to toss them in the trash, I notice that my waterlogged employee badge is still hooked to my belt loop, lanyard hanging limply in my back pocket.

I chuck it in the trash on top of my jeans.

Cora's taking her sweet time upstairs. I turn on a rerun of *Survivor,* which I know she'll appreciate when she gets back. I resolve to build a tomb around my jealousy. I can't let it interfere with what we have. She's the best—the only—friend I've got. I'll meet someone else, once the shine of the turn fades. The lift. Whatever. Because it has to fade eventually. Right?

I know now. This is the punishment I deserve. The cruel poetry of chaos swirls around me. Of course I bonded to a person who would never love me back. And now I'm trapped here. For life. Which is longer than anything I ever understood *life* to represent.

I pick up the metal trash can and hurl it at the green wall with all the strength in my devastated body. It leaves a jagged dent. I throw it a second time. Harder. My teeth quiver, and a horrifying, feral dirge I've never heard before explodes from my mouth.

In a heartbeat, Alonzo's at my door.

"Hey, what's happening? You okay?"

I'm so sick of people asking if I'm okay. How is anyone here ever okay again?

"Mia?"

I scream myself to pieces.

Alonzo approaches with his hands up. Slowly. One of them holds a needle.

"Shhh, it's okay—"

"Don't touch her." Cora's back, like a flash of light. She pushes past Alonzo and guides me toward the bed.

Alonzo freezes, but he's still clutching the needle, business end pointed in my direction.

"Mia, you gotta calm down. Okay?" Cora says. "If he sticks you with that thing they're gonna move you back upstairs, and you just got here."

"Doesn't matter. Here is here. I'm stuck."

"Mia, please. Do it for me."

She runs her nails through my hair. I bury my face into a pillow, steamy with humiliation. Don't want to look at her.

"I'll be around the corner," Alonzo says. A concession. But mostly a warning.

He shuts the door.

My clammy tears cool under my clothes, like waking in an icy sweat. "Wonder if we can ask around and find out where Lisa got that shot," I mutter into the pillow.

Cora's hand flexes. Scoring my scalp with her nails.

"Ow, ow, ow—"

"Fuck right off, I'm not letting you die."

She waits for my sniffling to subside. So quiet, so still, that if it weren't for her fingers in my hair I'd swear she floated away.

"Mia," she finally says. "There's something I've been wanting to talk to you about."

She stands to open the door just a crack. Peeks around the corner. Then shuts it again.

She sidles in close as I pull myself upright. Her voice is so small I almost have to read her lips. "Remember that book you found in my room?"

A fist seizes my heart.

"You ever read it?"

"N-no. But I know the basics—"

"Keep your voice down," she says. "This is important."

My entire being holds its breath.

"There's a group of people I know. They believe—and I do, too—that Saras are the next wave of human progress and someday, everyone's gonna pay for the way they've treated us. We'll outnumber them. They won't be able to keep us locked up anymore. If you die before that happens, I'll never forgive myself."

My heart slams back to life.

"When I first heard about the group . . . I dunno, I started looking at my life in a whole new way. I think they could help you feel better, too. Most days, they're the only thing that keeps me going." A shy smile slides to her lips. "And my boyfriend."

"David."

She hesitates. "That's not his name."

It takes all the restraint I've ever known to keep from screaming again.

"Actually, he's the one who started the group." My stomach shudders as she goes on, "This is a big deal, what I'm telling you. He trusts me and I take that seriously. People want to kill him, for all the stuff he's saying. He escaped from a center in Texas last year when someone put a hit out on him." She sucks in air, then whispers, "He wants me to do it, too."

I hold my breath, teetering on the edge of irrevocable trust. If I so much as blink at the wrong moment, I'll take us both down.

"I was gonna try to do it last month, but they took my phone when they moved me upstairs. I'm glad I didn't, though. Because now you can do it with me." She takes my stunned silence as a pact. "I wish we could leave today, but there's still a lot of planning that needs to go into it. Money, too. Nobody's ever gotten out of Forty-Eight before, and it's a lot harder to escape from New York than Bumfuck, Texas. I know they're probably gonna ask me for more cash. It's always five hundred here, two thousand there. I'm trying to scrape it together, but—"

"Cora."

My voice glows between us. Her mouth snaps shut, and I reach for her hands.

"I have money. I can help you."

NOW

I didn't realize I had stitches in my leg till I tore them. I think I was standing on the stool, stretching toward the window. Trying to pry away the plywood and punch through the glass. Was I *chewing* it? There are splinters of wood between my teeth. I'm not sure. All I know is at some point I hit the floor and the stitches split. I haven't managed to heave myself back to the cot. The floor is sticky with black blood. Mine.

A Sara at full strength might be able to pummel their way out of this room. But Devon knew I couldn't hack it.

It feels like I've been lying here a hundred years. I only stop screaming because my throat is smoldering and it hurts less to hold the pain inside. I crimp into a ball and massage my protruding ribs with my knobby knees. I'm losing weight like a slashed tire; rapid, assured destruction. A memory unspools: Mom on the stoop, an emaciated husk. She bolts for the car. *Sorry, baby.* I saved her. Cut my arm with the gardening shears. Nobody's coming to save me.

Knots of time come loose and slip from my grasp. I came here . . . when? Am I still in New York? Underground somewhere? I swear I hear trains roaring past. No . . . that's me. Screaming again.

This is a 1. Uptown. Local train.
The next stop is. Thirty-Fourth Street. Penn Station.
Stand clear of the closing doors, please.
Ding-dong. Ding-dong.
Stand clear of the closing doors, please.
Someone's blocking the door. Get out of the way, you're blocking the—

Door. The door, oh God, someone's at the door.

The floor shudders as feet pound toward me.

A pair of hands help me to a seated position as I gnash the dark void with my teeth. My eyesight faded hours ago, along with my strength, and I haven't been able to stand to put more wood on the fire.

Someone swings a lantern into my eyes. I squint with a painful gasp, blinking three faces into focus. Dr. Lacie. Gareth. Devon. But he hasn't come all the way inside. Just hovers in the doorway with a passive watchfulness. Like this is some slow-moving spectator sport.

Dr. Lacie finishes peeling me off the floor, tacky with congealed black resin.

Why was the train so late?

I need to pay attention. I'm going to miss my stop. . . .

Gareth moves to the corner, easing off his coat. Preparing to draw for me. Keeping a safe distance.

My head lolls. Dr. Lacie helps me up onto the cot and clucks her tongue in disapproval at my torn stitches. "Mia, I'm going to administer another sub-cu injection. Hold still—"

I always confused the local and the express. Sandy quizzed me but I kept getting it wrong. I never meant to get lost like this.

Dr. Lacie slides a needle into my cadaverous thigh and my butchered leg disconnects from my body.

I'm not sure when Devon came into the room but now he's standing next to her.

Still hasn't said anything.

I hope to God he doesn't follow me home, when I get off the train.

I think my stop is coming up next.

Gareth finishes drawing and hands the full reservoir off to Devon. Darts out of the room.

But I'm not watching him. All I can see is that bag in Devon's spidery hands. The gorgeous glow of its heat signature.

"I'm sorry," he says.

My fractured mind fuses back together like a nightmarish Picasso. What's he saying sorry for? I think I'm crying. Just want the bag. Please, please, please—the fucking *bag*.

He waits for me to meet his eye. Then relinquishes it.

I drink, and a rejuvenating swell prickles across my body—tide-like, pushing me back to shore.

Dr. Lacie starts repairing my stitches. Grateful tears slide down my cheeks as I pull from the bag. Devon returns my gaze with a gentle, anesthetizing emptiness.

"I'll have one of my girls find you some crutches," Dr. Lacie says after a moment, washing the hardened blood from my leg. "You'll want to use them while you heal. Takes about three weeks for rust wounds to fully close."

Girls . . . Who's she talking about?

Girls.

Cora.

My focus sharpens to a point.

I know where I am now. How I got here.

"I need to see Cora, right now," I say to both of them. "It's important."

I'm terrified, imagining what might have happened in my absence. What might have happened if she's been alone with him.

"Your friend is safe," Devon replies, an airy assurance to his voice. Takes a seat on the stool beside my bed. "She's just busy. You can see her in a few days."

I fix him with a different sort of stare, now that the blood bag is empty. Like there's a hidden message between the lines on his face.

"Busy with what?"

"She's helping Dr. Lacie with something."

Dr. Lacie pauses mid-stitch. Devon's eyes leave mine and sway to hers.

Before I can ask them anything else, she secures fresh gauze around my leg, pats my hip, and guides me to my back. "Don't try to walk again till I get you those crutches."

She packs her supplies into her cross-body kit and makes a sharp turn toward the door. She and I both wait for Devon to join her, but he doesn't.

"Margot, I'll meet you upstairs in a few minutes," he says, off her questioning glance.

I shoot her a pleading stare. *Please, don't leave me with him.*

But she's looking right through me. She nods, picks up the lantern, then bends toward Devon to peck his mouth on her way out the door.

Surprise catches in my throat. Of course, he gets perks from his people. But there's something about the way she just kissed him—an easy, lived-in affection, not the type of sinister carnality I figured went down at a place like this. Like they've been at this for a while.

A memory from Mom's phone stabs at my mind:

That bitch from Montana.

As she shuts the door and leaves us in the dark, Devon unlatches the stove. Starts loading it with wood. Doesn't say a word.

Maybe I'm supposed to say something.

He grabs a container of ski wax from the dilapidated shelf and shoves it in the fireplace. Pulls the lighter from his pocket and flicks it till the flammable paste catches. Tongues of fire stretch toward the dry wood.

He shuts the stove and returns to his seat as light and warmth bleed across the room.

"I really am sorry," he finally says. "We're trying to ration around here and usually go three full days. I didn't realize you'd be—"

"How long have I been in here?"

A gust of alpine wind throttles the thin, dark windows.

"Since last night. That's what I mean. I didn't think you'd be in such bad shape."

I interrogate his placid gaze. It felt like an eternity . . .

But I'm too exhausted to turn this into a fight.

"I thought about everything you told me. I believe you, Mia."

I swallow a mouthful of cold air.

"I mean, of course she's dead. I think I knew, all along. Just didn't want to face it."

At last, I nod. I wonder what changed his mind. I know better than to question it, though.

He moves the stool an inch closer, so we're eye to eye.

"I wanted her to pay for what she did. She cut me off at the knees. You don't know what it's been like, for us. Since then."

Guess that's one part of the story he still subscribes to. That's fine, though. Better he blames her than me.

"What Kayla told me sounds fucking awful," he says after a moment. "I'm sorry you had to see that."

I'm silent. Watching our heat signatures tangle with the firelight.

I withdraw, letting the space between us breathe. Desperate to change the subject.

"Three days is a lot," I finally say in a hoarse voice. "Why aren't you guys hunting?"

"That's what they expect us to do. Not worth the risk."

"But why ration if you've got people like Gareth?"

"We've got *three* people like Gareth," he corrects me. "There are two others. We used to have more. We've been . . . trying to replenish." His tired eyes slide off. "ADAPT looks different, online. All organized and shit. Meanwhile, the people who started it are hiding out in the fucking sticks. It was never supposed to be this way."

"I get it." I think that's what he wants me to say.

"Over the summer, Margot found this great little ranch up in Montana. All of us were gonna go in," he says, almost prayerful. Confirming my suspicions about her. "Two big farmhouses, twelve acres of land. Off the beaten path, but close enough to Bozeman that we could hunt. Would've been a good life. But we had to abandon ship 'cuz your mom knew where it was so . . . that's how we ended up here. Middle of nowhere. No electricity. Shooting up on the nights we don't eat."

My brow arches. "What, you mean like . . . heroin?"

"God, I wish. We take whatever Margot's girls can grab from the closest hospital. Runs the gamut. Fentanyl and oxy are hard to get lately, but propofol's decent. Helps you sleep through it. But most of the time you're just snorting Tylenol with codeine and hoping for the best."

The irony of Saras never ceases to amaze me. Our sustenance has to be pure as the driven snow to appease that delicate stomach. But the blood in our steely veins can take whatever the hell you throw at it. There's no such thing as an overdose.

Not like I'm itching to try, though.

"Anyway, I should've known you'd need to eat more. You're still healing. I'll have Gare keep hanging with you for the next few weeks. He'll take care of you, he's a good guy."

I think I know now, who made those marks on Gareth's arms.

It takes a moment for my mouth to shape the words "Thank you."

I wait for him to stand, craving the end of the conversation. But he doesn't move.

Something shudders between us. Like he's just sensed my unease.

But of course he has. He can see my eyes darken. I always seem to forget about that.

"Tell me something." He folds his hands into a triangle, where he rests his chin. "When this happened to you . . . was it something you wanted?"

"You didn't care whether I wanted it when you told Mom to do it."

He grits his teeth. I feel his energy shift, the way air thickens before a storm. God dammit, I need to shut my mouth and pull back. Can't forget who the fuck I'm talking to.

"I just mean—"

"Mia, that was her idea. Not mine."

There's barely a whisker of space between us. He lowers his voice.

"That was a really bad situation and I'm sorry for the way it—"

"That's not . . . No. That isn't what she—"

"Mia, listen to me. If you're gonna stay here, if you're ever going to *get past it* and live life on your terms, you need to know the truth."

I'm glowing with that strange, uncanny certainty again, the same way I felt when we first got in the car together. Like all my life's treasures are hidden behind a locked door, and he's dangling the key in front of my face.

"When we found the ranch, I said to her . . . 'Babe, your kid is grown. She can't take care of you forever. Let her live her life so you can live yours.' But she was too afraid to leave you behind."

I pull a thin, reedy breath. My Picasso brain flips upside down and all the pieces dislodge.

Or maybe they're falling into place.

"She told me you were pressuring her to do it," I manage to say.

"Because she told *me* she was going to, and once she did I knew we could finally leave. But I never supported it. I knew you'd be miserable." He holds my stare. "I knew how much you hated me."

There's a slow leak in me. Like he's just opened the scar where she bit me. That soft expectancy returns to his gaze. But I don't know what he wants me to say, after that.

"We don't have to talk about her. If it upsets you."

"N-no. It's fine." I've never had the chance to talk about this with someone who was there. Someone who knew her. . . .

"Like I said. Bad situation," he says. Opening the stove to stoke the wood with his boot. "It made me crazy, to see how you guys were living. I mean, you did what you had to do. She was free, and I had to respect that. Still. It just made me want to—"

it makes me want to light ur house on fire. you deserve better.

I can recite this argument word for word.

But I can't help but wonder if I was reading it backward the entire time.

"Point is," he says as he slams the stove shut. "You're allowed to be angry. I'm angry, too."

My voice erodes in my scratchy throat. "I'm not. I mean, we kinda didn't have a choice."

"*She* didn't. You did."

I quirk my head like a lost animal. And I am. Really and truly lost. How is this conversation happening? With *him*?

"There was something she told me last year. In confidence," he whispers. Like she might be listening through the cracks in the rotting wood. "I dunno, we were talking about her ex. Your dad. And—"

His hands meet his face, rubbing the pressure point between his eyes. Like it helps him dredge memories from that dark well.

"Tell me."

"I guess when you were like, thirteen or fourteen, he tracked her down and started calling again. He was asking about you. Wanted to meet you, or whatever."

"She never told me that."

"Course not."

I'm paralyzed, as if Dr. Lacie's shot just swam up the length of my body.

"It would've ruined everything," I murmur. Filling the blanks Devon's left. "If we met, and he wanted to be a part of my life, if he ever wanted joint custody—"

"Or full custody, once he found out about your mom."

"Yeah . . ."

"You say it would've ruined everything." The words melt in his mouth. "And yeah, it would have. *For her.* For you, it might have been great. Who knows."

The thought sticks in my head like shrapnel as he unfurls to his full height. Pops his neck to one side, then the other. At last, he's on his feet. Heading for the door.

Something deflates in me. Like I wish we weren't done.

"I'll bring Gare back around tomorrow night so you can eat. Just . . . don't tell anyone. Okay?"

"I won't."

"Lucky break, getting shot by that dumb bitch, huh?" A gallows laugh escapes his lips.

"What about Cora?"

"What about her?"

"Can she come with Gareth? Tomorrow?"

He drags a breath. Lets it out with a nod. "Don't see why not."

I almost smile . . . till he opens the door and memories of hunger and the black dark float through my body like toxic spores. Panic spirals up my throat. Against my will, I call out to him, "You swear to God you're coming back?"

"Don't worry, Fun Size. You're safe now."

I'm desperate for sleep, but my murky brain keeps flickering. Faster and faster, like strobes through fog.

Were there traces of these conversations in their texts?

Something I missed?

Does it *matter*?

She's gone. Being angry won't summon her back.

And maybe that's a good thing.

I wasn't allowed to have this before—this anger. Not after what I did. And I'm still not. This is a secret. Something to conceal under my skin, igniting the nerve endings in my quivering gums. I wish it *could* summon her back. I want to show her how deadly I've become. How I can be twice the monster she was.

I watch the embers blush in the stove as the healing darkness of sleep taps me on the shoulder. But I feel like I've forgotten something.

I wonder what changed his mind.

Why he decided to believe me.

Why I've decided to believe *him*.

((((

There's a rustle at the door, prodding me awake. I realize, as it opens, that it didn't click. Devon didn't lock me in this time.

Gareth enters with a tepid smile, trailed by Dr. Lacie, holding a pair of crutches. The end of another day in the dark. But this one felt more manageable. By a long shot.

"Best thing you can do to promote healing is start with some easy movement," she says as she leans them next to my bed. Barely looking at me. As if direct eye contact might set her ablaze.

Gareth takes to his stool and tightens the tourniquet as Dr. Lacie reveals a pair of black sweatpants and a clean thermal top under her arm. She tosses them onto my bed without a word.

I'm thankful. To both of them. Even if they're only doing it because Devon said so.

Dr. Lacie studies me, waiting for me to get changed. But the whole right side of my body smarts. The analgesic wore off hours ago. I make a pathetic effort to shimmy out of my ragged, bloody jeans.

"Uh . . . sorry. I could use a little help."

She's brusque, but at least it's over fast. She eases the fabric past my wound and yanks the stiff denim from my ankle. I draw a sharp hiccup of air, but say nothing.

Before helping me into my new pants, she inspects my dressing. Peels away yesterday's bandage. But this time, she doesn't inject me with anything to numb the pain. Her touch is volcanic.

"Where's the shot?" I moan as she holds my leg steady. Can't keep quiet anymore.

"Sorry. The clinic's a little understocked right now."

She starts flushing my wound with something that smells like vinegar, and I swear I can feel the stuff singeing my bones. I clamp my pillow between my teeth as Gareth offers me the blood bag.

"Here. This'll help."

I gulp it like oxygen as Dr. Lacie makes quick work securing a new roll of gauze around my leg. At last, the agony starts to cool.

As she pulls the clean sweatpants up past my hips, Gareth moves toward the door.

"Thank you," I make sure to say.

"Be back tomorrow."

I can't help but notice the jaundiced hollows under his glassy blue eyes. The gray pallor of his thin lips. My chest tightens in remembrance. He's probably doing double—even triple—duty tonight. And it's still not enough.

"Wait—" I call out to him. "Devon said Cora would come. Tonight."

Gareth frowns and arches a brow. As if he doesn't know who I'm talking about.

"You know. My friend. Who I came with."

"I'll see what's up," he says flatly. The hair on the back of my neck spikes. Something about the timbre of his voice. But he ducks out before I can ask him anything else.

As he shuts the door, Dr. Lacie's gaze finally snaps to mine. My heart stammers, like she's just trained the barrel of a gun on me. A quiet laugh escapes the crook of her upturned lip as her eyes rake over me.

"I don't think you look like your mother at all."

Dark laughter rises from me, meeting hers. "I've been saying the same thing."

She packs her first aid kit, thoughtfully tapping her incisors together. "I heard a rumor you forked over ten grand to bust out of Forty-Eight."

"It's not a rumor."

I peel off my filthy shirt. Her gaze digs a trench down my body.

"You know we have rules around here," she says after a moment. Surveying the shape of me.

"I understand."

"The kind of rules he's not gonna tell you about." Her marquise face sharpens as she chews the inside of her cheek.

"I told you. I understand." I hold her gaze as steady as I can, then change into the clean top. She needs to know I'm not a threat. That I'm not my mother. After a moment, she casts me a smirk of approval.

"Then we'll get along great."

The harsh *zzzzip* of her first aid kit fills the silence between us.

She starts sanitizing her hands. Like she might be preparing to leave. But I have to keep the conversation aloft, now that she's opening up to me.

"What's Cora been helping you with?"

"We're working on some research together," she replies after a moment. A smile crawls across her face. Not the fox-like sneer she's been wearing to address me thus far. It's earnest. Hopeful, even.

"That's really cool, I didn't realize you guys were doing research up here—"

"*I'm* conducting research," she's quick to correct me, then adds through her teeth, "Devon has other responsibilities."

She straps her kit back on and turns toward the door.

"I'd love to hear more. About what you're working on, I mean." She pauses, but doesn't answer. "I'm here to help, if you need it. Devon told me you're running low on supplies and stuff. I have a lot more than ten grand saved up."

Her thick lashes flutter like black moths. "How much more?"

A lie worms its way to my lips, all on its own. Just like before. "Like, five hundred? There was this trust I got access to. When my mom died."

If she thinks I've got potential as a piggy bank, she might let me be involved. Let me be with Cora. At the very least, it might keep her from slitting my throat with a rusted knife.

She stares me down and finally responds. "I'm researching how human stem cells react inside the bodies of Saras."

"They react by killing them," I blurt. "Like those shots."

She bristles, then smiles. A conspiratorial invitation. "Not always."

The door flies open before I can ask her anything else. Devon's just joined us. His energy is frenetic. But not the hungry kind. His wild eyes sweep right over me as I study the darkness behind him. Where I'm expecting someone else to be . . .

"Margot. Where the hell is the Chevy?" he asks, voice quavering.

"I sent Zach and Noah to Steamboat Springs," she replies coolly.

"You *what*?"

The tension in the room swells to a clot as Margot takes a pointed step in his direction.

"I sent. Zach and Noah. To Steamboat Springs. For bleeders."

His eyes swing to mine, then back to Margot, as he claws his temples and expels a breath. As if he's trying not to go nuclear in front of me.

"Why?"

"'Cuz we're starving and I'm sick of sharing my girls." Her voice is like satin.

"I mean *why fucking Steamboat*? It's way too populated—"

"Worth the risk if they come back with friends."

"Margot." His jaw goes taut, like there's a scream stuck to the roof of his mouth. "I told you I had a plan. I was handling it."

"Should've handled it faster." She brushes past him with a white flash of her elongated canines. He snares her wrist, but she shakes him right off. He *lets* her shake him off.

I'm not sure I ever saw him do that with Mom. Then again, I'm not sure Mom ever spoke to him that way.

Margot shoots me a loaded glance, a memento of her earlier warning, before she sees herself out.

As she slams the door, Devon reels his posture back up. I didn't think it was possible for him to shrink like that.

"Uh, you should take a couple laps around the camp," he says, clearing his throat, as though it will erase what I just saw. He hands me my crutches on his way to the door. "It'll help you heal faster."

"Wait—" I'd physically pounce if I had the strength. He spins to face me. "You said Cora would come tonight. Where is she?"

"Oh uh . . . I asked her to swing by. She said no."

My heart loses its balance and falls to my feet. "Wait, what? That's not possible."

"I'm sorry."

"That doesn't make any . . . What did she say?" A feral twinge shoots through my mouth. I anxiously jab my tongue with the tip of my exposed canine.

"Just that she didn't want to see you. And I didn't push it."

My mind goes blank. There's no filter. Only panic.

"You're a fucking liar." The words erupt from my lips, broiling hot.

His eyes darken like burnt holes. Everything inside me craters. *There's* the Devon I know. He holds my stare like he held my head under that bloody water all those years ago as my teeth slink back to my gums.

"I-I'm sorry." My voice sounds like it's coming through a phone made of string and a tin can. None of this feels real.

In an instant, that atomic flash leaves his eyes. Like I dreamed it.

"I understand." He attacks my shoulder with a reassuring squeeze. "I know she means a lot to you. Hope you can work it out."

From his mouth, it's like a bad omen. I shiver as he whirls out the door.

"Take your time getting up, okay?"

Sliding the crutches under my arms evokes a queasy sense memory. Last time I used them I was ten. On the road with Mom.

I hobble out into the cold, toward the fire pit. There's a group of a dozen or so gathered there, sitting in frostbitten lawn chairs. I can feel their eyes on me. *There she goes. Daughter of the traitor.*

Kayla bounds in my direction, from the opposite end of the camp. The only person who's not gawking at me stone-faced.

"You're up!" She falls in step with me. "How's your leg?"

"Shitty." I avoid her gaze as I struggle along. I scan the faces around the fire. Looking for Cora.

I was glad to see Kayla the first time. But her familiarity feels like a slap in the face now. It doesn't matter Devon's kept me fed. Given me a doctor. He's still telling lies. And Kayla backs him.

Across the camp, I catch sight of Gareth. He makes a large loop around the fire pit, eyes glued to the ground, hands in his pockets. Careful to avoid the gathering. He takes cover inside a trailer behind the main lodge.

As he passes, the entire group stops chatting and stares. Jaws reverently clenched. I peer over at Kayla and realize she's doing it, too.

"How long's it been?" I ask her, keeping my voice low.

"Fifty-one. I'm fine." It takes me a second to realize she's counting the hours. "My wave is tomorrow. It's been worse."

"Have you been rationing this whole time?"

"Just the past two weeks." Her raw mouth gurns with an aggression I haven't seen since the early days of Mom's infection. "When we first came up here we had Gareth, Margot's two girls Kat and Sophie, and seven others. They came from the outpost outside Omaha and we thought they were cool and everything was working fine but one day they broke out while everyone was asleep and started running down the mountain." She chatters on, as if talking will keep her from pulverizing her tongue.

"What happened to them?"

"Never made it out of the woods. It's life on fucking *Mars* up here. They got lost once the sun went down. We found their bodies a few nights later."

"God, that's horrible."

"Better than the alternative. If they'd made it to the closest town and told everyone where we were."

I almost make her an offer—to share Gareth with her, or something . . . till I remember what Devon said. I'm not supposed to tell anyone I have a designated bleeder. Which makes me wonder . . .

"Have Margot and Devon been rationing?"

She shakes her head. "They eat every night, but they take the minimum four ounces. Someone up here needs to keep their shit together. If they start spinning out, we're screwed." She sucks a pulpy wad of blood from her trembling lip like it's strawberry jam.

It's the answer I was expecting. Still, I don't understand why I'm worthy of cutting the line along with them.

"So. Here's the grand tour, I guess." Kayla starts turning in a circle. "There's my cabin I share with Bjorn and Teresa. We have room for one more, if you want to come bunk with us once you're all better."

"Thanks."

"I can introduce you, if you're feeling up to it."

"Maybe tomorrow."

Kayla nods. We both saw the way the other Saras were looking at me.

My eyes drift across the camp, trying to dodge those barbed stares around the fire. The glowing red cross above the clinic pulls my gaze like a magnet. Something flutters under my skin and tugs at my ribs.

Of course. That has to be where Cora's been.

"Kayla, I need to see Cora. She's in there, isn't she? With Dr.

Lacie?" Kayla's face is a mask. "Devon said she didn't want to talk to me, but that doesn't make any sense. She's my—"

Kayla looks askance, chewing her tongue again. "I'm sure she's just busy."

I try to compass through Kayla's bizarre body language. Her sweet, dismissive bell of a voice.

"How does Dr. Lacie have access to like . . . nurses and drugs and all that stuff?" If there's one thing I can count on, it's Kayla's historic propensity for gossip. All I have to do is stir the right pot to find out what she knows. Plus, I can tell she's dying to keep talking so she doesn't gnaw her lip to rags. "She must come from money or something."

"You'd think that. But nah, she's just some brainiac from rural Montana who got poached to lead a bunch of research at a Sara center in Austin a couple years ago," Kayla says in a hurried whisper. "But when she tried to launch trials they kinda laughed her out the door."

"She was in Texas?"

"Yuh-huh."

"So that's where they met."

"She helped him escape."

"Oh. Wow—"

"And I'm sure you can guess what he gave her in return." Kayla fixes me with an impish grin. An echo of that sly siren who once held court behind the bar. "Apparently, she was the first person crazy enough to ask him for it."

Kayla's arched gaze meets mine. We're both imagining it.

That bitch from Montana.

A gravelly groan from the bottom of the hill interrupts the intrusive thought. Headlights cut the evergreens as the black Chevy careens up the windy road, making double time around the hairpin turns.

Everyone around the fire scatters like insects, racing to be the first to greet the car. Kayla's no exception.

Two spindly, emaciated men leap from the idling vehicle, mid-argument. The younger and taller of the two, on the driver's side, wears a blood-soaked camo parka. The Saras flock to him, trancelike. One of the girls paws at his bloody coat, and he smacks her hand away.

"Get the *fuck back*—" he snarls, sprinting around the vehicle to pop the trunk. His partner follows, screeching in his ear.

"It's too fucking late, man! He's dead. You *know* he's fucking—"

The trunk springs open to reveal two figures. One squirms like a grub wrapped in silver duct tape. The other is motionless. Blood drools from the lip of the trunk into the snow, like a nightmarish shave ice.

In an instant, Devon and Margot are at the fringes of the group, parting them down the center with an almost biblical force. I hobble back toward the fire pit, watching from a safe distance.

Nobody says a word as Devon inspects the captives in the trunk. He nods approvingly at the writhing wad of tape on the right. The group turns to stone as he nudges the body on the left. The guy in the blood-soaked parka raises his shaking arms with a pitiful intake of anxious snot.

"Zach. What's your hour?" Devon asks without looking at him.

Zach lets out a shuddering breath. "Twenty-nine."

"Noah?"

The second, spotless man puffs out his chest. "Fifty." Then, he checks his watch. "Fifty-one."

"Look man, I'm sorry," Zach sputters. "I just . . . I couldn't fucking help it. We're not getting enough."

Devon closes the distance between them. Zach wilts under his gaze, sniveling. What's the punishment, for something like this? Is he going to tear into his face? Maul him like a fucking bear? I can't watch . . .

"Come see me in four days. Yeah?" Devon lowers his voice with tectonic intensity. "We'll talk about 'not getting enough.'"

"I'm so sorry, dude. Please, *please* don't do this—"

"Keys." Devon unfurls the palm of his hand.

Zach complies with a tearful gust of regret. Three of the other guys standing on the sidelines rally to restrain him. He howls as they drag him toward the main lodge. A well-timed choke hold shuts him right up.

"From now on, I keep the keys. Me and Gare are the only ones who leave the property. Understood?" He's saying it to everyone . . . but he's looking right at Margot. She flashes her teeth but says nothing.

As she stalks back to the clinic, I realize the door below the red cross is hanging wide open. We have an audience.

Three young women stand framed in the warm, electric gleam: a wisp of a waify blonde, a tall Black woman with sprawling curls . . . and Cora.

I tear toward her as fast as I can on my crutches. Kayla notices I've broken off from the group and jogs after me.

"Wait, Mia—"

She grabs for my arm, but I shake her off. We pass Margot halfway across the courtyard.

"Let her," she says. Holding Kayla back.

The two of them watch me like I'm in some sort of movie and they're on the damn couch stuffing their faces with popcorn.

"Cora. Oh my God—" Relief lodges in my throat. I drop my crutches so I can hold out my arms to her. "Are you okay?"

She doesn't return my embrace. Hardly even looks at me.

"Cora, what's—?"

I balance on one foot like a shivering seabird. She sighs and crosses her arms. Still won't meet my eye.

"Core, talk to me. What the hell is going on?"

"I went through your shit, Mia," she finally says, in a voice congested with hurt.

The other two women step back, giving her the floor. But they're still watching.

"What *shit*? What are you—?" Wait. My backpack.

I have hers, and she has mine.

"Look, I'm not sure what you saw. But I need you to know—"

"Pretty sure I already know everything."

The other two girls exchange a smug whisper.

"I found that notebook." Her voice cracks, like she might cry.

My heart batters my ribs. It's over. She must know why we're here. All the things I've lied about.

I dare to steal a glance at Devon, over by the Chevy. Helping Noah drag his captive bleeder to Gareth's trailer. Does *he* know? Has he known all along? If he does, what the hell has he been playing at?

Danger. Danger. Danger.

"I read all the stuff you wrote. Before we even knew each other.

What were you like . . . fucking *studying* me, or something? What even *is this*? Between us?"

Wait. This is about *her*. Not ADAPT.

"Core, listen. It doesn't mean anything. It wasn't—"

"You said I was 'whoring myself out.' That people like me are, and I quote, 'part of the problem.'"

I study the white glare of her shivering teeth. "I can explain," I say in a voice so tiny I'm not sure it's mine. Now I'm the one who's about to cry.

I can't support myself on one leg any longer. The other girls start whispering again.

"You know I was taking that stupid journalism class." My cheeks burn as I flail for my crutches on the ground. Cora just watches. Doesn't help me. "I wanted to write a piece about what it was like to live at a Sara center. For school."

"Is *that* why you were being so nice to me? For a fucking home-work assignment?"

I manage to curl a finger around one of the crutches and pull it under my arm, though I nearly topple over in the process.

"At first . . . yes." It feels like hell, but at least she's not accusing me of being a mole. "I thought you might be a good like, *subject,* or whatever—"

"What am I, some kind of zoo animal? You didn't even ask me."

"You're right. I should have . . . I'm sorry. But that was before I knew you, I mean *really* knew you. Before everything happened."

She responds with a hard, unflinching stare.

"Cora?"

The blond girl coughs in the raw silence that follows.

"Please. I'm sorry . . ."

"I'm not ready for sorry yet."

A chill slinks down my spine. Margot's right behind me.

"Inside, ladies. It's cold," she says. Floating past me through the door.

All three of the girls follow her, caught in her gravity.

"Core—"

Cora slams the door. Like we're back at the Sara center. Like we've never even met.

The evergreens groan in the frigid breeze as Kayla wordlessly sidles up to me. Maybe she's waiting for me to spill my woes—like old times at the Fair Shake. But I never told her my whole story back then, and I'm not about to start now.

I dig my crutch into the earth and turn, careful not to slip on the slick, dead pine needles.

All I want to do is run.

I fling open the door to my ski-shop prison. Stare at that crusted black puddle on the floor.

I called Devon a liar, but he was telling me the truth. He didn't lure her away or turn her against me. This happened because *I* lied. And there's nothing I can do to fix it. If our roles were reversed, I'd feel the same way she does. Maybe worse.

Silky entrails of our binding web unravel all around me. I can feel her separate from me with every passing minute, like she's running down a long, dark road.

But I knew, didn't I? Knew we'd have to separate at some point. That was the plan all along. But every time I imagined it, it was *me* separating from *her*.

There's nothing holding me here. Not anymore. I can't stay and watch him consume her. If I can find my way back to civilization, I can finally make that phone call to the FBI. There's still a way to win this.

Those rogue bleeders Kayla mentioned didn't fare too well out there, but I have a vague sense of the route Devon took, I've fed, and—most importantly—I have Daylights. I bend on a single, shaking knee to grab Cora's backpack from underneath the cot.

I don't know what I'm expecting as I hobble around the back of the lodge and make my way toward the tree line. A swarm of guards in ghillie suits, hiding in the brush? A barricade of bear traps and snares? I figure Devon's probably armed half the people here—Kayla being one of them. But they're not exactly patrolling the grounds.

The Saras are all circling Gareth's trailer, anxiously waiting to take the new bleeder for a spin. Hoping Devon will open the door and call out a name. They fuse into one trembling, voracious pack—a withering den of wolves. If anybody sees me escape, they're not about to chase me. In fact, they might not realize they've seen anything at all. I limp past the Chevy, where grisly stalactites of frozen blood hang from the back bumper.

I decide to steer clear of the dirt road. I'll follow it down, but stick to the wilderness. If Devon notices I'm missing, that'll be the first place he'll look. And he's a hell of a lot faster than I am, considering the state of my leg.

I swing myself along on my crutches, winding between the trees, using the moon as my lantern. Putting exhilarating space between my body and that awful camp.

I'm not sure how far I've gone—maybe a mile?—before I start to feel the cold. *Really* feel it. Adrenaline kept my blood pumping— kept me warm—the moment I decided to run. But I don't even have a proper winter coat—just Cora's stained leather jacket over my hoodie and the thermal Margot gave me. I need to stop and build a fire. Ride out the night, pop a Daylight once the sun comes up, and keep moving. Except—*no*. Fire is a bad idea. I don't know how far I've gone, but my guess is it's not far enough. I can't risk anyone at the camp seeing smoke. I need to keep walking. Stumbling. Whatever it is I'm doing. A sorry excuse for a getaway.

The crutches chafe my underarms, and there's an exhausted tremor in my good leg. Doesn't matter. Just keep going. Swing, step. Swing, step. Swing—

I slam my crutch, but there's no ground to catch it. I tumble down a rocky, snow-spattered mound. It's small. Barely a hill. I probably wouldn't have tripped at all, if not for the crutches. I attempt to brace myself—straightening and planting my injured leg.

I howl as my flesh strains against the stitches. I can't help it. The pain is so intense, so sudden and all-consuming. I slap both hands over my mouth to muffle the sound.

An owl answers back. Mocking me.

I stay that way, crumpled on the wet, icy ground.

The stitches are still intact. I'd be bleeding again if they weren't. The cold knifes through me with double cruelty, now that I'm sitting still. Snow seeps through my sweatpants.

I need to keep moving. Doesn't matter how slowly. If I get far enough, I can build that fire. I'll just keep walking till I hit something. A hunting lodge, or a forest ranger's station. I don't remember exactly how we got here from Clark, but I know it's out there somewhere. I've got Daylights and Cora's giant, unwieldy map. I can survive a few sunrises.

I ignore the yelp of my stitches as I engage my flaccid core and wobble to my feet. But as I pause to release a breath, my confidence goes with it.

Sure, I can keep inching along. And the sunlight won't kill me. But after twenty-four hours, I'm going to get hungry. If I try to eat squirrels or birds, I'll get sick. If I'm lucky enough to encounter anyone in the forest, I might guzzle their carotid before they can help me. If only I had someone like Gareth. A loyal, unlifted friend to follow me around like a dog.

I shove the crutches under my arms and force myself to take a step. Then another. My wound seethes with each movement.

ADAPT got one thing right. It's hard—no, *impossible*—for a Sara to survive on their own. Devon saved himself by building a family. Finding people he could depend on. Even Mom had someone: me.

I don't have anyone.

I shudder as a gust of wind threatens to knock me off my crutches and back to the ground. Those alien tears stand in my eyes, ice cold. I refuse to blink. Refuse to feel them.

Walk, Mia.

Swing, step. Swing, step.

I stumble again. This time it's a rock, buried under the snow. My stable foot catches the slippery edge, and my ankle gives way.

I'm back on the ground.

This time, I don't get up.

The tears on my cheeks harden into a freezing rime.

I close my eyes and Cora's face materializes. That gorgeous, furious flash of her teeth. She's not mine anymore. Never was. As if someone like her could ever be *anybody's*.

Devon was right, when he told me—like a confidant, a fucking *friend*—that she was done with me. That's just it, though. The way he talks. Like that game two truths and a lie. He's been playing it since the day we met.

I sift through everything he's told me since my arrival.

He said the woman at the Walmart shot me.

I didn't see the gun.

Only *told him* I saw it.

Still. It could be true.

He told me I'd only been locked up in that ski shop for twenty-four hours, even though it felt like a thousand years. But it's impossible to tell time when you're trapped in the dark with rust poisoning.

And then there's what he said about Mom.

What he told me *feels* like the truth. That's the worst part. I can't find the lie because there might not be one. Not when it comes to Mom. In the end, he knew her better than I did.

My body works overtime to fight the creeping hypothermia, but it's an angry ouroboros of pain. The wind kicks shards of dirty ice in my face, minute after agonizing minute.

I lift my ragged gaze to the moon, waning behind a sheath of fog. Try to brush the hair from my eyes, but I can't feel my fingers anymore.

I can't do this.

After all I've been through, all I've survived, I'm still that terrified child alone in Mom's Jeep, panicking and pissing her pants. Desperate for someone to protect her.

I see it now. What he's created.

Why they don't leave.

There's resentment. Infighting. Grudges up and down the mountain. But every family has grudges. And living with a grudge is better than dying alone.

Fog swallows the moon, like the slow dissolve at the end of a movie. I shiver and plant my crutch, dragging myself upright. Turn in the opposite direction.

Back the way I came.

MARCH 2024

"You have to promise you'll do everything I say," Cora whispers, pulling my blanket over our heads. I stare, transfixed by the light of her phone. "There's a reason I haven't gotten caught."

Discord is the only place official ADAPT business or gossip gets discussed. No exceptions. When Devon—a.k.a. David? a.k.a. the chatter he's hired?—talks to Cora on her socials, they avoid the topic altogether. If anyone at the center were to read their messages, they would paint a picture of an ordinary long-distance relationship. On Discord, people are free to anonymously discuss the movement. Every time she finishes checking in, Cora deletes the app from her phone.

"I never know when these assholes are gonna randomly search my stuff," she explains, scrolling through the chat. "So if you get an account, you gotta do the same thing. Even though you're on Two. You never know."

I read over Cora's shoulder as she downloads me on the latest news. The secret server is buzzing with helpful information—mostly about Red Markets, Daylights, and where to find both. There's also police-scanner activity. Whispers about recent escapes and public demonstrations. All the stuff the press won't publish is on Discord. It's got shades of the old Facebook group, but there's a razor-sharp, militant urgency to the conversation. This isn't about helping people navigate an incurable disease. It's about winning a war.

"The day before Thanksgiving, I sent them two thousand dollars," Cora explains under her breath. "They put me in touch with this guy named Bradley, who's gonna get us a car when we're ready to go."

"Oookay, well now he's got your two thousand dollars, but you're still here."

"That's the thing, I'm stuck. I haven't figured out how to get the Daylights. That's part of the deal—".

"Except you also *paid them*—"

"The Daylights are the only reason they'll take a risk like this. The money helps keep things secure. They told me to steal as many bottles as I could, but I can't—"

A knock at the door interrupts her. I throw off the blanket as Cora taps her screen and deletes the Discord app.

I'm expecting Alonzo. But it's Beatrice.

"Mia, I was hoping we could have a word. We've got some folks from legal in the building and they'd like to speak to you."

Franklin's throwing Cora under the bus.

He admits he attacked me, but he insists Cora lifted me—not him. Which means she should be serving an equal punishment, upstairs. The staff have definitely noticed I don't go anywhere without her, and vice versa, lending some credence to Franklin's claims.

"They just want to know *exactly* what happened that night, in your words," Beatrice says to me, perched at the opposite end of a long, sterile conference table.

"It was definitely him. Franklin was the one who—" I almost say *lifted*. "Who infected me. Not her."

"When we first had this conversation, you said you couldn't tell who it was."

"I could barely talk that day. My memory's a lot clearer now."

"You and Ms. Quinto have gotten close these past few weeks—"

"I mean, she was there for me on the worst night of my life."

"Mia," my lawyer pipes up, sitting beside Beatrice. Drinking a stale, oversweetened street coffee that burns my sinuses. "What do you know about the ADAPT initiative?"

I hold my breath. Not because of the smell.

"I haven't heard anything, what is that?"

"Simply put, it's a terrorist group. A school of thought that Saras should attempt to infect as many people as possible in order to tip the scales."

"Okay. Well. I don't think I've ever—"

"Mr. Stewart claims Ms. Quinto subscribed to some of these philosophies."

"I've never heard her say anything about it."

"Mia, we take what happened to you very seriously," Beatrice says. "And we just—"

"I don't know what you want me to say. Franklin was the only one who put his hands on me that night. And I don't know anything about this ADAPT stuff. I'm still trying to figure out how I fit in here, and Cora's helping. She's a good person. Sorry, but that's all I have for you."

My resolve is steady. But inside, I'm howling.

I find Cora back on Four, in her own room. She texted me and said she wanted to show me her "treasure map." She shuts the door behind me, holding a familiar padded envelope in her hands: her "birthday present."

She unfurls a massive paper map of the United States, the kind you see befuddled dads in old road movies wrestle with behind the wheel.

"After I sent that money to Bradley, someone sent me this. I asked why they couldn't just drop me a pin, but I guess phones are off-limits once we get going, so—"

"Cora, we have a problem. Potentially. I dunno."

She lowers her hands, limply holding the map at hip height like a paper skirt.

"Potentially? You *don't know*?"

"They're gonna question you again about . . . y'know. That night. And Franklin's been telling people you're uh . . . into this stuff."

"Into *what* stuff?"

I make a meek gesture toward the map. There's a highlighted route, from New Jersey to the Midwest. Along the way are a half dozen hand-drawn red stars. A Post-it stuck to the bottom.

"What did you say to them?"

"Nothing, obviously. But I'm worried we don't have much time. If they can prove you were the one who did this, if they move you upstairs for good—"

"Fuck," she hisses, her face two inches from mine. Anger I've learned to receive but not absorb.

"We just need to get this done. Now."

She nods, gripping the map in two trembling fists.

"Show me."

"Okay so, this is the outpost."

She pulls off the Post-it stuck to the bottom. An address in Nebraska.

"That's a long way from here."

"That's why they got us a car. Our first stop is this Dodge dealership across the bridge in Hackensack—"

"Where Bradley is."

"Yeah."

"Bradley who has your two thousand dollars—"

"That's the going rate, for a gig like this."

A moment passes. "Cora, where's Hackensack? Across *which* bridge?"

"The GW. It's in New Jersey."

"Do they expect us to just . . . *walk to New Jersey*?"

"Er . . . I guess so? We can't scan into a cab or take the train. We can do it though, we're pretty fucking fast."

"We can't *run*, are you insane? Every cop in the city will be looking for us. We'll give ourselves away in two seconds."

I sink to the ground, and she follows. Kicking a tube of mascara on the floor back and forth between her bare feet. There's an itch at the back of my mind. I grab the map from her.

"Can I hop on Discord? I need to ask your people a question."

"About walking to Jersey?"

I shake my head. "About the Saras who live in the subway tunnels."

While we wait for a response, our plan takes shape. The best, and really, the *only*, time to leave the building is during dinner. I saw firsthand how empty the halls are as each floor gets released to the dining room. We need a meal before we go. That's a must. After I eat, I'll sneak into the kitchen stairwell and wait for Cora to have dinner with the other Fours. Then we'll casually exit the building at the same time as the bloodletters. I rescued my old badge from those bloodstained jeans before the trash got taken out, and thankfully, it still works. I've tested it, stealthily pinballing into the staff stairwell and back out again during dinner. Nobody's seen me.

Then, there's the matter of stealing Daylights. I'll have to pull this off before I go to the dining room. The Daylights get locked up in a medicine cabinet underneath the nurses' station on Two every night, right before dinner. Alonzo changes the combination every Friday night, but only by one digit. If last week the combo was 41, 72, 20, this week it'll be 41, 72, 21, and so on. All I have to do is count the weeks since I last helped him put everything away. That, and distract him long enough to weasel my way in while everyone's at dinner. Cora says she'll run downstairs to tell Alonzo one of her neighbors is unresponsive in bed—like Lisa was. It's a shitty thing to lie about. But it stands a chance of keeping him occupied.

We grab a gulp of icy air in the courtyard after dinner. The temperature hardens me, inside and out, as I watch Cora from the corner of my eye. She lights up a clove and zips the jacket I gave her. Loosening this bond feels impossible. But I'll have to, if I want to finish what I started. I was wrong, when I thought all the fight had gone out of me. The dark, secret place I've been storing all my rage is exactly as I left it.

Cora gasps smoke in the wrong direction when her phone lights up. I wriggle in close to read over her shoulder.

Someone's responded to my Discord post.

> » Will meet u at the MTA maintenance entrance at the NE corner of 23rd and 8th Ave tmrw. Door will be unlocked for u btw 6–7pm but NO LATER.
> » PW is turtle.
> » Transfer funds tonite
> » We can do this for u for $10K.

"Shit . . ." Cora stares at the number onscreen. "Ten thousand dollars? That's insane. We don't—"

"It's fine." My voice is cold and smooth. "Tell them yes."

We pack in separate rooms. A private moment, almost ceremonial, to ingest our new reality like a dangerous potion.

Cora texts me from upstairs.

Going to see my kids on 9 one last time. do you
wanna come meet them?

I hesitate. This is a pure, tender part of her life. I shouldn't leave
my mark there, even a faint one. If everything unfolds the way it's
supposed to.

You go. I don't wanna take away from your time w
them. ♥

She comes back around 6 A.M. Quietly, like she thinks I'm already
asleep. As if that were possible on a day like this.

She crawls into bed and meets my stare: hard, burnished gold.
She's ready. We both are.

Something thrums in her silence. Her stare. An almost imperceptible murmur I hadn't noticed before, like the wink of a distant
star. I squeeze my eyes shut. Like all of a sudden I'm afraid. But the
hum just gets louder.

I'll never be able to translate a person's private thoughts. That's
not something a Sara can do. Still. It feels as though she's signaling
to me between breaths.

There is something she's trying to tell me.

Something I've been aching to hear.

My chest swells. Flowers bloom behind my eyes.

No . . .

It's too late now. I've already decided what this is. All the things
it can *never* be.

She reaches out to me. Runs her smooth thumbnail along my
bottom lip as I open my eyes.

No.

She slides her thumb into my slack, willing mouth. Questing
toward my teeth. My body betrays me.

Yes.

In return, I offer her my thumb. A bashful laugh rises between
us as we bite down at the same time.

I don't know what this is. Almost a kiss, but not quite. An oath.

I watch her face for a reaction. Her eyes blink closed as a soft sigh moves up her throat. The raw, fantastic pain of her bite shoots all the way through me, and I feel a dazzling coil of certainty expand and contract between us.

I sink in deeper. Aching to caress bone.

Her blood is different than the first time I tasted it—the time it saved my life. It's delicate like sugar water. Sweet, weak tea steeped in a cup of venom.

But I need more than this. This can't be the only part of her I'll ever—

She's pulling her thumb from my teeth.

Is it over? Already? No. Can't let this—

I seize the back of her head and press my mouth to hers. There's that liminal rush of terror as I wait for an answer from her body. Finally, she parts her lips for me. I realize I can't tell the difference between the taste of my blood and hers. It's one and the same.

An invigorating tingle rushes over me, like waking from a long, dark sleep, as I slip a finger between our delicious red mouths. I can feel her asking me for this. There's a ribbon of invisible light leading me to all the places she wishes someone would touch her.

I slide my hand down the front of her tight Lycra shorts. The ones she was wearing in that bare-backed, black-and-white photo in the mirror. I have every contour committed to memory.

I never thought my hand would be this steady.

This isn't me.

But it is.

She undresses us, and I lose my fear with each sip of her. The way that cold glass in my hand used to calm my frantic pulse.

She tugs my hair to guide me out from between her thighs and pulls me on top of her. Knows that's where I want to be. She drives those gorgeous claws into my bare hips as our bodies twine and tumble into darkness as one.

Wait.

Wait . . .

There's a sound I can't identify. An insistent throb that swarms my head, drowning out everything else. When she moans into my neck, I barely hear it.

What *is* that?

Faster and faster. Louder and more urgent. Screaming at me.

I know it's you. I can hear your heart beating.

She comes to pieces underneath me a second before I wrench my body away.

Both of us pretend to fall asleep.

At least, I'm pretending. Sick with unresolved longing and the memory of that horrible phone call on Christmas.

The way he spoke to me when he thought I was someone else.

Everything is mixed up and muddy in my mind and my body and I'm trying to find the joy, trying to bottle the thrill of what we just did and tuck it away someplace safe, but I can't.

I dress quietly. Trying not to wake her.

This should not have happened. Cannot ever happen again.

I'm going to destroy everything she believes in, everything she loves.

She turns from me, onto her other side. Like I can already feel her regretting me.

Or maybe that's just me, hoping she is.

☾ ☾ ☾

Two o'clock. I stand first. Her eyes are already open. At some point, she also got dressed. I wonder if she's going to say something about what happened. Even allude to it. I hate how relieved I am when she doesn't.

Showers. In separate rooms.

Fine. It's better this way.

I watch pearls of our blood fall down my body and circle the drain as I suck the finger where she broke my flesh. The spot healed hours ago. Trancelike, my other hand follows the water down between my breasts. Down to the place all my pain is lying in wait . . .

No.

I twist the faucet all the way to cold and shiver like my body's trying to shed a fever. Glare at the water till it runs clear.

Dinnertime approaches, and I double-check my backpack to straighten my twisting thoughts. I've made plenty of space for the pills. There's no leeway for distraction, no guardrails. Lose focus and we lose fucking *everything.*

Five o'clock. The afternoon guests and volunteers clear out. I catch Mandy's gaze as she steps into the elevator. Guess this is goodbye.

Five fifteen. Two gets called for dinner. I text Cora as I shuffle toward the dining room.

> **Omw to dinner, come down in 5 and grab Alonzo**

I hit send, and the elevator opens. Cora spills through the doors, eyes full of crocodile tears. Wait. What the *fuck*? She's early. She's not supposed to do this till I've eaten.

I try to catch her gaze, but she doesn't look at me.

Horror thickens in my lungs as she jogs toward Alonzo, at the end of the hall. Gesticulating with wide-eyed intensity. She's telling the lie. I let the other residents trickle ahead of me into the dining room. If she's doing this now, she's doing it for a reason.

Alonzo swipes his badge and trots up the staff staircase. As the door clicks shut, Cora finally meets my stare.

"What are you doing?" I mouth as she approaches.

"They're searching my room."

"Who?"

"That guy, that lawyer. And two of the nurses from Eight."

"You've got to be shitting me—"

Obviously, she's not. She's holding her backpack. Ready to go.

"But we have to eat first." I steady myself against the nurses' station. Like my legs might abandon me. "This wasn't the plan."

"Yeah well, new plan."

I bite down on my knuckle. Grinding my bone for maximum focus.

"Forty-one, seventy-two, twenty-six," Cora whispers.

"Right."

The medicine cabinet is more like a safe, nestled underneath the nurses' counter behind Alonzo's vacant ergonomic chair. My knees quake as I crouch down and meet the eye of the combination lock.

41, 72, 26.

I press the latch with my thumb. It doesn't give.

Okay. Breathe. Maybe my hand was shaking.

41, 72, 26.

"That's not it, that's not the fucking code," I croak.

Did I count the weeks incorrectly? Today is Saturday. He would've changed it yesterday. It's been four weeks since I became a resident here. Four changes.

"It was twenty-six. I counted. Four weeks. Twenty-three, twenty-four, twenty-five, twenty-six—"

"Wait. It was a Thursday night," she says.

"Yeah?"

"He changes it on *Fridays*. Count again."

I breathe out stale air, studying the lock through a wall of tears. "Twenty-seven."

"Go, go, go."

41, 72, 27.

Click.

There aren't as many bottles as I was hoping. Only about a dozen. They're probably due for a shipment. I hadn't planned to take their entire stock. Didn't want it to be blatantly obvious what we'd done. Plus, people need them.

"Do you think six bottles is okay?" I ask in a cramped whisper.

"They just said take as many as you can."

The faint beep of a scanned badge echoes across the hall. Someone's in the stairwell. We're wasting time. I waterfall half the bottles off the shelf and into my open backpack. Knee the cabinet shut and twirl the dial.

I grab Cora's arm and whisk her toward my room at full speed as the door to the stairwell creaks open. We peer around the corner. It's not Alonzo—it's one of the phlebotomists from the kitchen. But he'll be back down soon enough. And he'll know Cora just told a lie.

"We have to go now," I hear myself say. This is a mess. Neither of us has eaten and we won't be able to make a smooth getaway with the bloodletters when they leave the kitchen. But if we don't move and cut our losses, we might not get out at all.

The smell of the dining room taunts me as we creep out of my room and inch toward the staircase that leads down to the kitchen. I pull my waterlogged badge from my back pocket.

"Just run."

Cora grips my hand as I swipe the badge and we catapult into the stairwell.

We pour down the steps, two, three at a time. Skitter around the corner, past the double doors to the kitchen. Toward the street-level exit.

As I scan my badge one last time, an alarm blares. Boring through me like a chainsaw.

But the door gives.

Freezing wind assaults my face. We sprint against it, hurtling around the side of the building toward the drawbridge. If they start pulling it back, we're in deep water. Maybe literally. Jesus, how much of a head start did we manage? Ten seconds? Two?

We tear across the bridge as it grinds to life beneath our feet. Cora yelps, but she doesn't slow down. I keep the glimmer of Eleventh Avenue in my crosshairs, matching her miraculous speed. I didn't know I could move like this. Like her. Maybe we'll make it. Maybe—

The bridge drags us back as we bolt forward, and the cityscape warps like a disorienting Hitchcockian dolly zoom. I can't tell how close we are, or how far.

"Jump!" Cora shouts.

"Wha—"

She yanks me up and over the gap between the street and the drawbridge, roiling with murky whitecaps. It's only a couple of feet, but the terrifying, lightning-quick leap clobbers all the air out of me as we slam to the sidewalk.

I glance her way, and she's already righted herself. No time to relish any relief. She starts tugging me along.

"Wait, we gotta slow down," I hiss through my teeth.

"But—"

"Look at all the cars."

I'm grateful there aren't too many pedestrians on the river greenway, considering it's so cold tonight. But up ahead, on Eleventh, there's a lot of traffic whizzing past. It's more of a highway in this part of the city. Someone's bound to notice if we're traveling at the same speed, on foot.

Cora stops and shivers, hugging her jacket to her chest, as if she's just now realized she's outside. She protectively shrinks as she peers at the building behind us, then up at the fortress of skyscrapers.

Like she wishes she could run back the way she came, now that she's standing still.

"Just walk. C'mon."

We only have a few minutes before they realize we made it across the drawbridge and roll the thing back out, sending security along with it. Before the police know they ought to be looking for us. We're six blocks below Twenty-Third Street and three blocks west of the train station. But if we play this right, if we're invisible, we just might make it.

I link arms with Cora and shuffle us uptown, regulating her speed with each step. Her startled eyes bounce in every direction, and I remember it's been years since she's walked the streets of her city. I can't imagine the sensory overload. The dizzying miasma of light and sound is almost too much for me and I was only in there a month.

I once saw the saddest video of a seal who was raised in captivity, too scared to jump into the ocean when they released her to the wild. The trainers had to keep redirecting her. They finally just picked her up—this slippery whirligig of terror—and tossed her into the water.

I give Cora a reassuring squeeze as we walk.

"Shit, phones—" She digs into her backpack. I pull mine from my pocket and switch it to airplane mode.

From here on out, we're ghosts.

Walking uptown is easier than walking east.

There are more people once we cross Ninth Avenue, and even with the ferocious wind I can still smell each and every passing body. Whispers of bitter caffeine fill the air, burning my eyes and nose like hay fever. The deterrent helps, but still, I'm all too aware we skipped dinner. I realize I haven't been hungry since I became this way; never experienced the world like a Sara hurting for blood.

We reach the Twenty-Third Street station and spot the maintenance entrance on the northeast corner—an inconspicuous black door on the side of the adjacent building, slapped with an EMPLOYEES ONLY sign. It's supposed to be unlocked for us. We're on time. Still, I'm dizzy with nerves imagining what's lurking behind it.

Cora marches right toward it. I yank her back by the collar as a cloud of caffeine wafts past. "Hang on. People are watching."

"They're not."

"What do you mean? They're everywhere."

"Yeah, but they're not *watching*."

I take a nervous glance up and down the avenue; feet pound the sidewalk, making double time. Eyes are locked and loaded straight on, like everyone's picked the same distant focal point. It would be vulgar to look at anything—or anyone—for too long. But of course, I knew this. About New York. Everything in motion, everywhere, every waking minute. A hypnotic gravity that's stronger than fear.

"At least wait for the walk signal," I whisper. "Four . . . three . . . two—"

The orange hand at the corner blinks, and there's a break in the foot traffic. I hold my breath as Cora tries the door, and it gives way.

At first, it seems as though we're in a dark, dead-end utility closet, till a weak pool of light pulls my gaze, about twelve feet down. We're standing at the top of a spiral staircase. A jagged screech impales my ears as an approaching train hits a curve in the track, too close for comfort. I recognize this type of alcove from the night Jade and I made our emergency exit from the F train. We can access the perpendicular tunnel at the bottom of the stairs.

We take a tentative step into the depths. Then another. The whole staircase rumbles and sways in time with the passing train, and sparks fly from the tunnel, illuminating Cora's apprehensive face in fits and starts.

"Remember, look out for the third rail," I whisper, to her as much as myself, as the train screams away from the station and we reach the bottom. My eyesight comes to life in the dark as I point at the tracks. "That's it, right there. The silver one."

Icy metal meets my neck before we can take another step.

Someone's pulled a knife on me.

Cora shrieks, and a figure springs from the shadows to clamp a hand over her mouth.

The woman holding Cora wears a yellow vest and a hard hat over her frizzy gray locs. I can tell the person behind me with the knife is a man. I hear his labored tenor as he grunts in my ear.

But I can't smell either of them.

"No trespassing, ladies," the guy snarls, gathering my hair in his fist.

Cora blubbers something against the woman's palm, narrowing her eyes at me.

Right. "Turtle," I gasp. "Turtle, turtle, turtle—"

The woman releases Cora. But the man's still got me in his forceful grip.

"I said *turtle*." I writhe 180 degrees, trying to face him. He lowers his rusted blade but doesn't let go of my hair.

"Phones off. No flashlights," the woman says drily. Cora nods, and I try to.

She and Cora make their way into the tunnel, but the man's still holding me back. My stomach turns.

"You got Daylights?"

"Oh. Yes. But not a lot. We're supposed to sell them at the—"

Cora whirls around. "Dude, we paid you *ten fucking grand*—"

"It's fine, it's fine . . ." I mutter, digging into my backpack. I give him one bottle, careful to conceal the rest. We'll sell four and keep the last one for ourselves.

Finally, he puts the knife away. Pockets the medication. Cora meets my eye with an upturned lip and I shrug. What the hell else was I supposed to do? We should be glad that was all he wanted.

We skulk along in silence, following our guides in their MTA-worker disguises. Cramming into different alcoves to dodge the passing trains. At each station, we duck behind the concrete partitions, sprinting past prying eyes. The subway Saras can sense the trains approaching, and they know the location of all the cameras and employees. They only speak to tell us, "Express heading north in ten seconds," or, "Stay low, surveillance ahead." We breathe mouthfuls of oily exhaust and thick mildew. A heightened sense of smell is a curse down here. I wonder how the tunnel dwellers pull it off. Maybe you get used to it, over time. You get used to pretty much anything when you're in hiding.

At least the rats avoid us.

We hit Columbus Circle, a congested artery, and strategically veer into a network of quieter, smaller tunnels to avoid the light. I picture the scenery up above. We're at the southwest corner of Central Park—which I hardly ever visited. There's a pang in my chest as I realize I never immersed myself in this city I used to fantasize about. And now I'm leaving for good, a hundred feet underground.

We're meant to merge with the express tunnel and follow it all the way up to 125th. It's in this long, cloistered passageway that our guides pause and the woman asks, "Anyone hungry?"

Neither of us replies at first. No trains approach. It's silent aside from the squalid, measured drip of a leak around the corner.

A treacly scent dances toward me, cutting the stench of urban rot.

"Me." That's Cora.

The woman's eyes shift to mine. I shake my heavy head. I am not ready for this.

"C'mon, Mia. You should—"

"I can hold out."

The woman leads Cora into a shadowy vestibule up ahead. Her partner follows. I squint and detect two faint heat signatures—one fading fast.

"Stay here," the man mumbles over his shoulder. "Don't go trying to skip uptown by yourself."

I turn my back. As though that will keep me from smelling them. Hearing them.

I stare at a floor-to-ceiling scrawl of red and white graffiti on the craggy wall of the tunnel. It takes a moment before the disparate whorls of color gel into an image. It's that goddamn fish again, spattered with red paint. Someone's drawn a smug, toothy grin on its vacant face, like a grotesque, zombie-like piranha. More red dribbles from its open mouth.

A wet *snap* resonates from the vestibule. Cora whispers, but I can't hear what she's saying. My empty gut whines as I keep my eyes pinned to that perverted Darwin fish. Trying to anchor myself.

There's a tug of bitter longing at my core. I wish I were more than a girl cowering in a dirty subway tunnel, afraid of my own body.

But more than that, I wish Cora hadn't left me here alone. That she could *fight it*.

I know it's wrong to judge her for what she's doing. But I want to. I do.

I drag a breath of moist, putrid air. She and I are not the same. I have to remember that. This is who she is—what she believes. I can't compete with the image on that wall. The promise of blood without consequence.

She materializes, and our eyes lock. She wipes her mouth with the sleeve of her leather jacket. Leaving a stain.

We make our way above ground at the 175th Street station: the riskiest leg of the journey. Our guides help us sneak through the wrong end of an emergency exit, where we'll wait for the opportune moment to hoist ourselves up onto the platform.

Cora and I haven't exchanged a word since 125th. I think she knows I'm upset, but she doesn't know why, or how to make it better. Not that we've got time to stop and talk it out.

"You're gonna wait till the next train comes and watch the foot traffic," our female guide explains. We know by now we're never going to learn their names. "Hop up onto the platform once the last car clears and folks start heading up the stairs. There's a camera at the northeast staircase, so hug the wall as you round the corner."

I crane my neck to look at her and offer my thanks, but they've both vanished. There's only the faint acidity of cold blood, hanging ghostlike in the air. The sudden silence is unnerving.

"What the hell, they're not even gonna wait to make sure we made it?" Cora mutters.

"Shhh, there's a train coming. Get ready."

We stick to the paper-thin shadows just beyond the emergency gate, watching the passengers weave in and out of the station. A frail woman exits the train and starts humping a heavy suitcase up the stairs, one at a time. There's an elevator, but it's probably broken. My panicked blood boils. We can't stand down here much longer, we're too exposed. We have to keep moving.

"Fuck it," Cora breathes, and makes a break for it.

I gasp, swooping past the emergency gate and onto the platform beside her. The sloth-like woman on the staircase frowns. Looks right at us. Cora grabs for my hand. I swat it away.

"Follow signs for the bridge, to your right," I hiss.

But Cora's frozen. God dammit. Am I going to have to piggyback her all the way to New Jersey? On an empty stomach?

At that moment, a young man in janitor's coveralls descends. He waves to get the woman's attention halfway down the stairs. "Give ya a hand, ma'am?"

The woman turns to face him. Now, I take Cora's hand. Squeezing it like a punishment. "This way."

We slip around the bend, toward a passage that leads to the George Washington Bridge Bus Station. There's only one other person: a cyclist in head-to-toe reflective spandex, walking his bike. Dude must be freezing. Then again, if you ride your bike across a massive interstate bridge for kicks, the cold probably doesn't rattle you too much.

"I'm sorry," Cora whispers. Hasn't let go of my hand. Or maybe it's me who hasn't released her.

"Let's just walk."

We follow the cyclist at a safe distance as he exits the adjoining bus station. The bridge looms above us, a shimmering colossus of skeletal arches, like the mouth of a mammoth whale fossil.

The cyclist carries his bike up a rickety metal staircase, where the bridge's structure meets the road. I nod to Cora. We'll give him some space, then go the same way. I'd prefer to keep my distance from the glow of his neon spandex . . . and the smell of his sweat.

The rusty old stairs are riddled with holes and jagged edges. I shudder, imagining what it would feel like to fall and scrape my knee. Cora and I finally detach, moving in a cautious single file.

We reach the top and follow an impossibly slim pedestrian path, protected by warped, ancient metal rails on either side.

"No running, just like before," Cora reminds both of us, eyeing the cars as they rumble past.

"Mhmm."

"Just a casual, freezing-cold stroll to Jersey." Her eyes move over me, searching for the hint of a smile. There isn't one. "I really am sorry, for what I did back there. I kinda panicked—"

She thinks this is about how she hesitated in the train station. I didn't realize I was still radiating so much bitterness about her feeding.

"It's fine. I don't want to . . . Let's just get there."

"Mia—"

"I said it's fine."

We've just breached the riverbank on the New York side when a skirl of sirens explodes at our back. We slow our pace and turn, but don't stop moving.

"Are they coming this way?" My whole body is chattering.

"I-I'm not sure. . . . It almost looks like—" Cora squints. Her mouth goes rigid. "They're lining up. Like they're trying to block the bridge."

"Fuck."

"Do you think they're doing it on both sides?"

"Let's keep going and hope they're not." They're locking down the island. Trying to keep people—keep *us*—from getting out. They're less likely to block the opposite end. But we can't waste another second.

We walk as fast as we can without breaking into a run. Which is damn near impossible. The cars that are already en route are permitted to pass, so we keep up with them as the bridge behind us empties out. Tears thread across Cora's face in the icy wind. The distant red lights catch her hair like a fiery crown.

As we approach the other side of the river, something black and nebulous floats into my periphery. My shadow twin feeds me with a burst of courage, walking beside us on featherlight feet. I wonder if she's been here all along. Waiting for the right moment to make her presence known again.

Only taillights illuminate the New Jersey exit. Cars pass freely, and so does the lone cyclist ahead of us. I clamp a hand over my mouth to muffle a joyful shriek as Cora's eyes meet mine. We pick up the pace, running full-speed at last. The dark suburbs below await our arrival with open arms. I drop my resentment like a yoke. Forget my hunger. My fear. We're so damn close now. Cora meets my eye. I can hear her heart hammering, and mine answers.

Neither of us is thinking about what happens after this.

That's the thing about running full speed ahead. You might not see the cliff till you've run straight off.

NOW

We're having an important meeting tonight.

Kayla tells me this as we dig through a garbage bag of supplies from the outpost. Trying to find some clean clothes among the secondhand donations. I already know about the meeting, though. Gareth told me yesterday. The bleeder Noah abducted two weeks ago just died of an infection. Everyone's hoping Devon finally has a real plan to address the food shortage. Everyone who doesn't have a designated bleeder, anyway.

Gareth and I still meet for dinner every night. I've stopped questioning it.

I managed to reinfect my wound when I went on my little midnight sojourn. I'm off the crutches, but I still can't run. Margot examined my leg the night after my escape, and she could tell it was dirty. But she didn't comment on it. She probably wishes I'd run away. I don't think she told Devon about it, though. If he knew, there's no doubt he'd make sure *I* knew it. That's what I tell myself, anyway.

Even so, I've been keeping my distance from the two of them. Maintaining safety in numbers. I move into Kayla's cabin and try to keep myself occupied at night. My roommates and I chip ice from the freezing lake and melt it over the fire so we can do laundry. Noah enlists my help chopping wood. Like Kayla, he needs to ramble to keep his hunger at bay. He tells me stories about the Tucson Twelve—when there were twelve of them, anyway. Paul had a stomach of steel and once fooled a whole fancy restaurant of would-be victims by consuming an entire meal. It worked so long as he ran to the bathroom to throw up between courses. Bjorn, one of my roommates, is a trickster who once siphoned half the gas from the generators to run the old ski lift like some sort of amusement park ride. Devon made him go four days hungry for that one.

Noah's careful not to tell stories about Mom. Although part of me wishes he would.

All the while I swing the axe, trying my best to hit the same spot twice. I'm terrible at it, but it beats standing around and waiting for Devon to pluck me off and try to talk to me.

One night, he pulls me aside while I'm by myself stacking firewood. Scares the piss out of me when he materializes between the pines.

"Margot was telling me you offered to make a donation," he says.

"Oh uh . . . yeah—"

"Half a mil, she said?"

I nod and stammer, "My mom had this trust she left me."

His smirk is a sickle in the moonlight. "C'mon now. We both know she was broke as shit."

I clench the log I'm holding, and my jaw.

"Don't worry. If Margot were breathing down my neck, I would've said the same thing." He delivers a soft punch to my shoulder, like he's about to call me fucking "sport" or "kiddo" or something. "Your secret's safe with me."

I sigh with relief. Hanging a stiff, mild-mannered smile on my face. "Thanks."

As he slinks off, I think about mentioning Cora. I think about it every time I see him. But I know there's no point in asking about her. Not anymore.

The windows of the clinic are boarded up, just like the others. I can only tell the lights are on because of the low, constant drone of the generator. Otherwise, it's quiet. I linger whenever I pass, keeping my eyes peeled for a sign of life. Picking my loneliness like an inflamed scab. But Cora doesn't appear. None of the women do. The only people who come and go are Margot and her "girls"— Sophie and Kat. The stillness is unnerving. I can still feel Cora thrumming across the distance, but it's quieter now. A lagging counterpoint to my dejected pulse.

I have to remind myself she's probably doing something important in there, unlike me: trying and failing to chop wood. She doesn't want me to rescue her. Doesn't *need* me to.

Neither of us needs to be rescued. That's the other thing I understand now.

Even if I'd survived the wilderness and the cold and the sunlight, even if I'd made it to Clark or Steamboat Springs and found help, the two of us are fugitives. They closed down the George Washington Bridge to try and capture us. All this time I was hoping for a pardon, if I delivered Devon to the FBI. I was counting on their mercy. But I'm a Sara now. A Sara who's broken the law. Mercy is delusional. If I reveal myself, I'm getting locked up for good.

Night after night, I shear shards of kindling from a fallen tree with the edge of my axe. Like I can hack my humiliation down to a stump if I stand there long enough. I could have stayed in New York. Finished college, found a job. Fallen in love with a sweet, un-lifted, uncomplicated girl. Devon could have killed me. *Should* have killed me. I'm lucky to be alive. I'm safe, and I'm fed. Eventually, I might even be happy.

Maybe when springtime comes.

The sun goes down. Kayla and I bundle up and make our way down to the fire pit with our roommates Bjorn and Teresa, an on-again-off-again couple she met at Cloak and Dagger peddling pills. *Met.* Her words. They're snarky and shifty and don't seem to trust anyone except Kayla and Devon. They definitely don't trust me. They answer all my questions with a barbed "Yes" or "No" and appear to be allergic to eye contact. But they've seen the special treatment I get, and they know better than to question my place here. Same as me.

As Noah gets a blaze going, Gareth materializes at the door of his trailer. That's my signal. We try to be discreet about it. Even though everyone knows.

He's already got a cup waiting for me when I enter. Doesn't like to prolong our visits. We don't talk much. But I never leave without thanking him.

As I bring the chipped enamel camping mug to my lips, I glance across the compound through the window. A plume of exhaust pulls my gaze, wreathed with a soft yellow heat signature. There's an RV idling on the outskirts: a sleek, black behemoth hemmed with impenetrable tinted glass.

"Where'd that come from?" I point and ask Gareth.

"Pulled up late last night."

"Whose is it?"

"I have an idea. But it's not my news to share." There's a smile in his voice that doesn't reach his lips.

Across the way, Devon and Margot emerge from the main lodge and hike toward the fire. She's whispering something to him with a thin frown, but he's marching half a step ahead, not looking at her. It takes a moment to register across the darkness; he's looking at *me*. My gaze plummets to the floor as I swallow what's left in my cup and hand it to Gareth.

"Thanks."

He doesn't reply. Just sees me out and shuts the door. Locks it behind me.

I'm not surprised when I don't see Cora, or the other two women from the clinic—the willowy blonde and the long-legged Black girl. Like the three of them slipped through a hole in the world.

Devon scans our faces as I wedge between Kayla and Teresa. I brace myself for the weight of his stare. But his eyes sweep right over me.

"Is everyone here?"

I wait for somebody to mention the three missing women.

Should I?

I open my mouth, but nothing comes out.

Margot comes forward, like she's about to address the group. But Devon's already talking again. "Starting tonight, there are gonna be some changes around here."

The fire pops, spitting out sparks. Margot flinches and takes a step back.

I can't help but notice their stilted body language. Like a dance where both partners are fighting to take the lead.

"You're tired of this. I'm tired, too. But we've done good." He points to the black RV. "You've probably noticed we have a guest. If he likes the work we've been doing here, he's going to give us more money. A lot of it. And we've got Margot to thank for that."

He squeezes her hand and kisses it.

"Let's be real, we've got Margot to thank for a lot of things."

He holds her gaze as a modest smile softens the hard geometry of her face. Kayla starts to clap, and the rest of us cautiously join in. As though it might entice him to toss us a few more bread crumbs. Margot clears her throat like she's about to cut in, but once again, Devon talks over her. Dropping her hand.

"That said, and this is very important: Do not. Disturb. Our guest. Don't go creeping in the windows or knocking on his door. I cannot emphasize this enough. If he comes out to introduce himself, great. But he does his own thing, and whatever that *thing* might be, he's allowed to do it. Understood?"

Everybody nods. Waiting for him to tell us who it is. But he doesn't.

"Listen, guys. I'm proud of us. And you should be proud of yourselves." He focuses on each of our faces, one by one, like a benevolent game of duck, duck, goose. "We got through a hard winter. It wasn't supposed to be this way, and I'm sorry for that. But you pulled through. The worst is over."

His gaze lands on me. Smoke screams in my eyes, but I don't blink.

"I'll be back soon, okay? Try to stay off the ski lift this time. This isn't fucking Disneyland."

Bjorn is the first to laugh. Right on cue.

Devon smiles and spins on his heel, turning toward the dirt road. Only Margot moves to follow him. The rest of us are still salivating over those delicious words. *The worst is over.*

And yet . . . I'm surprised that's all he has to say. I was expecting real news. Not another layer to this blood-spattered matryoshka doll.

"Fun Size. Come with me."

My heart retches.

Kayla catches my eye, surprised to hear him call me by that old nickname. Everybody's staring. My feet are like lead.

"C'mon. I need you."

Nobody says anything else till we reach the top of the dirt road, where the Chevy is parked. Devon lets me catch up as Margot's uneasy gaze ricochets between our faces.

She shows me her back, building a wall with her body. Weaves her arms around his waist and whispers something I'm not supposed to hear. *Good luck,* maybe. I don't know. She kisses him, hard. I avert my gaze as she makes a show of slipping her tongue into his mouth. It's a lot. This is the second time she's done this in front of me. As if she thinks I need some sort of reminder. I hide my burning face in my scarf and grind dirty snow under my boot. A moment later, I let out a breath when I spot Gareth trotting in our direction.

I'm relieved he's coming. I think. Then again, I don't know what the hell this is. Why they need me.

Margot's eyes arc to mine as she finally separates from Devon and glides past. But I can't read her expression. She's gotten good at imitating that inscrutable vacancy of his.

Part of me wonders if we all have.

Devon tosses Gareth a set of keys. Thumbs toward the tree line, where the cube truck sits dormant. "Parked her back there."

At last, he turns to me. Smiles as he unlocks the Chevy.

"This'll be fun."

(((

Gareth follows us in his truck. I sit on my hands and bite my lips together as we rumble down the dirt road, mile after mile. If I'm quiet, if I'm just a statue riding shotgun, I can't piss him off. And yet, my silence seems to be the problem.

Devon toggles a cigarette from an open pack of Reds on the dash. Offers me one. I shake my head. Still haven't glanced at him.

I feel the jagged edges of uncertainty closing in around me. Does he know I tried to run? Is that why I'm here? I know he likes to play this game: See how long it takes me to confess. Catch me in a lie.

He cracks both our windows as he lights up. Sighs before he finally speaks.

"I didn't sleep with your friend."

I choke on a gust of wind.

"Actually, it might shock you to know I like to keep things professional around here. Plus . . . y'know. Margot." He takes a drag.

My red face swivels back in my scarf. "I don't know why we're talking about this."

"Sure you do."

I want to kick open the door and barrel-roll down the side of the mountain.

"Anyway, your friend Cora told me something interesting, the night we met."

"What, that she's got my fucking burn book?" I mutter.

"No, although that's . . . hilarious." A plume of smoke escapes his lips as the dirt road smooths out. "She told me what happened the night she lifted you."

I crumble in on myself, winding my arms around my shaking knees. There's a sharp tickle at the hollow of my neck.

"Oh."

"I know, now, why you didn't want to tell me. I'm sorry it happened that way."

I scratch the base of my throat. His eyes leave the road and meet mine. This time, I don't turn away.

"It was wrong of me to ask you. I hadn't earned it. Plenty of people have stories they don't want to share."

His neck cords as he drums the steering wheel. As if he's about to say something more but changed his mind.

"But yeah," he rebounds. "I didn't know what the deal was, between you two. Whether there was more to it."

"Uh-huh."

"Too bad about that fucking burn book."

"Guess so."

"Don't 'guess so' me, like I don't know how it feels to lose someone like that."

"It's not the same," I murmur. "I can tell she's still alive."

The ember of his cigarette glows in the silence.

"Mia. You're better than this. You think I don't see you creeping around the clinic every night?" He hisses air through his teeth. "You can't keep obsessing. You fucked up. You gotta own that and get past it."

A lapse falls between us. I swallow a thorn of shame, peeling away my sweaty scarf.

"So." He arches his brow. "Aren't you gonna ask me where we're going?"

"Fine. I'll bite."

He snorts. "That's cute. You're funny. That's why I brought you, by the way."

"'Cuz I'm *funny*?"

"'Cuz you won't. Bite. You've been eating."

We make a hairpin turn at a dilapidated stop sign and Devon digs into his coat pocket. Pulls out a phone. It's a dated, cheap flip burner. Like the one I found in Mom's bed.

He frowns, checking a text.

Guess there's one person here who *is* allowed to have a phone.

"Here's the situation," he says as he puts it away. His voice softens. Like he wants me to lean in. And I do. "I had one of my contacts in Omaha vet a group of bleeders for us. We're linking up with them tonight. I'm sure you heard what happened with the last group. We gotta have people we trust from now on, people we know are gonna stick with us. We're gonna chat with them and make sure everyone's being straight. That's why I need your help. You ate tonight. You can . . . y'know. *Discern*."

I nod. He snags my gaze.

"Has Gare been good to you?"

"Yeah." I know what he wants me to say next. "Thank you. Again."

We approach the ghostly borders of Clark. The Goodwill. Dawson's Dairy Farm.

"That reminds me," he says. "Something I've been meaning to ask you. It's something I ask everyone when they first get here, but . . . you and me kinda skipped the usual formalities. Didn't we?"

I'm expecting him to smirk at me. But he doesn't.

"When all this is over . . . what do you want?"

"What do you mean?"

"It's not a trick question, Fun Size."

"It's just . . . when you say *over*—"

"I mean when we're in charge of things. Who do you want to be?"

"Oh." I pick the gauzy fibers of my scarf. "I don't know yet."

"Everyone knows. Even if no one's ever asked, you always *know*."

"I mean . . . maybe I'll go back to New York?"

"And do what?"

"Um . . . I wanted to write, I guess."

"Wanted? Or currently want to?"

"I want to. I was gonna like, before all this happened, I thought I might do this fancy journalism program? I dunno." I fold my scarf into a triangle, like a tiny memorial flag.

"You sound so embarrassed."

"Because it is. Embarrassing. It feels dumb. Now."

"Your mom never let you go to college, did she?"

My breath catches. He's dangling those golden keys in front of my face again.

"It's not that she didn't *let* me—"

"You just couldn't."

In the silence, a memory glimmers. Jade at the bar. Seizing my hand. *There's only one other person in the world who knows what I've been through, and that's you. I'm not letting you leave.*

I need to keep talking about her. Every time we start, it's never enough. I don't know what to say to get him to hold that door open.

"It's interesting, looking back on how you guys did what you did—" He goes on, and a surge of reluctant gratitude fills my chest. "You were just a kid, but it's obvious you were the brains behind that operation."

"She did a lot. She bought the bar, she found our house—"

"Take a little credit where credit's due, would you?"

I shrug, conceding.

"One thing that kinda blew my mind though, when she and I were back together last year. Whenever she would talk about you? It was like you were still ten years old. And it was just the weirdest thing, when I finally saw you again."

"I remember. You came to our house and you scared the shit out of me."

He laughs.

I don't remember it being funny.

"Actually, that time, I thought you were Izzy. And that's not the time I'm talking about."

"The parking lot."

"No. There was one other time."

He pulls from the dregs of his cigarette.

"I knew you were at that show."

He means Cloak and Dagger. My nerves tighten. Even though it happened in another life, even though nothing he says can get me in trouble anymore.

"That's when it really hit me. How old you were. You were with this big group of people and you were drinking and you had this little . . ." He coughs. "You were wearing this *shirt*. I recognized it. It was your mom's."

Something slithers up my throat from between my frozen lungs. Something in the way his voice just changed.

"You just looked *so* . . . You looked happy. So I stayed out of your way and I didn't tell your mom. Didn't want to make the night all about you."

He smiles.

". . . Thanks, I guess."

I think I'm done talking about this now.

He tosses his butt out the window and reaches for another cigarette. A slight tremor in his hands. I hand him the pack. He catches me staring at it, like I'm waiting for him to offer me one, even though he already did.

"Take what you want. Don't be such a little mouse, that drives me crazy." He tosses the pack into my lap. "This isn't your mom's place."

I draw a breath like a blade. Paw around in the cupholder for his lighter.

"So uh . . . these bleeders." I grapple for an out. "How'd you like . . . vet them?"

His fingers flutter against the steering wheel as a smile plays on his lips.

"Can you keep a secret?" I hate the way my heart stammers as I nod. "They said they wanted to join us. And we said yes."

"You mean like . . . they want to get lifted?" I suck down a too-large mouthful of hot, scratchy smoke and fight the urge to cough.

"Exactly. They'll be loyal if they think we're gonna reward them later." I catch him glancing in the rearview. At Gareth's headlights.

"So we're lying to them."

"Think about our endgame, for a sec. Population inversion comes with a new set of problems. Mainly, we can't feed ourselves if we've absorbed our entire food chain. Like, we need to start looking at this as an agricultural challenge."

"Right."

His eyes drift from the road and lock on to mine. "Not everyone can be like us. Not everyone *should*. You get me?"

"Okay but . . . who gets to decide that?"

"Well, right now, we do. Eventually we'll have protocols. Benchmarks and tests—"

"Isn't that like . . . I dunno, *eugenics*?"

His offended stare crackles and he rolls his shoulders, like all of a sudden his clothes are too tight.

"Okay, obviously I'm not gonna *talk about it in public* the way I talk about it in front of you. You think I'm stupid?"

"Didn't say that." I shrink in my seat.

"I know what to keep to myself. You'll learn how to do that, too. Nothing matters more than what you *don't* say."

My neglected cigarette burns out between my paralyzed fingers. I twist the ends, revealing tiny worms of tobacco.

"But how are you supposed to get people to stop hunting? I thought that was like . . . part of the appeal?"

"Well, how would *you* solve it?" There's a practiced arrogance laced between the words. Like he expects me to say I don't know.

"I mean, maybe you treat it like a game or something. But it needs to be a game you can win."

He nods with surprised approval. A thoughtful tug of smoke. I catch him looking at Gareth in the rearview again.

I know I shouldn't ask. But I can't help it. "Did you make the same deal with Gareth? Lie and say you're gonna lift him someday?"

Devon shrugs.

"Why wouldn't you do that for him?"

"Look, there's a whole . . . when it comes to Gare—" His scowl loosens into something like pity. "He got clean to keep me alive. Back when this first happened to me. I offered him a way out. Guy's a fucking catastrophe without this. He needs it. And I need him. Sometimes a thing like this just *works*."

"But you're playing him."

"Mia, Gareth's not a value add. That's what I've been trying to explain to you. I've known him most of my life and I promise, he's *not it*." He holds my gaze. "He's not smart like you."

He's saying this to shut me up. This heady compliment spiked with unhinged camaraderie. It works, though.

I let the dismembered pieces of my unsmoked cigarette fly out the window. Hoping he doesn't notice.

We leave the Clark city limits and follow the desolate country road for another ninety minutes. When we hit Route 40, I start cataloguing the landmarks. There's a shack selling smoked fish. A billboard for whitewater rafting. A gas station. Not like I'm thinking of escaping on foot again. But I like to know where I am. Just in case.

Just in case what?

Nothing. Never mind.

It's another hour till we reach the motel. Gareth pulls up next to us in the parking lot and hops out of the truck, chugging a massive Gatorade. He looks more gaunt than usual in the weak yellow light of the NO VACANCY sign. Like he was able to hide behind all those shadows in the woods.

I can't imagine how relieved he must be, that we're doing this.

"The group's in room seven," Gareth reports as we approach. "Patti texted and said she left our keys in the usual spot."

"Owner here is a Sara," Devon explains as he locks the car. "Runs things kinda like your mom did. If you see her, she's okay."

I nod, following the two of them up a flight of stairs, to a room with no scanner. There's a cracked porcelain flower pot on the stoop, and Gareth lifts it up to reveal a key card. Cortisol claws the lining of my stomach as he unlocks the door. I know what we're here to do. But there's something else happening. Something I'm too small to see, from my vantage point.

I hesitate, instinctively planting my feet. Devon holds the door open for me. Waiting for me to move. When I don't, he places a gentle hand on my back and guides me inside. Shuts the door behind us.

Gareth opens a backpack and tosses me a roll of duct tape. "You know the drill."

I eyeball the curtains.

"So we're like . . . staying here?"

"Just for the day," Devon replies, inspecting the room: Wilting floral wallpaper, yellowed with age. Pockmarked wooden surfaces stained with water rings. A haphazardly made queen bed with mismatched pillowcases. He wrinkles his nose and yanks a pungent old coffeemaker from the outlet, shoving it out the door with his foot.

"Fuckin' A, Patti."

He whirls back into the room. I numbly spin the roll of duct tape around my wrist with a thousand-yard stare.

"Gare. She's supposed to have her own room." He says this to him, but he's looking at me.

"Oh. Patti didn't—"

"Patti knows."

"Okay."

"Go ask her for the other key. Please."

Gareth ambles out the door, leaving the two of us standing at the window.

That icy eel moves back up my throat as I dodge Devon's probing gaze. Now that we're alone, I understand why I was scared of this room.

I'm scared of what Mom would have done in this room.

"You good?" He fills the silence. Like he's just seen my anxious eyes darken ten shades of sickly green.

My teeth writhe under my gums. "Um . . . yeah."

Stale oxygen burns in my chest, as if I'm too afraid to breathe the air between us. He squeezes my arm. But quickly lets go.

"Gare will come grab you when we're ready," he says with a disarming, casual inflection that makes me wonder why I'm still holding my breath.

After all, he said I was supposed to have my own room.

I stare past his shoulder as he sweeps out the door. At my own reflection in the black window.

"Don't forget to do the curtains."

☾ ☾ ☾

There are twelve of them. A few sit on the bed, but most are on the floor. The youngest looks to be in his late teens. I feel like I've seen him before. Might have been one of the kids at the outpost. The oldest is a matronly woman in a tracksuit with thin silver curls encased in crunchy gel. A tiny raven-haired girl in fuzzy pink slippers sits on the floor in the far corner. When she yawns and stretches, her cropped sweatshirt rises, exposing her navel. It sticks out like a little flower bud. There's a disorienting jolt in me, like the first time I noticed that adorable gap between Jade's front teeth.

In a way, she reminds me of her. A reflection of a reflection.

She reaches into her pocket and pulls from a vape that smells like grapefruit. Or maybe that's just the smell of the room.

Of them.

Gareth and I wade through the crowd, trying to find a place to sit. But Devon is standing. Maybe I should do the same. My eyes land upon a familiar face next to him: Shea from the outpost. She quirks her brows with a smug tilt of her head when she sees me. I'm sure she knows who I really am, by now.

"Everybody, this is Mia and Gareth." Devon brings us forward, and the sea parts to let us through. I don't say anything. Don't even wave. Feels profane, somehow.

We start by having each person introduce themselves. Where they're from, why they want to help us. A theme starts to emerge. Over and over, they monologue about a breakup or a death in the family. Money problems. Dead-end career. Shitty parents.

Colin, the boy from the outpost, says he can't wait to see the look on his drunk-ass dad's face when he shows up to bleed him dry. Chelsea, the girl in the fuzzy pink slippers, wants to "lock it down" at twenty-five so her looks don't fade, make all the right investments for the next hundred years, and buy a mansion in the Hollywood Hills. Vicki, the woman with the crunchy gray hair, is recently widowed. She confesses, tragically earnest, that she wants to get into politics and write new, better laws for Saras. She's scared she's getting too old to start a new career, but she can pull it off if she freezes time for herself. "My husband ran out of time to do what he really wanted in life. I wish I could've given him a gift like this."

Her words go through my heart and out my back.

I never thought of it that way. Like a gift.

Which only makes me feel worse for helping Devon lie to them.

We're listening to the last person's story—Emerson, who was living in their car in Seattle—when I hear Devon's voice in my ear. I jump. Didn't realize he was standing so close.

"See anyone you like?"

"We're not taking them all?"

"I mean for you."

With a shiver, I remember what Franklin told me the night he cornered me in Cora's room. He wanted to *request me*. Wanted me to request *him*.

When Mom and I made this agreement fourteen years ago, there wasn't any kind of deliberation. I didn't even think, when I grabbed those garden shears.

But apparently there's a lot I don't know about sitting on the other side of the table.

It starts to make sense a few minutes later. When Devon passes his knife around and asks everyone to cut their wrist.

"Gently though, yeah? If you're looking for the suicide cult, you're at the wrong hotel."

Dark, nervous laughter fills the room.

So does the smell. That gooey orange-blossom sugar high.

Now I know why he asked me to be his number two. I'm gasping between gritted teeth and I already ate my fill tonight. I can't imagine how the others would have handled themselves.

"I know Shea already asked you all the important stuff," he says as the group encircles us, cupping their bloody wrists. All the light-hearted magnetism leaves his voice. "But if you're lying, if you're drinking alcohol or coffee or popping pills or any of that shit—" He takes his gun from his belt. I realize this is the first time I've seen it. "We're about to find out."

He glances at me, then Shea.

Of course. Someone has to taste the food for the king.

My gaze skates over to Shea. What do we do if they make us sick? But her face betrays nothing. She's all in.

My pulse thrashes in my gums as Colin approaches and offers me his blood-soaked wrist. All the anxiety flees my body as I press my lips to his creamy skin. I've never fed directly from anyone's veins. And it's different.

Really different.

First there's the warmth. The complexity of the drink. Every second the blood cools outside the body, it loses its potency. I didn't know. How could I?

Maybe I didn't want to.

The needle provides a clean sort of decency. Civilized separation. Safety, too, if the bleeder doesn't know the person they're feeding. But this is a trust fall. None of those things matter tonight.

The scorch of serotonin steals my breath as the walls of my heart hum with a gorgeous, incendiary sense of self-worth. I know it's just chemicals. But . . .

I pull my lips from Colin's wrist. The room wobbles. Devon looks like he's staring up at me from a pool of water.

"Um, he's clean," I croak.

I let Colin pass so Devon can confirm. He's quick and efficient. Knows to pace himself. Gareth bandages Colin's wrist when he's done.

"Thanks, man. We appreciate you." Gareth's voice is a distant rumble.

Two more people step up. One for Shea, one for me.

I try to follow Devon's example. Just a sip. Don't go crazy.

Another pair approaches. Better. I think I can manage not to embarrass myself.

Shea has Emerson next. I've got Chelsea.

She hasn't made the cut deep enough. Like she was scared or something. I ease the soft, slick gills of skin apart with my teeth. She yelps, and it echoes across my bones.

I have chills all over and for a second, I'm sure she's just poisoned me.

But there's nothing different about the taste.

Well, no. That's not . . . It *is* different. Just not in a bad way.

She's clean.

Better than clean.

Oh . . .

Okay.

I should stop now.

Going to stop.

. . . Now.

I bite down instead.

"Easy . . . easy—"

Devon's hand is on my neck. Gently prying me away. There's a tear creeping down my cheek. A vibrant ache between my legs.

Chelsea giggles, uncomfortable, from some faraway place. I'm staring at her rosebud navel again.

"Clean?" he whispers.

"I think so?"

Not me, though. I need to get the hell out of this room.

The walls expand and contract with my shaky breath as he steadies my shoulders. Wipes the blood from my bottom lip with his thumb.

Something passes in the air between us. A pact in a language I don't yet understand.

"You look tired," he says.

"I-I'm fine." The high is starting to subside, like shaking out a numb foot. My eyes rivet to the islands of blood staining the musty old carpet.

"Go get some rest. Shea can take it from here." He hands me the key to my room. "This one's yours."

I have questions, but they're all scrambled nonsense. I just nod and pocket the key. Don't want to stay here another second.

I shuffle toward the door. Into the slow boil of approaching daylight. As I turn to shut it behind me, I see Gareth bandaging Chelsea's wrist. Devon never took his turn.

A shower feels like a good idea. It's been almost a month since I last bathed at the Sara center. Ten-second scrubs in a bucket of melted lake ice don't count. I turn on the water and face myself in the mirror with a tattered sigh. Blood seeps through my shirt, leaving faint, sticky kiss marks down my chest as I yank it off. I just want this night to end.

As I fold in half against the water-stained Formica . . .

The door clicks.

I knew, of course. Knew there was more than one key to this room. I see her in the mirror. "Hey." She waves with her bandaged wrist.

I stare at Chelsea's reflection as she approaches, but I don't turn. Like watching an eclipse through one of those pinhole projectors.

"You need to go."

But she's still coming toward me.

"Please leave. Now."

She reaches the place where the carpet meets bathroom tile and unfurls the bandage from her wrist. I spin to face her.

"Listen, I haven't done anything like this before and I'm really not sure if I—"

She presses her wrist to my lips, but I'm slow to surrender. I train one eye on the door. As if I'm expecting it to open again the instant I turn my back.

"What's wrong?" she asks into my neck.

I hate it, but I push her wrist away. "I just . . . I need to know we're alone."

"It's okay. He told me."

My insides lurch. "Told you what?"

She lifts her head. Startling me. As if I'm expecting someone else. Jade?

Cora.

"He said you'd be nervous."

When I don't react, she peels her sweatshirt up over her head. Closes the space between us till our hips are touching. I feel the nuzzle of that little rosebud against my bare skin and my legs start shaking.

"Listen, I really, *really* think you should go—"

She raises her wrist to my mouth again. The scent of her wound brings those exquisite tears back to my eyes.

I am so, *so* tired of fighting all the goddamn time.

I slide my tongue across her bloody gash, back and forth, deepening it with the sharp end of my tooth, as she reaches behind my back with her free hand to unclasp my bra.

I bite down and the whole room shudders.

"God, that's so fucking good," she whimpers.

She might be lying. He might have told her to.

But at this point, I don't care.

☾ ☾ ☾

Red dissolves to gray dissolves to darkness, wave after gorgeous wave. I ride the undertow of viscera and feel my eyes rattle in the back of my skull as we lap from each other till we're blackout drunk.

There is more blood than there should be. More than her wrist. That's all I really know.

Until we're finished.

Until I catch my breath and the velvety aftermath hardens.

"Um . . ." Oh my God. There's *so* much blood. . . .

Oh my God. Oh my God. . . .

A slaughterhouse scream explodes from my throat.

Chelsea bolts upright. Wrapping a sheet around her thigh to clot the wound. "Holy shit, you okay?"

The scream goes on and on and on and—

I collapse to the bathroom floor. Chelsea hobbles in after me. When I start retching into the toilet, she holds my hair back.

"Do *not* touch me." My teeth are out and that's on purpose. I need her to be scared. So this never happens again.

"Shhh, it's okay. I'm fine. You're fine."

I stare into the toilet like a scrying bowl.

"I promise, I didn't have any coffee or alcohol or anything like that. You would've known when you—"

"That's not what I'm—" Shit. Here it comes. I shudder. All my bones are rattling.

But my body refuses to relinquish the blood. It's just acid and pain. Over and over. Like I'm trying to turn myself inside out.

She's still holding on to my hair.

A memory of Cora blinks across the horrible void. Cradling me on the bathroom floor. Up on Seven at the Sara center.

I spit and hiccup and sob all at once.

"I won't tell anyone," Chelsea whispers after a moment. "Like, if you have a girlfriend or something—"

"I don't have a *fucking girlfriend*."

It's so much more. She has no idea. I could have killed her. Maybe he wanted me to. I'm not sure what stopped me.

"*Please* leave," I moan into the toilet, creating a pathetic echo chamber all around me.

"Okay. I'm sorry," she whispers. Finally lets go of my hair.

I curl into a towel and sleep naked on the bathroom floor. Can't get back into that bed.

I dream about a purple couch that used to be blue.

Wake up screaming.

)) ((((

We drive back to the mountain. He's not speaking.

Maybe he's waiting for me to say something. I have no idea. It's going to be a long night.

He saw her get into Gareth's truck with the others. Knows I didn't kill her. If that was even the point.

I should ask him.

Jesus fuck, ask him *what*?

I feel hollow. Like he stole something from me, but I don't know what. Or how.

He wasn't even there.

After a few minutes, he tosses his pack of Reds into my lap.

"Thanks," I mumble, cracking the window.

He unzips his heavy winter coat and tosses it to the back seat. I do the same. The air is warmer tonight. A hint of spring for the first time.

I want to cry. But I smoke instead.

"So uh . . ." Devon finally breaks the silence. "I figure you probably want to have a little chat, huh?"

"About?"

He hesitates, then spills with a mouthful of smoke. "Do you remember what I told you, that night?"

". . . What night?"

"The night you found her."

My stomach curdles. It's like he watched a bootleg of my nightmare.

The night you *killed her.*

"Do you remember, Mia?"

"No," I reply like a knife.

"C'mon, you're not a kid anymore. We're both adults now and it's time for us to talk about this."

"*Why?*"

"Because you still hate me and I can't fucking stand the way you look at me."

He pounds the wheel and the car skids to one side, scraping the shoulder. He readjusts his grip as I drag my knees to my chest.

"When I saw how you were with that girl last night—"

"Please stop—"

"Just listen. Your mom and I had this . . . *understanding.* Between us. When we met. I gave her an out, but she decided she was okay. Until this one night—"

"That's not true, she didn't know, you fucking *tricked her*—"

"Mia." There's that steady, still-water voice again. "How could she *not* know? We were together a whole month, maybe more, before it happened."

". . . Before you made a mistake."

"So you do remember."

I don't want to look behind this door ever again.

"You get it now, right? How that can happen?"

I pull from the cigarette with all my might, till my lungs itch and spasm and force the smoke back up my throat. The closest I'll dare come to an admission.

"I do have one question, though. If you don't mind," he says.

There's no point in giving him an inch. He's already taken the mile.

"Why didn't you lift her?"

"You said we weren't supposed to."

"Well, maybe she was special. Maybe you wanted to break the rules."

"Is that what you wanted me to do? Break the rules?"

"What I *wanted* was for you to have some fun for once in your life." He wets his lips. "Did you?"

My face burns as he laughs. I don't know why, but after a moment, I start laughing too. Like he yanked it out of me.

An invasive feeling riots through me—a horrifying warmth that doesn't belong.

I feel like I'm losing my mind. Or signed it away, when we started this twenty-four hours ago.

"You might not believe it, but there was a time me and Izzy were happy," he goes on. Quieter now. God dammit, I thought we were done discussing this. "We were making a family together, y'know? Margot wasn't a part of that."

I have nothing to say, so I let the rumble of the road speak for me. We pass the gas station. Smoked-fish shack. Whitewater rafting.

"I'm still angry at her. I know we both are. But . . ." He lets out a breath and impales me with the corner of his eye. "I'm really glad you came to find me, Mia."

I try not to react as the truth avalanches over me. Mimic that impenetrable mask of his.

Of course.

It's not an accident, when he uses my nickname. He knows why people called me "Fun Size." I can still hear that strange cramp in his voice, when he described seeing me in her clothes at Cloak and Dagger. Everything makes sense, now.

He's trying to slot me into the empty space she left behind.

He misses her. And how could he not? She never would've spoken to him the way Margot does, or tried to siphon power from him. She fit perfectly in the palm of his hand.

I know, now. Why he didn't kill me that night in the woods. Why he's kept me happy and fed. But also why he starved me. Left me bleeding on the floor of the ski shop for three days.

Because he did. I fucking *know* he did. He lied, when he said I'd only been there one day.

All that pain, all that helplessness—just like the first few nights of the lift. A moment in the dark where you're reaching out for someone—*anyone*—to breathe life back into your body. To claim you.

He engineered the perfect reenactment. And he's not finished.

And maybe—horribly, inescapably *maybe*—I've somehow shown him I'm willing to reciprocate. But I'm not. If I did, he's the one who manufactured it. Just like he manufactured everything else.

My ragged mind shorts out. Shimmers back to life on the seventh floor of the Sara center. Cora with her hairbrush. A warm blanket around us. *Survivor* on TV. Cora changes the channel. Now it's *The Wizard of Oz*. As if Mom is here, too.

I'll just stay here. This is where I live, now.

What have you learned, Dorothy?

If I ever go looking for my heart's desire again, I won't look any further than my own backyard. Because if it isn't there, I never really lost it to—

"Hey, we're gonna stop here for a little bit." Devon pulls over to the side of the dirt road.

My mind wails, trying to collect the crumbling pieces of my fantasy. Can't breathe past the tears in my tight throat.

I glance over at the clock. 5:37 A.M.

A spike of fear goes through me. "The sun's gonna be up soon."

"We got time."

Time for *what*?

He looks over at me. And I guess I'm crying. I don't know.

"Whoa, hey. What's going on?" His gentle voice repulses me. "I just wanted to show you something cool. C'mere—"

He opens his door and trots over to my side. I'm motionless.

"I used to go camping around here when I was a kid," he says through the crack in my window. "This is a great spot to watch the sun come up. Thought you might want to see it."

He digs into his pocket and produces an envelope. Shakes out two white rectangular pills.

"Shea gave me the last Daylights they had at the outpost."

I open the door, if only to get a closer look at the pills. They're a different color than the ones I've been hiding.

He pops his and holds it in his cheek with a smile. "I thought I'd save them for a special occasion or something, but I didn't want to wait. It's been fucking *ages*."

He presses one into my palm.

"They don't look like the ones we had in New York," I finally say. Rubbing my tears away with my sleeve.

"There are a few different formulas floating around. They're all safe, though. C'mon."

I roll the pill across the ridges in my palm. The thought of the sun warming my face again feeds me with rejuvenating hope. Such a small thing. But that's the power of scarcity. The small things flood those shrunken spaces. I just wish I were doing this without him.

Wish this didn't feel like some kind of trap.

But maybe it's not. Based on the way he's swooping through the brush to reach the switchbacks. The jittery spring in his step.

"There was this like two, three-year period when I was a kid where my dad moved back in. We were living in Boulder," he says as he forges ahead. "He had this janky old camper that my mom fucking hated. He kept it parked in our driveway and a lot of times that's where he slept, when she didn't want him to come inside."

"Uh-huh . . ." I engage absently. Following him up to the trail. Still squeezing the pill in my fist.

"But yeah, those two summers, we took the camper up to Wyoming. Came around this way. Him and me. Not my mom."

I'm watching him. Waiting to see what the pill does, if he starts acting different. He's down to his T-shirt but he doesn't look like he's cold. I wonder if that means anything.

"After that, I started coming here on my own sometimes."

He trudges up the first switchback. Peers over his shoulder at me. "How's your leg? Can you run yet?"

"Don't think so." I focus on the horizon instead of him. A thin schism of amber breaks in the east.

"It's all good." He hangs an arm around me. Doesn't notice my wooden posture. Or if he does, he's ignoring it. "We'll get there when we get there."

The mountains have a crisp, cerulean glow all around them. Like adding white paint to blackest blue. I don't know what to do. The pill is getting soggy in my palm.

"I came up here last summer, when I was trying to figure out . . . y'know. How the hell we'd survive this."

I nod. Waiting for him to remove his arm from my neck.

I steal a glance at his forearm, swinging in my periphery. Those crude, green-gray stick-and-pokes. There's no sign of disruption on the skin. No discomfort in the approaching sunlight.

The number 167 leaps out at me, etched across his wrist: nearly identical to Gareth's tattoo, except for the color. Gareth's was a clean, sharp shade of black. All of Devon's look like faded old bruises.

Or scars.

They're the same queasy color as Cora's rust injury. I realize I've never looked at them before. Not really. Most are on his left arm and wrist—at least a dozen. Maybe more.

Self-harm masquerading as art.

As we bend around another switchback, gooseflesh explodes down my legs and encircles my feet like shackles. All my body hair stands on end, like I'm caught in the cold. But I'm hot. Broiling hot.

I need to take that pill. Now. Unless it's already too late. Unless . . . Shit—

I stumble, and he catches me. A flash of annoyance in his eyes. "Okay, now what?"

My forehead weeps with sweat. I unfurl my fist to reveal the pill.

"Why didn't you take it!"

"I-I don't—"

"Do it, right now."

I nod. But still, I can't bring it to my lips.

"Mia. It's a *Daylight pill*. What the hell do you think I'm trying to—?"

"I just didn't want to . . . I was waiting to see if—"

"Will you please just take it before your fucking face incinerates?"

His gaze bores into me. I stuff the pill into my mouth and cradle it under my tongue. It dissolves quickly. Already warm.

"That hurts, you know," he says after a moment. Pulling me back to my feet.

"What?"

"What you just did. You don't trust me."

He stalks ahead as the pill swarms my system. I can tell it's working almost immediately.

I feel stupid. Like turning on the lights after a bad dream.

Two truths and a lie.

I still can't tell the difference. I wonder if that was his approach with Mom, too. If she was able to withstand it because those shining truths just felt so damn good in comparison. I realize now, how lucky I am that I can't love him the way she did. He can't drown me. I can tread water till the end of the world.

And it might come to that.

I trail him for the next hundred paces as the drugs kick in and the shivering subsides. I think I can finally relax enough to feel happy about seeing the sun. But it's a force-fed happiness. It's eating the whole cake to prove how grateful you are, knowing you're about to be sick.

Up ahead, a hazy blush rises between the peaks, streaked with sherbet orange and faded sapphire. My breath catches. It reminds me of Tucson.

I still don't understand how I can long for a place that brought me so much pain. But I do. I think I always will.

"On the left." He points. There's a flat pewter rock, covered with scratches. Initials. Proof of life.

He sits there. I don't. He pulls up his knees and hugs them for warmth, staring at the sun.

"Over there is where I scattered my dad's ashes."

He doesn't offer anything else. I can tell he wants to say more, but he wants me to throw the ball back. Wants me to want it.

A question reluctantly leaves my lips.

"How'd he die?" I half expect Devon to admit to his murder.

"Someone killed him."

"Someone?" So, yes.

"A woman he was shacking up with. Shot him in the head with a rusted bullet."

His eyes pull mine. Knows he has my attention now.

"I didn't know your dad was a Sara."

"You never asked."

"Is that why your mom made him sleep in the camper?"

He laughs, brushing the dirt from his boots. "Nah. She made him sleep in the camper 'cuz he was an asshole."

"How old were you when he . . . uh—"

"It wasn't the way it was with you." He answers the question I'm insinuating. "He abandoned ship when I was about thirteen, so we weren't in touch, by the time he got it."

"Oh."

"It was a good fifteen years before I heard from him again. I'm out in California at a dead-end job, letting Gare crash on my couch after rehab . . . and that's when he calls me. Says he's in town and wants to meet up."

Stripes of light stretch across the rock. The sun is livid in his tired eyes, but he doesn't squint or make a shield with his hand. He lets them burn.

"Of course, I drop everything to see him. That's the shitty thing, about shitty parents. You can't help it, you miss them. But it's not really *them* you miss. You miss how it felt to hope things might get better. Before you knew they wouldn't."

Finally, I sit down on the rock. He's already made space for me.

"So we meet up at this hotel bar where of course, he doesn't order anything. And he starts . . . talking at me. Saying how he

wished he had something to leave me when he died, and that he'd
finally found something worth passing down to me. Told me to
come upstairs and he'd give it to me."

"So you just . . . let him do it?"

"You think I had any idea what was happening?"

At last, he breaks his staring contest with the light. Turns his
bleary eyes on me. "He left me, after. Only thing he told me was to
keep out of the sun. I didn't have another Sara to help me, or the
Facebook group, or . . ."

Something comes loose inside me and floats through my veins.
"Why would he do that?"

"I think maybe . . . he wanted me to figure out how to be strong.
On my own."

I let the silence settle around us like dust.

"Three years later, he turned up dead. In Utah, actually." He
gives me a pointed look.

There's a bitter taste in my mouth as I stare down the cliff, to the
place he probably dumped that can of ashes. Even Devon's godaw-
ful father got a funeral.

"So," he says. Rising from the rock. "Now we're even. You
earned that story. Only two other people have."

"Gareth and Margot?"

"Gare and your mom."

I shudder, like something's just swallowed the sun.

He takes a step past me. Against my will, I reach for his hand
and pull him back.

Why, I don't know.

But the look he gives me makes me sure I'll live to regret it.

"You can't tell anyone I brought you up here," he says after a
moment.

"I won't."

He lifts me off the rock. Turns my hand over in his, studying it.
Then lets it go.

"We need to get back."

We're only about an hour behind Gareth. He would have arrived
at the mountain just before the sun came up. Morning streams

through the evergreens. Neither of us has spoken since we got back in the car.

Everyone else will be asleep. My roommates will know he gave me a Daylight pill. Another perk of my gilded cage.

I'm privately spiraling about having to see Chelsea again. Wondering what people will think went on last night. And not just with her.

I'm already rehearsing the placating speech I'll deliver to Margot. *I swear to God, nothing happened.*

. . . Right?

We make our final approach on the dirt road. Devon extends an arm toward me. When his hand comes to rest against the back of my neck, I hardly feel it. I detach from the world as he works his fingers between the knots in my hair. Rubbing the base of my scalp. The three-minute drive to the top of hill stretches paper thin, like time itself might snap and unravel.

He finally releases me to grab the steering wheel with both hands and park the car. It takes a moment for my numb, unfocused gaze to lock back on to reality.

For me to notice the hatch of the cube truck, hanging wide open.

I step out of the car, and the stench smacks me like an open palm. My shoes meet the bed of bloody pine needles, soggy as a wet sponge, displacing a drove of engorged black flies. Devon's eyes shoot to the red handprints on the side of the white truck. Gareth is gone. So are the bleeders.

"You've got to be *fucking*—" He gulps his horrified words, storming around to the front of the truck.

"*Gareth*—!" he shouts across the camp. Racing past the cold, burnt-out fire pit. My feet fuse to the dank red ground.

He sprints to Gareth's trailer and pounds on the door. No answer.

"We need to find them. C'mon—"

But I don't move.

A fuzzy pink slipper in the dirt draws my gaze.

I gasp into my knuckle and bite down as Devon bolts past me, toward the main lodge. I'm still staring at that slipper in the dirt.

She's gone. Chelsea's gone and the last thing she ever did was let me use her.

Devon slams the door to the lodge and the screaming match starts immediately. So loud I have no choice but to listen.

I have heard this fight before, in a different key.

"Where the fuck are my bleeders, Margot?"

"Where the fuck were you*?"*

A crash. Someone threw something. Could have been either one of them.

"Hope she was worth it." Even through the wall, Margot's words drip with venom.

"Get off my dick and answer the fucking question, Margot." The temperature rises in his voice. *"What happened. To. My* bleeders*?"*

"What the hell do you think happened? That truck pulled up and they didn't stand a chance. Everyone is starving—*"*

"You were supposed to be watching *them*—*"*

Another resounding crash. Something shatters.

"They're your *fucking family, Devon."*

A rustling sound at the front of the truck snatches my attention. Like someone's still alive in there. I inch forward, holding my breath . . . and Gareth's pale, blood-dappled face appears in the window. Hyperventilating on the floor of the cab.

Our eyes meet through a simmering curtain of flies. I don't want to imagine what he's just seen. What Devon's going to do to him when he leaves his hiding place.

I hold his stare and inch toward the door. Reaching out to open it. It's locked. When I tap on the window, he shrivels in terror. I've never seen a grown man look so small.

I withdraw. He wasn't ready to reveal himself, when Devon called his name. And he's still not.

"I'm sorry," I mouth. He doesn't react.

I wish he'd run. Now might be his only chance. But if he runs . . . I don't eat. A pang goes through me and I turn my back. Shuffling across the bloody dirt to my own cabin.

I'm careful with the door, trying not to let any light in as I worm my way through.

Teresa, Bjorn, and Kayla sit in a circle on the ground. Hunched over Vicki.

Or . . . well, that *was* Vicki.

I can't look away, like someone's pinned my eyes open. They don't notice me. Don't so much as glance in my direction.

As my vision adjusts to the darkness, I realize there's a fourth person on the floor between Teresa and Kayla, sharing in their filthy glee. A boy, with a mop of black curls and sparkling shark's eyes. A stump where his left hand ought to be.

I know him. I've known him since I was ten years old.

Pyotr. The boy from Saratov.

He breaks his trance and peers up at me. Like he's stepping out from behind my computer screen. Pixels thickening to flesh and bone.

He's impossibly small—a brittle sapling of a bloodstained boy. I'm twice his size. Still, I'm petrified. Can't get away fast enough. As if I've forgotten what I am.

I stumble out the door and race toward the forest. Toward the lake.

I peel off my grimy, bloodstained clothes and wade into the freezing water, curling my toes in the silt and slime. Letting the cold numb my bones. I walk farther and farther, till only my eyes crest the surface, watching the lodge through the trees. Like I'm waiting for it to explode.

Behind the clinic, something pulls my gaze. Half buried in the melted snow.

Burnt-out remains inside a powder-blue hospital gown.

☾ ☾ ☾

The next three days are a cruel, black blur.

Devon leaves with Pyotr and his handlers in the RV. Doesn't tell anyone where he's going or when he'll be back.

Gareth is too traumatized to give blood. To anyone. Still, he doesn't run. Stays locked in his trailer. Margot withholds Sophie and Kat from us. She seals herself inside the clinic with them.

And Cora.

I know she's in there. Alive. It's weaker now, but I can still feel that live wire of warmth, humming through my hunger and despair.

She's also in danger. But I don't need our bond to know that.

All I can think about is that tattered blue hospital gown. What could have happened to the person inside it.

We've all eaten our fill, so the starvation is a slow burn. Sometimes that's worse, though. When it creeps up on you. Kayla has gum and cigarettes, but Zach steals her whole stash. The two of them fight like dogs over the last piece of Doublemint. She bites his pinky finger clean off the bone, chews it up, and spits it back into his face.

I fantasize about another escape. But the idea is fleeting. I'm too afraid Devon will reappear the instant I hit the woods, as though he'll feel my betrayal under his skin like an unscratchable itch. Besides, I still can't run.

And I'm not about to leave Cora behind.

On the second bloodless night, I leave our shivering fireside huddle and take a slow, shaky lap around the clinic. Stand below the boarded-up window, listening to the hum of the generator.

There has to be a way to figure out what they're doing in there. To reach her somehow. I wander around the back of the lodge and spot a second, smaller door, past the screaming red haze of the neon cross. I run my hand along the contours of the molded wood, detecting soft vibrations on the other side. A faded old sign reads MEDICAL OFFICE, accompanied by a reindeer with a despondent frown and a bandaged foot.

I feel the clamor of my desperate heart in my throat as I press my ear to the wall. I can sense the lights are on, but I'm not sure if anyone's on the other side. I try the door. It's locked. As expected. But I might be strong enough to kick a hole through the rotting wood, or yank the doorknob right off. Everyone's so sick and distracted they might not even hear me. Or if they do, they'll think I'm just spiraling from withdrawal and lashing out.

I start tugging at the doorknob. The ancient screws twist and grind against the wood. Harder. Just a little more. A slimy black wood chip dislodges. As I feel it start to submit to me—

A bolt on the other side creaks. The doorknob turns.

Click.

That's a gun.

Kayla appears, silhouetted by the cruel flicker of weak fluorescents. She raises her silver snub-nose.

"Get out."

"Kayla, what the hell?"

She doesn't reply. My blood hisses as she points the gun between my eyes and walks me backward down the path, slamming the door behind her.

"You know what they're doing in there, don't you?" I ask under my breath, once she's marched me all the way to the tree line. Finally, she drops the gun. Shoves it back into her holster with a tired grimace.

"Look, I'm sorry. I didn't mean to . . . Margot said she doesn't want anybody bothering them right now."

"Bothering *who*? Who else is in there?"

"Cora's okay. Just know that."

It's slight, almost undetectable. But I think I see her shudder.

"Kayla," I whisper. "I found something. In the woods."

Her hand creeps back to her holster. "What kind of something?"

"I think you know."

She taps her teeth together in the anxious silence.

"Please. You have to tell me what they're doing in there."

"What good does it do, to tell you? Then you'll just know. And he'll know you know. You'll *fuck yourself* by knowing."

A gust of wind steals whatever heat was left in my shivering body. "So it's bad."

"Didn't say that."

"You say a lot, saying what you won't say." As if I don't know who taught her that.

Finally, her face thaws. "I don't want you getting hurt. Okay?"

She grabs my arm and starts pulling me back toward the fire. My body follows, but the rest of me stands guard under those black windows. I wish I could send Cora a sign. Some hopeful, telepathic smoke signal from the only pure part of me that's left. I wonder if she still feels me, the way I can feel her.

I never left you. I never will.

I'm going to find a way through that door.

Night three. Devon comes back just before midnight.

The RV is parked farther away than before—about a quarter mile down the dirt road. Deliberate distance.

Two cigarette cherries hover in the dark like demon fireflies as he hikes toward us, Pyotr at his side. I'm hardly surprised to see the little boy smoking. Not after what I saw him do on the floor of our cabin.

The delirium phase of our hunger has started to set in. Bjorn is blathering on about sasquatch tracks and Teresa's holding a fistful of her own hair, staring, fascinated, at the bloody follicles. I'm chewing my fingertips raw, sucking my own useless life force. Hanging toward the back as the group flocks to Devon with mothlike devotion.

He scowls and holds them at arm's length. "Don't think for a *second* that I came back for you."

Kayla doubles over and wails as he shoves past. Bjorn reaches out to grab his arm. Pyotr spins like a top, teeth bared, and gouges the poor bastard's cheek. Bjorn whips in a circle with a heinous shriek, trying to get the kid to let go, but he doesn't. I draw back, wishing the shadows would eat me alive. Hoping Devon hasn't seen me.

"Hey."

Too late.

"Follow me."

Of course, I do. Beats a fucking hole in my face.

Devon turns to Pyotr, still tearing into Bjorn like an overripe melon. "Pyotr. *Davai.*"

The boy drops Bjorn and scurries to keep up with us. Teresa sobs and falls to her knees beside him. He'll heal. Eventually. But he's too nauseating to look at straight on.

The three of us walk toward camp, leaving the traumatized herd at the top of the dirt road. Then, as though struck by a brilliant solution he'd never thought of before, Devon brightens and pivots back around.

"Okay, fine. How 'bout this." His voice twinkles with sadistic levity. "You may go down the hill—*one at a time*—to eat in the RV. Pyotr's people are feeling generous. Kayla's first. Do not go until she comes back. Kayla, you choose who goes after you. And so on. She has my permission to shoot anyone who cuts the line."

Kayla's face is a beacon as she races down the hill. Pyotr laughs. Devon shows restraint, but I can tell he wants to.

"You okay?" He peers over at me as we walk.

"Fine." I braid my arms over my chest to keep my shivering under control.

"Who is she?" Pyotr points a petulant finger at me. He's still got a faint accent, but it sounds like he practices. He's had over thirty years.

"Mia. A good friend." Devon slings his attention back to me. "Pretty sure our guest needs no introduction."

"We've met" is all I have the strength to say. Walking at their pace is hard enough.

"Jesus, look at you. . . ." He slows down and grips my shoulders. Sweeps the hair from my ashen face and secures it behind my ear. I want to snap off his finger and chew it to a pulp, like I saw Kayla do to Zach. "When's the last time you ate?"

"You know."

"Gareth hasn't helped you?"

I don't want to throw Gareth under the bus. He's been through enough. "I was just like, trying to show solidarity. I dunno."

"That's nice. But stupid. I need you to eat, we have a busy night ahead of us."

He marches me over to Gareth's trailer. I hate how relieved I am, even if he's going to force him.

Pyotr stares at me with an innocent, detached fascination as we walk. "Your hair is pretty."

"Uh . . . thank you?"

"I had a nanny with nice red hair. Aleksandra."

"Oh. Is she still your—?"

"It turned gray when she got old. I liked her much better, before it turned gray. I put her in the lake."

Devon snorts. Shoots me a look that tells me I probably don't want to ask any follow-up questions about Pyotr's nannies.

My head spins. I remember what Cora said about the children up on Nine, at the Sara center. Stuck in time, with brains that never finished growing. This guy's been eight years old since the Cold War.

I wonder how a child amassed enough wealth to travel the world in private, Sara-safe jets. That has to be how he got here.

"C'mon, Gare." Devon punches his door. "Up and at 'em."

Pyotr smiles at me and tugs my sleeve. "I'm going to see Dr. Lacie now, but I'm very happy to meet you."

He skips off toward the clinic. When he knocks, someone lets him right in.

I stare after him, reeling, as Gareth finally appears. I have to admit, he looks a little stronger, now that he's had a few days off.

He's standing taller, and those hollows in his face have started filling out.

"Mia needs to eat," Devon says, looking past Gareth's vacant stare. He breathes out. Slowly. "Lemme get ready."

He shuts the door and locks it. Not about to risk another starving Sara in his orbit.

Devon moves to follow Pyotr across the camp, then turns to meet my eye. "Tonight is really important. Make sure you have as much as you need, okay?"

Dread coils around my lungs. I'm so sick of his surprises. Plans he doesn't explain till we're halfway down the fucking rabbit hole. "What's happening tonight?"

But he's already gone.

Gareth sits with me while I drink. We don't usually do it this way. Don't draw it out. But I sense his unease tonight. Like he wants to talk to me.

Blood from a cup can't begin to compare to what I had for my last meal. But maybe this is better. Maybe it will help me forget.

He watches me sip from my chipped mug. In a flash, I'm back at the old dinner table. Sitting in the wrong seat.

"How long have you known about Pyotr?" I ask, if only to uproot myself from the past.

"Been hearing about him ever since they tracked down his handler. Back when Margot was working at the center. I knew the kid was gonna come through at some point, but I didn't think it'd be so soon." He removes the tourniquet and rubs his biceps. "Guess things are moving quickly."

"What *things*?"

"You know. Our study. The one he's funding." I can't help but notice how he uses the word "our." "After that, Inversion. Eventually, anyway."

"How does Pyotr have all this money?"

"He gets himself adopted by rich women with a charity addiction and kills their husbands." Gareth chuckles darkly. "Spend thirty years murdering oligarchs, eventually you're gonna wind up with a pretty fat stack."

I finish what's in my cup, but I'm still licking my lips. Gareth sighs.

"More?"

"No. I don't want you to—"

"It's fine." He reaches for his tourniquet.

"I'm serious. I don't need it. I know you don't feel good. I know how hard this has been."

Gareth's pale, tired eyes widen to shining marbles. Like he's about to cry.

"It *has* been hard," he chokes out. "Shit, what happened the other day—"

"Not your fault."

"I tried to stop them."

"Of course you did."

He leans across the table. I meet him in the middle.

"Whatever he's planning tonight, it has to work," he says. "He can't hold on much longer. None of us can."

"I know."

"Back when he was having Margot's girls steal all that hillbilly heroin? Y'know, to help everyone ride the food shortage?" I nod as he stares into his quivering hands. "He knew I couldn't be around that shit. But he told me I had to suck it up. He never would've done that. Before all this."

I absorb the ache in his exhausted voice. He caresses the fresh pinhole in his arm like a lover . . . before he catches me staring.

He clears his throat. "It's gonna be worth it, though. Anyone he lifts is gonna get treated like royalty. Just gotta hold out a little while longer."

I wish I didn't know the truth. He doesn't deserve to be strung along like this.

There's a knock at the door.

"We can't let this fall apart," Gareth whispers as he stands to see me out. "Whatever he asks from now on, you gotta do it."

"Gare—"

"Promise me."

The door opens. Kayla stands there, luminous. Like she wasn't on her knees bent double thirty minutes ago. That unnerving, crooked picture smile is hanging on her face again.

"Mia, can I borrow you?"

Kayla wordlessly delivers me down the hill, to the RV. She guides me up the stairs and opens the door . . . but doesn't follow me inside.

"I gotta go help out in the clinic," she explains off my questioning glance. "I'll see you in a little bit. Don't be nervous."

My heart goes limp and slides down the length of my body. "Wait, don't be . . . ? Kay, what's—"

A blaze of white light inside the RV pulls my gaze. I turn, and in that moment Kayla vanishes. Leaving me on the stair. I hear a flurry of expectant whispers inside. Some in English, others in Russian. Margot. Devon and Pyotr. A few others I don't know.

"Fun Size, c'mon in."

My feet reflexively shuffle forward at the sound of his voice—a fine-tuned Pavlovian instrument. I hate myself. Hate whatever this is.

The RV is warm and spacious, pulsing with electricity. Pyotr's team hovers in the nearby kitchenette: Six middle-aged Russian women with heart-shaped faces and blond hair. Whispering among themselves. The sweet aroma from their most recent feeding hangs in the air. This must be Pyotr's loyal squad of bloodletting nannies. Wonder how many he's "put in the lake" since 1990.

I walk into the bright, amplified glow of three tall stage lights, weighted down with sandbags. In the center of the room is a camera on a tripod: one of those tricked-out DSLRs, like Alyssa had. A curvy brunette in a striped pantsuit applies lip gloss in a compact mirror, sitting in a canvas folding chair across from Margot, Pyotr, and Devon. The three of them share a tufted leather sofa.

This is some kind of interview.

I breathe a sigh of relief. I don't know what I thought this was going to be. Why Kayla was tasked with delivering me to him. Then again, I'm still not sure exactly why I've been summoned. Am I supposed to be on camera or something?

Margot snares me with her gaze as I hesitate in the doorway. Scowls and flashes her teeth.

"What is she doing here?"

"It's fine, I asked her to come." Devon stands and guides me over to the kitchen.

He's completely transformed in the past hour: clean shaven, with his wild hair cropped at the nape of his neck. Someone's put him in a black turtleneck, and I can tell he's not comfortable and wearing it like a costume. Still, he's fucking glowing under those lights. I can't stand it. Margot's stepped things up as well, with wings of black eyeliner and a freshly pressed white coat. Pyotr fidgets in his doll-sized designer suit, mussing his neatly combed hair.

"We're making a big announcement tonight," Devon whispers. An inch too close to my ear. "It would mean a lot to me if you just like, hung out. For moral support. You know?"

"Um . . . Sure. Okay."

He replies with that wolfish grin and a tug of my hair.

Margot's still staring at me, stone-faced.

"Hey, Everleigh," he calls out. "C'mere and meet Mia. The one I was telling you about."

The brunette woman in the pantsuit scurries over, extending an enthusiastic hand.

"Mia! It's so great to meet you. Everleigh Saunders."

I shake her hand, guarded. She doesn't smell uninfected, and I don't feel any kind of pull to her. She must be one of us. She has the kind of generically beautiful features that make me sure I've seen her on TV before, but I can't place her.

"Mia, I'm really glad you and Everleigh are finally meeting," Devon says. "You could learn a lot from her."

"Oh. That's . . . cool. Thanks—"

"We need to get started," Margot mutters from the couch.

"Ready when you are," Everleigh chirps.

Devon moves off, following Everleigh to the camera.

"Uh, wait—" I hiss at his back. "What do you want me to do, exactly?"

"Just hang. Like I said." He fixes me with a performatively anxious grin. "I really appreciate it."

"Devon. The stream is up," Margot snaps. He acquiesces and trots to her side. But he's still looking at me.

He's trying to distract her and throw her off her game. Why, I don't know. But that's what this is. Why he wants me standing here. He's trying to weaponize that jealous streak of hers.

My canines creep forward as the stream goes live and Everleigh makes her introductions. But I keep my mouth shut.

"So, let's go all the way back to last January." Everleigh sets the scene with laid-back ease. "Dr. Lacie, as I understand it, you and your husband met when he volunteered for one of your trials at Salvation of Austin, is that correct?"

I stifle a snort. *Husband?* Since when?

"Yes. He'd been following my research for the past few years and had a lot to say. I was uh . . ." She meets his eye and forces a smile for the camera. "Happy to continue the dialogue."

He picks up her hand and holds it in his lap. They're both wearing thin gold bands I'm sure I've never seen before.

"Hence the reason we're all here tonight." Everleigh entices Margot to go on. "So we can *all* continue the dialogue."

"Absolutely." Margot leans forward. Like she's about to reveal a secret. "Charles Darwin says, 'The crust of the earth is a vast museum.' The natural processes of extinction and renewal define life on this planet, and our own births and deaths are a microcosm of this rhythm."

Devon stiffens, and so do I.

I have heard this monologue before. I've *read it.* On that bot-poached social media graphic, back when I was digging for evidence at the Sara center.

On the Origin of a New Species. By Devon Shaw.

"When you think of it that way, there's nothing novel about Sara-tov's syndrome at all," Margot continues. "We've known for years that this is a highly nuanced condition—both a virus *and* a genetic mutation. But we don't talk about the latter. The medical community is hesitant to view Saratov's through the lens of mutation because, well . . . once you do that, you have to start asking some extremely sobering questions. But we're not afraid of those questions."

I'm fighting the urge to laugh aloud. I wonder if I should, just to ruin the stream.

I don't know why I didn't see it before. She's the brains behind ADAPT. Not him. She's the one with the medical degree. The one who asked for this.

Did I seriously think he sat down and read *On the Origin of Species* cover to cover while he was locked up? That a person like him could even *understand* it? This whole time, he's had everyone fooled. Including me.

I remember thinking I could never know who he really was. This elusive revolutionary. A ghost you feel but never see. But I've known him all along. Nothing but an imposter wearing the idea of himself as a disguise.

I sink into a barstool at the counter, and it creaks across the silence. Margot's gaze swerves from Everleigh to me, and Devon lets go of her hand. It's subtle, over in an instant, but I notice the glitch between them. He flashes me a smile. Margot makes a face like she just bit into a hard lemon. And he hurls himself into the conversation.

"What we do here is empower people and offer a different viewpoint. As in, you're not *sick*. You have a gift. And you deserve to live a full life."

"And what do you have to say to those who claim your agenda is a little less wholesome than that?" Everleigh knits her brow.

"Those claims are unsubstantiated," he replies. "There are problematic people out there who keep trying to put our stamp on things we had nothing to do with. It's too easy to mimic someone on the internet. That's why we wanted to sit down with you, in person. We're done subscribing to this narrative we didn't write."

I shudder as he stares down the lens. I don't think I've heard him speak without cursing the entire time I've known him. He's like a different person. But of course, he's not about to relinquish his power. He's matching Margot's eloquence, word for word. Committing to the disguise.

"When I wrote the first draft of that epilogue, my intention was—"

"*Your* intention?" Margot nudges him with a flirty grin. But her voice is radioactive.

He picks up her hand again and laughs. Doesn't bat an eyelash. "Hard to know where she ends and I begin sometimes." God but he's fucking charming when he needs to be.

Margot drives her nails into his palm. Still smiling.

Everleigh reads the room and swoops in with her next, and most vital, query. "So, tell us. What makes tonight special? Why did you choose this as your first, official public appearance?"

They peer over at each other, locked and loaded. Wondering who's going to fire first.

Devon wrests his hand free and places it on Margot's knee. "I think I ought to let Dr. Lacie take the lead here."

Margot flinches. Another subliminal curve ball. He's *letting* her take the lead. But she's not about to surrender the spotlight, now that she's standing in it.

"Last year, I authored a study that had the potential to upend the way we understand Saratov's syndrome. Unfortunately, I wasn't permitted to explore human trials." She clears the bitterness from her throat. "But thanks to the ADAPT network and our incredible friend Pyotr Kuznetsov, we've been able to make it a reality. When we talk about helping people live full lives again . . . this is what we mean."

My heart flutters. *The study.* She's finally going to tell me what's become of Cora. What's been going on behind that locked door. Hope glimmers from some faraway place, a thousand miles in the distant dark. I wring my hands, watching her. Waiting . . .

As Devon interrupts again.

"Evolution, as we understand it, hinges upon the ability to multiply, right?" The words rush out of him. "Mutations occur across generations, over thousands of years. Saratov's syndrome closes that gap. We know this. But a side effect of this mutation is sterility. Saras can't have children. We multiply in a different way. Unfortunately, this fact gives naysayers a pretty solid foundation. One that's hard to argue with. What you have here is the mule problem: they're not their own species because they're sterile. Can't pass on their genes. If you can't do that, you're just an anomaly. The scientific community puts us in that same category, which makes it easy to dismiss any hypothesis we try to make about our place in the world."

He talks so goddamn fast. Knows stupid people are impressed by fast talkers.

But I'm picking up every little piece. And every little piece weighs down my soul, like a pocket full of stones.

"But now . . ."

I know what they're doing in there. What's happening to Cora.

Everleigh's eyes glisten as understanding breaks across her face. She parts her lips, but there are no words.

I remember Mom, crying at the dinner table, saying how much she wished she could give me brothers and sisters.

I think of Cora in the car, sharing bittersweet memories of her uninfected friends who became mothers. Ingrid at the Sara center, forever mourning the baby she lost the day she got sick. Knitting blankets till her fingers were numb.

This changes everything.

No wonder Dr. Lacie's superiors were so afraid to let her run a trial. And it's no wonder Devon wanted her to succeed and gave her everything she asked for: His blood. An army. Commitment.

Well. Almost everything.

"Hang on," Everleigh whispers. "I need a second. . . ."

She draws a trembling breath and makes a steeple shape with her fingers between her eyes. Devon relishes the emotional interruption as blood storms my ears. All I can think about are those scorched remains in the woods. I need to know how far they've gotten. Whether anyone's had a child. *Who.*

"Is this real?" Everleigh asks.

Everyone nods except me. What's "real" here is relative. I know that.

"How?"

"Come with us and we'll show you," Margot says, and rises. "You can meet them."

I'm a tumbleweed of nerves as we hike toward the clinic.

"Gonna need you to cut the stream while we walk," Devon says to Everleigh. "No identifying landmarks."

"Oh my God, of course." She hits pause, keeping the camera slung around her neck.

Margot hangs back with Everleigh, indulging her awestruck questions, as Devon and Pyotr march ahead of us. I'm hovering somewhere in the middle, lost in the fog of it all.

"Pyotr's associates helped us find a fantastic lab in Moscow," Margot gushes. "We send them the samples and—granted, this is a very simplistic way of putting it—they're able to 'shock' them back to life using human stem cells."

"You wouldn't call that cheating?" Everleigh asks.

"Would you call IVF cheating? It's the same idea. All the genetic material belongs to the Saras in our study. It's their flesh and blood. We're just giving it a friendly nudge."

"Whose is it?" I whirl around.

I'm too embarrassed to ask the real question grinding against my skull.

He said he didn't sleep with her. But the ugly thing I'm imagining . . .

"Whose is what?" Margot gives me her best imitation of Devon's blank stare.

"Whose . . . *genetic material?*"

"The women in our study. Two of them are pregnant. One's at three months, the other's just shy of five."

Not Cora. Couldn't be. We haven't been here long enough.

"A healthy network of anonymous donors takes care of the rest."

"So nobody we . . . *know.*"

"Not for a trial." She curtly weaves past, keeping pace with Everleigh.

"I'm sorry I couldn't tell you," Devon says in a quiet voice, stopping to let me catch up. I approach him like an electric fence. "We were afraid you'd spook her and try to talk her out of it. It needed to be her choice."

"Right."

"You of all people should know how much she wants this."

I hang my head. All this time, I thought Cora was a prisoner. My stomach is syrupy with shame.

We reach the clinic, and Everleigh readies her camera. Pyotr leapfrogs ahead of us as Devon unlocks the door.

"If it's a boy, we're going to name him Dmitri," Pyotr announces from inside. "If it's a girl, Larisa. After my mommy."

"Oh my God . . ." Everleigh whispers, entering the space like a holy monument.

I step up behind her. And the interior takes my breath away. I see now, why Devon's had the rest of us living in squalor. Every dime they had went into this sterile, gleaming hospital in the bowels of the wilderness.

But before I can take it all in, before I can scan the room for a sign of Cora . . . a piercing shriek cuts the reverence.

I whip around the corner and follow Everleigh into a room with six spartan cots in it—two rows of three. In the center stands a young woman I've never seen before: a hollow-eyed, skeletal phantom in a hospital gown with withered, graying flesh and hair like twigs. A small but noticeable swell protrudes from her gown. Someone's tried to make her look presentable and camera-ready; she's wearing makeup that doesn't match the rest of her.

In her hand is a silver snub-nosed pistol.

And the scream . . . that's not her. It's Kayla, from the opposite corner of the room. Because that's Kayla's gun she's pointing, right at the camera. No, not the camera.

She's pointing it at Devon.

"Edie," Kayla whispers, an awful tremor in her voice. "It's okay, honey. Just give it back. Slowly."

The woman, Edie, doesn't flinch. Doesn't even look like she's breathing.

Kayla inches toward her, then hesitates. Searching us for guidance.

Dr. Lacie hovers behind Devon, her frozen face a rictus of terror. Pyotr cowers under one of the beds. Everleigh lets the camera fall to her side, but the red light indicates she's still rolling. Then there are the other girls: the two I saw with Cora that first night, buried against each other's necks, too afraid to watch. And Cora. Halfway out of the bathroom on the far side of the room. Skin and bones, with that same awful, washed-out pallor. She sees me. And my entire being howls.

"Edie." Devon takes a step toward the young woman. If he's afraid, it's nowhere on his face.

Her arm shakes. She steadies it with her other hand. He takes another step.

"I want you to think."

She nods as a tear falls down her cheek. But still, she keeps the gun raised.

"You don't want to do this to me."

God dammit, what is she waiting for?

She starts lowering her arm. Devon breathes out and opens his palm.

"Good girl. Just give it—"

The gun goes off.

She moves so fast nobody sees what she's pointed it at. Until it's too late.

She's turned it on herself.

The room capsizes in a vortex of screams. I don't want to look at the pieces of Edie's shattered skull, at that sluggish tide of rust-tainted black blood, but I can't shut my eyes. Devon lunges for the gun on the ground and holds it out in front of him. Now, he's terrified.

"Nobody move," he barks, hoarse with anguish.

As he turns, scanning each of our faces, Everleigh jolts upright. She skitters toward the exit, camera thumping against her breast like a second heartbeat.

She kicks the door open. Thinks she's fast enough. She's so scared she almost is.

But Devon is faster. He fires two rounds, dead center at the back of her skull, hitting the same spot twice.

His aim is exquisite. I immediately know—have *always known*—that he was the one who shot me in the woods that night.

I lose myself in the middle distance as the grisly devastation carousels around me.

Pyotr rocks back and forth under the bed with his hands over his ears, blubbering in his mother tongue. Margot sinks to her knees, hypnotized by the horrible black tributaries creeping across the floor.

And Cora. Cora's just staring at me, hugging the wall for support as tears pour down her frail, haunted face. Her lips move. I miss it the first time, what she's trying to say. But when she repeats herself, I see it. Over and over, like a distress signal.

Help me.

☾ ☾ ☾

"I need everybody's guns. *Now.*"

Devon kicks a smoldering branch with his boot, belching sparks into our stricken faces as we slink around the fire.

Kayla's inconsolable, hunched on a rock, away from the light. Hasn't cleaned Edie's blood from her face yet.

Coats and pockets open. Slowly. Noah drops a revolver to the ground. Gareth, too. Teresa relinquishes two: hers and Bjorn's. Four more people add theirs to the pile. Devon gathers them and starts emptying each clip with trembling hands. Doesn't say a word.

I didn't realize how many of us he'd armed. He trusted us.

"If they come for us, if we *fail*—" He's not yelling anymore. Just sounds exhausted. He presents an empty clip and tosses it into a black trash bag. "You've lost your right to an easy out. And you know what? I think I'm good with that."

He hasn't glanced my way so I don't know if this includes me. Still, I'm here. Submitting to his rage with the rest of them.

"I want to watch you *starve* till you chew your hands to fucking *stumps*." He punctuates the words as each clip hits the ground. "Watch you *burn* with a rusted *pike* in your ass."

Kayla's breath hitches from her dark corner of shame. His gaze slices toward her, then back to us.

"You're all *leeches*. You want to stand next to me and say you're a part of this while you watch me do all the work. I do *everything*. For *you*."

He hoists the black bag over his shoulder, like a rail-thin, demonic Santa Claus.

"And I'm fucking sick of it."

He turns to leave and picks up a flaming log with his bare hands. Chucks it across the camp with a heart-twisting snarl.

As he stalks off, I spot Pyotr, scurrying down the hill toward his RV. His terrified sobs echo through the trees.

I help Kayla over to the lodge. She produces a key . . . and unlocks the medical office. The door I was trying to open the night before.

She lets me in and slumps to the floor. Catatonic, with her head between her knees. I shut the door behind us and lock it.

Her voice is so soft it hardly registers. "I-I was doing Edie's makeup. I don't know when she took the gun. Maybe when I went into the bathroom. I took it off for a second, but—"

"I believe you."

She keeps her face pressed tight against her knee, like she wishes she could fold in on herself so many times she disappears. There's something that looks like bone stuck in her hair.

I turn in a circle. Absorbing my surroundings. There's nothing here but a cheap wooden desk with a laptop and a refrigerator in the corner. The fluorescents quiver, like they're trembling in sympathy. Behind me, Kayla's breath stutters in and out.

I sit down at the desk and lunge for the laptop. Maybe there's still Wi-Fi coming from Pyotr's RV. They had a strong enough signal to host a livestream. Maybe I can blast out some sort of SOS email, or log in to my old socials. But no networks show up when I open the settings.

I lose myself in the desktop's whimsical pink gradient as despair unspools from the center of my chest.

There's not much on here. Just a few folders. I notice each one has a name.

Claire
Ava
Edie
Meg
Daisy
Cora

I suck in air and double-click.

It's a chart, logging dates and body temperatures. Two columns that read "INJECTION #1" and "INJECTION #2." All the way up to today.

I open the folder labeled "Meg" after Cora's. Her log ends on March 14. DECEASED in bold red lettering.

Cora and I would have arrived at the camp one week later.

I open the rest of the folders. A second girl, Claire, was logged as DECEASED four days ago. But before that . . . she was pregnant. Seventeen weeks along.

The lights flicker as the refrigerator hums behind me, pulling my gaze. Bile rises in my throat as I shuffle forward. Like I know what I'm going to find when I open it. But I can't help it.

Two small red cases rest on the shelf. Both labeled FETAL REMAINS.

Stiff globules of black blood cling to the lid of the larger container like stale, sticky syrup. A taste like rotten fruit fills my mouth as I slam the fridge shut.

"After they die . . . that's when they ask for my help," Kayla whispers as I sink to the floor beside her. "I take the bodies to the woods before the sun comes up. Once the light hits them . . ."

My lungs deflate. Those Saranasia shots are still sewn into the lining of my backpack. I wonder if Cora still has them. What she could have done, had she known.

"They keep trying. But their bodies can't survive it." Kayla's voice strains. "And Margot won't let them leave."

I had a feeling it was going to be something like this. But hearing it. *Knowing* it . . . it's like I can never know anything else, ever again. I'm empty. All that's left is the hot, feral residue of rage.

"I wanted to tell someone," Kayla goes on, face still pressed against her knee. "And I was going to. But then I realized. Everyone already knew. Except you."

"Kayla." When she lifts her head, her eyes shine with fear. Like she knows what I'm about to say. "It's not too late. We can help them."

"Don't—"

"Listen to me."

"You listen to *me*. I told you I didn't want you getting hurt. This is what I meant. You can't trust any of us."

"Even you?"

She's shivering. "Jesus Christ, Mia. Why the hell did you come here?"

"I think you know."

She answers in a choked voice that's almost a whimper. "Your mom."

I nod.

"Mia, that story I told you. About how it happened to me—"

"It wasn't true?"

"No, that's how it went. But like . . . God, and I've *known this*, all along. That was a two-person job. He didn't *save me* when she fucked up. That's how they would do it. How he told *us* to . . . One person would attack and be the bad guy. Then someone else would come and rescue you." She exhales with a bleak laugh. "Double the loyalty points."

I match her crestfallen stare.

"I thought I knew your mom. I mean, she wasn't perfect. We both know that. She could be a real fucking bitch sometimes," she says with a pained laugh. I sigh in agreement. "But he turned her into something *so* much worse."

I nod, staring into the void of the boarded-up window.

"There's something seriously wrong with him, Mia. Like, I don't understand how he can just . . . *do what he does*. To so many people. Like it's nothing."

Weak light whispers through a hairline crack in the wood. I can't help the first thought that burns across my mind: *Now go get some tape. And fix the fucking window.*

"I've only ever lifted one person." Kayla's voice tiptoes. Like she's been afraid to say this aloud. "This girl, Melissa. She was young, like barely eighteen. We met at Cloak and Dagger when she asked me to buy her a beer. She got herself killed when we were en route to Colorado. She took a knockoff Daylight that didn't work. I still think about her every day. I *feel* her, like there's a little speck of her still floating around inside me, y'know?" She folds both my hands into hers. "It's the same way I feel about your mom."

My throat thickens with emotion as I meet her eye. "We need to get out of here. We have to be ready in twenty-four hours."

Kayla nods. "Before anyone else dies."

I was going to say, *Before we lose our nerve*. But I keep that to myself.

TONIGHT

Kayla and I burn daylight in our stuffy bunker. Trying to ignore the haunting hum of that horrible fridge. By the time the sun goes down, we have a plan.

The risk is molten in me. I know how easily everything could backfire. But if I slow down to calculate my odds, I won't act. Just like the night I first tried to run. I can't help but wonder, if I'd made it out, whether I could have saved Cora weeks ago. Whether Edie and Claire would still be alive.

Both of us need to have something to eat before we get started. Which means Gareth will be the first link in our chain. Plus, there's something I need to ask him. Something I haven't told Kayla, because I'm afraid she might talk me out of it.

I survey the camp for a sign of Devon or Margot. The Chevy is still here. But they're not outside. In fact, nobody is. For the first time, the fire pit is dark.

There's a chance Devon could be in Gareth's trailer. A chance this whole thing could start ripping at the seams before we take a single step. But when Gareth opens the door, he's alone.

He's surprised to see I've brought a guest, though.

"Gare, we need to talk to you. Can we come in?"

He scans the perimeter. "You seen him tonight?"

"No."

"I don't think he's come out at all."

"Good."

The three of us sit at his lopsided plywood table with a lantern between us. I share my camping mug with Kayla. Gareth doesn't ask questions or remind us of the rules. I think he understands. Tonight is different.

"Gare, there's something I have to . . ." I push the mug toward Kayla. It feels crude to drink his blood when I say this. "I'm just gonna pull the Band-Aid off. Devon told me he has no plans to lift you. Ever. I'm sorry. I thought you should know."

Kayla shoots me a startled glance. I knew I was going to catch her off guard. But I need to do this.

I watch Gareth's face for a reaction. His mouth twitches, like he's about to say something. He glances down at his arms. At the minefield of scars.

I follow his gaze to that black "167" on his arm.

"What'd he say, exactly?"

"He uh . . . well, he has all these ideas about who should become a Sara and who shouldn't. He said he didn't think you were smart enough."

Gareth removes the tourniquet and pulls the springy ends apart like a tightrope. Sighs as he lets it snap back and hit him in the wrist. "The two of us would be dead, if we didn't have each other. I dunno if he told you."

"He kinda told me everything."

"Nothin' sacred anymore, huh?"

"I'm sorry."

Kayla's eyes darken with that telltale shadow as she catches my gaze. *The fuck are you doing, Mia?*

"You know, I did the same thing for my mom," I say. Softly, like I'm trying not to startle him. "For thirteen years. I lost a lot of time, but—"

"It was never gonna be a *loss,* if he kept his promise—"

"Gareth, he doesn't care about that. He has no problem writing checks you can't cash."

He replies with a slow nod. It's time to twist the knife. And I learned from the best.

"When you told me how he treated you, when he started bringing the drugs in . . . I thought, how could he do that, to someone he calls family? Someone he says he loves?"

Gareth pulls his sleeves over his stippled arms. I can see the tears brimming. I hate leading him to the edge like this. Then again, I'm only telling him what he already knows.

"We're leaving, Gare. Me, Kay, and the girls from the clinic. We want you to come, too. It's time."

I watch Kayla from the corner of my eye as she tilts her head with the slightest of nods. She gets it now. If anything goes wrong out there, we're going to need blood.

Gareth's mouth is a long, grim line.

". . . How?"

It's not a no. But it's not a yes, either.

"We've got a dozen Daylights. All we need is a head start." He doesn't react. "I promise, we can protect you."

Still, nothing.

Kayla nudges my ankle with her shoe. She and I both know what I need to say next.

"We can lift you. Once we're free and it's safe."

I don't want to do it. But I don't want to lie to him, either.

"I don't have a lot to offer you," he says at last. "He keeps the keys to the truck. And I only have a phone when I'm out on official business."

"We can manage on foot. Call for help once we hit that gas station outside town."

He wets his shaking lips. "He has Daylights too, you know."

"Does he have any left?"

"I know Shea gave him a couple. Some of them were for Pyotr."

"And we took two on the way home that day."

"Right." He hisses out air. "Either way. A head start will be the most important thing."

"He's gonna sleep right through it. As long as we don't let anything wake him up."

He's massaging that fresh pinprick on his arm again. "Can I decide in the morning?"

Kayla and I exchange an unsettled glance. This isn't the answer we needed. But any hitch in my confidence is likely to dissuade him further. I stand, if only to regain some dominance. "Seven A.M. Don't be late."

It takes him a long time to nod. I swallow to push the nausea down. Praying I haven't flung my faith in the wrong direction.

◖ ◖ ◖

One of Margot's two nurses, Kat, opens the door to the clinic. Her frazzled gaze ping-pongs from Kayla's face back to mine. Red eyes cloudy with exhaustion.

"Aw, sweetie." Kayla takes her in with a sigh. Only I recognize its artifice. "You doin' okay?"

"What do you want?"

It's probably better if I take over. "Is Dr. Lacie inside?"

"Yeah, but she's resting."

"That's okay, we can wait." I take a step toward her. She shrivels. Like I hoped she would. Technically, I am number three around here. In the absence of Devon or Margot, someone like her should defer to me.

"Devon says it would be a good idea to come by and keep everyone company. Just . . . y'know. To lighten things up." I wasn't planning to tell this lie. But who is this lowly, unlifted nurse to challenge his request? When she doesn't flinch, I add, "You look like you could use a break."

Her head droops, and she nods. Opens the door to us.

"I need to search you."

"Of course."

Her hands are shaking as she pats us down, and I make a show of sniffing her neck when she leans in close. Trying to keep her from glancing down my bra, where I've hidden the Daylights. She scuttles aside with a sharp intake of breath.

"I'll let the doctor know you're here."

A faint, brown blush stains the floor where Edie bled out last night. Kat deposits us in the main bunk before she sails toward an adjoining examination room.

Three girls remain. Listless in their beds. Our presence barely even registers.

"That's Daisy," Kayla whispers, pointing to the girl with the sprawling black curls, her ballerina legs pressed to her chest in a taut egg shape. "And Ava." The waify blonde sleeps on the cot beside her, shivering under a pile of blankets.

Cora sits up in bed, on the other side of the room. It looks like it takes all the strength she has just to lift her head. She mouths my name, and I rush toward her.

Kayla clears her throat as a warning, but nothing's going to stop me. Cora's limbs are like reeds—all brittle, jutting bone—when she reaches out to hug me. She smells like antiseptic and decay. Acrid and upsettingly sweet.

The other girls stir as I hear Kat and Margot speaking in low voices on the other side of the door. Kayla meets my eye. We might not have much time.

"Where can we talk?" I whisper in Cora's ear.

"U-uh . . . I don't—"

"Do you need a shower?"

She gives me a dazed, quizzical look that melts into understanding. "Yeah. That sounds like a good idea."

She wobbles to her feet, and Kayla helps me support her. "Bathroom's over there." She points a feeble finger toward a nearby alcove.

Daisy sits up and stares at me as we pass. I try not to hold eye contact. She knows something's up. Might even recognize it as hope. But I'm not ready to trust anyone but Cora. Not yet, anyway.

"I'll stall them." Kayla scurries toward the exam room after Kat as I pull Cora into the bathroom, shut the door, and turn on the water.

She collapses onto the shower stool in the corner, exhausted. Just lets the water pelt her. Doesn't even take off her gown.

I scoop the Daylights from my bra and reveal them to her. She nods with recognition, eyes at half mast. I shove them into my pocket, then remove my shirt and pants and push them toward the door. The shower occupies more than three-quarters of the room, and I can't afford to let our provisions get wet.

I fall to my knees in my underwear, clasping her hands. Water pounds my spine, fat and cold. I'm waiting for it to warm up. I realize it probably won't.

"You shouldn't have come here—" Cora rasps.

"Fuck right off, I'm not letting you die."

She lunges forward and her lips meet mine. It's a frail kiss. Two shivering mouths afraid they'll never meet again. But it revives every dying part of me. Her shoulders hitch, and when I open my eyes, she's crying.

"I'm so sorry, Cora. When I wrote all of that—"

"Doesn't matter."

"No, it does. It was wrong and I never meant to hurt you. Please forgive me."

"I love you so much—" It's a quiet tremor of a confession. Like a goodbye.

I steady her wet face between my hands. "Core, here's what's happening. I'm giving you six Daylights. At seven o'clock tomorrow morning, when Margot's asleep, you're going to take one. If Daisy and Ava want in, too, we have enough. But you need to be careful, when you ask them. Make sure nobody hears you."

"Ask them what?"

"If they're coming with us."

"Coming . . . where? How are we supposed to—?"

"All you have to do is take your pill at seven. Does the front door lock on the inside?"

"Just the outside. I think we can get out. But Mia—"

"We have to trust each other, okay? Just like the night we left the Sara center. As long as we work together, we got this."

"But . . . we're not strong enough. And Ava's pregnant. You'll see, she can barely walk. If anyone comes after us—"

"They won't."

"*He* will."

"Only if he knows we're gone. Seven o'clock gives us twelve and a half hours to get ahead. Two pills each. There's a gas station I saw a few nights ago. We'll stick to the woods till we get there."

"Then what?"

"Find a phone. Call the cops." I shrug. "Beg for mercy?"

"Like we'll get any."

"You'd rather wait and see if we get any from Devon?" I hold her gaze. Something rises in me. A reckless faith that starts to feel like certainty. "We have something they want, Cora. We have *him*. Don't forget that."

She doesn't reply. Just shudders and folds her spindly arms against her concave belly. I know. *I know* . . .

"They lied to you. And they used you. Someone has to answer for that."

I move in beside her on the bench. The water plasters her gown to her freezing-cold skin.

"You'll have a family someday. Maybe not the way you thought. But you will. That's my promise to you."

Her shuddering is contagious. I'm trying not to cry. Trying to be strong for her sake. But maybe that's what it is, to be strong for her. To sit here in the cold, together. Let it spill over both of us.

"I don't love him," she whispers. "I never did. I know that now."

"It's okay—"

"It's not. I was so fucking stupid, Mia. . . ."

I wring the water from her thinning hair and kiss her cheek. That little black jewel at the corner of her eye.

"All you did was want something you couldn't have. You're not stupid. You're human." I rise to turn off the shower. "He's a monster."

There's a stack of stiff, shopworn towels on the shelf above the bench. I wrap one around her shoulders and fold another around her hair.

"I was hoping I'd get a chance to tell you," she says as I help her to her feet. "I had the craziest dream a few hours ago. Someone woke me up and I thought it was Kat, so she could give me my shot. But it was your mom."

I freeze with the towel wound halfway around her head.

"You've never met my mom."

"No, I know. That's why it was so weird. It's not like I know what she looks like. Like . . . maybe it was *you* but in my head I knew it was *her*, you know? Anyway, she was fucking *pissed*."

I catch my breath and dress, robotically, as she goes on.

"She started trashing the clinic. Smashed up all the machines. Took the needle out of Kat's hand and stomped on it. It was insane."

Needle. "Wait. Cora, do you still have my backpack?"

She nods.

"If you open the front pocket, you'll see a hole I stitched back together. There are two Saranasia shots inside."

"Oh. Shit."

"Now you know. If anything goes wrong."

A knock at the door. Three times in quick, irritated succession. "Cora?" It's Margot.

I jump into my pants and grab the Daylights from my pocket. Tuck them into the towel around Cora's hair.

"Just . . . hold still, I guess?" I stare at the precarious hiding place with a knot in my stomach. Cora nods. And Margot flings the door open.

I'm thankful for the cold shower. Easier to disguise the way we're both shaking.

Margot's pointed gaze lands on me. Then slides to Cora.

"Mia," she mutters. Scanning Cora up and down. Like she knows to suspect foul play but isn't sure where to look. "Didn't know you were in here."

"Just trying to help out. I know everyone's tired." I place a hand on the back of Cora's neck to keep her head steady as I guide her toward the bunks. "If you need anything else, you know where to find me."

"That's . . . very thoughtful," she replies through her teeth.

I ease Cora back into bed, squeezing her hand. We both know this is it. If this is meant to be, the next time we speak will be tomorrow morning.

I scan the room for Kayla . . . but she's already gone.

"Thank you, Mia," Margot says, like a razor on bone. Holding the door open for me.

I wish I could turn to catch one final glimpse of Cora. But it's safer not to.

I shuffle outside, stomach swirling with the thrill of what I've just accomplished.

A smirk slides to my lips as Margot shuts the door behind me and I tongue the sharp tips of my teeth.

I hope I never see that bitch from Montana again.

A cold breeze rakes my damp hair as a light but unwelcome springtime snow falls between the trees. No problem. Won't stop us. We'll dress in layers. Bring extra for the girls. Kayla's got that big bag of donations.

An owl perches on the roof of the lodge and fills the silence with its song. But other than that, the camp is quiet. Like nobody's even here.

I assume Margot gave Kayla the boot and that she's already returned to the office. But when I try the door, it's locked. I start knocking. "Kayla? You in there?"

No response. Something shudders in the trees. But not the wind. I squint, searching the darkness, before I knock again.

"Kay? C'mon, it's me—"

Still there's nothing. God dammit. Where did she go?

I realize I don't hear that owl on the roof anymore.

I start turning in a circle. Scoring my lip with an anxious canine . . .

When a crunch in the frost cinches my heart.

I already know who's behind me. And it's not Kayla.

"Mia—"

I have no choice. I have to face him. Wear that inscrutable mask one last time and pray to God it's enough.

"Don't say anything," Devon whispers as I open my mouth to interject. "Just come with me."

My mind chafes against his silence as he grabs my arm and marches me around the lodge, toward the front entry. I wonder, with a gust of terror, whether he's already caught Kayla. Whether Gareth went to him and squealed right away. Tears stab my eyes.

Stupid, stupid. How could I have been so *fucking* . . .

He leads me up the steps of the ramshackle A-frame. The soft, moldy wood is slick with fresh snow. As he unlocks the door, I study his expression in the moonlight. His eyes are muddy and unfocused, meandering between my face, the door, and his feet. His head lolls. Just enough for me to realize something's *off*. He's tense as a grenade, but half asleep.

"Um . . ." I mumble in the doorway. I need to stall till I have my bearings. "I was looking for Kayla. Do you know where she—?"

He drags me through the door and locks it behind us. My mouth goes stale with panic.

For a moment, we just stand there. He's gripping my arms so tight his hands are starting to shake. I survey the room from the corner of my eye. Wondering if there's another way out.

There's a mammoth stone hearth illuminated by a few shards of smoldering wood. A crooked moose's head watches us from the mantel with dead, glassy eyes. A camping lantern on the abandoned, dusty bar provides the only other light, and our shadows spread grotesquely across the cracked, dented walls. Stacks of tattered chairs hem the room like scaffolding, and the floor-to-ceiling windows are plastered with black trash bags. The carpet is a graveyard of unwashed clothes and gun clips. A limp, unmade air mattress sits in the corner. Beside it he's stationed a tarnished old bar cart, littered with tightly rolled dollar bills. Different prescription bottles surround a telltale patch of cloudy white residue. I can't tell what they are. But I don't think they're Daylights.

Finally, Devon's bleary eyes rivet to mine. "You know what's gotta happen now. Right?"

"I-I don't . . . what's gotta—?" I swallow a sour mouthful of dread.

"Pyotr's gone. We shouldn't have let him run." He sighs, still squeezing my shoulders like a vise. "Should've shot him, too, when we had the chance."

"Y-yeah."

I flex my elbow, hoping I can coax him loose. But he just grips me tighter.

"Here's what we need to do. You with me, you listening?"

I nod. The safest thing I can do is let him talk. It doesn't seem like he knows about the plan. But he might be starting to form one of his own. . . .

"You know what Margot's trying to do to me," he slurs, breathless. "If Pyotr tells anyone where we are, she'll throw me onto the fucking fire. This is a fucking *arms race,* babe. They're gonna bomb us to hell and back if we don't drop one on them first."

My hackles ignite. I'm not sure if he knows it's me he's talking to. . . .

"I need to know who's still on my side."

"I mean . . . they don't really open up to me. I think you know that."

"Kayla does. And Kayla knows fucking everything about everyone, doesn't she?"

I shake my head, glancing around the room. I don't know how to escape this conversation if I can't even follow it. His grip slides down my arm, and my heart drops with it. This reminds me too much of Franklin. The way he's clutching my hands. Filling the conversation with questions I can't answer. I have to stay in the driver's seat this time. Can't turn my back. Not even for a second.

"Mia." He swivels my chin to meet his.

Guess he *does* know who he's talking to. I'm not sure if that's better or worse.

"Who's still with me?"

"I-I mean . . . I am." That's what he wants to hear. Right?

Or did I just relinquish the driver's seat, by saying that?

"Here's what we need to do. We have all the guns. We have the trucks—"

"Right—"

"There's one girl in the clinic who's pregnant. Ava. We have to take her with us. If we save her, we don't need Margot anymore. We don't need *any* of them." I inch backward as he closes the space between us. "But we gotta do it tonight."

"We don't have enough time. Tonight," I wheeze. "I don't know where you're trying to go, but the sun's gonna be up in less than—"

"We've got Daylights."

"How many?"

"You and me can split the last one—"

"What about Ava?"

"We've got the truck. I'll drive that, you take the Chevy. She can hide in there, and that's where we'll sleep till it's safe to hit the road again."

I feel like I'm on the same drugs he is. Everything he says makes my horrified pulse race faster and faster.

"Devon. Just so I'm clear. What you're proposing is . . ."

"Cleaning house."

I extract my hands. He stares, wounded. "You'd seriously kill everyone? Even Gareth?"

"He's changed. I don't know why, but I don't like it."

"How the hell are we supposed to do this without someone to feed us?"

"We'll hunt."

"And get caught in about two seconds." I pull up my posture. Hoping I've started to gain some ground. "Plus, without Margot, Ava's gonna die. She needs proper medical care. Don't be stupid." It feels good to call him that. Even if I'm just playing my part.

He exhales, reaching behind his head to cradle his neck.

"Don't do this tonight," I pour into the silence, trying to control my quavering voice. "Wait one more day. We can make a better plan."

At last, he nods.

"But you *would* do it. Right?"

I know I'm supposed to say yes. And I almost do, when he reaches for me again. Brushes a tendril of my hair. I catch his outstretched hand in mine and hold it as tight as I can to keep him at arm's length.

"You're a good girl. Y'know that?" he whispers, absently tonguing the points of his teeth. There are tears standing in his eyes. I don't know if he's about to cry or tear my throat out. "You're better than her, you always were. She was always so fucking selfish. But not you."

I'm still driving against his grip to keep him from taking another step. I know what he's about to do. It's hissing from his body like static as I fight to hear my own thoughts.

"Rip me open with that pretty little mouth. It's what you fucking want, isn't it?"

He pushes against my palm till my shaking elbow finally submits and the barrier between us falls.

Why, why, *why* do they do this? These men who claim to know what I want—*who* I want—and how I want it. Can't they see all I ever wanted was for them to leave me alone?

Maybe they do. Maybe that's the reason.

If I run—if I reject him—he will be angry. The kind of angry you don't live to tell about.

But this *cannot* happen. There is nothing, *nothing* in this world that could ever make this okay.

His breath hits my face and terror wrings my throat.

There's only one thing I can think to do.

I raise his hand to my mouth, blocking his kiss, and squeeze his finger between my teeth. Drawing blood.

He shudders as his forehead comes to rest against mine, and a surprised croak escapes his lips. I back away. Inch by horrified inch. Stretching his arm between us, keeping his finger hooked in my teeth. I'm not sure how long I should let this go on. All I know is this needs to feel like compliance. Without complying.

His blood is thick with chemicals. Like hard, metallic water from a rusted pipe. Nothing like that sweet drink I took from Cora that long-ago night. I choke it down with my revulsion. But his eyes are closed. A stoned smile on his lips. My heart holds its breath. This could be just as dangerous as letting him kiss me. Maybe worse.

He stumbles, realizing how much I've pulled away, and swoops toward me. When I try to back up, I hit the craggy stone wall of the hearth.

My canines slam his skin, hitting bone. He jolts with a sharp inhale and wrests his hand away. But he's still smiling.

He shakes his bloody finger and opens his eyes. Twines his arms around my waist. Ice-cold hands taunt the edge of my shirt.

"What else you got for me?" His voice is sugary with perversion.

My mind collapses till only one thought remains: *Run*. He can kill me if he wants. I'd rather die than find out what happens next.

I slither down the wall and try to weave around him. But it only makes him hold on tighter.

"Stop," he purrs into my hair. "What makes you think I'm gonna hurt you?"

I angle myself to knee him between the legs. Feels pathetic, but it's all I've got. As I raise my foot, there's a jingle of keys. The door unlocks.

I want to scream. Someone's just saved me.

Margot.

She discloses her teeth, clenched in disgust, as Devon releases me.

Nobody moves. I'm waiting for her to start shouting. Maybe hit him, or throw something at his face.

But she's not even looking at him. She's still staring at me.

He unfreezes first. Sheepishly sucks his bloody finger. Fucking laughs.

He doesn't care anymore, if she knows. That much is clear. But she's made a crack in the moment. And I can squeeze through.

"Get out," she seethes.

And I do.

My skin tightens and twists as I sleepwalk across the camp, like my body's trying to exorcise an evil black ichor up and out of my pores. I can barely hold myself upright.

To my relief, Kayla's unlocked the door to the office.

"Oh my God, where have you been?" She rushes over to me. I stand in the dark. The snow in my hair melts down my skull. "Mia?"

"I-I was looking for you . . ."

"Sorry. I was scoping out the work shed around back. There's a lot of nasty, rusted shit in there so I figured, in the absence of guns—"

I gaze past her shoulder, into the void. Deflating. If I'd just waited for her to come back and hadn't panicked and made so much noise, maybe he wouldn't have heard me and then maybe he wouldn't have—

"Where were *you*?" she asks again.

I'm waiting to cry. Desperate for it. But my body's tapped out.

"Mia?"

". . . Let's just get the hell out of here."

TODAY

We huddle on the floor together. Staring, unblinking, at Kayla's watch. The final moments dissolve. At 6:50, we take our pills. At 6:59, we open the door to a scintillating blanket of white. It snowed more than I thought.

"It'll melt, right?" she whispers.

I think I nod. I was hoping it would have already. Footprints could be a problem. But we've taken the pills. And we don't have enough to try this again.

She draws a ragged breath. I know she's scared. She doesn't trust the Daylights, and I don't blame her, considering what happened to Melissa. I take a deliberate, reassuring step into the sun. Letting her get a good look at me.

Movement behind the lodge pulls my gaze, and Gareth creeps out of his trailer. Meets my stare across the distance.

A swell of courage fills the terrified hollow in my heart. We're really doing this.

The three of us meet in the middle and make our way toward the clinic without a word. Gareth perspires through his parka. I can smell it. Every few paces, he catches the corner of my eye. Like he's sizing me up. I don't know what he's hoping to see. What a reliable person looks like to him. All the same, I square my shoulders and take the lead.

Kayla's got a sack of warm clothes for Ava, Daisy, and Cora. My backpack is stuffed with rusted yard tools. I know I'm not winning a gunfight with a hand trowel. But it's better than nothing. Besides, there isn't going to *be* a fight. All we have to do is walk.

My eyes reluctantly magnetize to the front door of the lodge. I know he's still in there. I wish I could torch it with my gaze. We take the long way around so our footsteps don't resonate.

We reach the clinic and stand in a row. A gut-wrenching vigil.

It's quiet. Too goddamn quiet. Birds sing and the wind whistles through the pines. But there's nothing else.

I feel exposed, like I'm dead center in someone's crosshairs.

Kayla brings her shaking lips to my ear and whispers, "Shit, what if Margot is awake in there?"

"I don't think that's where she is."

Kayla raises a questioning brow. But I don't feel like explaining how I know. Gareth cranes his neck, grappling for snippets of our hushed conversation.

"Okay, well what about—?"

A bloodstained arm shoves the door open.

Cora squints in the sunlight as it bounces off the severe white snow. Shuddering in her thin, gore-drenched gown with my backpack slung over her shoulder. I'm buzzing with fear as I rush toward her. But that's not her blood. It's falling from her chin, rorschaching down the front of her dress.

". . . Sophie and Kat," Kayla finishes her thought.

Gareth buries his mouth into the crook of his elbow. Like he's going to throw up.

"Get changed," I whisper to Cora. Snagging the sack of clothes from Kayla's stunned grip.

After a moment, Ava and Daisy timidly emerge. Daisy's gown is soaked through, like Cora's. But Ava is clean, aside from her red, trembling mouth. Too weak to fight. I'm glad she drank, though. They'll be stronger, all three of them, now that they've done this.

An older version of me would have wished they hadn't. But anyone who stands in our way today is asking for it.

Cora strips naked with a hard-shell stare, flexing her bare toes in the snow. The other two follow her lead. Gareth takes a respectful quarter turn, still breathing into his arm, as they tear into Kayla's bag.

I don't have to tell them to hurry. They know. They yank shirts over their gooseflesh and zip up pants that swallow their shrunken waists. Ava's barely showing. I can only tell because the rest of her is so thin by comparison. It's hard to believe such a feeble body can carry a child.

Then again, she's not supposed to be able to. The entire reason we're here.

The girls swap shoes with each other, quickly trying to determine their sizes—or the closest thing to it.

"Give me your gowns," Kayla says. That's a good call. The less blood in the air, the better. She balls them up and buries them in the snow. Slides a nearby garbage pail on top.

Cora seizes my hand. Daisy and Ava step forward.

"Hope you know what the hell you're doing," Daisy mutters as she shoves her shoes on. Cora cuts her a glare. But she's got every right. I'd say the same damn thing.

"*Shhh.*" Gareth whirls back around, dread burning in his eyes.

I turn to face the dirt road—where I know it is, anyway. Under the snow. The ice beneath my feet is already starting to liquefy in the sun. Maybe we'll get lucky and we won't leave a trace. Maybe we're smart enough and strong enough and I'll be picking up the phone at that gas station later tonight. I wonder what I'll say when the police answer. How long till the low, predatory drone of helicopters fills the air.

"This way," I mouth to the group. "Stay off the road but don't lose sight of it."

I take a step. Cora's still clinging to my hand. It's cold and her grip is weak. But she's with me. She's alive. And we're walking out of here together.

We're about a quarter mile down the hill when I realize Gareth is falling behind.

He lingers halfway behind a tree, gazing at the edge of the camp just past the ridge. I leave Cora's side and backtrack toward him.

"Hard part's over, Gare. All we gotta do is walk."

But he's staring straight through me. I reach for his arm, and he twists it away. Heaves a breath he can't keep down.

"It's okay, he didn't hear us. I promise, he's not gonna—"

He sears me with his panicked stare.

"I know this is hard. But—"

Gareth backs away. Slowly. Till he runs. Slipping through my fingers in a hellish instant.

Holy shit.

"Gare—"

He kicks up a cyclone of snow, bolting back up the hill.

No.

I sprint after him as my scar groans and my injury rises from the dead. I tear through the awesome pain, flailing toward him. Trying my damnedest to be gentle.

"Please, *please* don't do this Gareth—"

He elbows me down the hill with a blaze of wild, terror-stricken strength. I hit the ground headfirst, and my nose absorbs the impact. I feel it splinter underneath me.

I try to right myself. But before I can find my feet again, Kayla roars past like a bullet.

There's no time to protest or hold her back. I forgot what it's like, to watch a Sara go full-out. That gorgeous, diabolical precision.

Gareth shrieks. The piercing sound volleys through the trees. Lodges between my lungs.

Kayla slams his face against a rock and grinds it to gristle. Keeping his neck pincered in her ruthless jaw. Blood sprays in all directions. Splashing our jackets and shoes. She's half his size, but she holds her ground as he spasms and struggles, squeezing his rib cage between her knees till the bones give way with a fat *snap*.

At last, he's still.

Kayla rolls off him and leaps to her feet. Massaging a cramp in her thigh.

"We should drink," Cora whispers. "Before his heart stops."

"We don't have time for that," Kayla replies. Can't help but lick her lips, though.

"She's right. He screamed," I murmur, horrified. "We gotta go."

But I can't move. Like the snow just hardened to ice around my feet.

Tufts of blood-matted silver and gold hair litter the ground. I think of the night Mom and I found chunks of a dead javelina strewn across our driveway. Mauled by a coyote.

He deserved better.

He never understood.

But that's his fault. Not mine.

Blood coats everything like an oil slick. A siren's song of sweet, steamy vapor dances on the breeze. I want it. I know we all want it. But we're open to attack if we stay another second.

"O-okay." I clear my throat as my bruised face burns and my nose knits back into place. Everyone's looking at me. Because they think I have a new plan.

"Um . . . there's a creek up ahead."

At least, I seem to recall seeing one, the night of my failed escape.

"We'll follow that instead of the road. Snow's gonna melt faster alongside the water."

We can't wait for our footprints to fade. Not if Gareth's scream woke him up. My pulse peals in my ears.

"We gotta run now." I look to Ava, Cora, and Daisy. "Try your best, okay?"

Adrenaline numbs me like a narcotic. Cools the fire in my leg. The faster we go, the easier it gets. Devon kept me so small and so weak I didn't realize I'd won this much strength back. I'm not quite hitting the same gear I did the night we left New York. I might never recapture that speed. Still, I'm flying. Like a dream I've been too afraid to believe.

Cora meets my stride, but her breath is short and labored. We're going to need to take breaks. That's okay. This is the most important leg of the journey. Just need to put distance between our footprints and Gareth's remains.

Relief rushes over me when we reach the creek. We wind along the rocky riverbank, where wet, sunbaked stones protect us from the snow. Sweat glows on Cora's brow. I unzip my jacket. The warmth is like a promise.

Ava is the first to stumble. I skid to a stop and help Cora steady her.

"We need a breather." Daisy shudders.

"Thirty seconds?" Kayla catches her breath. Tying her coat around her waist.

I shake my head as Ava's quaking legs buckle. I catch her full weight.

"She's not gonna be able to do this," Cora whispers in my ear.

"N-no, I'm fine." Her voice is sturdier than the rest of her. "Just . . . give me a minute."

Kayla nudges Cora aside and lifts Ava's sagging shoulder. "C'mere. We'll carry you."

She means the two of us. I'm not sure my leg can handle it. But it's our only option.

Ava pulls a sharp breath. Convulses against me. Grinds her teeth as her eyes roll back. Cora yelps and Daisy dives toward her, cupping her gray face in her hands.

"C'mon, Ave. Stay with us. We got you."

Ava nods, fighting for control. A pearl of blood falls from her nose. Kayla fidgets, scanning her periphery.

"Mia, we gotta—"

"I know."

Ava gulps air, pushing through the turbulence. Her lungs are creaking. I can't imagine the pain she's feeling. How long she's been feeling it. We hold her as tight as we can to tamp her body down. Can't carry her if she's seizing like this.

"Breathe, Ave. Almost through," Daisy keeps encouraging her. "You're so fucking strong, girl."

"You're gonna be home soon," Cora adds, a pang in her voice. "Your mom's gonna be so happy to see you—"

Ava nods, frantic. Growling past the final throes. Finally, the episode tapers. Just enough for Kayla and me to lift her off the ground. I've got her legs hooked on either side of my neck. Kayla has the rest of her, slung piggyback over her shoulders, facedown. She's too weak to keep her thighs cinched around Kayla's waist. Can't hold herself up.

"Fuck yeah." Daisy squeezes her hand. "That's how ya do it."

Ava whistles out air. My heart twists, spurred by the bond between them. These girls have been to hell and back together. Almost back, anyway. Soon enough.

☾ ☾ ☾

It's harder to run now. We're doing the best we can. Stopping when we need to. More than we want. But we're moving.

The sun climbs in the sky as the creek widens and the current intensifies. Kayla slows her pace to check her watch. We've been gone almost three hours.

"Think we're in the clear?" she grunts over her shoulder.

"Not ready to make that call." I adjust Ava's legs. "But we need to find the road again. I don't know where we are without it."

"It's close though, right?" Cora pipes up.

We all slow down. Once again, everyone's eyes land on me.

"Uh, well. The road runs east to west. Right now, we're facing south." I think. Fuck, I can't believe we made a go of this without a compass. Not like anybody had one. Like he would've *let* anybody have one.

"So then . . ." Cora turns in a circle. "Never . . . Eat . . . Soggy . . . Waffles."

I snort. Can't help it. Feels good to laugh.

"East takes us *to* camp? Or away from it?"

"Away."

"Okay." Cora takes up the lead. "The river's curving in that direction. So we might be fine. Do you remember hearing it, when you were on the road?"

"No. But that doesn't mean we're off base. I saw a sign for white-water rafting." My gut churns as I try to reassure myself. We're definitely lost. But maybe not *hopelessly* lost.

We trudge onward. Starting to jog. Till Ava moans and loses her grip on Kayla's neck. We catch her like a basket before she hits the ground.

"I think we should walk," Daisy says. It's not a suggestion.

Kayla and I gather Ava back into our arms as heat rises in my cheeks. I know we're all thinking the same thing. We've messed this up. *I've* messed this up.

But what choice did we have? There was no time, no other way.

Cora rubs my shoulder. Like she hears the guilt humming all around me.

Thirty minutes later, the river curves in a new direction, deeper into the trees. Cora grinds to a halt. I want to collapse to the dirt and scream. Not at her. At myself. For trusting Gareth. Letting this happen. If he hadn't tried to run, we wouldn't have followed the creek.

"That's it," Daisy grunts. "The river's not helping."

"But we have to follow something," Cora fires back. "We don't want to go in circles."

"This is *insane*. We're just . . ." Daisy's lip quivers. "We're wandering around in the middle of *nowhere*—"

"Better than where we were."

"What's gonna happen when we run out of Daylights? When we get hungry?"

I hang my head. Kayla adjusts Ava's body, nodding at me to set her down for a second. As we gently help her unfold and sink to the ground, her breath catches with a thick, viscid snarl.

Cora and Daisy spin to face us as despair swims up my veins. She's seizing again. Worse than before.

The cheerleading starts. *You got this, girl. We're almost through. We're gonna make it.* But this time, she can't hold her head up. Her eyes are two white globes, bouncing in time with each nightmarish convulsion. Her jaw snaps open and shut as her hands spasm into useless, frozen claws. She's chewing her tongue to a pulp, destroying herself faster than her body knows how to heal. Foamy red viscera pours down her chin. She breathes, convulses, and chokes again. A horrific loop of suffocating agony.

"Ava . . ." Daisy yanks off her shoe and tries to wedge it between her teeth. But it's too late. The damage is done. She's asphyxiating. There's too much blood. Her lips are two blue bruises.

We watch. Helpless. Hoping beyond hope she'll turn the corner. But she doesn't. She's not going to.

"Cora . . . My backpack."

Cora's teeth chatter as she tosses it over to me. I tear the front pocket open and split the stitches with my nail, revealing the two Saranasia shots wrapped in their haphazard toilet paper cocoon. Still intact.

"No," Daisy cries when she sees what I'm holding. "Please, no—"

"We can't let her suffer," I say without looking at her.

"No, no, no. Core, please don't let her—"

I glance at Kayla. She draws Daisy into her arms and locks her in place. "Don't watch."

Daisy wails into Kayla's sweater but doesn't fight her. Doesn't turn around. Ava starts rolling away, kicking up slush and mud. Smothering herself against the dirt.

"Help me," I say to Cora as I grapple for Ava's ankle. "I don't want to mess this up. I need a vein."

Cora flips her over as gently as she can, taking a beating from her spastic legs. She pushes her hair aside and points to her neck.

"Okay?"

"Oh God. Yeah. Okay."

Tears pour down Cora's cheeks as she gives Ava a kiss on the forehead. I take that as my cue. I want this done quick and done right. I'll never forgive myself if it's not.

I plunge the needle into Ava's left jugular. Hold it till every last drop is under her skin.

It's fast. Chemicals flying to the rescue like a flock of angels.

She twitches. Her eyelids flutter. Fists go slack.

And she's gone.

Cora crumples against me. Shivering so hard I'm terrified she's about to have a seizure of her own. Daisy twists in Kayla's arms and howls. Kayla releases her, dragging her knees to her chest. Pressing them against her eyes. Daisy holds Ava's heavy head in her lap.

And that's where we stay. For how long, I don't know.

Doesn't matter.

If he finds us here, he's not taking us alive.

Sunlight streams through the trees in shimmering stalks of pink and amber. Auras and shadow. Snow and sky.

Cora stands and starts gathering stones along the riverbank. Daisy follows her lead. I secure the last remaining shot in my backpack's front pocket, then join her with Kayla.

We fill Ava's jacket, pants, and shoes. Weighing down her fragile body. It doesn't take much.

The sun will come for her soon. We've only got about two hours left on these Daylights. But she deserves more dignity than that.

There's another reason. One nobody wants to acknowledge aloud. But we can't leave her here if Devon passes through. Not if it helps him find the rest of us.

As we lower her into the water, Daisy whispers, "I'll tell your mom you were on your way. I'll tell her you're sorry."

Everything inside me unravels. My tears are a tidal wave. Kayla and Cora brace me on either side.

☾ ☾ ☾

We need to move. Anywhere. Forward.

"We've got to try and find that road." Kayla rallies us. "We're gonna need another pill soon. That'll get us to sunset. But after tonight—"

The three of us nod. No way in hell we're trying to race day-break.

"We should take the second dose now." Daisy squints into the pine-fractured sun with a frown.

"We've got time on these," Cora says. "This is the good shit, from New York. They *say* six hours, but you can get seven."

"I thought four was the limit."

"On the old formula. We got to test out the new stuff."

"I just think I'd feel better if I took mine now."

"You shouldn't," I interject. Traipsing ahead. "It'd be a waste."

"How do you know if it's not working anymore?"

"I mean . . ." I think back on my sunrise hike with Devon. Those bizarre half memories when I was desperate to leave my body. "I think you'll start to feel really sweaty and light-headed—"

"That's the thing though. I already do—"

"'Cuz we've been running," Cora hisses.

"That's not what I—"

A gunshot rings through the treetops.

Nobody moves. Nobody breathes.

A second pop follows. Louder. Closer. Like whoever's firing is moving fast.

Really fast.

"Maybe someone's out hunting," Kayla stutters. "Someone we can—"

"Kayla." The harrowing look in Cora's eyes says it all.

Terror crackles across my body as I unzip my bag and seize a rusted, three-pronged cultivator. It's small. Stupid. So goddamn stupid.

"Listen, those are warning shots," I whisper. "He's not aiming at us because he doesn't want to kill Ava."

"But Ava's already dead," Daisy chokes.

"He doesn't know that yet."

My gaze swings upward. Into the trees. Then back to Daisy and Cora.

"How fast can you—?"

"Mia!"

Oh my God. Oh my God.

"You fucking bitch—"

I can't see him. But he's close. Close enough to gouge me with that murderous voice.

We didn't leave any footprints. It had to be Gareth's blood. The stench of it on our clothes. I should have known. We *all* should have known.

"Don't. Move." I toss my backpack to Cora and scramble up the tree like a cat with a death wish. Clenching the cultivator's rubber handle between my shuddering teeth.

I curl around a pine bough to disguise myself. It bends precariously against my weight.

And he's there, seething on the riverbank. Like something dredged up from hell.

All at once, I'm ten years old. He's pounding up the stairs to my bedroom as I dangle one foot out the window. Mom screams, begging me not to jump. Begging him not to kill me.

Cora's eyes flick up the tree. I wish she'd stop looking.

Devon swerves toward them, gun drawn.

"You're two down. Where are they?" He trains the barrel on Kayla.

"I-I dunno, we got separated—"

I need him to move another foot toward the tree. He's so close. . . .

He frees up one hand and claws the back of her neck. Pressing the gun to her chest.

Whatever he was high on last night faded a long time ago. He doesn't flinch. His clear eyes shine like blades.

Kayla shifts backward with her arms raised. He moves with her. Toward the tree.

"C'mon, Kay. Talk to me."

Now. It's got to be now.

I yank my weapon from my teeth and let go of the branch. My stomach hits my throat as I plummet and the wind lashes my face. I was a lot higher than I thought. Which makes it a lot harder to aim this thing.

I fight to steady my arm against gravity as my feet slam his spine. He falls face-first into Kayla, who tumbles into the river.

The gun goes off in the water, skimming the surface like a nuclear skipping stone. My ears ring and for a moment all I can hear is my own galloping heart.

We struggle. All three of us. A tangle of arms, legs, and teeth. I'm fighting to keep purchase on the cultivator. We're all so quick. So strong. So scared.

I drive the rusted prongs into Devon's calf, stabbing holes in his pants. He donkey kicks me in the teeth before I pounce upward to pin down his hips.

He thrashes, trying to buck me off, as I hook him with the cultivator a second time. Digging jagged red tracks up his thigh.

Daisy and Cora bolt toward us, seizing both his arms. Cora takes a massive bite from his shoulder, through his down jacket. Bloody feathers fly through the air.

At last, Kayla worms out from under him. Wheezing for breath.

That's when I realize: He's not holding the gun anymore. He must have lost his grip when it went off in the water. The current's already carrying it away.

"The gun, the gun—" I hiss at Kayla. "Go find the—"

But she's limping. Slumped against a rock, moaning into her sleeve. Her femur is bent at a sickening right angle. It'll be at least an hour before she can walk on it again. Forget running.

I only took my eyes off him for a second. Maybe less. Just to glance at her.

He clenches his chest and flips onto his back, punting me across the riverbank. Knocking the wind from my lungs. He rockets to his feet, shakes Cora from his shoulder, and bites Daisy's hand with a horrific *crunch*.

"Where's Ava?" he barks, tossing the two of them to the water like gasping fish.

Nobody speaks. If he thinks she's still alive, he won't kill us. Not yet.

I have to run downriver and get that gun. It's our only chance. Whoever has the gun wins.

He knows it, too.

I bolt, and my injured leg fires back. Doesn't matter. He's got rust in his bloodstream. He'll be slower. I can beat him.

My eyes sweep the current as I run. Desperately seeking a glint of silver. The staccato of his footsteps at my back.

I spot something, winking at me under a dam of twigs. I wade into the shallows.

Fuck, it's a beer can.

I turn, and the ball of my foot slides against a flat, slippery stone.

He catches my hair in his fist. Winds it in an excruciating circle and drags me backward, using his free arm to squeeze my elbows to my chest and restrain me from behind. Horror swirls in my blood like hot poison. I am so much smaller than he is. Every time, I forget.

"Enough," he says in my ear. Slow and steady, like he's trying to talk me off a ledge. "You can't keep fighting me like this."

He's not going to kill me. He can't. Not without a weapon. And not till I tell him where Ava is.

But he can make me wish he would.

"Why, Mia?"

"You know," I growl through my teeth.

"No. Why did you think it would *work*?"

I squint, searching the riverbank for the others. I can't see what they're doing. Whether they're coming for me.

I hope they don't. I hope they run.

"It's gonna be okay. Just tell me where she is."

His lips brush my neck. I know what happens next. When he parts them. I squeeze my eyes shut.

It's not gonna kill you. Not gonna kill you. Not gonna—

His teeth meet my skin and sink down, down, straining against my nerve with horrible, electric insistence. A siren wails through my veins. Explodes up my throat.

This isn't like what Franklin did. I was prey, then. Anesthetized for a submissive death. There's no twilight sleep waiting for me this time. No death. I'm going to feel it all. For as long as he wants.

Blood surges down my collar and pools like boiling hot mud

under my clothes. My vision flashes red, and I swear I can feel all my atoms breaking apart. Floating away like a thousand spider hatchlings on the wind.

For a fleeting, dreamlike moment, he pulls away. Swallows.

"I hate this. You know that, right?" he says, into my wound. His voice throbs across my body as my brain blinks in and out. Not really here. Unclasping, clawing back. Detaching again.

"I can stop. I can take you home, right now."

My knees buckle, and he crumples to the ground with me. Doesn't let go.

"Just tell me where she is."

I gaze at the sky, grainy like white sand. But I can't keep my head up. My muscles are shredded, desperate to recalibrate.

There's no movement on the fuzzy horizon. They're gone.

His teeth reconnect. Scraping my soul from my skin.

As a fresh howl gurgles up my mutilated throat, his jaw loosens. My eyes stumble open.

Cora stands at his side with the Saranasia shot lodged in his neck. Her thumb rests on the plunger. About to press down.

Each passing moment flickers like a snapshot, quick as a gasp then gone. Stop-motion at the speed of sound.

He lurches around to face her, releasing my limp body. I watch, upside down in the dirt. Clutching my raw, slick wound for dear life.

Devon smacks Cora with one hand and yanks the needle from his neck with the other. He stares at it, on his knees. Knows exactly what it is.

Cora hurls back toward him, arms outstretched. Wrestling him for the injection. He tosses it over his shoulder as she leaps on top of him. Drags his nails across her face. She answers back, seizing his wrist in her teeth. I'd help her if I could. Get up and retrieve that shot. But I'm paralyzed. My devastated body is working overtime to repair itself. All I can do is try to remember how to breathe.

I stare, spellbound, as channels of blood melt the snow, snaking toward the river. Listening to them tussle and screech like dogs. I've got to stand. Got to finish this. But I can barely wiggle my goddamn toes.

Cora starts panting. Devon gains the upper hand. Rolls on top of her and wraps both hands around her thin, gray neck.

"Cora—" My voice scorches my throat like hot coals.

I drag myself to my knees with a guttural moan that jolts my half-dead flesh back to life.

I meet Devon's disbelieving gaze, unblinking. Keeping one hand on my wound and the other on the ground to steady myself as I rise.

At that moment, there's a hitch in his flinty stare.

Sweat glimmers on his brow.

His trembling grip on Cora loosens, and he draws a frayed breath that sounds like it hurts. Wet and dry at the same time.

I have heard this sound before.

Cora squirms out of his grasp as he wilts and falls to his side. He unzips his coat in a ferocious panic and starts scratching at his arms and his chest.

He had one pill left.

It was the old formula.

If he's been chasing us since this morning, since Gareth screamed . . .

Cora bolts to my rescue and helps me stand. We watch him, arm in arm, as he staggers upright. He surveys the surrounding wilderness, drunk with primal, blackout panic. Starts weaving toward the trees. As if the shade will help.

But he doesn't get half that far. His legs are too weak, and he can't make it ten paces without another scratching frenzy.

He turns to look at us, his eyes two manic, bloodshot orbs. "Help me find it."

He means the shot.

He stumbles in a circle, searching the red mud. Mopping sweat from his eyes.

"God dammit, Mia, please."

I take a step toward him.

"Yes. Yes. C'mere." He doubles over, reaching for me as I shuffle forward. "Thank you. Thank you. I'm so sorry, I never meant to hurt you, I never—"

"I need to tell you something."

He gapes at me. "Mia, please. The shot."

"*I* told the police about Montana. *I* tracked you down." I bite the words off. One by one. "I came all this way to watch you burn."

"N-no." His eyes dart between my face and the ground. "That doesn't make any—"

"Come on. You knew." I hold his frantic gaze. "But you let it happen because you needed someone other than yourself to blame when everything fell apart."

"But . . . *why*?"

"Because of my mom."

"Bullshit. You hated her."

"Doesn't matter. You killed her."

"*You* killed her!" The burst of emotion saps all his strength. He clutches his hobbled knees. Flexing and clenching his shaking hands. Sinks back to the ground.

"Your *mother*." He hacks blood. Drags a labored breath and releases it with a laugh. Pure, uncut black wickedness. "Was a dumb, worthless piece of ass who threw you to the wolves to keep my dick wet."

He's waiting for me to react. But I don't. He's going to burn to death with those words in his mouth.

"God. *Fuck*—" He grips his shuddering scalp as it starts to blister. His hands turn red. Then purple. Heat auras tornado around his body. "Please, *please* just fucking help me—"

I hear Cora whimper at my back. I almost forgot she was standing there. I turn to glance at her. And a flash of glass by her foot pulls my gaze.

The shot.

As I lunge to pick it up, something plucks the taut strings in my chest.

Something he said last night. When he was the worst kind of honest.

He said I was good. Unselfish. Better than she ever was.

His scalp starts to crackle and split like bone-dry mud. It's finally starting. The chemicals can't hold the light back any longer.

He sobs on the ground. A boy shattered by his sorry excuse for a family. Who made him sick and called it a gift.

"O-oh. My God. You found it." He stares at the shot in my hand. "Thank you, thank you—"

I take a measured step toward him. Then another.

"*Hurry—*"

His face falls as my eyes narrow. He realizes what's happening before I do.

"Mia. Please. You can't let me die like this."

I clench the injection in my fist.

"That's what *she* would have done."

He's right. It is.

I place the shot on the ground. Between his face and my shoe.

Seven seconds on the clock.

He extends a desperate, blackening hand as I stomp down. Tiny, jagged crystals scatter before his eyes.

He screams. A bloodcurdling coloratura that takes my breath away.

"One."

"No, no, *no—*"

"Two. Three. Four."

"*Mia—*"

I'm going to watch this time. Every last second.

"Five. Six."

I squint through the swirling auras, searching for the exact moment his body surrenders. I never pictured it like this. Such ominous, perfect beauty.

"Seven."

Nobody talks about what happens at eight seconds.

For someone to know it takes seven seconds, someone had to be watching. Someone had to be there for eight.

Someone stared at those desiccated entrails, where eight seconds ago there was a voice and a mind and a body brimming with purpose and desire and pain.

Nobody talks about what happens after you pierce the pitch-black heart you've been hunting like a trophy. I thought I'd be drunk with satisfaction. Thought it would feel like collapsing over the finish line in a blaze of glory. But there's nothing.

I can't look at him anymore. Whatever he is now.

Whatever he was to me.

Not my father.

Not my friend, or my lover.

What?

I don't know.

The person who forced me to grow up. Who stole thirteen beautiful years of my life.

Well.

They might have been beautiful. I'll never know.

I'll never know how much of what he said was true. How many times my mother lied to me. What might have been, if he'd never spoken to her at the fireworks that night.

But here is what I do know.

My mother loved me. In her way. The only way anyone can.

She brought me into a cruel world, but that wasn't her fault.

All she ever did was trust the wrong man.

In that way, there was nothing special about Devon at all.

Somewhere along the line, before I was born, she learned the wrong lesson about love. Learned to believe things she knew couldn't possibly be true.

And she never unlearned it.

She could have. Probably should have, when she became a mother.

But she was so young. Younger than me. I can't imagine. She was so lonely. So confused. Delicate, like a thing you want to hide behind bulletproof glass. Maybe that's what her mother tried to do. It failed, of course. Same way it failed for me. The way it fails for everyone.

I was all she had. Before she survived because of me, she was surviving *for* me. I was the only thing holding her back from him. Those dark promises and dazzling lies.

I do not forgive her for what she did to me. The way she hijacked my childhood and shunned the woman I became. But I forgive her for the places she found solace. Even the places I'd never enter myself. I know who she was, and I know who she became, as intimately as I know every scar on my body. Scars that still itch. Even rupture when I don't expect them to. But there's room for forgiveness between the edges of my pain. Maybe someday, I'll be able to live in the space where two truths meet.

I mean, I think I'll have to.

Because now I know. Nothing will take that pain away.
Not even watching him die.

((((((

Kayla and Daisy catch up to us. We wordlessly take our second
dose of Daylights.

I know what I have to do. I have to find that cell phone.

Cora helps me slowly, carefully pick up his jacket, encased in
a rind of sunbaked gore. We pinch the stiff material between our
fingertips. Unzip the pockets. There's his lighter, keys, and a pack
of cigarettes on one side. The phone is on the other.

Cora tosses it to me. I hand her the blood-spattered cigarettes.

She sparks one up. Offers the pack to Daisy and Kayla. They
watch, transfixed, as I hold up the phone and pace in a circle for
service. There's one bar.

"Remember," I say before I dial. "By the time they get here, no
matter how hungry we are, we suck it in. We're not the monster. We
killed the fucking monster."

Cora throws her arms around my neck and plants a bloody kiss
on my bruised cheek.

9 . . . 1 . . . 1.

A marble-mouthed woman with a Midwestern drawl answers.
"Routt County Sheriff, whatsyer 'mergency?"

"Um . . . Hi. I uh—" I can't believe this is happening. "I'd like to
report the whereabouts of a wanted criminal."

"D'you have eyes on the individual at present, ma'am?"

"I do. He's dead."

EPILOGUE

Fifteen years later, New York hasn't changed. And yet, everything has. The storefronts. The marquees. The laws.

Not the energy, though.

We would have been back more often. But our hands have been tied. At least, they were those first three years. When we took our punishment. As expected.

What we didn't expect was what would happen after those photos came out. How one image could change our whole life.

Cora and I were coming out of the courthouse in Colorado, a few minutes after sunset. All these people were camped outside. Cameras and gawkers. Our lawyers liked to keep us away from all that. Always tried to hustle us past. It was a hard day. Both of us cried on the stand. As we traipsed down the stairs, I grabbed her wrist and kissed her, right in front of everybody. I only did it because we hadn't been able to touch all day. They kept us on opposite sides of the courtroom. People snapped photos. There's this one really great shot, where the streetlight haloes our faces and you can see the moon rising over the courthouse and the mountains in the distance.

We blew that one up and printed it out in black-and-white. Hung it over the fireplace.

Everything changed, after that picture.

We did time at a Sara center in Denver. Nothing like Salvation of Manhattan, with their designer furniture and tropical plants. It was a no-perks situation. No Daylights. No phones. But we had each other.

People started writing to us. Real, handwritten letters. We kept every one. Actually, I don't know where they are at this *exact* moment. We're in the middle of moving. They might be in storage. But we held on to them. I'm sure of that.

Some of the people who reached out to us were ADAPT devotees. We had to be careful with them. Technically, we did not kill Devon. And that's the story we stuck with. But they were already sympathetic to our cause, after hearing what we had to say in court. Over the course of three years, they helped us build an appeal. In return, we helped them build a community. That was all they ever wanted, really. Devon was a means to an end. The only person who was organizing. Till we started doing it.

The laws are evolving. If you hurt someone, you go to prison. Like anyone else. Nobody needs to die to keep Saras alive. Never did. Closing the centers has been a winding road, though. People will always fear what they don't understand. But we haven't given up. We've always been good at sniffing out loopholes.

The years melt away like spun sugar. It's taken Cora nearly a decade to graduate law school. And I'm still trying to finish this goddamn book. I'm pretty close, though.

The apartment we found is on the eleventh floor of a creaky prewar complex on West Sixty-Eighth Street. The kind with a gilded garbage chute and—probably—a couple of ghosts in the boiler room. She's excited. New York is home for her, after all.

I still don't want to take the subway. I bought us a car. Have not yet told Cora how much it's going to cost to park long-term.

I never expected us to come back here permanently. And maybe it won't be. Permanent. But we've made a yearlong commitment. Tomorrow, we're going back to Salvation of Manhattan—which is still in operation—and bringing home two kids Cora met on the ninth floor all those years ago. Someone from the center has to come to our apartment for an assessment every three days. The fucking *hoops* they've made us jump through.

For years, I tried to talk her out of it. They kept telling her no, and I couldn't bear to watch her get rejected, over and over. We couldn't get the lawyers to look away from the liability. Sara kids represent the murkiest part of the new laws. Which is why Cora studied it. Why it's taken her so long to get her degree.

We are part of a pilot program. *Her* pilot program.

I've never been so proud.

I am also scared shitless.

I promised her we'd be a family. I meant it. Of course I meant it.

But every time we visit the kids—Violet and Ramon—I fold in on myself. Don't know how to talk to them. How to process the things Cora's told me about them. Ramon is eleven, with a face of delicate, barely-there peach fuzz and an encyclopedic knowledge of every Pokémon there ever was or will be. He has an issue with the shower. Gets so panicked they have to sedate him so he doesn't stink. He's bitten every nurse he's ever had. Violet is eight. She's like a little church mouse. Loves to read. Plays piano. Doesn't sleep during the day. Never could. But she's also up all night. She's hypervigilant, and her circadian damage has made her an emotional minefield. They're trying to regulate it with medication. Keeping her consistent with Daylights helps. But Cora has warned me we're in for a roller coaster of sleeplessness.

Which is why I ask her again, the day before they move in, if she's prepared. If she really, *truly* wants this.

Of course, she's never flinched. I don't expect she will today.

She loves them. Effortlessly. They occupy her every thought. This day is huge. Bringing them home.

I don't know what I feel.

But I made her a promise.

I know what I'm scared of. I'm not an idiot.

I have no idea how two people whose parents failed them can succeed at this.

But I also know I can do scary things. I've done a lot of them.

The first night is nice. We watch cartoons and play Clue. Violet sets up her keyboard and plays us a song she's writing. We've decided not to force Daylights on them if they don't feel like it. Especially while we learn Violet's sleep patterns.

We climb into bed just before dawn and crank our noise machine. Even on the eleventh floor, the city traffic during rush hour resonates. Violet's still awake, reading in the living room. Ramon passed out an hour ago.

"Should we like . . . I dunno. Make up the couch for her or something?" I peer around the corner. The little girl has dutifully secured the blackout curtains. She sits with pin-straight posture in Cora's green velvet study chair. Every few seconds, she glances up from her book and scans her surroundings with dark, watchful eyes.

"She'll go to her room when she's ready. Don't worry. This is just what she does." Cora pecks me on the cheek. Yawns and curls into bed.

I linger in the doorway. Her tiny figure calls to me. Something in the way she can't finish a paragraph without glancing over her shoulder.

But Cora is right. She heads to her room a few minutes later. Maybe she'll sleep if the rest of us do. She's had a big night. Must be exhausted. I turn off the lamp and slip into bed. Cora's already dozing. I guess she's more like Ramon, in that way. That's nice, though. I love that they have small things like that in common.

A scream slaps me awake. I'm on my feet in an instant.

I still forget where I am. Sometimes I wake up in Tucson, standing at our big picture window. Waiting for the Jeep to come rolling over the hill. Or in the kitchen at the Salt Lake house. Taping down the curtains before the sun comes up.

I'm on my way across the apartment before Cora even opens her eyes. Violet's in her bedroom, balled in a blanket on the floor in the dark. I turn on the light and she screams again.

"I'm sorry. Lemme just—" I smack it off.

If she sees me, she's looking right past me.

"You wanna get into bed?" I finally ask. Not sure I should approach her. What did her therapist say again? What are the physical boundaries, when this happens?

Cora will remember. She'll be here in a minute. This is her territory.

My heart races as I wait for her to intervene. Is this how it's going to be, every day?

Violet sniffles. Chews her fist and draws blood.

"Um . . . do you wanna like, put on a movie? Or—"

"Can we go outside?"

"Oh. I'm not sure if we're supposed to—" That's one of our rules, for the first week. These are indoor kids till the psych team at the center tells us it's cool to take them on short, simple excursions.

But she's already on her feet. Blanket draped over her head like a little shepherd.

Cora appears in the hall. Watching us. I'm waiting for her to take over. But she doesn't. I feel like I'm being tested.

"Hang on. I have an idea. But you need to take a pill first. The sun's gonna be up soon." I study her shifty gaze. "Is that okay?"

"I guess. If you're with me." She wipes her nose with the back of her bloody hand.

I lead her to the kitchen and clean off her face. We sit at the breakfast bar, sucking our pills. Just staring at each other.

Cora passes through and casts me a sleepy, crescent-moon smile. "I'm gonna take her to the roof. That's fine, right?"

She nods. Reassuring warmth blooms from her like a sweet fragrance, drifting across the room. I still don't know how I got so lucky. How we got here.

She closes our bedroom door, leaving us alone.

"Tongue check," I say to Violet. That's something I *do* remember the therapist telling me. She doesn't like the taste of the Daylights. We have to make sure she finishes, every time.

Violet's tongue droops comically, like a slobbering dog. She's being cute. But the tears in her eyes keep rising. Still in the throes of whatever darkness comes to call when the light creeps in. Most kids are afraid of the dark. But most kids aren't Sara kids.

We ride up in the elevator, side by side. She's still got her blanket tucked under her chin. Has vehemently refused to put on a coat. The nights have been pretty crisp lately. Hopefully she'll be warm enough.

It's October. Almost my birthday. Hers is two months later, to the day.

Our rooftop is modest but well-equipped. There's a little vegetable garden. A patch of turf where the dogs can pee. Couple of picnic tables.

There's not much to do up here except look at the skyline. But really, what else do you need? We stand at the ledge together. Gazing downtown in silence. The sky is milky with early-morning fog. A daisy chain of traffic wends up Eighth Avenue.

"We weren't allowed to go on the roof," she finally says.

"Well, we're allowed on this one."

"I like it."

"Good, I'm glad."

"Are there dogs who come up here?" She points at the potty patch.

"Sometimes."

"I wish we had a dog."

"They're not very nice to us."

"I know."

"I mean, we could try though." I crack a smile in her direction. "Listen, you can train a dog to do anything if you give them bacon."

"Did you ever have a dog?"

"Nah. Me and my mom were cat people."

I haven't thought about Cheddar in ages. I hope he found a good home. That he died fat and happy, with no memory of the traumatic night he divebombed through our window.

I realize this is a story I might tell her. There are a lot of things I could tell her. Not the worst things. But the things that give me context, color, and shape. Things I might not have even told Cora, because they weren't relevant. Because Cora isn't a child.

When I lost everything, I was already on the verge of leaving my childhood behind. I was ten. There was no time to reclaim my youth. I was going to have to grow up one way or another. At the time, speeding things along didn't feel like too much of a sacrifice. As if I had a choice.

But Sara kids are different.

It won't be easy, and I'm not about to delude myself. I can't undo what's been done to this girl. Nothing can. But I can help her get her childhood back. If she'll let me.

"When I'm tired, we can go inside," she says after a moment.

"Are you tired yet?"

"No. But I think I will be."

"Well, just let me know."

"Can we do this again tomorrow?"

"For sure."

"Where's the Metropolitan Opera House?"

"Oh. Um . . ." I glance over my shoulder. "Up there? I think?"

It's been a while since I've been back. And I don't really know this neighborhood.

"Which way is east?"

"Well, if that's downtown, then we're facing . . . which way?"

"I dunno." She chews the threadbare, fringy corner of her blanket.

"Never. Eat. Soggy. Waffles." I point out each direction as I turn in a circle. She laughs.

"That's dumb."

"Yeah, but it helps."

"South," she finally answers.

"Good. It's important, to know that stuff. When we go out in the world."

And we will. I'm not hiding her. I make a silent promise over her like a prayer.

Sunlight slips between the concrete giants guarding us to the east. To my surprise, she pulls the blanket off her head.

I bend to meet her gaze.

"You gonna be okay?"

ACKNOWLEDGMENTS

Every time you sit down to write a new story, it takes you somewhere you've never been before. Sometimes you get there, enjoy the view, and head home before it gets dark. Other times, the sun goes down and you realize you can never go back the way you came and you're going to have to live *here* now. This was one of those. Thankfully, I didn't go it alone. You never do.

Bottomless gratitude goes out to my editor Kelly Lonesome and my agent Liz Parker, without whom Mia's journey never would have continued. I never meant to write this book, but God, I needed to. Thank you for making sure I had that chance.

Thank you as well to the unassailable team at Tor Nightfire, who have worked so hard to make sure the Night's Edge series has reached the people who need it most. To Katie Klimowicz (the brains behind both these stunning book covers), Jordan Hanley, Kristin Temple, Alexis Saarela, Valeria Castorena, Michael Dudding, Jeff LaSala, Rafal Gibek, Jacqueline Huber-Rodriguez, Heather Saunders, Devi Pillai, Lucille Rettino, Will Hinton, Claire Eddy, Eileen Lawrence, Sarah Reidy, and every single person who ushered these books into readers' hands. I'd also like to extend my gratitude to Elena Stokes, Brianna Robinson, and the passionate, thoughtful team at Wunderkind PR. It takes a village. Er . . . a coven?

To all the booksellers who hand-sold and supported *Night's Edge,* made cute TikToks (I'm lookin' at you, Mando at B&N Kirkland), and stuck it on an endcap with a recommendation. You change authors' lives, every time you do this. To every incredible reader who has tagged me on social media, designed art (Kayleigh McKee, you are a genius!), told a friend, and reached out to share their story with me . . . you make me feel seen when you see these characters. Thank you from the bottom of my heart.

An embarrassment of brilliant minds and trusted friends touched this manuscript at various stages and left their mark: Hilary Clifford, Christina Keach, Colleen Scriven, Molly Lyons, Hannah Rosner, Janel Parrish, Amanda Mortlock, and Emmy Yu. Thank you for giving me the hard notes, validating me, and/or both. To Jac Schaeffer—who helped me "free the angel in the marble" as we crafted a television pitch and I started to see all the enormous possibility in this world. I treasure every pearl of wisdom you've ever dropped for me.

On that note, I also owe a world of thanks to Melissa Darman, who handled my burgeoning TV career with so much patience and grace she deserves a medal of honor, and Adam Cooper, who always helps me make good choices.

To all the incredible authors I've met this past year who have offered me sage advice, hype/blurbs/inspiration, cocktails, or all of the above. This includes (but is NOT limited to): Nat Cassidy, CJ Leede, Catriona Ward, KC Jones, S.A. Barnes, Cassandra Khaw, Brea Grant, Sunyi Dean, Delilah S. Dawson, Scott Thomas, Erika T. Wurth, Alexis Henderson, Damien Angelica Walters, Sadie Hartmann, Philip Fracassi, Johnny Compton, Scott Leeds, Nina Nesseth, Hildur Knútsdóttir, Chuck Tingle, and Olivie Blake. I will probably get to know many more of you by the time this is published. This community has meant so much to me. They say it becomes impossible to make new friends once you hit your thirties. Whoever "they" are, they have clearly never written a horror novel and met a hundred other weirdos whose brains work the exact same way.

To the wildly talented Hannah Bonner, who allowed me to use her gorgeous poem "Lethe" as an epigraph. To the estate of the brilliant Mary Oliver, for "The Uses of Sorrow." To Alyssa Kurtzman, who directed and edited the absolute perfect trailer for this book (and also made sure we didn't get arrested for filming on the New York City subway). To my friends who traveled with me or gave me a special place to write this past year: Gautham, for Sedona. Dawn, for Mammoth. And Caroline, for the *entirety of America*. I can't even tell you how much I needed those trips while I was writing this.

To Mom, Dad, Patrick, Sallie, Jim, Sarah, Jared, Ana, Aunt Ree and Uncle Iggy (who never fail to call me from Spain and sing me a heartwarming, congratulatory tune). Thank you for seeing me through all the twists and turns of the past few years and supporting my work, even when I told you a deeply upsetting vampire pandemic probably wouldn't be your vibe. Sorry if this one got weird (again). I'm glad you still love me.

Lastly, to Sam. Thank you for always making sure I had a soft place to land. I know this was a lot. You let these characters crash on our couch rent-free for the past three years without complaint. They were terrible roommates. Thanks for putting up with them. More importantly—thank you for being my family and making a home with me. It's all I've ever wanted.

ABOUT THE AUTHOR

Lee Jameson

LIZ KERIN is the author of *Night's Edge*, and a playwright, screen-writer, and graduate of the Rita and Burton Goldberg Department of Dramatic Writing at NYU Tisch School of the Arts. She is also the author of *The Phantom Forest*. She lives in Southern California.

Instagram: @lizkerin
Website: lizkerin .com